ERRANT EXPECTATIONS

A Pride & Prejudice Variation

by

A.S Bishop

In Dedication

To my husband Michael.
You keep me going, even when
I fall flat on my face.
You laugh, but you pick me
up while you do it.

To my Mum, pestering me to finish so you
can hear the end of the story - sometimes
annoying, sometimes needed.

Thank you

Both

PROLOGUE

I hope you are enjoying your time with our Aunt Gardiner's relatives as your letters have suggested. I cannot say that I do not envy you the experience, but I would wish to share the pleasures such as you have named, visiting tea shops, hunting for new booksellers, discovering new parks, only with you, who might help me feel more at ease. Perhaps, we may journey one day to Bath together, you as my guide. However, I am cheered to hear you will soon be returned to Longbourne, for your absence has been sorely felt.

Needless to say, time has passed much as it ever does, with the turning of the seasons, the daily rituals you know I find so soothing, our father's unceasing retreat to his book room when his female relatives become lamentably loud. If only all of us could escape so easily.

It is both fortunate and not, that there has been rather more furore of late, what with so many changes in such a short space of time having taken place. No doubt you have had some of this related to you from our eldest sister, but I am sure she was unfailingly kind and gave you little to discern, other than Jane seems well amenable to the Netherfield tenants. One in particular, Mr Bingley, has paid our sister much attention, and if our mother is to be believed, they are well on the way to being wed. I cannot divine if this is the case or not however, as I forever struggle to catch the tone of conversations when I am playing chaperone to Jane and Mr Bingley. I will say, that Mr Bingley is persistently cheerful, even when faced with a sister who has looked unfavourably upon Meryton, yet even

*Miss Bingley has been heard to call Jane a 'dear, sweet girl'.
I shall leave this to you to discover the truth, as I trust your
judgement in such matters.*

*Our youngest sister begs leave to beseech you to bring
her some particular trifle she has mentioned in one of her
missives. Now that I have done so, Lydia also insists I inform
you of the militia's arrival. I was intending to do so, but you
can comprehend Lydia would have you be informed in her
words and not mine.*

*Apologies, I shall not further the topic, other than
to say that Mr Bennet has not deemed it necessary to make
much change to how our household is managed, even with an
increased number of unknown gentlemen in the area. I must
admit to being somewhat alarmed by this and did attempt to
make some suggestion to altering the freedoms our younger
sisters were permitted. I was not met with success, and so
sought Jane's aid in attempting to steer Lydia and Kitty to less
flighty displays, but our eldest sister would not see the harm.*

*Forgive me, I feel this has been a lamentably dour
missive, but I felt it necessary for you to understand the
household upon which you will re-enter. There has been
nary a sensible word said and my attempts to focus upon my
music has been much affected. Thank you for sending me the
compositions you discovered. It was a handsome gift and had
I the opportunity, I would have devoted much time already
to its study. While the melody at first appears quite simple,
a further glance reveals the complexity. I look forward to
practising it with you when you are home.*

*I must finish here as our mother wishes to call on Lady
Lucas and insists I attend as none of my sisters are present.
I shall ask to call in on Mrs Greenings on my return and thus
attend to your injunction to check up on her health and that of
her children.*

*Do not hasten home, no matter how I have articulated
matters. You have been my steadfast and ever-beloved guide
into womanhood, yet you deserve to be away from our
mother's continual complaints and the persistent demands
our father places upon you. I would not have you end your*

adventures prematurely.
All my love and affection
Your sister,
Mary

CHAPTER 1

Mrs Philip's Parlour, Meryton November 19th

Elizabeth listened to Lieutenant Wickham's account of his history with a Mr Darcy, a guest of the Netherfield tenant's, with an air of startled disbelief.

"What a wretched tale, Lieutenant Wickham. Surely, you must have some grounds for legal redress?" she was not precisely sure of the legalities of wills, and inheritance laws, but, perhaps her uncle Philips would be able to explain such matters in order for her to comprehend. That is if she wished to find a way to offer aid.

However, the truth was, Elizabeth struggled to display genuine interest in such a new acquaintance's past trials. Her role as mediator, moderator and mentor within her own family was more than enough responsibility and left her little solitude to dwell on her own concerns. Her attendance tonight, at her aunt's card party the very evening of her return, was not how she had wished to spend her first night home, yet here Elizabeth sat, quietly attentive to a handsome stranger discussing his ill-treatment. Her astonishment on the whole was not feigned, the content of such private dealings, and the Lieutenant's comfort in his disclosure made no clear degree of sense. Furthermore, the officer's delivery was so smooth, so practised, a kernel of doubt grew. Nervous tension ran down her spine, and Elizabeth shivered to dispel the feelings, shifting in her seat as her company continued to betray his sentiments.

"...myself has been scandalous; but I verily believe I could forgive him anything and everything, rather than his disappointing the hopes and disgracing the memory of his father."

Bemused, Elizabeth allowed her thoughts to wander, ruminating on her return to Longbourne, almost perfectly timed to coincide with that of her father's cousin, Mr Collins. Ever since the moment her foot touched the gravel driveway of Longbourne, there had been not a moment of peace. She had spent the past summer in the company of her aunt Gardiner and cousins, while they visited her aunt's brother and his family, in Bath. Her uncle had wished to gift his wife with an extended holiday, but had not had the time free to accompany her, as such Elizabeth happily agreed her aunt with minding her young cousins. Aunt Gardiner's brother, Henry Thompson, owned a successful law practice, and he, his wife and two daughters had been exceptionally welcoming to Elizabeth, granting her an open invitation to remain as long as she would wish. In thanks for her company and support, aunt Gardiner had encouraged Elizabeth to extend her visit some two months, granting her the time to explore as she had not been free to do while managing her cousins.

Lieutenant Wickham chuffed deprecatingly, while his words continued to flow. Understanding her role as mere listener, spared the gentleman little attention thinking contentedly of her aunt's nieces, Evelyn and Rebecca, girls of sixteen and fourteen summers. The girls had been excellent company throughout her rambles around the many streets and shops of Bath. While they were both young, still somewhat easily excited, neither had displayed the lack of decorum and propriety her own juvenile sisters so often did. Evelyn and Rebecca had become dear friends, offering easy rapport, without judgement or condescension, such that she was exposed to within Longbourne's walls. To return home and be met by such a voluble and unknown gentleman as Mr Collins, and now the officer seated so attentively beside her, was a decidedly discordant finale to what had otherwise been a most pleasurable summer.

But it was not just the excesses of Mr Collins Elizabeth had to abide, but those of her family too. Lydia and Kitty had been in raptures detailing the many officers they had become acquainted. Her mother had appeared most discomposed, her handkerchief flapping wildly, as she announced how well Jane would be, situated but three miles away with Mr Bingley in Netherfield. To that, Elizabeth had been keen to discern Jane's thoughts, but her sister was still somewhat weary from so recently rising from the sick-bed. Alarmingly, neither of her parents had concerned themselves with the care of their eldest daughter, Jane having become unwell while a guest of the new neighbours. But thankfully, Mary had felt it her sisterly duty to tend Jane. As for her father, Mr Bennet had been quick to observe how pleased he was to have her home, only to disappear the moment he crossed Longbourne's threshold.

Lieutenant Wickham, unaware of Elizabeth's distraction, so absorbed with his story, complained plaintively, "-could not believe my misfortune, to have joined a militia regiment within the same county my once-childhood friend now occupies!"

Elizabeth returned to the present, and with a sigh, resumed her part of the conversation, "Chance plays its hand in all things, Sir. I can only view matters from a woman's vantage, but could you not see your way to moving beyond past grievances? Or mayhap, as you are so newly joined, could not a redeployment be considered?" Elizabeth rambled, not really thinking long upon the matter, and with little interest in encouraging further intimacy with the handsome officer. For all his good looks and charm, his manners were too smooth, too contrived, and Elizabeth was uneasy to be so singled out on their first ever meeting.

"Lieutenant Wickham! Come, play lottery tickets with us! You too, Lizzy!" Lydia's bright tones broke into the heavy atmosphere that had developed in her corner.

With a welcoming smile, Elizabeth answered, "Excellent suggestion Lyddie, you are ever so good at the game, so I shall leave Lieutenant Wickham to your less than tender mercies!" she teased, to which her youngest sister could only brightly laugh, before tugging the gentleman away.

Breathing a sigh of relief, Elizabeth moved to an even quieter corner, while keeping a steady eye upon her sisters. Lydia was a darling girl, so bright and cheerful, her chestnut locks catching the candle-light and giving her hair a russet hue. Her dancing blue eyes, lighter than their eldest sister Jane's, often gleamed with merriment. In contrast to Lydia, was Mary. Her clever and most devoted sister claimed hair so dark it was almost black, but was in fact a very dark mahogany. Mary's bright blue eyes, matched Jane's, were easily overlooked due to the spectacles her sister required, yet they sparkled whenever Mary's passionate nature was roused. Most disregarded her quiet middle sister, but Mary was simply focused upon her interests, almost to the exclusion of aught else. If only their father would employ a music master, the girl would be hard won away from her musical studies! Having remained home this evening, Mary possessing no interest in cards, so it fell to Elizabeth to keep vigil over her family without her sister's quiet yet astute observations.

"There you are Eliza! Have you been hiding away in this gloomy corner a-purpose?" Charlotte snuck upon Elizabeth.

"Heavens, Charlotte, you caught me unawares!" heart pounding, Elizabeth clutched her chest in reflex.

Apologetic, Charlotte took the seat beside her, and perhaps hoping to ease her friend, talked of her occupations the three months Elizabeth had been away.

"John has little enjoyed his time away at school, but has made many friends who have had occasion to visit. I cannot say my brother has excellent taste in companions however!" Charlotte muttered, her furrowed brow indicative of her low opinion.

Bumping her shoulder, Elizabeth laughed lightly, and Charlotte smiled in reply, only to tease, "You, however, are scarcely back a full day, and are already making conquests of all the well-favoured officers we are surrounded by!"

"No doubt you are referring to Lieutenant Wickham?" Elizabeth asked, coolness shading her tone, "Presumably you imagined some romantic tete a tete between the two of us, but to that I must sadly disappoint."

"Have I offended, Eliza?" Charlotte asked worriedly, her eyes flicking between Elizabeth's, attempting to assess the cause of her ill-temper.

Tucking an errant coffee curl behind her ear, Elizabeth softened her tone, "Not entirely, dear friend. But please, accord me the civility of not imagining romantic intrigues with every gentleman's glance." Looking away, Elizabeth continued to study the mixed company her aunt had collected for her card party. The Netherfield tenants were not to be seen, her aunt not feeling an invitation would be little welcome. But there were Mrs Long's nieces engaged in conversation with a Captain Carter, while Lieutenant's Denny and Saunderson were set to a table with Maria Lucas and Kitty. Jane, looking a little distracted, playing with Lydia, Mr Collins and Lieutenant Wickham. There were others, but sighting the principles allowed Elizabeth to relax somewhat.

Turning back to Charlotte, "You must understand, being back in Meryton, tis interest enough for the gossips, without adding further grist of rumour and speculation."

"What is amiss?" Charlotte's brow furrowed deeper, her dark golden hair caught up simply behind her, intelligent hazel eyes searching Elizabeth's toffee brown ones. "You are out of sorts this evening, tis most unlike you."

Another sigh escaped, and Elizabeth felt the weight of fatigue drop heavily upon her brow, "You must not fret, I am in a most disagreeable temper and should not be out in company. Yet there has been little pause since my return, and the pervasive *noise* has felt as if I'm stuck in a downpour."

Charlotte nodded sympathetically, her lovely gaze softening in understanding, "Could you not have remained at home this evening?"

"Mama would not permit both Mary and I to do so, therefore as payment of my extended absence, I allowed my sister to take her ease. She has more than earned the reprieve." Elizabeth could not see her middle sister set in her place, when only a little participation on her part would suffice.

"While I can attest Mary has been a most diligent companion to Jane, as Mr Bingley grows in your sister's acquaintance, I am grieved Mr Bennet did not see fit to shield you from your mother's bidding." Charlotte, practical to a fault, but with a gentle heart carefully protected, always bore an excess of frustration towards

Elizabeth's father and his lackadaisical manner.

Saying nothing in her father's defence, Elizabeth asked instead, "Will you meet me tomorrow, by the stream that leads to that quiet wooded copse?"

Charlotte rose, nodding as she did, then tugged Elizabeth up by her hand, "I recall the place well, so I shall meet you tomorrow, near eight?" At Elizabeth's nod, her friend continued, "Very well, now let us settle to a table, I'm of a mind to partner you at whist, for I know you are fiendishly clever at the enterprise, and am therefore assured of our success!"

"So, tell me, what has *the jewel of the county* so out of sorts?" Charlotte teased.

Elizabeth had been home a day complete, the excitable and *voluble* nature of her near constant companions, the peace and tranquillity of nature, in addition to the solid and reliable presence of her dear friend, was as a balm to her serenity. While Lydia's behaviour was somewhat a consequence of her age, the same was not the case for the Bennet matron, and though Elizabeth was a social creature, happy to adapt to a range of circumstances, it was necessary for her to balance such occupation with solitude. Nonetheless, Mr Collins had been a shadow forever at her shoulder, and it was easy to comprehend the motive, while honourable, would not have him desist. Mrs

Bennet's many leading remarks also suggested that her mother was in favour of a match with her father's cousin. Mr Collins was destined for disappointment, Elizabeth thought darkly.

Before addressing her friend's concern, Elizabeth remarked, "Bath is by no means a haven for one such as I who enjoys to ramble, but one aspect I do dearly miss, is the quantity of tea shops available, for would it not be somewhat more snug to be ensconced in one currently?" Elizabeth watched as the clouds scuttled by on this grim November morning. The weather was hardly ideal for any lengthy sojourn, but nor could Elizabeth stomach the thought of remaining caged with her restless family. Quietly, she continued, "I do believe I visited near enough them all these past few months."

Charlotte sat quietly next to her on the wall of the little stone bridge, a mid-way point between either home. "Eliza?" she prompted when more time had passed without her attending.

"Patience, dear Charlotte, despite this chill weather, I am basking in the peace nature has oft provided." Elizabeth bumped her shoulder against that of her friend's, "I could not bear to remain within Longbourne's walls, and walking alone would only leave me to fester in my thoughts."

"Is it the handsome officer from last evening that has you so out of sorts this morning?" Charlotte slyly enquired.

"Hardly!" she snorted in frustration. "You can be somewhat preoccupied with my romantic life, and I have had enough of that at home as it is." Elizabeth huffed, still refusing to return Charlotte's assessing gaze.

"You cannot fault me for noticing that the very day of your return, the handsomest officer in the militia regiment singles *you* out on your very first introduction! Lieutenant Wickham must have displeased you excessively for you to not feel flattered and admired."

Waving away the officer's name, Elizabeth replied with little control over the ire aimed upon the absent man, "Pah. I grant you the gentleman possesses a pretty face, yet I would no sooner grant a relative stranger the power to disturb me, than I would allow Mr Collins to succeed in his questionable courting!"

"But you were caught up in private conversation with Lieutenant Wickham for half the evening, much to the dismay of many a lady present, your sisters chief amongst them. Did he truly not command qualities upon which he could please?"

Rolling her eyes in exasperation, Elizabeth explained, "Indeed, the gentleman can flatter and please, his manners everything one would expect. But I am little interest in discussing a stranger's unhappy history, something to do with a friend of Mr Bingley? Mr Darcy I recall?"

At Charlotte's nod and interested and expectant look, she continued, "There was some mention of not meeting the terms of his father's will, leaving Lieutenant Wickham unsupported. I am ill-inclined to lend credence to the tale however, for it was all delivered so perfectly, too easily tripping off the tongue! The Lieutenant was too quick in confiding his private dealings on first meeting. I will not malign the man, but nor will I allow my trust be so easily won! I am in no hurry to prove myself so foolish and simple."

"How peculiar!"

"My thoughts exactly! Now, that is not what I asked you here for, but I am pleased you will cease to imagine any interest on my part in that quarter, so may we retire the topic of Lieutenant Wickham henceforth?" Elizabeth entreated, her soft, warm brown eyes pleading her friend for clemency.

Charlotte's husky laugh broke free. Elizabeth heaved a sigh of relief and settled in to unburden herself, hoping for some wise counsel from her treasured friend. "Thank you for meeting me this morning. I know you are much occupied with that of managing your mother's home, but since my return, I have come to the horrifying realisation that I am guilty of a terrible sin."

With a careful glance, Charlotte quietly asked, "And what is this terrible sin?"

"I am in possession of many a fault and

flaw, but perhaps chief amongst them, is that of sitting idly by while my parent's lead my sisters down wretched paths." Her gaze had turned hazy with internal reflection and so missed the raised brow that was a mimicry of her own quizzical expression.

"What has led you to this belief? Was it seeing the contrast of another family with daughters and how they deport themselves?" Of course Charlotte would cut to the heart of the matter.

Elizabeth smiled brightly when thinking of Evelyn and Rebecca, "While I will not deny they are a very different type of daughter than my sisters and I, and that seeing how mannerly and well the girls behaved made the realisation all the more bitter, it was not that. No, the truth is, from the moment of my arrival, the minute I stepped a foot from the carriage, I was greeted almost violently with the swell of others demands and expectations, and little appreciation for my weary state." Elizabeth paused to sum it up succinctly, "Jane greeted me with a glowing radiance I had not witnessed in her before. I must attribute such to this Mr Bingley fellow." Ticking the names off with her fingers, "Kitty and Lydia shrieked to be heard above the other in regards to the many handsome officers they had met since the militia had encamped here. And Mrs Bennet? Well, poor mamma was enervated with her raptures over

Jane's beauty being the means of saving us from the hedgerows, while simultaneously pushing Mr Collins in my direction and saying ever so many out of character praises for my person. I surmise she has some intent to foist my father's cousin upon my notice in the hopes I am to wed him and thereby save *her* from those dratted hedges!" Elizabeth fumed at her mother's scheming, then with a shrug continued, "And my father, while greeting me warmly, reminded me only a moment later that I have much to accomplish considering my extended absence!"

"You have not mentioned Mary or how Mr Collins received you?" Charlotte astutely asked.

Smiling brightly at the thought of her quiet and overlooked sister, Elizabeth answered, "That is because Mary was not present. Unlike the rest of my family, Mary had been discharging my duties to the tenants in my absence, and so was only able to greet me upon her return. And my sister is not one for overly loud demonstrations, yet she was long in releasing me from her embrace, so I take from that she was much pleased to have me home. As for Mr Collins? Well, I little like the man, but perhaps that is because he is fond of offering empty flattery. Mary suggests he has shown more interest in my company than he had in hers, however Mr Collins will have to accept disappointment in his quest to gain a wife from the Bennet daughters."

"He said that? That he is seeking a wife?" Charlotte asked with more intensity than was custom.

"Aye, his intent was made abundantly clear over the course of his first meal with the Bennets." Elizabeth answered with her own peculiar expression. "Why does this pertain to our conversation?"

Now it was Charlotte who fell quiet, and so Elizabeth indulged the silence as she kicked her heels against the stone bridge as she waited.

"Would you be averse to Mr Collins making a match *outside* of Longbourne?" were the words that broke her quiet reverie a moment later.

"Truthfully?" Elizabeth asked, looking her friend full on, "I would not, but do you mean to imply *you* would take on the gentleman?"

"Would it be so wrong of me?" Charlotte asked stiffly, "To have the chance of a home and children of my own?"

Alarmed, Elizabeth explained, "Of course not, but the man is hardly sensible!"

"He has an honourable occupation and is set to inherit more-"

Elizabeth's eyes flashed for a moment, until with a conciliatory gesture, she wrapped her arm about her friend's waist, still seated upon the bridge as they were, "Forgive me Charlotte, I meant no judgement upon you or your wishes. And while I will admit that you are correct, Mr Collins *does* have an honourable occupation, and yes, upon my father's death, will inherit Longbourne, I meant only that such decisions should not be made rashly. Only look at my parent's and you can comprehend how ill such things can result." Charlotte nodded in forgiveness, but said no more, "I will not encourage your suit, *but* I will not impede it either, dear friend. It is not for me to judge, but so long as you are content with your decisions, then so too shall I be."

Charlotte finally reciprocated the one-armed embrace, until with a tug, pulled them both off the wall, their rumps painfully cold from the stone, "Agreed, dear Eliza. And thank you. So, you have related how your family greeted you, but not how that implies you are at fault. Where does the connection lie?"

Sighing deeply, Elizabeth explained, "I am as a foil upon which they push from in varying ways. For Jane, her beauty is all the more apparent when in contrast against my own dark appearance, yet I cannot acuse her of such abuse with any intention. For Mrs Bennet, I am her least compliant child and so she has the perfect pretense to behave as she does, I try her nerves most attentively!" Elizabeth rolled her eyes. "For my younger sisters, I am dull and all the things they wish to avoid, no matter how often they are scolded to ameliorate. And my father treats me as a son with nary a privilege of such!" Another deep breath pulled in, and she then went on to say, "I am happy to be home, but I cannot let my family continue as they are. If Jane is soon to wed, perhaps now would be the opportune time to canvas making the changes that would see my sisters improve their education."

Relieved to have worked through her thoughts that had troubled her ever since she returned, Elizabeth felt tension unwind from her shoulders While it was not her duty to enact reforming her family, nor was it acceptable for matters to remain as they were.

Charlotte quietly agreed and promised her support in whatever way she could, but it was enough Elizabeth had vented the weighty thoughts, Attempting to steer their conversation into lighter topics, Charlotte cheekily asked, "Now, tell me what your thoughts are of Jane and Mr Bingley?"

Elizabeth laughed without restraint, pleased to be in company with such a dependable friend, "Oh, Jane is utterly under this Mr Bingley's power, that is not in question. All that is left to discern, is if the gentleman feels similarly. What do you make of it?"

From there, the two friends wended their way to Longbourne, where presumably, Charlotte would begin her quest to win the hand of the not so fair gentleman.

CHAPTER 2

Darcy watched as the two ladies finally moved away from their spot on the bridge. It had not seemed his morning could have gone more awry than it did when his horse threw a shoe on the way back to Netherfield, only for Darcy to become a little turned around on his slow return on foot. This was rendered false, for by the very stream he had paused to gain his bearings, his horse tethered back upon the lane some ways, two ladies settled in to converse, leaving him trapped as an unwitting audience to their private discourse!

What wretched beginnings, even more so when Darcy caught his name spoken, causing his temper to fray further. Yet not a moment later, all had been wiped away as Darcy stood in silent shock. Further surprises followed! Now, as he strode back to his horse, Darcy attempted to process everything he had just heard. First, it was apparent that the missing Bennet daughter had returned home. Second to that, from the sounds of her eloquence and wit, the lady appeared to be intelligent and capable, an unequal burden taken upon her shoulders. To this, Darcy could empathise, all too familiar with heavy encumbrances to bear so early in life.

Darcy guided his horse thoughtfully back to the road he had discovered, navigating his way leisurely towards Netherfield. Bingley would be delighted to discover his own interest in the refined Jane Bennet was reciprocated, much to the chagrin of his sisters. There too, Darcy had been surprised, for it had not been apparent that Miss Bennet was particularly enamoured, but Darcy could hardly call himself an expert in lady's expressions. To this, he wished his friend well, and would remain clear of interfering, no matter how Miss Bingley repeatedly pressed him to do so.

If discovering this was all that Darcy had heard, perhaps his pace would not have been quite as sluggish, but there was more that the Bennet daughter had unknowingly revealed. Concern for her sisters, their conduct, showed a loving regard for her family's welfare, despite how they disregarded it themselves. This 'Eliza' Bennet also would not encourage a match simply because it would see her family secured, yet her account had dismissed financial means to concentrate upon a harmonious union that would see neither party unhappy thereafter. What a novel occurrence, that not all ladies were driven by ambitious and materialistic means!

Just as Darcy reached Netherfield's long winding drive, did he finally admit why the lady had become so distinct, so admirable, sight unseen. Her questioning Wickham's tale, his charm, dismissing his appearance, to see to the heart of the matter. Admittedly, having his name so cavalierly brushed aside was refreshing, but hearing this Bennet daughter failing to succumb to Wickham's lies had restored his mood. What a marvellous creature. Darcy could not wait to take her measure in a more direct manner. Perhaps he could encourage Bingley to deliver the invitations to his ball directly, and with that, Darcy handed over his mount to the approaching stable hand and hurried indoors.

After a hasty wash and change, Darcy descended the stairs and made his way to the dining room. His morning ride having gone so verily askew, he had entirely missed breakfast and was only just in time to sit down for lunch, so it was some time before Darcy had attention to spare.

"I say, Darce, you've more the Hurst about you, eyes only for your plate!"

"Charles!" Miss Bingley cried, a look of horror spread across her face.

Darcy smiled at Hurst, who up until now had been quietly seeing to his victuals, and having caught his gaze, Hurst raised his glass in salute before resuming his attention to the food before him. The bluff gentleman preferred to keep his biting humour sharp, and hidden from those unknown to him, but Darcy knew Hurst's rapier wit delighted in sharpening itself upon his sister-by-marriage.

"See Caro! Neither Darcy nor Hurst have aught to say on my remark, therefore, neither can you." Bingley chided his sister, but the ease with which he dismissed her was never comforting to witness. Bingley was too inured to Miss Bingley's behaviour, and so little noticed how ill-tempered a creature she was. The entire time Miss Bennet and Miss Mary had been under Netherfield's roof, Miss Bingley's mean arts and allurements had been a sore trial, but if he were honest, little had changed with their departure.

"Now then Darce, where have you been all morning? I asked the stable-master when you were not at table for breakfast, but he said you had not yet returned from your ride." Bingley perhaps did not note how eagerly his sister followed his enquiry, but a spark of mischief lit in his breast, causing him to deliberately adopt his severe expression.

"Achilles threw a shoe on my way back, benighted nuisance." Darcy kept Miss Bingley in his peripheral vision, not wanting to miss her expression, "Forced to walk over three miles in total I'm sure, what with getting lost. Kirk was most displeased to point out my boots were six inches deep with mud in some places! However, having had a most miserable morning, I caught a delightful sound carried on the wind, that of a lady's laughter. Worked immeasurably in cheering my spirits." Darcy internally winced, hearing himself sound like Bingley was almost painful to bear.

Witnessing Miss Bingley's appalled expression made it worthwhile. So he continued, happy to be paying Miss Bingley in arrears for her poor civility to the Bennets ladies, "Did we have any plans this afternoon? I thought it might be prudent for you to deliver the invitations around personally. What do you think of calling in on Longbourne directly?"

Bingley's face was everything his sister's was not, and his friend could not agree more violently than a man in the first rush of romance, Darcy thought cynically. For sure, he would never be so transparent as his friend, but perhaps being more open was not necessarily so wholly evil as he had previously believed. For if it were not for the fault of overhearing a private conversation, Darcy would still consider Miss Bennet unaffected by his friend, and it appeared he himself should have considered that not everyone affected to display their feelings as openly as Bingley. Overall, his morning had been over-full with discoveries, and perhaps, with this visit to Longbourne, more was to come.

Caroline Bingley was heartily displeased. Her brother's leased estate was to be the first step in the Bingley's ascension to the first circles, not only through her brother becoming a landed gentleman of wealth, but for her debut to Mr Darcy as a proficient and deft hostess. Yet nothing was as it should be. The society was abysmal, the house itself was nothing of any merit, and her brother continued to dance attendance on his *dear angel* Jane Bennet, who, while quite lovely, was as a milksop to the beauties to be found in London society. To add even further insult, the dratted girl had fallen ill under her roof, forcing her to `do the pretty` with Jane Bennet and her mouse of a sister, else Mr Darcy think her errant in her role as mistress.

Now, here they all were, off to call upon those self-same Bennets and worst of all, Mr Darcy had gone from his customary aloof behaviour, to some dark facsimile of her brother! All because of some wretched laugh he had caught on his wreck of a ride this morning!

It was not to be borne. Caroline had worked too hard, had bragged too loudly, to permit Mr Darcy free of her clutches. She had every expectation of leaving Meryton an engaged woman, regardless of the gentleman's wishes upon the matter.

Hurst quietly watched his sister-by-marriage as she entered the coach, followed swiftly by her brother, and finally, and most surprisingly of all, Darcy too.

His wife sidled up beside him as they stood by the window watching as the carriage departed.

"What do you make of that my dear?" he asked his wife, wrapping an arm about her waist.

Louisa looked him full on, her face filled with worry lines, put there by her devil-woman of a sister, "I do not like it Geoffrey. Tis not like Mr Darcy to willingly be so sociable and for that, you can be sure my sister will have marked the aberration."

"To that," Hurst bent to kiss his wife's brow, "I cannot deny, however, your sister has been deluding herself for some time when it came to that gentleman. I say, we make of this, an opportunity, to suit all our tastes!"

His wife continued to look worried, so he persisted, "Will you not enquire my dear?"

"As to that, I am sure you wish me to query, but I mean to thwart you instead!" Hurst could finally see the soft light in his Louisa's eyes that bespoke her own simple and sweet nature.

"Then I shall delight in regaling you with my designs over tea, whereby you may pretend to attend my every word, and I may content myself in believing myself well heeded!"

Louisa laughed gently, her mirth a small thing, so hard to discover, so buried beneath her sister's harping and scheming. It was only between the two of them, that he ever truly saw his *genuine* wife, else wise the woman he married disappeared under the strength of her sister's character. Steering them away from the window, Hurst settled his lady to her embroidery, while he attended some much-needed correspondence. Caroline was not the only one who could scheme.

Elizabeth and Mary were quietly working in the music room when shrieks could be heard from Mrs Bennet, such that the two sisters could no longer concentrate upon their tasks. Eventually, the expected summons from their mother had both girls tidying away their sheet music and joining the other ladies in the parlour. Jane was seated demurely by an unknown gentleman of reddish blond hair, and open, happy features, who sprung from his seat at their entrance.

Beside their mother was a lady full of stiff courtesy, failing to rise in greeting, choosing to dip a condescending chin in welcome. The lady was dressed ridiculously for a call, wearing a rich silk in a potent pink that clashed terribly with her reddish hair. A relation of the gentleman beside Jane? By the window, a man of tall height and breadth, his appearance impossible to discern with the light streaming in at his back. Her younger sisters, Kitty and Lydia, had claimed their usual place at the small table furthest from the fire, attention consumed by the bonnets set before them. That left Mr Collins in the armchair beside the fire, the one nominally occupied by their father.

Mrs Bennet chimed loudly, "Oh, bless me, I quite forgot! You have yet to meet my next eldest daughter! Lizzy, this is Mr Bingley, who has taken up residence at Netherfield. And this is his sister, Miss Bingley. And there is Mr Darcy" Mrs Bennet waved a lace handkerchief to the window, "friend of Mr Bingley's."

Elizabeth startled at the sound of Mr Darcy's name, but carefully bobbed a correct curtsey as her mother introduced her round. Jane blushed slightly when Mr Bingley hurriedly retook his seat, but before Mary could accompany Elizabeth to the one remaining settee, their mother claimed her aid in seeing to the disbursement of the tea things. Elizabeth gently nudged her sister into her assigned task and took a seat beside Jane, the one not occupied by Mr Bingley.

Mr Darcy moved quietly to the chair beside her, while Miss Bingley frowned her displeasure with her present company. Mary accomplished her work without saying a word, leaving Mrs

Bennet to chatter away at Miss Bingley, while the brother consumed all of Jane's attention. Once finished, Mary eased herself into the space beside the disagreeable lady, a slight frown of concentration marring her features. Her dark mahogany hair was pinned up fiercely, the heavy locks too thick to take a curl unlike Elizabeth's own mane that possessed a soft wave, which presented its own inherent problems. Smiling gently in encouragement to Mary, Elizabeth attempted to direct their mother onto less brash topics, her eyes alight with intelligence and good humour.

Mr Bingley gamely encouraged Mrs Bennet to talk of local acquaintances, causing Elizabeth to wince, while Mary caught her eye and smiled at the sight, only to nod towards Jane, who seemed enraptured by Mr Bingley's generously good-natured replies. Her mind busily considered the match between her fair sister and the new neighbour, considering the little intelligence she already possessed, comparing it against what was presented before her, yet Elizabeth continued to be polite and inserted a fair comment or two, softening Mrs Bennet's somewhat selfish opinions.

"I beg of you, Mr Bingley, to not think so of the Lucases. My dear mother, has long been competing with Lady Lucas as to who can host the most successful dinner party. And as neither will admit defeat, long may this feud continue!" Elizabeth laughed softly as she caught her mother's eye a-purpose, "But nor will anyone in the neighborhood crown a victor, for all agree it is to the neighbourhood's advantage, that these two ladies continue to host exceptional dinners!"

Her mother's frown melted away at the careful compliment hidden in Elizabeth's words, and happily allowed the conversation to flow away from her at last.

"I hear from your sister, that you have been a companion to relatives in Bath. Were you able to take some time from your duties to enjoy the bustling city?" demeaned Miss Bingley.

Instead of a like-minded reply, Elizabeth marvelled, "Why Miss Bingley, I regret to inform you, that no duty other than familial, took me to Bath, and so content was I in my company, that I was only too pleased to extend my visit, when induced to do so by those I resided with. It is altogether agreeable, to share with those harmonious, a passion for experiences old and new. I enjoyed myself immensely and my mother was only too happy to spare me in order for my time away to equal some three months complete!"

Mr Darcy's rapt focus was perturbing, but the delight Elizabeth took in depreciating Miss Bingley's condescension overcame any scruple, for Mary's letters had recounted in detail, the frequent attempts to humble the Bennets at Miss Bingley's hands. With casual indifference,

Elizabeth noted how attentive Mr Bingley was, and so curious was she about him, could not help but note Jane and her companion talk quietly, their attention so markedly fixed upon the other. Accordingly, Miss Bingley inserted herself into her sister's small circle, a silent prompt given to her brother, to which Mr Bingley proved impassive.

"Is aught amiss Miss Bingley?" Elizabeth politely enquired, protective of Jane's interests.

"No, nothing Miss Eliza, I was just wishing to remind my brother of the visits we have yet to make." Miss Bingley sniffed disdainfully, and her attention shifted to the as yet silent Mr Darcy.

Following her lead, Elizabeth could account, now that she had seen him clearly, to be uncommonly good-looking, his jaw and cheek bones sharply delineated against the backdrop of his inky mane. His nose was slightly askew, adding a roguish charm to his appearance, while his stone-grey eyes pierced Elizabeth as they in turn studied her.

"While, it is late in-" Elizabeth began, only to have Mary stiffly interrupt.

"It is Elizabeth" Mary asserted, her blue eyes locked upon her cup, "Not Eliza, Miss Bingley."

The lady's dignity allowed her no verbal reply, yet Miss Bingley's entire posture screamed offence. Mary said no more, but refused to look up from her cup, however it was clear to

Elizabeth, Miss Bingley's manners provoked her sister's correction. Into this silence fell Mr Collins like a lead weight, as he stood by Mr Darcy's side.

"Am I aright in thinking you are Mr Darcy of Pemberly in Derbyshire? Related to my esteemed patroness, Lady Catherine de Bourgh of Rosings Park?"

Mr Darcy's darkly alluring features aligned themselves into a severe expression, stone eyes and granite cheeks made the gentleman fiercely imposing. There was little softness in the great man, but that of his unruly curls against his brow, ears and neckline. Yet Mr Collins, lacking in acuity, unable to detect the cold disdain emanating from the statue of a man.

"I am." Was the curt reply given to the half-witted rector.

"Oh! What fortune is mine! To have the distinguished honor to inform you that your good lady aunt, Lady Catherine de Bourgh, and jewel of a cousin, Miss de Bourgh, were in excellent health but four days hence!" Mr Collins would have continued if Mr Bingley had not spoken louder than was his usual, mentioning his intention to host a ball.

"Oh, how you honour us Sir, though I do imagine-" Mr Collins began, only for Mrs Bennet's words to over-run him.

"Oh, Jane! Does not Mr Bingley do you such an honour!"

Lydia and Kitty's squeals of delight were

muted, having the joy shared between them, making them for once more restrained than they normally would be, but Elizabeth merely rolled her eyes at Mary, causing her sister to smile in genuine amusement.

"-honour of the first set?" Mr Bingley's words filtered to Elizabeth in time for her to catch Jane's reply in the affirmative, setting Mrs Bennet off once more in happy expectation, their mother's imagination needing very little fuel to fire her flights of fancies. Briefly Elizabeth caught sight of Miss Bingley's unhappy expression before the bulk of Mr Collins person intruded into her awareness.

"My dear cousin, would you honour *me* with the first set?" Mr Collins pompously asked, the happy expectation of a positive reply evident, as he confidently looked upon his fellow guests, rather than Elizabeth herself.

Mary sent a troubled look her way, and her stumbled thoughts crashed around her head. Poor Mary struggled through such occasions and therefore the ball would be a trial for her next young sister. Elizabeth would work with Mary, she vowed with determination, help her manage accordingly so that some pleasure could be had from the evening for once. As she made her vow, Elizabeth also promised herself to speak with both Kitty and Lydia, in the hopes of making some improvement in that quarter. Offering a tiny smile of reassurance Mary's way, the stone gaze of Mr Darcy caught her attention. His expression was impossible to comprehend, however her study of the gentleman was interrupted by a coarse cough from Mr Collins. A stifled snort followed, Miss Bingley's attempt to cover the sound encompassed everything that was false and shallow.

Frustrated to be caught in a web of such a public setting, Elizabeth decided she would not fall victim to her mother's machinations, and instead, with a sweet, yet mischievous air, replied to the repellent request, "Mr Collins, what a compliment!" Keeping her gaze pinned upon the overbearing rector, "Yet I fear you may call into question, your honourable vocation within the local society if I were to accept! I would hate for you to recieve a negative reception for failing to honour the *hostess* of the evening, as is surely more appropriate, when that self-same lady is present." Ensuring the appropriate contrite expression, Elizabeth continued, "Indeed, how would it look if the Bennet's took possession of all the young gentlemen to the area for the first set, and thereby snub our neighbours? For they will one day be yours, Sir." With a sweet look at her mother, who appeared furious with Elizabeth's refusal, she proceeded, "Why mama, it would be conceited to so disrespect the hostess. I would be mortified to offend such a new acquaintance!" Her colour was high, and she knew her youngest sisters watched in rapt entertainment, but they could be managed later. For now, it was imperative Mr Collins not assume a positive reception, not when her friend Charlotte wished to attain success with the gentleman.

The room seemed to hold its breath, paused as if to discover how Mr Collins would receive such direction, for the gentleman stood before her stupefied, his thoughts muddling through his vacuous mind, until with a burst of animation, Mr Collins turned his eager eyes upon Miss Bingley, who could not recover her disgusted countenance swiftly enough to conceal her displeasure.

"Of course! Why, my cousin is indeed correct! How foolish of me to behave so poorly, when the lady is before me!" Mr Collins smiled benevolently down upon Miss Bingley.

Feeling some added motivation would be needed, especially if she were to encourage Mr Collins towards Charlotte, Elizabeth was ready to continue when Mary spoke up.

"Yes Sir, my sister has the right of it. You must consider it your Christian responsibility to perform your duties as a gentleman to the benefit of the closely knit local society you find yourself in. I am sure your patroness would approve."

Mr Collins gaped at her reticent sister as if he had never seen her before, but then he returned his attention of moments before,

"Miss Bingley, I must beg your pardon for my inexcusable disregard! Please, would you do me the honour of standing up with me for the first set?"

The silence stretched, Mr Collins request having created an anticipatory air, full of expectations, disbelief and humour. Even Mr Bingley and Jane waited to see how Miss Bingley would answer. The lady contemptuously glanced away, and with nominal grace accepted, causing her brother to almost snort a laugh until he managed to check the impulse. Elizabeth turned away from Mr Bingley's struggles and instead was caught in the power of Mr Darcy's gaze. Perhaps it was her imagination, but for a brief glimpse of restrained mirth, the solemn gentleman's manner seemed marginally lighter. With an almost imperceptible dip of his head, it appeared the stone-giant admired her deflection. What a peculiar man.

Darcy was at pains to keep his true sentiments to himself. If he were to glance just once towards his friend, the tight grip he had upon his amusement would be lost. It had taken all his strength not to react to Bingley's snort of laughter, but he had maintained it. Until now, Darcy had been in a bemused state, as the visit progressed much as he would have predicted, with Mrs Bennet flattering his friend, praising her daughter and attempting to thaw the ice surrounding Miss Bingley. But throughout it all, the unknown Bennet daughter's words whispered through his mind, softening his perception. His once hard opinions of the youngest Bennets seemed especially affected, for they were of age with Georgiana, and he would not want a stranger to view his sister as coldly as he had done the Bennets.

While his impression had softened, the true surprise came in the form of the missing daughter herself. Miss Elizabeth's beauty caught him completely unawares and instantly gained his admiration. She was of a petite frame, and despite her feminine figure, there was a lightness to her movements. But it was watching her eyes, the caramel-brown glowing with some inner fire that captivated him. Her dark brown hair was merely bound up, but no matter the simplicity, with Miss Elizabeth, the whole of her, her manners, her appearance, her intellect, her *light*, was mesmerising.

Then to witness her evade Mr Collins and entrap Miss Bingley. Darcy felt troubled by how deeply one meeting and one overheard conversation had affected him. Perhaps it was the novelty of meeting someone who had failed to succumb to Wickham's charm. Perhaps it was watching Miss Bingley be so expertly sidestepped, and so sweetly too, for there was naught amiss with her reasoning. Darcy felt in uncharted waters. Why could he do nothing but study this woman? What magic compelled him to draw nearer, like a flower turning to the sun?

"If you will excuse me, I shall leave you all to Jane's delightful company. Mary?" Miss Elizabeth stood, hooking her arm through that of her sister's.

Darcy watched the black scowl fall upon Miss Bingley before she pasted on a benign expression, and henceforth continued to interfere in her brother's and Miss Bennets conversation. Of Mr Collins, no one paid any heed bar Mrs Bennet, and even she seemed ill-pleased by such attentions. Darcy rose abruptly, moving across to the window, hands placed firmly at his back, while his whole attention remained fixed upon Miss Elizabeth.

"-that is beautiful work!" Miss Elizabeth praised, causing her younger sister to flush with pride, her reflection in the glass providing him the perfect spot to observe, "I do believe, Lyddie, that is the stitch Mary demonstrated?" A quiet murmur, "I thought so! It does look marvellous, and how clever of you to dress a bonnet with such details!"

The youngest's strong tones followed, "Tis not for me, silly. This is for Mary! As her current bonnet is simply *hideous*!"

Darcy glimpsed Miss Mary's dark

expression out the corner of his eye, turning his body as if noting something of interest through the window he stood by. Nerves jangled, and he controlled his breathing, fighting his feelings of awkwardness.

"Why Lyddie, how kind! And look, the blue ribbon brings out Mary's eyes! What a thoughtful gift!" Miss Elizabeth's words were all true, validating the younger girls seemed to calm them, while Miss Mary studied the bonnet in question, intently. "Yet, perhaps Mary could save such a fine construction for Church? She would require something simpler perhaps, for every day?" Miss Mary looked up, a nod of agreement her reply, "Maybe a soft green to highlight her dark hair?"

Darcy watched as Miss Lydia studied her sister, "Oh, I have just the thing! Only, tis one of yours!"

Miss Elizabeth smiled slightly at this, "Then why do you not fetch the item, and if tis one I am willing to part with, I will happily leave it for you to remake."

Miss Lydia whooped energetically before dashing from the room. Miss Elizabeth quietly spoke to Miss Mary, before the younger, quieter sister, followed in Miss Lydia's wake.

"Now Kitty, I can see you think I have not noted those incomplete sketches in that folio. No, do not frown so, as I have no intention to offer a scold. Instead, I have a commission for you."

Before Darcy could listen further, Miss Bingley rose and announced their need to depart, to which his friend could only comply, his longing glances in Miss Bennet's direction resembling that of a puppy. As he made his way across the room, he stopped by Miss Elizabeth's side without understanding what he would say, but then he surprised both himself and the lady when he asked, "Might I have the pleasure of a set Miss Elizabeth?"

Her beautiful brown eyes, sweet and rich, blinked once, before she quietly consented to reserve him a set. The third. He bowed, then swiftly stepped from the room, ignoring Mr Collins, else he be trapped in banal conversation.

As he entered the carriage, his thoughts were filled with Miss Elizabeth. Her love for her family was expressed in every gesture, her careful guidance and gentle encouragement. How swiftly would his sister have recovered from this summer's disappointment under such sisterly care and affection? Someone who openly expressed tenderness in delightful little ways, instead of cool, controlled instruction. Georgiana would benefit from her own Miss Elizabeth. But with a family like the Bennets, it was not possible. Regret wrenched deep in his chest.

Darcy's disappointment was hard to hide, and Miss Bingley was only too quick to assume some commiseration with him, that the indignity of such people was too much to tolerate, and only the very little pleasure she would have in showing how such an event as her ball was to be conducted, gave her any relief. Darcy had not meant to interrupt, but queried where they were next to call, only for Bingley to say with the time, the remaining invitations would have to go out by post. This left Darcy somewhat dissatisfied, as he would not be able to carefully inform Miss Lucas about Mr Collins parsonage, something he assumed she would be much interested in, considering her marital aspirations. The poor woman. While he would not judge Miss Lucas for her intentions, he could not celebrate a union with such a fool as was Mr Collins.

CHAPTER 3

Netherfield Park, Hertfordshire November 20th

Over dinner, Darcy was forced to endure Miss Bingley's continual sniping, her equanimity little improved from their time spent at Longbourne. Bingley remained affable throughout, until with a final exasperated sigh, he muttered something that Hurst cheerfully caught.

"What's this?" Hurst chortled, "Caroline has a partner already for the first set?" His eyes alighted upon Darcy with some expectation, to which he was quick to deny. "If not Darcy, then who?" Hurst queried.

Miss Bingley looked away, colour flushing her cheeks, which only served to tickle Hurst further.

Bingley gave a hearty sigh, "The Bennets have a distant cousin visiting, and on receiving their invitation, the gentleman wished to claim a dance from one of the Bennet daughters. Miss Elizabeth, having only just returned to Longbourn was singled out, yet in answer, the lady quite rightly claimed that it was somewhat tactless to request a dance of a member of their own household, when the hostess of the event was present." Here Bingley paused to take a sip of his wine, yet Darcy would wager it was an effort to tamp down the memory of his sister's reaction. "Therefore, with very little hesitation, Mr Collins requested Caro's hand for the first set, to which of course she was obliged to accept."

Hurst's baffled expression, having not met the man, most likely thought his sister by marriage was demeaning the connection to the Bennets, unaware of how truly ridiculous the pompous rector was.

Unable to contain her outrage, Miss Bingley ranted, "It was that impudent chit, Miss *Eliza's* doing!"

Bingley intervened, sensing his sister's composure was shaky at best, "Nonsense Caro, Miss *Elizabeth* was extremely conscientious to think not of herself, but of her family as a whole. It is true, that with my own attentions to Miss Bennet, the local matrons could take a decidedly poor impression of the family, leading to some harm to the Bennet's standing in the community. Admittedly, Mr Collins could have requested *a set* rather than the first, but tis done now."

Darcy had admired Miss Elizabeth's quick

deflection, but in truth, the local society would *expect* Mrs Bennet, knowing her character for what it was, to keep the majority of male attention upon her daughters.

"The officers of the resident militia! They, too, are to be invited to the ball, so there will be more than enough dance partners! That Miss Eliza was being deliberately provoking!" Miss Bingley screeched.

Hoping to defuse the mounting tension, Darcy cleared his throat, "I disagree Miss Bingley. Miss *Elizabeth* was no doubt, disconcerted by the rash actions of her father's cousin, and sought to ameliorate any potential offence you rightly were entitled to feel. The lady's *kindness* in thinking of others before herself, in encouraging Mr Collins to think of his duty was commendable. It is unreasonable to apply censure upon one for how the gentleman assimilated the guidance and its subsequent application." Darcy sipped his wine, grateful that there was only the dessert course left to partake before the ladies would withdraw. Much more of Miss Bingley's vitriol and Darcy would lose his appetite.

"Well...that is..." Miss Bingley sputtered.

"Excellently put, Darcy!" Bingley saluted him with his glass, causing Hurst to chuckle and down his own wine.

"How rare it is, Darcy, to hear you speak well of the fairer sex!" Hurst noted, the canny intelligence he carefully hid, peeking through.

"Exceptional, more like," Miss Bingley cattily commented, "Miss Eliza must be another candidate for such musical sounds made of a morning."

Hurst sputtered into his refilled glass, while Bingley turned red and gasped like a trout. Darcy attempted to restrain his own errant expression, but his consternation must have been apparent when Miss Bingley glanced his way, her confusion clear. The vivid imagery of what could *cause* Miss Elizabeth to be vocal early in the morning was difficult to shake from his mind. Unable to fathom the faux pas she had committed, it was Mrs Hurst who steered the conversation into safer waters, talking of arrangements of the upcoming ball. The men collected themselves enough until the ladies withdrew, at which point, loud guffaws could be heard from the dining room.

Elizabeth exited her father's book room, happy with what she had managed to accomplish. In her buoyant state, even Mr Collins bumbling attempts to pay court to her, could not dim her sense of achievement. Therefore, it was much to her dismay to discover the presence of several officers taking up seats in her mother's parlour.

Lieutenants Wickham, Denny, Saunderson and Mr Collins large bodies made her mother's furniture look small and dainty in contrast, but the happy welcome she received on entering did little to mend her opinion.

"Miss Elizabeth, how lovely it is to see you again!" Lieutenant Wickham was the first to reach her side, followed swiftly by Mr Collins who sent the officer a dark look. "I must say, calling upon Longbourne has become manifestly more pleasurable since your arrival."

"Cousin Elizabeth, how glad I am to have your company while these officers entertain your younger sisters." Mr Collins volley was met with a raised eyebrow from said officer, who gallantly bowed her into the room.

Catching Jane's eye, Elizabeth silently questioned her sister, who did nought but shrug her delicate shoulders. She huffed, Jane forever perceived the world with gentle eyes! Finding Mary, Elizabeth sent the same silent query, for her to shoot a speaking glance to the Lieutenant at her side. So Mr Wickham was the instigator of this visit. As they reached her youngest sister animatedly discussing a prank one of the officers had suffered, Elizabeth nimbly secured a central position, flanked by Lydia and Kitty, who smiled happily at her. Smiling brightly back, Elizabeth bided her time patiently.

"Miss Elizabeth, have you space on your dance card for the upcoming ball? I have it on good authority that you have been much in demand."

Elizabeth frowned in puzzlement at Lieutenant Denny, and answered with an arch sweetness, "Now Lieutenant, with three younger sisters, I am sure you do not wish to incite further contention into such exciting activity?" The officer glanced away, a rosy hue painting his cheeks. Feeling she had slayed one head of the hydra, Elizabeth studied his companion, "Lieutenant Saunderson, I hear from my sisters that you intend to be a dedicated career military man?"

"That is indeed my calling, Miss Elizabeth." The Lieutenant's gruff tone was at odds with his fair-headed complexion, the officer no older than her eldest sister, she was sure.

"Do you have much training that must be rehearsed?" Glancing between the officers, then further about the room, Elizabeth hoped her implication was apparent, "Or are they more relaxed in the militia than the Regiment?" She knew this was not so, not when Bath was filled with a host of wounded soldiers and recuperating officers, many having risen from one service to the other. Off paying calls upon the local ladies was not chief amongst those expected tasks required from servicemen.

The Lieutenant looked discomfited, sending his own silent appeal towards his older compatriot. "I cannot speak for the Regiment,

Miss Elizabeth, but I have not found the militia to be a relaxed outfit." Lieutenant Wickham failed to display any contrition at this obvious avoidance of duties.

"Oh Lizzy, you need not worry about such things! I am sure the officers are all so dashing and charming *because* they achieve all that nonsense so swiftly, leaving them plenty of time for parties and balls and dancing!" Lydia's girlish tones spoke of her innocence, her delightful energy spreading smiles about the room, Elizabeth included.

"While I would that were the case, dear one, I do believe we should permit these good gentlemen to be on their way, as we would hate to be the cause for them to face any unpleasantness from their commanding officer. Is that not so, Jane?"

Jane startled, agreed nonetheless, and therefore, without much trouble, the house was almost free of unwanted male guests. Of Mr Collins, there was little to be done. With the room mostly to themselves, Elizabeth captured Kitty by her hand and tugged her into the music room across the hall, closing the door hurriedly to prevent Mr Collins from joining them.

"What is it Lizzy? Why do you pull me about so?" Kitty whined, her matching dark hair to Elizabeth's tossed slightly askew with her slumping into the settee. Elizabeth laughed and joined her, tickling Kitty until she giggled and pleaded for mercy.

"There, much better! I do so hate to see you sad, dear one." Elizabeth tucked a coffee coloured curl behind her sister's ear. "I have something of which I wished to discuss with you, and you alone."

This she knew, had the anticipated effect, causing Kitty to perk up considerably, "What?" She fairly bounced in her seat, her excitement palpable, "What is it?"

Her laughter escaped once more, Kitty's infectious lightness catching her up in a like-minded spirit, "Hush, and I shall tell you." Kitty quietened, "I have spoken to father this morning, and he has agreed, so all that is left, is to seek your own approval of the scheme." Kitty began to speak, but Elizabeth hushed her with a raised hand, "Sssh, patience Kitty. You are aware I have developed a strong friendship with our aunt Gardiner's nieces, and it is for them I would wish you to send the sketch of Longbourne to, but that is beside the point." Elizabeth babbled, "I have suggested, and been granted permission, for *you* to visit our aunt's family in Bath, and all that is left to discover is if *you* would wish to go?"

Elizabeth patiently waited for Kitty to review her thoughts, familiar as she was with her slower pace, a contrast to that of their much quicker witted younger sister, Lydia. While many thought Kitty silly, it was hard for the girl to appear to advantage when constantly outshone by her more vivacious siblings, and Lydia was perhaps the most spirited creature in the county! It took her sister a little while before she asked, "Would this be for me and me alone? Or am I to travel with you or Mary?"

"This would be for you and no other. I grew very close to Evelyn and Rebecca, to such a degree that they became as sisters to me, and while I would delight in returning to visit them, I feel it only fair that another gain the benefit of travel, meeting new people, experiencing new places." Elizabeth then shifted from encouraging, to something a little firmer, "There is however, some conditions to this visit. The girls are not yet out and still have a governess, therefore, so to would you be considered." Speaking quickly, as she could see Kitty's ire rising, she hurriedly went on, "Not that this would affect your standing here at home, but while in company and a guest of Uncle Thompson, you would be under the authority of their governess, Mrs Ashley."

"Is this some trick?" Kitty carefully asked, "Are you only offering me this so that I can learn something?" tone sharp and wary, Kitty stared back at Elizabeth with similar brown eyes, her younger sister, a taller, sleeker version of herself.

Smiling widely, brow raised in her own picture of mischief, Elizabeth answered, "Am I that cruel, Kitty? To make you go away because I think you untutored?" Kitty's stance softened, but the wary look did not leave her eyes, so Elizabeth huffed and looked away. The music room was a simple, unadorned space, not filled with lace or messy work-baskets. A mere green settee, small slightly ornate table, and the pianoforte. That was all. But in this room, Elizabeth had found it easier to enjoy some peace. So too, for Mary. And here, she decided she would explain more of her reasoning, more than she would have before her time away.

"Very well sister, I shall relate my intentions, but I beg of you not to interrupt, which I imagine will be no easy feat. You are surely aware, that both Jane and I have benefited from our time with our aunt Gardiner. Her lessons, and her guidance, have been the means for which Jane and I model our conduct. That behaviour, that deportment and correctitude is not the same for you and our youngest sister. Your lessons were not so excellently guided and as such, there is a *wanting* displayed in your manner, that reflects poorly upon the Bennets as a whole." Kitty's mouth burst open in rejection but again, Elizabeth stopped her with a raised hand, "Please Kitty, bear with me, for I truly do not mean to denigrate or rebuke." Her words softened further as Kitty sat back with a defiant grunt, "So while I have always been aware of this disparity, the glaring truth of it was made clear while away in Bath, witnessing how the girls I was visiting behaved. But then I considered, how is it fair to fault you and Lydia, when you have never been given the opportunities that have been afforded Jane and I? As such, with some little conversation with our aunt and uncle Gardiner, and today our father's permission, I have sought for *you* to experience some wider society. Does it matter that there will be some alteration? Is it of not more worth that you gain the opportunity?"

As Elizabeth concluded her speech, Kitty wrapped her arms about a cushion and tucked it close against her body, chin resting upon the top. Her eyes stared off into the distance, her thoughts hidden. Then, without lifting her head, Kitty asked, "Will Lydia and mama be told why I am to go? Will not Lydia demand her share of the pleasures Bath has to offer?"

"Kitty, our father has agreed, so whatever you decide, our mother and sister will be told only what you wish. And it matters not if Lydia wishes to take your place. Tis *you* who has been afforded this opportunity, and you alone." Elizabeth's words were full of love and reassurance, hoping to nurture the tiny bud of her sister's individual spirit, the desire to be set apart from her sisters and be seen and valued upon her own merits.

"Very well, I shall go. But Lydia is not to be told all that you have shared with me!" Kitty warned, then a thought sparked behind her eyes and she asked, "If you are sending *me* off to Bath to further my education, what are you considering for *Lydia's* benefit?"

"Lydia requires a far more cautious hand, considering she has our mother wrapped about her little fingers."

Kitty snorted, and Elizabeth smiled in agreement, "Yet, our aunt and uncle are aiding me in discovering what is to be done. There has been talk of one of our aunt's cousins may be well situated to guide our youngest sister, but nothing has been decided."

Shrugging, Kitty moved on, "When am I to go? Am I to have new dresses? Who will travel with me?"

Happy to have soothed her younger sister's concerns, Elizabeth answered any and all questions, stating she would leave with their Gardiner relatives, following their visit this Christmas, from there, her aunt's brother would come to London and bring his daughters to be introduced. In regards to new dresses, Elizabeth encouraged Kitty to join her in rifling through their combined wardrobes, to see if there was any that could be made over to better suit. Being of similar colouring, but somewhat shorter and fuller figured, there were some selections made that delighted Kitty enough to keep her excited. Elizabeth kept to herself, that her aunt Gardiner had made some fabric choices already, in preparation for one else two dresses being made for Kitty while she visited with them in the New

Year.

Netherfield Ball November 27th

Darcy watched as the assembled guests milled about the ballroom and adjoining drawing rooms. Having grimly avoided the behest to join the Bingley's in the receiving line, he studied the assembled guests as they roamed, well aware he was waiting for a particular set of chocolate curls to appear. Their meeting over a week ago had remained with him, trailing his thoughts like the train of a woman's gown. His mind filled with the sounds of her melodic laughter, warm words, gentle signals of affection, all of which Miss Elizabeth displayed with such ease and without guile.

Prior to meeting her, before he had overheard that open and private conversation between two close friends, Darcy had not thought of anyone in the surrounding area charitably. He had been dismissive, disregarding the derogatory comments made by Miss Bingley, and deaf to any of Bingley's foolishly warm sentiments. Yet, the shade, or perhaps the light of Miss Elizabeth's honesty made him perceive his company differently.

Sir William volubly talked amongst the officers, Mrs Goulding caught up in rapid conversation with two young ladies, and Darcy realised, none of these people had foisted themselves upon his notice. Not like they would, and *did*, in town. Perhaps for the first time at any event he had attended, Darcy allowed himself to relax. To twitch his lips in a semblance of a smile as he witnessed the officers react to the entrance of the Bennets, but then he himself fell into the void, sinking into sweet brown eyes, animated in admiration for her surroundings. The decor had barely registered, but through Miss Elizabeth's genuine regard, did he acknowledge Miss Bingley had assembled a refined ambiance. He knew, from having born witness to it all, that much of the work had fallen heavily upon the staff of Netherfield, and so the true accomplishment of the evenings finery could hardly be attributed to Miss Bingley, but the lady *had* brought it all together.

Darcy forced himself forward, manoeuvring through the ebb and flow of the assembled guests with practised ease, until at last he reached Miss Elizabeth's side.

"Good evening Miss Elizabeth, Miss Mary, Miss Lucas. I hope you are all faring well?" was his dull inquiry, at odds with how he felt, as if on the precipice of a cliff, the dark depths below him, and cold angry skies all about.

"We are all well, are we not?" Miss Elizabeth gestured to her companions, who nodded, without speaking, "Yet I must admit to some relief of finally attending tonight, as for after, we shall no longer have to bear listening to my younger sisters' excitement unabated!" her words were a tease upon the absent members of her family, causing Darcy to glance about to locate them.

They were easily spotted, for while Miss Bennet was beside her parents, close to the entrance, most likely in wait for Bingley, the younger two were amidst a sea of redcoats. Once again, a familiar disdain attempted to overcome Darcy, but a soft enquiry from his present company brushed such concerns aside, like a feather duster sweeping away the cobwebs.

"For shame, Eliza, you should comprehend that your suffering will not abate, not with Lydia and Kitty's continual gleeful recollections to contend with!" Miss Lucas's tease caused Miss Elizabeth to share a commiserating grin with Miss Mary, before the lady turned to him, brow raised.

"Have you managed to enjoy your time here in Hertfordshire?" the noise and volume of people attempted to steal the sweet sound of Miss Elizabeth's words, but Darcy caught them nonetheless.

"It has not been quite what I anticipated, but Bingley has an excellent property upon which he may choose to purchase and develop further, or maintain for the duration of his lease to endeavour to gain some experience as a landholder." Once again, his words were drab and sober, yet his audience maintained polite expressions nonetheless. None battered their lashes, or fluttered their fans, no coy titters. It was refreshing, he realised.

"Mr Bingley has oft mentioned to our sister, how reliant he has been upon your counsel these past few weeks." Miss Mary quietly remarked, her gaze avoiding his own.

Miss Elizabeth smiled gently at her sister, before turning to him with arch sweetness, "That is very generous indeed, Mr Darcy. For has it not meant you have been kept from your own tasks and home, in order to offer aid to a friend?"

Miss Lucas quietly interjected, "We have heard of your estate being quite significant, surely you will wish to return in order to manage it directly?"

Darcy stiffly explained how he had been maintaining a regular correspondence with all his business endeavours, therefore, he hoped, that there was little aggregation, that his time away would have generated.

"I cannot deny that I have many interests that need overseeing, but I am confident in the capability of my agents, stewards, and staff, that my instructions and directives will be ably managed." Darcy wished to thump his own brow, much as his cousin would, at how utterly tedious he sounded. Yet he must give the ladies their due, none had looked grieved to be caught in conversation with him, and not one lady had managed to flatter in the manner Miss Bingley had perfected. Overt flattery was utterly aggravating to endure.

Hoping to redirect the conversation away from himself, Darcy asked Miss Lucas, "Have you been introduced to Mr Collins, Miss Lucas?" When she acknowledged she had, Darcy attempted to discuss a topic he hoped would be of interest, "I am not sure if you are aware, but Mr Collins patroness, is my aunt, and as such I am very familiar with Rosings, the surrounding area, the parsonage and the many tenants. I visit annually at Easter to see to any necessary estate matters."

Miss Lucas's surprise at his offering personal details almost set him back, until with a glance at Miss Elizabeth, she encouraged the topic with a series of questions that exemplified, that while Mr Collins could hardly be a desirable candidate, the gentleman would be marginally improved through partnership with an excellently sensible woman.

The first strains began to filter through, and as such, couples moved to cluster about the ballroom, awaiting the arrival of their hosts. At which point, Darcy recalled Mr Collins was to be partnered with Miss Bingley and a bubble of mirth attempted to escape, carefully concealed by an abrupt cough. Accidentally, Darcy caught Miss Elizabeth's eye, and the sight of her biting her lip in restrained amusement almost completely overturned his composure, but his discipline held. His heart, however, felt infinitely brighter, enjoying a shared moment with toffee-brown eyes, like polished bronze, sparkling back at him.

Elizabeth felt lighter than she had since her return to Longbourne, missing her new friends just slightly less, now that she was enjoying good company and the prospect of lively dancing. Charlotte had masterfully managed Mr Collins into asking her for the second set, and currently all five Bennets had evaded the punishment of standing up with their male house guest. This was indeed a mercy, as Elizabeth watched the gentleman take another wrong turn in the dance, setting Miss Bingley's cheeks to flaming in suspected temper.

She attempted to ignore the performance, encouraging Mary to converse with Mr Darcy, a somewhat tedious process, but it allowed for the first dance to pass and witness the pleasure of how naturally Jane and Mr Bingley were partnered. Their cheerful temperaments fairly glowed from them, and the sight of her sister's happiness brought a radiant smile to her.

Eventually, some of the officers braved the tall and darkly well-favoured gentleman at her side to request of her a dance, to which she happily complied, and from a quiet word received from Mr Darcy, Mary was escorted to their mother's side. Yet even while she was caught up in her activity, her attention seemed to stay tangled up in the prospect of her next partner. Her attention fixed upon his stern countenance as he stood stiffly to the side, Miss Bingley caught up in conversing with his profile. Not once did the gentleman turn to her, his brief replies to her commentary failing to discourage Miss Bingley. She was relentless, it seemed. A spurt of annoyance grew deep in Elizabeth's breast for the quiet gentleman.

Disgruntled with nuisance women like Miss Bingley and their ambitions, Mr Darcy was a source of some curiosity, what with having heard something of the gentleman from Lieutenant Wickham. As awkward in social settings as her sister, Mary, her heart softened towards the dour gentleman, perhaps dangerously so. Elizabeth was more than aware, from the cut of his clothes, to his very deportment, that Mr Darcy was out of reach, unattainable for a mere Miss Bennet.

Her dance concluded with easy rapport, Elizabeth smiled brightly as the officer encouraged her to accept his hand for a latter set, but well adept at handling over-eager attentions of coltish males, she cleverly deflected the application. There was an interim pause to permit the musicians some reprieve, and so Elizabeth carefully guided Mary forward into easy conversation under Charlotte's direction, while she waited patiently for the next set to begin. A strange sort of fluttery excitement blossomed in Elizabeth's body, making it difficult for her to attend the slight conversation Charlotte was conducting. And then he was before her, leading her to the dance and Elizabeth glimpsed her neighbours reaction, the general surprise and amazement such a simple event as being asked to stand up with a gentleman did not warrant.

Looking to her partner for some explanation, Elizabeth was silenced by the quiet intensity of the gentleman before her. Mr Darcy seemed as if he had been plucked from some gothic novel, where he could play either the tortured hero or the cunningly devious villain, that Elizabeth could not fathom what to make of the man. Hoping to discover more, Elizabeth set to sketching the character of Mr Darcy.

"Forgive me, Sir, but our dance appears to be something of a sensation. A rather peculiar consequence. Is there some defect to your character that would make our performance somewhat exceptional?" Even Jane looked surprised as she moved through the set with

Captain Carter.

"To that, I can offer little, save that I have scant interest in the activity, there being slight occasion to exhibit ere now." shocked Elizabeth to silence.

Turning to circle the gentleman beside her partner, Elizabeth returned to her position opposite Mr Darcy, she collected her wits enough to enquire, "Do you mean to tell me, that of your time in the neighbourhood, *this* is the first occasion you have chosen to *exhibit*?"

Aghast, Elizabeth failed to note Mr Darcy's stone mask descend, too busy studying the guests who had set to whispering amongst themselves, but worst of all was the calculating gleam in her mother's eyes. This was a disaster. Elizabeth knew all it took for her mother to hear wedding bells, was for a gentleman to step in the direction of her daughters, let alone single her out to dance with them and no other, therefore, she urged, still not looking at her partner, "Please Sir, do me the honour of asking *anyone* else to dance tonight!"

"I beg your pardon?" The icy reply caught her attention, matched perfectly with the stone visage from this monolith of a man. It would be hard to interpret that expression as inclination in any light!

"I intend no disrespect Mr Darcy," Elizabeth smiled at her sister, while her eyes pleaded with her partner, "but if I am the only lady to whom you engage in dancing, then you encourage the gossips to imagine some partiality. However, if you ask just *one* other, then this will be nothing of note, and we may therefore spend time in one another's company without inference and speculation." Elizabeth thought she sounded polite, not at all encroaching, but still Mr Darcy failed to warm in his expression.

Yet his words offered some reassurance he would comply, "Do you mean to suggest, that in order to suspend any suspicion of interest, I should hasten to ask another to stand up with me, and thereby allay any gossip?"

The set had almost concluded, time seeming to have sped up, stealing the joy of partnering with such an agile and graceful individual. However, she chuckled lightly, and nodded, attempting to perfect a mildly interested look, but nothing that would feed further grist to the mill.

"Then, permit me to escort you back to your sister, so that I may request a set." Mr Darcy gestured with his hand to where Mary stood, still in company with Charlotte. A slight quirk kicked up his lips, and Elizabeth breathed easier at last, but felt the tension had failed to free her from the fog that descended just then. "I thank you, Miss Elizabeth, for a most enjoyable half hour. I do not usually find it thus, but you do a credit to your dance instructor."

"Thank you, Mr Darcy." Elizabeth swept a curl back from her cheek, niggling shadows trailed across her vision, "I thank you for thinking of my sister, she does not do well in busy events such as this, and as such, often retreats to the sidelines when she must attend." Elizabeth dipped a curtsey and stepped lightly away, thankful Mr Darcy had neglected to offer his arm, despite how her vision wavered and his aid would have been appreciated. Her mother would imagine every civility as something more.

"Mary, dearest?" Elizabeth tapped her sister upon her shoulder, and was happy to see her so at ease, an uncommon occurrence.

"Miss Mary, would you permit me the honour of the next dance?" Mr Darcy's voice was gruff at her side, but the gentleman had banished his stone persona for a more neutral one, so it was impossible to discern if her words had truly offended the man. Frustrating as it was, Elizabeth was heartily relieved to see the back of Mr Darcy, while simultaneously sad that she could not see the gentleman asking her for a second. As he escorted a bemused Mary to the floor, Elizabeth fought feelings of admiration, concern, and pain.

"Why Eliza, I do believe you have made a conquest!" Charlotte quietly uttered.

Appalled at encouraging any further gossip, Elizabeth laughed brightly and batted the comment away, yet she could no longer ignore the beginning of a burgeoning headache. Charlotte's astute gaze reflected her concern, but before she could raise a query, they were interrupted.

"Why, Eliza Bennet, I do believe you have managed quite a feat!" Miss Bingley's insipid coo failed to mask the lady's unease, and was uncomfortably uttered loud enough to garner further attention.

"Not at all, Miss Bingley, I merely think Mr Darcy is more at ease at an event hosted by his close friend, do you not agree? It would be foolish to presume anything more." Elizabeth's temper remained concealed by her casually dismissive answer, but the escalating tension aggravated the dull ache to throb within her head, her eyes blinking ineffectively from the candlelight.

With a flash of her fan, Miss Bingley commented in a superior tone, "How wise of you to ascertain, Miss Eliza. Such astuteness of mind is so rarely evident in young ladies of late, their imagination so very rapid, to jump from a dance, to admiration, from admiration to love, and then from love to matrimony! How relieved I am to discover you are not so lost to such self-delusion. How refreshingly independent of you." Ordinarily, Elizabeth would have sported with the woman, but her pain made her thoughts sluggish.

"Forgive me, Miss Bingley, but to what purpose do you affirm my own sentiments?" She rubbed a finger against her temple, hoping to ease the pain pulsing behind her eyes, closing them for respite and therefore missing the flash of something in Miss Bingley's expression.

"Merely pleasantly surprised, Miss Eliza. In addition, I have heard such accounts of you from your sister, as to make your character something of an interest. That, and you have quite a *delightful* laugh." Miss Bingley uttered, her emphasis upon Elizabeth's laughter puzzling. "Dear me, you seem to be feeling a little discomposed, may I fetch you something for your relief? A glass of wine perhaps?" Miss Bingley's concern, saccharine sweet, made Elizabeth grit her teeth, but still kept her temper under good regulation.

"Tis nothing Miss Bingley, and I thank you for your care."

Charlotte's arm came about her waist, "Perhaps some quiet would help, Eliza? Truly, you look quite pale."

Elizabeth agreed, unwilling to be a burden to her family, and perhaps a little peace would permit her to remain until the end of the ball.

"I have just the place for you to withdraw. Let me fetch a footman who can escort you." Miss Bingley seemed almost ecstatic that Elizabeth felt unwell and wished to withdraw for some time, and so, without any delay, Elizabeth found herself tucked away in the quiet library, where the pounding of her head calmed when she reclined upon the settee.

CHAPTER 4

Hurst watched his sister by marriage as she hastened to her brother's side, an expression as insincere as the lady herself. Suspicion wormed in his mind, and he turned to his wife, "Louisa, do you have any notion," Hurst gestured with his glass towards Caroline speaking quietly to Bingley, "what that is about?"

His wife followed his arm and frowned, "I cannot say husband. Caro has been decidedly ill-tempered this week and I think it has much to do with Mr Darcy's comment of some days ago."

Hurst struggled to recall what could have set his nuisance of a relation off in her scheming.

"Remind me?" he pleaded.

His wife grumbled, "That one regarding a lady's laughter he overheard?" When his wife saw he recalled, she continued, "Yet I fear, that much has overset her, especially when Mr Darcy failed to agree that an entanglement with Miss Bennet would be disadvantageous to

Charles. The gentleman has remained firm in his stance to not interfere in my brother's romantic endeavours. Furthermore, Caroline has raged almost daily of the ignominy of her first dance being sabotaged by Miss Elizabeth's calculating, daring to imagine that the lady has set her cap for the self-same gentleman. How my sister has concocted such intrigues, or why, I cannot say. It has been a difficult week, husband."

Hurst patted his wife's hand in sympathy, well aware Louisa had suffered Caroline's temper during the preparations for tonight. After some careful thoughts, he gathered his wife's arm up, "Come, I do not like this unsettled feeling your sister is giving me. It is best to be close at hand with the hope to ameliorate her actions."

"Hurst! She is hardly so terrible as that!" His wife furiously whispered, but a snort of disbelief was his only reply.

Darcy concluded his quadrille with Miss Mary, pleasantly surprised by the young woman's conversation. The lady had not once flirted with him, had instead reminded him much of himself and his sister combined. Miss Elizabeth's younger sister possessed his own unfortunate discomfort in a crowded setting, merged with a love of music, much as his sister.

It was a strangely comforting diversion, however it failed to distract him from the underlying truth that Miss Elizabeth was sensitive and considerate enough to discourage speculation regarding either of them. Darcy felt the irony of being drawn to the one woman who does not attempt any such contrivances, a boon and yet it could not help draw him further under her power. While admittedly relieved Miss Elizabeth was as unusual as he first suspected, there was a modicum of offence and disappointment. Terribly frustrating, for was he not always complaining of women pushing themselves into his notice? Miss Bingley was hardly the worst!

Darcy returned Miss Mary to Miss Lucas's side, noting the absence of the lady who had been on his mind near constantly since that overheard conversation.

"Miss Lucas, is Miss Elizabeth not with you?" he cursed himself the moment the question left his lips. Far too revealing, and yet he still desired to know Miss Elizabeth's whereabouts.

"Unfortunately, Mr Darcy, my friend is suffering a mild complaint, as such, Miss Bingley had her escorted to a quiet place to rest, in the hopes she would be restored enough for the duration of the ball."

Darcy nodded, concern for Miss Elizabeth wrinkling his brow, witnessing the silent communication passing between the ladies, indecipherable to him.

"You need not worry Mr Darcy." Miss Mary quietly divulged, shaking Darcy from his agitation, "Lizzy often suffers megrims, they are not truly a cause for concern. Tis a regular complaint she endures."

Darcy acknowledged Miss Mary's words, but preoccupation with the subject did not abate. Desperate to detract attention from his fascination with Miss Elizabeth, he attempted to engage his company, "What think you of books?" Good heavens. Darcy mentally thumped his skull. As much as he loathed inane chatter, his failure to practice the civility had never been more apparent if he was to judge from the strained aspects of Miss Lucas and Miss Mary. Both ladies must think him an utter clodpate.

"If you are an avid reader, then you would do well to converse with my father, Mr Darcy. He is best pleased when he is surrounded by his books." Miss Mary's words, spoken without inflection, Darcy imagined carried a vague hint of disdain for the Bennet patriarch.

"I had not known that to be the case, and therefore must thank you for pointing it out to me. Yet, if I recall, you are not often found without a book?" Darcy asked, hoping to steer clear of any contentious topics.

Miss Lucas, attention divided between Mr Collins, who had appeared at his side, attempting to intrude upon his conversation, and her younger companion, unfortunately brought the unwelcome party into the conversation, "You are correct, Mr Darcy. Mary is quite the reader, and tis perhaps both her biggest strength and biggest weakness."

"How so?" Darcy asked, aware Miss Lucas meant no insult, and was intrigued to discover her opinion. From his peripheral vision, he noted Miss Bingley making her way towards him, followed closely by her sister and husband, both looking somewhat serious.

"Charlotte means that I would much rather read than spend an evening at such a frivolous event as a ball, with the insufferably tedious process of meeting new people, followed by the unknown discomfort of being forced to either dance with someone unpleasant, or to be neglected and relegated to a piece of inconsequential furniture." Miss Mary did not seem offended by her friend's comment and seemed very comfortable in stating her opinions so unequivocally. Her perspective, while controversial, was entirely understandable when considering her unfortunate circumstances, surrounded by lively, pretty sisters, forever compared to her detriment. What this would mean for her future, Darcy was unsure.

"While you might enjoy an evening where conversation was the order of the day, more rational dear Mary, it would not be a ball if it did not primarily consist of dancing." Miss Lucas smiled warmly at the young lady, who nodded once, but was not permitted speech by the arrival of Miss Bingley and her family.

"I must say, Sir, you dance divinely, which of course is hardly surprising, when one considers the elevated circles you must move in. And to think, you have condescended to bestow your generous attentions to my less fortunate cousin, who is perforce, outshone by her more radiant sisters! And to think, you have recognised my in-" Mr Collins managed to offend, denigrating his host's family, while flattering with servility; it was altogether a repulsive display, one which he was actually grateful for Miss Bingley arriving and intruding upon.

"There you are Mr Darcy! I almost could not detect you, so hidden by these ladies flocking to your side." Miss Bingley made a snide look towards his companions, both of whom seemed to ignore the insufferable implication, "I cannot locate my brother, and he is set to dance with one of the ladies standing just there by that potted palm." Miss Bingley vaguely gestured to the whole room. "Would you assist with discovering his whereabouts? I would not usually ask, but as I am familiar with your dislike of dancing, I am certain you will not object to missing the exercise."

A dark look descended, well versed in

'missing relative' intrigues, an attempt at a compromise, and therefore a stinging rebuke rose to his lips. Hurst inserted himself before Darcy could speak, "I think it would be better if I aided your search, do you not agree Darcy?" Hurst looked him in the eye, and he was assured Miss Bingley's ploy was unsupported. He would not have to break with Bingley over his sister, not when Hurst had little liking for the lady and was more than willing to foil the woman's plans.

Surprisingly, Miss Bingley welcomed her relations involvement, "Why Hurst, thank you. I did not think to ask, as ordinarily you are too far in your cups to be of much use." The waspish comment was brushed aside, and instead the lady went on in a more conciliatory tone, "I cannot think an extra set of eyes will do any harm. Why do we not begin?"

Darcy, stiffly remarked, "I shall search the library and study. You and Hurst can search the drawing rooms." But before Darcy could move away, Miss Bingley clutched his arm.

"Mr Darcy, you are hardly one to encourage my brother to return to dancing, and if we leave the two of you in some corner, you will keep Charles all to yourself, much as you do near every evening. No, I shall come with you and Hurst can search the drawing rooms, Louisa will go with him, will you not sister?"

Mrs Hurst sighed and agreed, pulling her husband away to begin. Darcy gritted his teeth, enraged anew over the woman's machinations.

Yet from the silenced group, came Miss Mary's words, "I shall accompany you Sir. I need to ascertain if Lizzy is well enough to return." Miss Mary moved towards the library, familiar with the layout of Netherfield after her stay here while Miss Bennet recovered from her illness.

Miss Bingley almost preened in contentment, leaving him confused. Surely if the woman sought to entrap him in a compromise, the presence of Miss Mary would thwart her efforts? They searched the study only briefly, the dimly lit room clearly empty. The library was only further along the corridor, and they reached the room to discover the door was locked. The housekeeper presumably wished to deter guests from lingering outside of those rooms set aside for the ball. Miss Bingley fetched a footman to locate the key and without much trouble, the door was unlocked. His heart dropped to his feet at the sight that greeted them.

There, in the room was Miss Elizabeth asleep on the settee, and there sat his friend, head in his hands, in the armchair Darcy favoured. They were alone. In a locked room. In Bingley's eyes Darcy saw the pain of heartbreak and agony of being an honourable gentleman. Miss Mary's quiet gasp was the only sound to be heard. Bingley looked away from Darcy and instead spoke quietly to the lady's sister.

"She was asleep when I entered. I have

not tried to rouse her as she was awfully pale to begin with. That has not changed." Bingley's words were flat. Lacking that joie de vivre he had possessed ever since they first met.

Miss Mary moved further into the room, Miss Bingley and he fixed at the door, neither entering, nor leaving. Darcy watched as Miss Mary bent over her sister, brushing away a lock of hair, the gesture soft and full of sisterly compassion. A look of sorrow accompanied the gesture, the lady wise to the significance of how her sister was discovered. The touch had the desired effect of rousing Miss Elizabeth and Darcy had the torturous pleasure of watching her awaken. The gentle fluttering of her lashes. The deep breath and soft exhale, and then her eyes, those luminous deep bronze eyes, catch upon her sister, watching a loving smile bloom, small. Perfect.

His breath seemed locked in his chest. Until Bingley stood and moved towards the sisters. But with a quick reversal, backed away, his hands dragging through his hair, tugging the locks from his scalp. A startled cry of concern escaped Miss Bingley, the first made since entering. Darcy watched the woman pale, a flash of something in her eyes, there and gone in a blink. A wretched thought arose, and Darcy studied his hostess with cold cynical eyes. Miss Bingley glanced once his way, before darting from his side, rushing towards her brother.

"Oh brother! What is this? What happened?" Demeanour was at odds with her jubilant expression, especially as his hostess settled her attention upon the Bennet sisters, "You poor thing, Miss Eliza, to be ruined in such an awful fashion! Oh how horrible for you both! And, oh...poor Jane! Charles, oh what tangled trouble!"

Again, harsh questions tugged at Darcy, the choking squeeze about his heart overlooked in favour of studying the participants in the room as if watching a play. Anything to distract him from the twisted reality that Miss Elizabeth was to be lost to him. She was already lost, his thoughts reasoned. Miss Bingley's machinations aside, Miss Elizabeth was never his, his thoughts argued cruelly. Yet this, this scene was most certainly orchestrated by Miss Bingley, for her own benefit, Darcy was near certain.

A cough at his back had Darcy turning to note the entrance of Mr Bennet. The gentleman studied the occupants of the room just as he had, before quietly stepping in and shutting the door behind him.

"Mary, is Lizzy well?" Mr Bennet queried. His quiet voice like a gunshot in the tense room.

"She has one of her megrims father. Tis why she fell asleep." Miss Mary's words conveyed no judgement, but a hard look pointed in Miss Bingley's direction was eloquent enough. He was not alone in his suspicions.

"And you, Sir? Are you well?" Mr Bennet coolly asked, his dark brown eyes astutely assessing his friend's agitation.

"I have been better, Sir." Bingley looked Mr Bennet square on, not hiding his state, but doing nothing that would injure the only true innocent party.

Miss Elizabeth stirred from her seat, "Father, pardon my confusion." Her voice was quiet and faint, absent of its usual vitality, Darcy thought, "I am not precisely at my best, but could it be explained what has everyone so distressed?"

Mr Bennet moved further into the room, standing by his daughter's side and taking her hand in his, a soft fatherly look of love and concern etched upon his features.

Miss Bingley's words dropped like rocks in a river, "My brother and you were alone in this room, Miss Eliza. For some time, it would seem."

Darcy *knew* this was the stratagem of the woman, but he could not fathom *why* Miss Bingley would hurt her brother in this fashion. If Miss Elizabeth was a lady Miss Bingley could not like, it made little sense why then she would contrive for her to become related by marriage. Darcy watched Bingley stiffen his spine, a look of determination fixed upon his usually amiable and lively features.

"And how, precisely, did this come about?" Mr Bennet, did not look towards his daughter, but instead upon their host.

The room's quietly burning fire in the hearth was heard to crackle and snap, a fitting backdrop for the drama playing out before him.

It was, however, Miss Elizabeth who broke the quiet, "Forgive me Father, I needed some time away from the noise of the assembled guests and so Miss Bingley was kind enough to arrange a footman to guide me here to rest and recover. I must have fallen asleep, but I cannot account for anyone else's presence."

Mr Bennet patted his daughter's hand, her sister seated quietly beside her, almost forgotten, yet it was Miss Mary who comforted Miss Elizabeth, wrapping a supporting arm about her waist, her other hand tightly grasped in her own. Lending her strength, while offering the assurity of affection and acceptance.

Bingley, on the other hand seemed an isolated island in comparison to the fortress of strength and unity presented by the Bennets, his sister standing apart and offering no words or gestures of sibling affection.

"Yes, child, I do not fault *you* for the current predicament, but I am still waiting upon Mr Bingley's explanation." Mr Bennet's gaze was hard, unyielding, and Bingley gulped at the stern character he faced.

"Ahem, that is, I received word," here Bingley looked towards his sister, "that an express had arrived, and so I went to discover it's whereabout.s My housekeeper informed me,

Mrs Nicholls that is, that she had been directed to leave the missive in the library rather than have the courier disrupt the ball. As I entered, I did not immediately detect Miss Elizabeth's form, and so I stepped further into the room, hoping to locate the missive swiftly and return to my guests. However, the door swung shut behind me, and must have locked upon impact." Bingley attempted to straighten up, his bearing not as strong under the patriarchal and protective examination he was subjected to.

Mr Bennet studied his friend, intellect reflected in penny brown depths. Darcy could not fathom the gentleman's thoughts, too busy with his own whirling tempest of emotions and sentiments. This could not come about. Everything in him rebelled at the almost mandatory outcome that was demanded of Bingley. The idea of watching the woman who had fascinated him since he first heard her voice, tied irrevocably to his long-time friend, was abhorrent. Pulse racing, Darcy felt helpless, watching a play and angry with how the story was unfolding, desperation bloomed to effect a change. A part of him *knew* this should not, could not, occur.

"Ah, that does seem," Mr Bennet glanced around, encompassing himself, his daughters and the two Bingleys, "mightily convenient, does it not, Miss Bingley?" Mr Bennet's voice was filled with sly inference everyone in the room understood, causing Bingley to shift focus upon his sister with a furrowed brow.

Darcy felt as if he were furniture, his presence unnecessary to everyone else, but vital to himself.

"I know not of what you speak, Sir." Miss Bingley's voice carried contrived innocence, and Mr Bennet snorted in disbelief.

"Hmm, well," Mr Bennet looked away from the woman, turning his gaze lovingly back upon his daughter, "I'm afraid my dear Lizzy, it looks as if you have been unwillingly and *accidentally*, compromised, and by your sister's beau, no less."

Miss Elizabeth's voice rose in denial, and Darcy could not help but admire her integrity, not scrabbling to gain a foothold in a profitable union, "Father, please, no one need know!"

Sorrowfully, Mr Bennet claimed, "Ah, but I am sorry my child, as Mr Collins is, as we speak, discussing your own absence, referring frequently to that of our host as well. I imagine the entire neighbourhood is somewhat aware by now."

Bingley looked thunderstruck, "What?!" his pallor reflected his distress, no doubt consumed with thoughts upon the lady who had caught *his* attention from the moment they met. How would Miss Bennet feel about this difficulty?

Mr Bennet taunted, "Yes, I am afraid that is the truth of it, for why else would I be here, if not to determine the matter myself?"

Bingley looked defeated as he strode forward, "Then I know what must be done."

Panic rose in Darcy's breast. He could not let this happen, "Bingley, wait!"

His friend paused his steps, near enough to Miss Elizabeth, that Darcy could take them both in, in one glance. Bingley, beleaguered and resigned, empty of hope, while Miss Elizabeth appeared on the verge of flight, her expression screaming denial and panic. The same that beat in his own breast.

"Miss Elizabeth," Darcy focused his thoughts upon the young lady, heart racing at what he was about to do, "I am reasonably confident, when I say, you would rather avoid marrying the man who has been so attentive to your elder sister since their first meeting?"

Miss Elizabeth's gaze was hazy and unfocused, her grip upon her younger sister's hand tight, knuckles white, "Correct, Sir."

"Then I propose a solution."

Mr Bennet's eyes danced, alight with humour, and Darcy felt a flare of anger with the gentleman; there was nothing of amusement to be found.

Bingley prompted him, his pause having elongated longer than Darcy realised, "Yes?" he almost barked.

"You can choose to whom you shall be wed." Bingley's mouth dropped open, while Miss

Elizabeth still could not discern his meaning, so Darcy clarified, "You can wed, as your father put it, your sister's beau. Or," he paused to stiffen his resolve, "you can marry me."

A squawk of outrage came from Miss Bingley, the flurry of her skirts bespoke her agitation, "What!" she cried, "No! That is not possible!"

Mr Bennet chuckled gleefully, delighting in observing Miss Bingley's performance. With a desperate wheeze, the lady attempted to pull upon his arm, to which Darcy shrugged free with patent disdain, disgusted with her.

"You have no say in the matter, Miss Bingley. This does not concern you in any fashion."

Her face paled, her hand shakily coming up to her mouth as if to stem a silent scream. Darcy removed the woman from his attention and focused solely upon the lady who could become his life partner, his wife.

"Miss Elizabeth?" he softly enquired, moving closer.

"Whyever would you choose to do this?" the soft query again marked her as different from what he was accustomed to.

Stepping further forward, until he was on bended knee before her, he took the hand held by her father, who gave it up with a pointed look, "Miss Elizabeth, Bingley is a dear friend, and while he would do the honourable thing and wed you, it would inevitably make more people unhappy than the affair warrants. By marrying me, we can prevent such misery, and instead decide our future together, ourselves, free of encumbrances. Is that not a fitting resolution?"

Darcy had never wished to propose to a woman under such conditions, but from his perspective, this was the only option he could accept. He held Miss Elizabeth's hand in his own, her gloves preventing him from the feel and touch of her skin, but already he felt connected to this divine being. Could feel threads binding them together, and perhaps he was conceited enough to think she would be foolish to refuse, but Darcy was almost certain Miss Elizabeth would make the only choice he would accept. Him.

Miss Bingley hissed to her brother, before standing at his side and urging him to see reason, "Please Sir, Mr Darcy. Your honor is not engaged, nor is that of my brother's! You need not sacrifice yourself like this. I am sure some quiet arrangements for Miss Eliza can be-"

"Hush Caroline," Bingley barked, his temper blazing, evident in manner and tone, "there will be no more words from you. And of course my honor is engaged–what the devil do you take me for? To cause ruin to a lady and turn my back would be a disgrace! How you can think that of me, I cannot comprehend! Instead, leave us, so that matters here can be concluded. I will be a moment behind, so do not utter a word of what has occurred, do you understand?"

Mutely and with a marked degree of temper, Miss Bingley left them, the library door slamming against the wall.

"Mr Bennet, if you are content to manage matters here I should follow my sister. If I am ne-"

Bingley was interrupted by Mr Bennet, "Go. And as you instructed your sister, do not speak of these events, for I shall know how to act if matters do not go as I imagine they will. But Mr Bingley?"

His friend paused, standing at Darcy's back, he knew not what his expression held when Mr Bennet spoke next, "There will be no further dances with *any* of my daughters until everything has been settled, is that clear?"

With shuffled steps, Bingley followed after his sister. Without slamming any doors.

"Now then, Lizzy child, I do believe Mr Darcy deserves an answer, do you not think?"

Her hand remained lax in his, her eyes staring off unfocused, leaving Darcy to study her in closer detail than he had been permitted to do before. Her eyes, a sweet toffee, or as shiny as a new coin, were shadowed with pain and concern. Her pert nose and slender chin made her appear almost elfin in looks, but matched with her glorious coffee coloured hair, bound up with ribbons and pins, Darcy could not help but imagine a future staring into those magnificent eyes of hers. Her skin, blemish free, demanded his fingers trail across its surface, to feel the tantalising glide of silk against his fingertips. Miss Elizabeth was a siren, her scent, her appearance, the sound of her voice! She had to say yes. No other outcome was acceptable to Darcy.

Elizabeth felt the pulsing throb of her headache swell behind her eyes, her restorative sleep vanquished by the stress of her circumstances. In pain, wracked with worries, indignant with the whole farce, and here Mr Darcy stood. Kneeled. She could not look at him overlong, not after his words of common sense and practicality, leaving no warm sentiments for her to cling to. Nothing as sweet as being delighted by her appearance, enchanted with her character.

No. Just simple, cold, hard, truths.

With a quiet sigh, she acquiesced to her fate, "Thank you Mr Darcy, I would be honoured to marry you."

Those words sealed her fate.

They were the last she uttered to the gentleman in question before he nodded, kissed her gloved hand and rose to speak to her father, quietly off to the side. The pounding in her head made concentrating impossible, and so in defeat, she slouched back against the seat.

"Lizzy, shall I summon the carriage?"

Nodding, Elizabeth kept her eyes closed as she felt her sister rise and move away, her gentle voice melding with the lower tones of the two gentlemen. Thoughts of what she had agreed to attempted to flit across her mind, but the pain batted it all away. Tomorrow would be soon enough. Without realising it, Elizabeth slipped back into a restless slumber, only stirring marginally when she felt herself carried.

"Ssh, go back to sleep. I am merely conveying you to your carriage. Your sister is here with us." Mr Darcy's words were a soft rumble against her ear, causing a shiver to race through her, blasting away the pain of her megrim. The next she knew the cool night air kissed her skin, followed swiftly by the familiar safety of the Bennet carriage, and then the soothing comforting embrace of a sister. The darkness appeased the pulsing pain, and sleep beckoned with such a sweet feeling of bliss, that Elizabeth was helpless to do aught but answer its call.

Morning sunlight filtered in through her bed curtains, a tickle of cold air against her bare feet. Slowly, Elizabeth roused from her slumber and felt the blessed absence of pain in her head. Her courses would begin today, ensuring she would suffer an entirely different sort of pain, but at least that was somewhat more manageable, she huffed to herself. Thoughts of last night drifted into her mind, and Elizabeth bolted up in consternation.

She had agreed to marry a man she had met *twice*! This was intolerable! She knew nothing about Mr Darcy, other than he was in possession of an independent fortune, had remarkably good looks, and a long-time acquaintance of his had blackened his name before she had even met him. On the other hand, he had come to her rescue, saving her from having to wed a man who was most assuredly in love with her sister, who would have been heartbroken to see the man *she* loved tied forever more to Elizabeth, all because they had been in a room together, unchaperoned! The ridiculousness of her situation was felt keenly, and Elizabeth knew the only way to overcome the tumult of her thoughts was to engage in a long and unhurried walk through the beloved countryside, letting the chill call of nature banish her worries.

With practised ease, she slipped from the bed covers on silent feet, not disturbing the slumbering Mary who had most likely kept her company to ensure Elizabeth's well-being. She looked fondly down upon her younger, peaceful, and reserved sister and felt the first stirrings of panic. Who would take care of Mary when she was not here to do so? Who would ensure the tenants homes were kept in reasonable condition, else her father completely overlook the matter? How would she encourage her younger sisters to embrace a more decorous manner of conduct, while not losing their natural temperaments?

Hurriedly, Elizabeth dressed in an old and familiar day dress, the lacings manageable unaided. Her undergarments were from the night before, and so, pulling on a thick pair of stockings, Elizabeth slipped from the room, her sister unaware. Accustomed to early morning rambles, Elizabeth avoided the many creaks and groans the floorboards possessed, and reached the back door through the kitchens. The cook merrily sent her on her way, handing her a small parcel of food, wrapped carefully in a napkin. Tucking it into her pocket, Elizabeth dressed warmly for the November chill, escaped outdoors.

The sweep of fresh air against her skin shocked her into full wake-fullness, sweeping away the cobwebs of sleep, as if it were mist burned away by the heat of the sun. Striding across the back gardens, Elizabeth slipped through a break in the hedges and pointed her steps towards Oakham Mount. The wide expansive views the modest rise would afford her, the perfect place to pause and collect her thoughts.

The chill weather attempted to steal the warmth from her thick redingcote, a gift from her aunt, in a rich emerald green, such that Elizabeth almost blended in with her surroundings. Her hands, covered in thick mittens her mother had knitted, knowing full well her need to escape out of doors even in winter. Elizabeth felt an upwelling of affection for her mother. Mrs Bennet had attempted to learn how to conduct herself as a gentleman's wife, without support or encouragement from her husband. Yes, she was a trifle vulgar and had no awareness of how truly voluble she could be, but her driving force was the well-being of her daughters comfort and security.

Elizabeth could only guess how her mother had reacted to the news and dreaded the calls for her salts, as Mrs Bennet felt all the raptures of finally having a daughter married off. That it was to be Elizabeth, her most contrary of daughters, would merely make her mother relieved, she laughingly concluded. She reached the peak quicker than was customary, but Elizabeth nonetheless paused, realising how out of breath she truly was. Her walk must have been swifter than usual, her thoughts providing the power with which to speed her steps. She found the familiar rock she had labelled her throne once when she was younger, when she felt all the excitement of the world laid out before her.

Now, that world seemed very small. She brought her knees up to her chest and rested her chin upon them, her arms wrapped around her legs, hugging her warmth close. She was soon to be ripped from the comfortable home she had always known would never be fixed. To a man she barely knew, let alone loved. The promise she had made with Jane seemed almost entirely a lifetime ago. So much had changed since she was a girl of thirteen summers.

Her indomitable spirit chased away her gloomy thoughts and attempted to reason her way through. Elizabeth made a mental tally.

One, she had always known she would have to marry, so there was hardly a reason to be troubled on marriage itself.

Two, she did not know her future husband, but perhaps what she *had* seen, could provide her some comfort.

Three, Mr Darcy had voluntarily stepped forward to save her reputation and his friend, with no obligation prompting his actions. His honourable nature was starkly at odds with the story Lieutenant Wickham had woven around him.

Four, this situation was at the hands of Miss Bingley, perhaps as punishment for her dance with Mr Collins.

Five, by marrying Mr Darcy, the path remained clear for Mr Bingley to continue to court Jane.

Six, Mr Darcy's appearance made him a considerably better candidate for marriage than Mr Collins, who had seemed as intent as ever to be in her company, regardless of Charlotte's attentions.

There was more to consider, but the quiet, the soothing lull of a winter morning, birds song, wind rushing through the branches; nature embraced her and silenced the ever-spinning chaos of her thoughts, and as such, Elizabeth lost all sense of time. The chill weather had her slowly returning home, her belly only marginally satisfied with the cook's parcel. Eager to sit down to a proper plate and a restorative cup of tea, Elizabeth blustered into Longbourne, a slightly blousy look about her, causing her father to smile wryly at the sight. Mr Bennet having already completed his breakfast, was presumably waiting on her return. Also at table were all her sisters bar Lydia, the loud tutting of her mother at Elizabeth's disarray had her kissing the matron's cheek in apology, but the sight of Mr Collins kept her mother's tongue still.

"Good morning everyone, I must apologise for my tardiness, I was lost to the peace of a fresh morning, but the chill was enough to hurry me home now that it has served its purpose!" Elizabeth cheerily greeted, pressing a kiss upon her father's brow as she passed.

Fixing herself a plate, Elizabeth gratefully seated herself at Kitty's side, her sister having thoughtfully prepared her a cup to her preference.

"Good morning Lizzy. I am relieved to see you well." Jane's soft greeting gave no hint of concern for aught but her health, leaving Elizabeth to assume, she knew little of last evening's events.

"Good morning." Mary quietly greeted, before returning to the book in her lap, her dark head dipped low.

"I cannot credit you had the misfortune to be struck with one of your headaches in the middle of the ball! Lydia and I could talk of naught else but how it would ruin the evening for us all! How relieved we were to hear father say we were to remain and that Mary would see you home. It would have been wretched of you to have caused us all to miss out on all the fun!" Kitty's bright chatter would ordinarily have made her offer a wry comment, but Elizabeth merely nodded to acknowledge her younger sister's exuberance. She was young enough to be forgiven her selfish inclinations.

"Yes, dear. Your father was very good to have not insisted we all return home. It would have been inconsiderate of you to cause Jane not to have remained the full night! As it was, it was unfortunate enough that the *host* disappeared from his own ball!" Her mother's voluble tones invoked the vestiges of her megrim, but Elizabeth was further disturbed to hear her mother talk of Mr Bingley's absence, knowing full well how much her mother relished gossip.

Sipping her tea, Elizabeth failed to reply, only to suffer further mortification when Mr Collins rose from the table, and bowing in her direction, began, "My dear cousin, I was certainly dismayed to discover you were brought low by ill-health, yet am happily pleased to see that you have suffered no lasting indisposition. I am well acquainted with ladies and their delicate constitutions, and consider it one of the misfortunes those of the fairer sex must suffer. It is therefore incumbent upon me to see your ailment as an indication of your delicate nature, and therefore will be ever mindful of your habitude." Mr Collins bowed again, not as low as the first time, and on rising gestured to Mrs Bennet, "Your good mother was kind enough to provide me an account of your ailment being of long-standing and that I was to not be alarmed you would suffer overlong. However, as I can see you are restored to your usual excellent health, I would be most gratified if you would indulge me in a private conversation, such that I think it will provide immeasurable happiness to all."

The table stilled, attempting to absorb the mass of words and sentences Mr Collins had just levied upon them. Once all had reached the same conclusion, there was such a clamouring of noise that Elizabeth closed her eyes in dismay. Her headache was on the edges of returning in full, would consume her if she did not find some peace in which to restore herself.

Looking to her father on opening her eyes, Elizabeth strived to ignore her mother's happy cries of support, and Kitty's failure to contain her giggles. From Jane and Mary, Elizabeth ignored their worried looks, and focused only upon her father. In his eyes, she watched the light of glee dance, and *knew* he would not discourage Mr Collins, and with his silence, did Elizabeth comprehend that her obligation to Mr Darcy, was not yet shared.

Discouraged, Elizabeth answered Mr Collins, a silent prayer of strength in her thoughts, Elizabeth attempted to deflect the situation she could easily envision, "Forgive me Mr Collins, but I must aver this conversation until I am entirely restored. I am not at liberty to disclose the full particulars, but in truth, following my meal, I have only the intention of seeking further rest and recuperation." Her mother's frown caused Elizabeth to rush on and proclaim, "Perhaps, being a man of the cloth, and so accustomed to ladies *delicate* constitutions, you are familiar with the need to *time* relevant conversations appropriately?"

Mary bit her lip, brow furrowed as she attempted to comprehend the insinuation. The truth was, Elizabeth had no doubt Mr Collins was unaware of her womanly difficulties, but the very idea, the suggestion that he *did* in fact know, would inflate his self-conceit and make it impossible for him to claim otherwise.

Rising from her chair, her appetite vastly diminished, Elizabeth excused herself and hurried away to her room. The silence she found there was interrupted moments later by the admittance of not just Jane, but Mary also. Elizabeth hazarded a guess that Kitty would hurry to inform Lydia of this morning's events.

Netherfield, November 27th

"What the devil were you conniving, Caroline?!" Hurst fairly roared, his face fixed in a fiercesome scowl.

Caroline ignored her sister's husband, her misery placing her in the darkest of moods. Everything had gone afoul, but how?

"Caro?" Louisa touched her hand, drawing Caroline's attention away from her vacant staring out the bay of windows streaming light in. The hustle of servants restoring Netherfield to order following last night's ball failed to garner any interest.

Pulling her hand away from her sister's touch, "I have nothing to say, Louisa. I cannot explain how Charles found himself in the library where Miss Eliza had withdrawn!" Her words were empty of bite, lacking conviction, and it was clear neither Hurst nor Louisa placed any faith in her answer.

Hurst, more energetic than Caroline had ever witnessed, crossed to the decanter once more, and Caroline could not help her disgusted sigh. The man could never be without his spirts!

Ignoring her angry family, Caroline looked away once more. Yes, she had manipulated circumstances to place Charles in the library with Eliza; it had seemed so fortuitous when the stupid chit claimed an indisposition, placing herself in the perfect situation to create a scandal, and thereby ruin her, and the Bennet's reputation, in one fell swoop! Charles, Caroline knew, would be hard-pressed to carry through with the union, not when he had his doltish head turned already by Jane Bennet. And it would have been so easy to convince him to give up the place, leaving his insipid *angel* and the rest of her pathetic family in their dust! Yet, somehow, everything had become twisted. Instead of just Mr Darcy as witness, there had been dull Mary Bennet, followed swiftly by the usually indolent Mr Bennet, who proved to be anything but! It had been a miscalculation to place Charles in that room, Caroline decided, for of course, Mr

Darcy would protect his dear friend, but she had been *sure*, so certain, that Mr Darcy would have arranged a small compensation to the impudent girl, placing Charles in Darcy's debt, and showing the Bennet's for the mercenary creatures that they are.

A soft groan, followed the growl of frustration, before Caroline finally let loose, "How could he do this?!" thumping the arm of the seat, "What was Mr Darcy thinking to agree to such a...a...mésalliance! To see that...that...*viper* as Mrs Darcy! Mistress of everything that should be mine!!!" Anger and grief warred for supremacy, and Caroline allowed her head to drop into her hand, elbow resting on the arm of her chair. Yes, she had schemed, plotted, manoeuvred, everything, to capture Darcy for herself, and it had all come to nothing. To worse than nothing–for now she would have to bear witness to Eliza Bennet marrying the man Caroline had pinned all her hopes and dreams upon.

It just was not fair!

"Caroline!" Hurst's bark made her jump, and she turned her own black scowl upon the fool.

"As it is clear you have paid no heed to my words, I shall take this opportunity, now that I can see you are attentive, to congratulate you." The wretch jeered at her, forcing Caroline to vent her ire.

"For what, am I to be so lauded, Hurst?" Her words snapped out like the flick and coil of a whip.

A doltish chuckle, "For Darcy's marriage! You have finally succeeded in getting your quarry to the altar!" Hurst's mirth grew, "Tis just a shame *you* are not to be the bride!"

Ignoring the loud guffaws, Caroline rose as if to depart, only for Louisa to halt her. "Geoffrey, that is not why we are here, now is it?" Louisa smiled softly, "You cannot blame him, Caro, not when you have spent the past three years so assured of your future, despite never achieving a modicum of encouragement." Her sister raised a hand when Caroline attempted to argue, silencing her words before they fell, "No, tis time you listened sister. You may say whatever you wish, but we all know that last night was by your design. Charles was so very upset, Caro. And hurt. That you could use him so ill shows a side of your character that is hard to accept." Sighing deeply, her sister continued after a moment, seeing that Caroline had nothing to add. "With our brother's departure to London, he has asked Geoffrey and I to depart for Hurst's estate, with you." A sense of welcome relief assailed her, and Caroline smiled broadly at her sister, only for it to fall when Hurst intervened.

"Do not look so content sister dear, for I have been given the *privilege* of seeing you settled, one way or another." Hurst settled himself to his seat, propping his feet up on the footstool before him. "I have agreed to Bingley's request, and as such have invited a number of friends to join us at my father's estate for the Christmas period." His look sent a shiver of revulsion through her, his accompanying words depressing her spirits, "And if you reject any genuine proposal of marriage offered you, you will be set up in your own household, to live off your portion, with no support from either your brother or myself. Have I made myself clear Caroline?"

Somehow her misery had magnified, and Caroline left the room for the solitude of her own chambers. How did everything turn out so foul?

CHAPTER 5

Longbourne, November 27th

"Lizzy?" Jane softly enquired, "Is your head paining you once more?"

Collapsed as she was upon her bed, Elizabeth discerned Jane's sympathy, however possessed little desire to confront an inquisition from her sister.

"From Lizzy's prone state, not only has her megrim returned, in tandem with the start of her courses, the addition of enduring an uncomfortable and entirely avertible incident with little paternal concern, had put our dearest sister in a wretched state! To all this, Lizzy has endured an untenable state of affairs through the vindictive machinations of a spiteful woman, ruining what was to be a pleasurable night!" Mary's words were uttered with ferocity, and as the loss of her composure was unusual, Elizabeth repositioned her head in order to witness the occurrence. Her blue eyes glimmered much in the way a clear spring shimmers in sunshine, but her tense posture bespoke of agitation, as she moved about the chamber tidying the disarray, her hands rigidly sorting and setting aside Elizabeth's possessions, her cheeks sporting twin flags of colour.

"Why Mary, whatever do you mean?" Jane sunk against Elizabeth on her bed, hands softly plucking out the Elizabeth's hastily placed pins, moving through the locks with soothing care and attention. Elizabeth closed her eyes in pleasure, and forgot about Mary's revealing words.

That was until Mary clarified, "I apologise Lizzy, Jane, but this...this game of our father's frustrates me endlessly. He could have prevented Mr Collins from speaking, especially now that you are engaged! But no, our father wished to be amused, to witness you depress Mr Collins marital pretensions. Observing us all, as he always does, as if we are exhibits in a....a....!" Mary growled.

"Menagerie?" Elizabeth helpfully supplied.

"Yes!"

The stillness of Jane's hands indicated her sister's surprise, "Lizzy? What does Mary mean? How can you be engaged?" Voice filled with bewilderment and a hint of hurt incited Elizabeth to shift anew to study her beautiful sister's face, regret churning in her stomach, for her words were sure to cause Jane pain.

Sitting up, Elizabeth ignored Mary's movements, "Tis true, I am afraid. And the circumstances do not profit from a good memory. I would wish for you to not have your judgement altered, but I would prevent your suffering pain of any sort if I could." Elizabeth grasped Jane's hand, "I am engaged to Mr Darcy."

Jane's eyes widened in shock, her hand coming up to obscure her mouth, "How can this be? You have had little opportunity to be courted by him, let alone become engaged!"

Elizabeth tried to laugh, but the bitterness of spirit she suffered, especially following Mr Collins 'eloquence' this morning, made the effort lamentable. They had been acquainted almost as long as she had known Mr Darcy, yet the former's daily presence had made little headway in improving his character, whilst she knew little enough of the latter.

Before she could explain, Mary bluntly disclosed, "Mr Darcy provided Lizzy with an alternative to marrying Mr Bingley, after we discovered him and our sister in a locked room together. All of which was contrived by *Miss Bingley!*" Mary sneered the last with so much contempt, Elizabeth feared placing the two of them in a room alone together, ever.

Jane paled at their sister's words, expression ranging from shock, to painful despair, only to rush towards denial. "That cannot be true! Miss Bingley would not do such a thing. I cannot believe it of her!"

"While I cannot truly recall how events developed last night, I *can* state Miss Bingley was the one who instructed the footman on where I could be allowed some respite in solitude. And if I recall correctly, it was some wild goose chase in pursuit of an *express*, that had Mr Bingley in the library, where I rested." Elizabeth shrugged, knowing her sister would refuse to judge Miss Bingley poorly.

"Lizzy was truly discomposed from her megrim Jane, and so has little recollection of what occurred prior to our admittance to the library, how Miss Bingley delighted in collecting Mr Darcy in pursuit of her *missing* brother, my own addition to the search marking her appearance with an air of giddy triumph! I would go into detail, but the memory- the recollection would serve me little to recount at present." Heaving a great sigh, stilling her movement, Mary gave her attention to assessing her elder sisters, "Permit Lizzy to gain some true respite, and we can bring some tea up later, before talking more on the topic." Mary's conciliatory gesture was welcomed, regardless of how little Elizabeth liked leaving Jane with such heavy worries burdening her.

Nodding slowly, Jane agreed, her eyes dark with trepidation.

Elizabeth watched them depart, heart

heavy, and head aching, body shifting with the onset of her courses. With effort, Elizabeth undressed properly and settled back to bed, further sleep would do little to help her situation. However it would keep Mr Collins away, and for that, Elizabeth was resolved to be content. Later she would confront her father and discover what her future held.

Elizabeth woke much later in the day than she had expected, and yet fatigue still weighed heavy upon her, summoning a maid for warm wash water, hoping to feel somewhat improved following. Once she had some bread and butter with a cup of tea, Elizabeth descended the stairs and headed for her father's book-room. As much as she would wish to delay *this* conversation as she had Mr Collins, Elizabeth needed answers about what fate awaited her.

She knocked upon her father's door, and heard her father's call to enter.

"Ah, there you Lizzy. Feeling more robust?" Her father's teasing would have cheered her before, but now, all she could picture was his mischievous smile as he watched Mr Collins application to seek a private audience.

"I am, indeed, feeling more *robust*, father. And so, I think I feel up to comprehending my situation in detail. Would you not agree?" Elizabeth kept her tone light, understanding how little her father liked the heavy complaining his wife so relished.

"Ah, my little Lizzy, you were exceptional this morning! I never doubted your capacity to outwit Mr Collins, but I must claim compensation for having had the man fill the air with his noise ever since!" Mr Bennet's complaint, Elizabeth ignored.

"While I am gratified by your confidence," Elizabeth settled into her customary armchair, a partner to the one her father most often occupied, rather than the seat behind his desk. "I reject your application for compensation. You, who is better situated, better informed, placed the burden upon my shoulders, and therefore must accept the repercussions without complaint." Elizabeth looked her father in the eye, a brow rising slightly in answer to his own. The two of them maintained a close bond, not just of similar temperaments, but in managing the burden of the estate between the two of them. And while her father claimed her as his favourite, Elizabeth suspected this was because she ably took it upon herself to carry out those tasks and duties he so little liked, leaving him to his much-loved books.

"Touché, child. You are obviously much restored, if you are so well-equipped to trade words with your dear father. Yet I imagine tis not Mr Collins that has brought you to my door." Mr Bennet raised his glass, before taking the armchair opposite his daughter. "Well, I am waiting for the inquisition I am sure to face, so out with it."

Elizabeth pursed her lips, annoyed her father would insist on prolonging matters. "As you wish. The last I could recall, I agreed to marry Mr Darcy in place of being compromised by Mr Bingley's error. If that is the case, then why have you yet to announce it to my family?" Her eyes flashed with ire, and colour bloomed in her cheeks, regardless Elizabeth knew it was futile to rage upon Mr Bennet, he would merely mock such a display.

"Then you recall correctly. You are indeed engaged to Mr Darcy, and if it had been up to me, I would have announced the betrothal last night. Yet your betrothed would have me delay." Elizabeth was more than a little surprised it was at Mr Darcy's behest that her father had remained silent. She had not expected that, and therefore softened her displeasure towards her father. "I can see you apprehend that I would have managed matters differently little Lizzy, and you are correct. But I do not think, after hearing Mr Darcy's explanation, you will quibble over his reasoning."

"Then I shall ask for the explanation from him directly, when he calls. I assume he is to call?" Elizabeth asked with a touch of her usual spirit.

"Alas, that is not to be the case, child."

Elizabeth frowned, and her father continued, "No, do not scowl so. Mr Darcy and Mr Bingley both departed for London today, each for different reasons. In your betrothed's case, he is to see to arranging a Special Licence, and to address your settlement papers. Given Mr Darcy's account, he believes he shall return by the beginning of December."

"So I must continue on as I ever was, then?" Silently, Elizabeth's mind whirled, then a sudden thought clarified, "Why then, if there is no scandal, or potential rumours circling, must I wed at all?"

"Lizzy, I credit you with more sense than this." Her father's displeasure was difficult to bear, "You heard your mother this morning. Word has spread already of Mr Bingley's unusual absence from his own ball, and there are some who have connected your own absence to that of his. It will take little tinder to set this small spark ablaze, I assure you. I would not wish to part with you under the best of circumstances, no one else is half so able as you, my clever girl, but in this, my hands are tied."

Reality realigned, and Elizabeth acquiesced without further complaint, yet the looming spectre of Mr Collins intruded, "Forgive me father, but I have still to hear the reason for keeping quiet, especially when I must endure Mr Collins!"

Her father chortled heavily, his frame

shaking, "His efforts at wooing are perhaps the next most entertaining thing to occur, after your mother's continual claims of Mr Bingley's credit." Elizabeth looked away, always hurt when her father would dismiss her concerns with nary a word of support, comfort or protection.

So Mr Collins was to be for her to manage, and Elizabeth could only think of one person who would aid her in diverting the rector.

Once her father had calmed, Elizabeth settled to attend Mr Bennet's explanation, "*Mr Collins* is the reason why Mr Darcy wishes to keep things concealed for the time being. Being connected to his aunt, the revered Lady Catherine de Bourgh– the irony of this still tickles me now, Mr Darcy is concerned that my cousin would hasten to inform his patroness of your connection. And it is that great Lady, that Mr Darcy wishes to deny any knowledge of your engagement until it is a fait accompli."

"But, why?" Elizabeth, uneasy with the need for secrecy, felt dishonest and disloyal to her family.

"Because, and this is the gentleman's own words I employ, *his aunt would object most strenuously, and would consider the union ill-qualified.* I must say, I am somewhat disappointed that I shall not obtain the privilege of meeting the great woman myself." Mr Bennet looked comfortably entertained by all that had been canvassed, a sentiment which Elizabeth did not share.

"Very well, I shall now know how to act, but do not imagine that I will gratify you with further entertainment on account of Mr Collins. I shall take my meal in my rooms tonight, and tomorrow I hope to manage the matter." Here, Elizabeth rose, intending to return to her room for the remainder of the day, "I had hoped to find you reasonable, that you would see fit to shield your daughter, but depend on it, father, I will carry my point with Mr Collins, and there will be very little said that will dissuade my course."

She quit the room, grateful to have escaped encountering the afore mentioned gentleman she wished to avoid, yet frustrated by the inability to speak with the one man upon whom her future happiness depended. Her room was comfortably arranged with pastel pink papering, adorned with a white floral motif. Her furniture, a modest bed, a closet and dressing table, neatened by Mary's earlier efforts, provided her familiar comfort. Yet it was to the little writing desk Elizabeth turned her steps to; her intention to write Charlotte and her aunt seemed the best way to manage her time in isolation, for further company would do little to erase the tumult of her thoughts.

She dispatched the note to Charlotte swiftly, then considered what she could say to her aunt Gardiner. Despite the injunction to render the issue concealed, Elizabeth *needed* her beloved aunt's words of wisdom at this turning point of her life. She was at a crossroads, and feared taking the wrong path. Her aunt's wisdom, her very real warm regard for Elizabeth, placed her as the solely suitable source of support.

Longbourne House
November 27th

Dearest Aunt,
I write to you following a rather turbulent evening that saw my life alter course in such a fashion that I am still unequal to the task of truly comprehending the full extent of those repercussions. I assure you I speak not in such inflammatory terms without due cause, and therefore beg leave to explain in full.

I had not been home for more than a full day, when I was introduced to an officer, a Lieutenant Wickham, who took it upon himself to importune me with a tale of such wretched circumstances, I could not help feeling disturbed to be so informed on so immature acquaintance. Throughout this tale of lifelong rivalry, between two men of different status, I was informed that the villain of this story, was in fact a recent acquaintance of my family, a Mr Darcy. When I canvassed the topic with my sisters, they claimed no true depth of understanding of the great man's character, merely stating he was a gentleman of good looks, but reserved temperament, little interested in conversing with anyone outside of his immediate party.
With little interest in the matter, I dismissed the Lieutenant from thought, consumed with more relevant matters pertaining to the welfare and support of my own family. You are aware, as we have discussed so recently, of my hopes to improve my sisters situation, and as you know, Kitty welcomes the opportunity to explore a society outside that of Meryton.

Therefore, with so slight an inclination, there was no need to ponder overlong upon the subject of one so little connected to my own circle. Yet when I met the very same gentleman the day following Lieutenant Wickham's tale, I observed only that of what my sisters described. A gentleman little tempted to engage in conversation, so you can predict how surprised I was to be requested to stand up with Mr Darcy, that self same day!

There was no further contact between our households the week prior to the ball last evening, which I suspect heightened my own expectations for the event. The prevailing rains kept us all housebound, and I assure you, the time passed at a crawl, nigh on an eternity when faced with Mr Collins and his empty flattery. There was a slight incident involving my father's cousin, and I think that one action set Miss Bingley, the hostess and sister of Mr Bingley, the gentleman who has leased Netherfield, and in whom Jane seems enamoured, against me.

I shall not use this missive to relate the dances, the dresses, or even to describe the evening itself, all I shall say, is that my sisters and I were well pleased to enjoy a lovely evening until a megrim of mine struck long before supper was called. This in partnership with the knowledge that Mr Darcy had neglected to dance with <u>anyone</u> until myself, and you will comprehend that my concerns relating my mother's propensity to loudly exclaim her opinions unrestrainedly, only served to exacerbate my condition.

Miss Bingley offered a room to rest within, so that my family's delight in the evening would not be suspended on my behalf. I thought only kindly upon the lady for her thoughtful consideration, only to be proven false, when by some design, Mr Bingley became entrapped in the very same room, while I lay sound asleep. Through some means, Mr Darcy, Mary and Miss Bingley were the ones to discover the situation, waking me from my repose, where still assailed with pain, and therefore my wits were not at their best. Miss Bingley seemed delighted by the situation, her glee, however soon turned to

consternation, when with the arrival of my father, and before
Mr Bingley could utter words better left unsaid, Mr Darcy
stepped in to provide an alteration to my compromised state.
Miss Bingley's cry of denial would have been welcome justice
if it were not for the unequivocal fact my ruined state would
harm my sisters, the very concern I had been considering
almost the entire summer I was away.

I was not equal to the task of following much more of
the events that occurred, my megrim having had sufficient
time to bloom once more, and therefore, with Mary's help, I
returned home. Now I must face a Mr Collins who seems intent
upon offering me his hand, while my father admits we are
under an agreement to keep last evening's event concealed
until Mr Darcy and Mr Bingley return from London, whereby
then my fate will be publicly revealed. Engaged. To a man I
have met only twice!
Forgive me aunt, but I beg of you to provide me some
guidance, some counsel of what I am to do, how I am to act, for
I can no longer trust my own discernment.
Your troubled niece
All my love
Lizzy

The next day dawned with an icy drizzle, keeping Elizabeth confined to the house, and therefore awaiting with dread, her first encounter with Mr Collins. Throughout breakfast, all her sisters were at table, surreptitiously watching Mr Collins for signs of a repeated request, Lydia seemed to be bouncing in her seat, her nervous thrill of expectation setting her as the silliest girl in the county. Elizabeth kept her focus upon her plate, feeling all the trouble of her monthlies, the pain of which made her oblivious to Mr Collins prolific speech on such nonsensical points as to the cutlery being nothing so fine as that of Rosings Park. The man was ridiculous.

This time, when Mr Collins rose and moved to address her directly, her father spoke up before the gentleman could, "Pardon me, Mr Collins. But I ask that you not impose upon my daughter currently. I promise you, that as my daughter claimed, you are a man who is adept at offering ladies little pieces of flattery at the opportune moments, but as you can see, this is not to be one of those times." Mr Bennet gestured to Elizabeth, who seemed frankly astonished at her father's consideration. Perhaps yesterday's rebuke pierced his fatherly conscience, but Elizabeth doubted it would be a lasting alteration.

Mrs Bennet was not to be quieted, however, "My dear Mr Bennet, as a woman myself, I can attest, that some *moments* are indeed better timed than others" Here Mrs Bennet smiled sweetly at Mr Collins, who it seemed, was struggling to follow the undercurrents of the conversation, only able to grasp he had been denied his petition from someone whom he could not argue. "Yet I feel, that a circumstance of *this* nature, would be wholly welcome."

Mr Bennet smiled wryly at his wife, and Elizabeth could see the smallest shred of admiration twinkle in his eyes. "Mrs Bennet, you are of course, correct, and far be it from me to argue with a lady." At this, all five daughters blinked in surprise, for it was rare indeed to hear their father genuinely compliment their mother. "Yet as the head of this household, it shall be as I deem."

Mr Bennet rose from the table, leaving six ladies quietly surprised, the sight of which seemed to encourage him to laugh unrestrainedly as he took them all in. He ambled away to his book room, and Elizabeth shook her head at her father. His delight in provoking his family was a character flaw she both loved and loathed in equal measure.

"Ahem, forgive me cousin Elizabeth. I cannot contradict your respected father, and therefore I shall defer my appeal until Mr Bennet gives his permission." With that, Mr Collins sat back down to his plate and resumed eating, while his eyes flitted about, fixing upon nothing, his thoughts seeming to rush through his head at such a pace as to make speech impossible.

Lydia snorted a giggle, and Elizabeth instinctively scowled at her youngest sister, not appreciating her mirth in the awkward affair. Tempering her scowl, Elizabeth instead rolled her eyes, to which Lydia smiled brightly once more, her petulant expression smoothed away. She would need to ask her father to follow up with their aunt Gardiner about Lydia visiting her cousin. Relieved by her father's support, Elizabeth endured a dull and quiet morning within the embrace of her family, that was until Charlotte arrived, her sister Maria at her side.

"Good morning all, I hope we are not interrupting?" Charlotte's overly bright tones, her looks having been tended to with particular care, caused Elizabeth to bite her lip in relief.

"Good morning Miss Lucas, how good of you to call when the weather is this dreadful." Mr Collins seemed to become enlivened by Charlotte's flattering attention, while those assembled looked on with apparent comprehension.

Mary flicked a glance over to her, and Elizabeth smiled widely in reply, causing her sister to nod in acceptance, before she rose and excused herself to her music. Maria settled herself with Kitty and Lydia, the former sharing her recently agreed upon plans to travel to Bath. The news had somewhat upset Lydia, until with a shrug she opined that with the Militia's presence, she would be wroth to leave the county. As the younger girls were contentedly discussing Kitty's trip, Jane arranged to pour for everyone, leaving Charlotte at Elizabeth's side and plying careful and flattering attention upon the only male present.

The truth was, having been alerted to Mr Collins intentions via the missive Elizabeth had despatched yesterday, Charlotte knew she would have to work particularly hard to rearrange Mr Collins designs. As Elizabeth promised, she would not inhibit Charlotte's purpose, she would also work to ensure others could not interfere. Seeing everyone was happily engaged, she slipped from the room, and after a quiet word with their reliable and wonderful housekeeper, Mrs Hill, Elizabeth knew her mother would not be present to raise a dispute.

Time spent with Mary in the music room passed swiftly, the two of them happily practising their festive carols, until Mrs Hill informed them that Mr Collins had been encouraged to dine and reside the night with the Lucas family.

"I see you have managed to divert disaster once again, Lizzy. I am impressed." Mary uttered once Mrs Hill had departed.

Elizabeth moved away from the instrument and slumped upon the settee, "I have not played matchmaker, I assure you. I have merely provided Charlotte the opportunity to succeed in her purpose." feeling flat and lifeless, Elizabeth gloomily dispelled the notion of playing matchmaker to one such as Mr Collins.

"Peace sister, I meant no insult." Mary soothed, her fingers playing lightly over the keys. While Mary had a vast knowledge of music, her passion for the accomplishment far superseding that of Elizabeth's, her sister's struggle to *feel* the mood of the compositions made it difficult for her sister to play to her own gratification. Elizabeth's talent was modest at best, music simply an escape from her mother's excitable chatter when the weather was foul, especially during the winter when the weather was not conducive to permit freedom from the house.

"I cannot account for the wish to tie myself to a man I cannot like, nor respect," Elizabeth verbalised, needing to make sense of everything, "but Charlotte is a practical and resourceful woman, who I am sure has considered the matter fully." Elizabeth gazed despondently outside, her own fate tied to a man *she* barely knew, made her more than a little saddened and dispirited. "But who am I to judge?"

"Indeed, Mr Collins does possess a suitable profession, and with being the heir to Longbourne, her choice would give Charlotte cause to be content. I cannot claim any true *knowing* of Charlotte's character, but I would not call her imprudent, and therefore must attest, her difference in temperament would make being married to a man of such narrow-minded views, and pompous conceit, far more acceptable."

"Agreed." Tone flat, Elizabeth listed further considerations, "Plus when you factor being the eldest in such a large family as the Lucases, her lack of fortune, Charlotte's own desires, the match would provide an outcome that would satisfy both parties."

"But not our mother." Mary softly teased, to which Elizabeth could not help but snort a laugh. "How do you fare, Lizzy?" her sister enquired, and Elizabeth's humour broke.

With a stifled sob and a further hug of her pillow, she falteringly answered, "Poorly." Wiping her eyes, Elizabeth kept her gaze fixed upon the scene beyond the window, "If I could have but spoken with Mr Darcy prior to his departure, I would feel at least partially comforted by *one* further instance of knowing the man before we are to wed! But that was not to be, and instead I am here, struggling to comprehend what mischief motivated Miss Bingley in her actions that evening?" Mary shrugged accepting Elizabeth's valid distress, but before more could be said, Jane entered, a missive in hand.

"What is it Jane? Who has written you?" Elizabeth worriedly asked, for Jane looked pale and uneasy.

"Tis from Miss Bingley, she says they are to depart for London this very day, and that Netherfield is to be shut up." Jane looked up from the letter, before handing the page across to Elizabeth, while she took the seat beside her. "Here, you read it, for I assume it concerns you just as much as it does myself."

Elizabeth took the page, and began to read, her heart racing, her own temper needing little encouragement to flare in regards to that dratted woman. Scanning the words, sentences began to leap out, and so Elizabeth uttered them aloud.

"I do not pretend to regret anything I shall leave in Hertfordshire, except your society, my dearest friend; but we will hope, at some future period, to enjoy many returns of that delightful intercourse we have known, and in the meanwhile may lessen the pain of separation by a very frequent and most unreserved correspondence. I depend on you for that." and then, further on, *"When my brother left us yesterday, he imagined that the business which took him to London might be concluded in three or four days; but as we are certain it cannot be so, and at the same time convinced that when Charles gets to town he will be in no hurry to leave it again, we have determined on following him thither, that he may not be obliged to spend his vacant hours in a comfortless hotel."*

Jane broke in, "It is evident by this," added Jane, "that he comes back no more this winter."

Elizabeth could not agree, not knowing what she did of the situation. But if it was to be so, she could not help be thankful that Jane would not be tied to such a wretched creature as Miss Bingley.

"I can see you do not agree, but you have not read further, please, continue." Jane urged.

"Mr. Darcy is impatient to see his sister; and, to confess the truth, we are scarcely less eager to meet her again. I really do not think Georgiana Darcy has her equal for beauty, elegance, and accomplishments; and the affection she inspires in Louisa and myself is heightened into something still more interesting, from the hope we dare entertain

of her being hereafter our sister... My brother admires her greatly already; he will have frequent opportunity now of seeing her on the most intimate footing... Charles is most capable of engaging any woman's heart. With all these circumstances to favour an attachment, and nothing to prevent it, am I wrong, my dearest Jane, in indulging the hope of an event which will secure the happiness of so many?"

"What do you think my dear Lizzy? Is it not clear enough? Does it not expressly declare that Caroline neither expects nor wishes me to be her sister; that she is perfectly convinced of her brother's indifference; and that she means (most kindly!) to put me on my guard? Can there be any other opinion on the subject?"

Closing her eyes at Jane's inability to discern people's true intentions and motives, her prevalent gentle disposition made it inconceivable that anyone would scheme and plot for their own benefit. "Jane, I would have you take that letter, and burn it, so that the words do not torment you more than they have already." Lifting her head, still clutching the paper, she continued, "I am not at liberty to reveal the full particulars, but as Mary stated the other day, Mr Darcy has made a commitment that will see him return. This commitment is not one I can openly discuss at my father's instruction, and therefore I ask you to be ready to accept that Miss Bingley's words, her high-flying *wishes*, are nothing more than that. Wishes. You will not have an overlong period of waiting, I assure you, so please, disregard this, burn it, so that none of this knowledge is passed on to our mother."

Jane studied Elizabeth, pain etched quietly upon her features, Elizabeth's own torment easily evinced, "While I can agree that I know not of the *commitment* Mr Darcy has made, that does not mean *Mr Bingley* is unattached."

Agreeing would only hurt Jane, but Elizabeth could see neither of them would accept the other's view, and so, in sisterly affection, both accorded the other the respect and right to think differently. Mary remained silent throughout, eventually returning to her practice. Jane tucked her letter away, returning with a work basket for the both of them to keep occupied. The day passed quietly on, and with the absence of Mr Collins, dinner returned to its familiar ruckus, conversation flowing one over the other, and Mr Bennet content to tease and torment his womenfolk without fear of interruption.

The peaceful interlude continued into the next morning, with Mr Collins silently consuming a large breakfast, and Mrs Bennet studying the latest fashion plates her daughters had collected for her. With an alarming speed, Mr Collins rose from the table and stated he would be busy for the majority of the day, and hoped to join them all that evening. His absence once again allowed the familiar patterns of Longbourne to return, and Elizabeth was free to roam that morning, the weather, while chill, had remained dry. She could feel an undercurrent flowing beneath all her interactions with her family. An air of appreciation she had overlooked, having been consumed with everyday concerns and disputes. The knowledge that she was to leave all this behind, to face new challenges, new faces, new places, made her heart ache with the oncoming loss of all that was familiar. Time spent in both Jane and Mary's company, happily discussing everything *but* gentlemen, and with Lydia and Kitty at her side, Elizabeth set about completing her Christmas shopping for her family. The distraction of officers meant that both her sisters paid her purchases little attention, but with the promise of a warm drink and new gossip, all three of them arrived upon their aunt's doorstep with a warm reception. In her heart, each moment felt like a long goodbye. To the places she had grown up with, the shops she had frequented, the paths she had walked.

However, this peaceful interval was shattered the next day when Sir William Lucas, his wife Lady Lucas and Charlotte visited. With one glance, Elizabeth smiled to see her friend's content, if expectant expression. A careful glance to Mrs Bennet, and Elizabeth understood such caution. Mr Collins stood about, uttering words of welcome and solicitation, and ultimately making a nuisance of himself. Happy as she was for a break in her routine, it was a rude shock to Mrs Bennet to be informed of the Lucas's news.

"Good Lord! Sir William, how can you tell such a story? Do not you know that Mr. Collins wants to marry Lizzy?" was Mrs Bennet's stark reply, her words falling into the room like lead shot from a gun.

Sir William's happy nature, his good breeding bore the remark and attitude of Mrs Bennet's with complaisance, Lady Lucas less so. "My dear Mrs Bennet, while I cannot attest to Mr Collins previous intentions, I can most certainly confirm that the gentleman is promised to my Charlotte, and has been for the last four and twenty hours."

Mr Collins was also swift to deny his intentions, "My good lady, while I will not deny that my esteemed patroness, Lady Catherine de Bourgh had counselled me to make a match with one of your daughters, it seemed apparent to me, that my suit would perhaps not be as welcome as one would wish. Additionally, with the curtailment of my application for your daughter's hand being made by my respected cousin, one could not help but be made aware of other, more receptive ladies, who would welcome my application for their hand." Here

Mr Collins paused, brushing his hand down his front, while his eyes darted towards Elizabeth.

If the gentleman thought he was to witness some air of despondency, he was to be little appeased, for Elizabeth maintained her cheerful disposition, well-disposed to think kindly of Mr Collins for having the intelligence and wisdom to perceive in Charlotte, such a desirable partner in life. Seeing the light of chance, now extended earnest congratulations, putting paid to the exclamations of her mother and sisters. She was readily joined by Jane making a variety of remarks on the happiness that might be expected from the match. The visit passed further, with very little said by Mrs Bennet, but a dearth of words was not to be the problem, when two such voluble individuals as Sir William Lucas and Mr Collins spent time in company, and so it was much later before all had departed, Mr Collins in addition. They were to make further calls before the rector took his leave the next day, and Elizabeth wished them well, hoping the swifter they left, the sooner the caveat of her own silence could be lifted.

Her mother remained silent all afternoon, but none were unaware of her unhappy state, a veritable storm in a teacup brewing beneath her matrons cap. Later that evening, absent Mr Collins, Mrs Bennet persisted in her disbelief, feeling herself sorely misused by all parties. For Mr Bennet, the matter provided ample amusement, and therefore, he spent much of the evening provoking his family with comments regarding the next mistress of Longbourne.

CHAPTER 6

Meryton December 2nd

Darcy watched as the Meryton streets came into view, his carriage rumbling past hardly significant to the people carrying on with their daily lives. His conveyance absent ostentation outwards, while within the comfort of passengers was ensured with plush seating, large windows, lined with thick fabrics, adjusting the light depending upon the passengers wishes. Prolonged journeys were no trial with room for long legs, such as Darcy possessed. He ignored the passers-by on the streets, even as he searched the faces and figures for one in particular. His week away had been fraught with struggles, and thoughts of Elizabeth had provided meagre comfort.

His sweet, quiet and shy Georgiana, distressed by the circumstances of his rushed marriage, refused to be comforted by thoughts of a much-awaited sister, her anger a foreign entity Darcy had never witnessed. Georgiana had spoke of little else, happy to have the support of their Fitzwilliam relatives, eager to ply attention to the unfair situation, hopeful their counterarguments, alternative solutions were to be considered. Darcy had endured it all, gritting his teeth to keep his sister from noting his own consternation and disappointment in his families behaviour. Anger towards Miss Bingley, who foolishly wrote to both her brother and *himself!* The letter was burned with barely a word read. Towards Bingley, Darcy had little to say for how often his friend had been warned of taking too kind a turn towards his sister. If the man had been more firm, held true to his principles, the manipulations his sister employed would never have come to pass.

From managing his family, the rush between solicitors, Doctors Commons and fulfilling Mr Bennet's directions, this return journey was the first peace he had managed to obtain. As Meryton fell away, and the carriage turned towards Netherfield, Darcy nudged his quiet companion.

"Bingley, did you remember to write to Nicholls?" he enquired, worried they were to enter a house closed up for the winter.

A quiet sigh alerted him to Bingley's morose mood, weary from the bitter condemnation and self-recriminations he had endured this past week, "I did. You need not fear on that score, Darce."

While Darcy forgave his friend his current mood, it was little consolation to see Bingley so low. His friend was paying dividends on his earlier complaisance. Bingley had endured pressure to give up Netherfield, to look past his interest in Jane, who Miss Bingley asserted, thought little of her brother. Miss Bingley also adamantly denied entrapping her brother in the library, blaming the servants, even going so far as to imply *Miss Elizabeth* was responsible! The woman was incorrigible! Her efforts from her time at Netherfield to the letters she had written almost daily, Bingley had been weary from the conflict. Encouraging Bingley to form and trust his own opinions had been more work than Darcy was prepared to provide, and so assured him of his belief that Miss Bennet, was in essentials, much as himself, reserved in company, and did not display her heart on her sleeve. To this, Bingley bitterly complained "Well she will be little inclined after all of this, is she?! Caroline's actions have affected the future of her most beloved sister!"

To that, Darcy made no reply.

Now, hours away from seeing the Bennets again, Bingley had succumbed to dark thoughts, saying little and leaving Darcy consumed with his own concerns, in no position to offer a crumb of comfort. His departure had been necessitated by Miss Bingley's untrustworthy behaviour, a small voice confessed his retreat was cowardly. Hiding. Delaying the moment he would see Elizabeth, face her in the cold light of day, uncertain of her true sentiments. Darcy acknowledged he had run away rather than face such unequal affection, but he had no direction for how he was to go on with the woman, there was no precedent for circumstances such as theirs. His own fascination had begun the minute he had heard her discuss Wickham in the most off-hand terms, and had only developed since then. For her, it could hardly be the same.

"It looks as if we have reached Netherfield. Darce," Bingley stirred himself from his seat, "Do you think she will hate me now?" Bingley's plea was not something Darcy could assuage.

"You are best to discover that for yourself, my friend." Was all he could say before they left the carriage and entered the house.

"Welcome back, Sir." Nicholls, the butler, a greying, thin fellow, almost equalled Darcy's own height. "Would you wish to refresh yourselves first, or would you rather partake of a light repast?"

Bingley, paused his forward motion, looking helplessly across at him, but Darcy would not answer. This was Bingley's home, not his.

"Err, ahem, I think it best we refresh ourselves first, then take a light lunch...in the study?" Flustered, Bingley dragged his hand though his hair, nervously tugging the length. He would struggle with premature baldness if he kept pulling it as he'd been inclined to do lately.

"Very good, Sir. I shall have the cook send up something in about an hour?" Nicholls, unfazed, nodded, then swiftly departed.

Darcy and Bingley each made their way to their rooms, cleaned up, and were back in the study in less than half an hour. Bingley's restlessness had not abated in that time, exacerbating Darcy's own anxieties.

"Good god man, cease your infernal pacing." He groaned when his strained patience wore thin.

"Hah!" Bingley pointed, a look of triumph washing away his restlessness, "Now you can perceive how damned frustrating it is to humour such disturbance!"

Abashed, Darcy could not deny that movement had been his familiar habitude whenever he suffered tumultuous reflections. His London study carpet could bear testament to such, following the conniving actions of his sister's one-time companion and the foul villain who had once been his child-hood playmate. However, his current consternation, what disturbed Darcy, was how *measured* his introspection was. Yes, he was concerned with his reception, but the *correctness* of his actions, the *knowing* that he had made the right resolution– that was not a sentiment Darcy sought to assess in too great a detail.

"Yes, yes, I am insufferable. You have pointed that fact out to me on many an occasion, but good god man, do *you* even comprehend why you are so uneasy?"

"Why else, but that Miss Bennet will now have the lowest of opinions of me! Of my relations! And who could fault for such! *Who* would wish to be connected to such a one as my sister?" Hands once more in his hair, Darcy was momentarily distracted thinking of a bald Bingley, "I tell you Darcy, I have never before suffered to be embarrassed by my connection to trade. Yet this week, I cannot help but to believe Caroline's desperate social climbing would not be half so bad if it were not for our background!" Bingley's voice rose with every exclamation, into which a maid entered, bearing the afore promised repast. Nervously, the girl visibly debated continuing on into the room, or a possible retreat.

Bingley turned away, cheeks flooded with colour, allowing the poor maid to shuffle in and accomplish her purpose and depart, post-haste. Darcy, unaccustomed to playing the soothing companion, was sure Bingley would be as mute as himself when the time came to speak with Miss Bennet, without offering some words of consolation.

"Come, Bingley, sit down to eat." The two

gentlemen took their seats, "If, and I do mean *if*, Miss Bennet has taken a dislike of you, then you are more than charming enough to woo her back. I have seen you accomplish such with ease, time and again, and with the absence of the most offensive person in your party, there will be no impediment to your advancement, other than the lady and her family. Which is just as it ought to be."

Darcy had piled his plate with enough food to keep his mouth occupied, but before he began, he had one last titbit, "Additionally, I should also relate, Mr Bennet has *not* disclosed my engagement with Elizabeth, that is, he assured me he would delay any announcement until his cousin returned to Kent."

Bingley looked up from picking at his food, bemused, "Whyever not?"

"Because," Darcy took a drink of his mulled cider, appreciating the restorative warmth, "Mr Bennet's cousin, is *my* aunt's rector. And if *my aunt* discovers recent events, most notable of which, my engagement, you can be sure she will be a force to be reckoned with. And *that* I have no wish to contend."

Bingley nodded in agreement, and both men quieted as they fixed their attention upon their sating their appetite, thoughts alike, consumed with one Bennet daughter or another. Once complete, and still with little said between them, they summoned their mounts to attend to matters of the heart in one case, and to settle matters complete, in another.

"Jane! Jane!" Their mother called, her shrill tones aggrieved, an irritant to the ear, and thus inciting one to remedy the cause as swiftly as possible, "Oh where is my Jane! For he is *come*!" Jane and Elizabeth shared a sympathetic smile, and appeared in the hallway outside Jane's room.

"I am here Mamma, what is it? Who has come?" Jane descended the stairs, guiding their mother gently back to the parlour and out of the chill hallway. Elizabeth followed, her own mind grasping just who *he* might be, and wondering if the gentleman came alone.

"Mr Bingley of course! Why, Jane, you look in such disarray!" Mrs Bennet fussed at Jane's hair, to which her sister quietly humoured, before she was conducted to a seat, "Never matter, you have such looks, that even thus, you are too beautiful!"

Elizabeth rolled her eyes and took her seat, content to be customarily dismissed from her mother's attentions.

Jane's eyes pleaded with her sister to situate herself at her side, yet with an unapologetic shrug, Elizabeth refused to be moved from her location in the window seat, chill though it was. Jane would have to deal with Mr Bingley as she saw fit, especially now that she was aware of all the particulars. Mr Collins departure yesterday, rescinded her father's agreement for discretion, but still Mr Bennet made no announcement, and the truth was, Elizabeth felt relieved. The longer less was said, then perhaps the need to wed Mr Darcy would no longer be required. Her foolish heart thudded in distress, and Elizabeth could not define if the thought gave her pleasure or pain.

Mrs Hill arrived at the door, announcing, "Mr Bingley, ma'am, and Mr Darcy." Once accomplished, the housekeeper departed to arrange for tea without being instructed.

"Good afternoon Mrs Bennet, Miss Bennet, Miss Elizabeth." Mr Bingley appeared nervous, bowing to each lady in turn.

Before Mr Darcy could add his own greeting, her mother erupted, "Oh, Mr Bingley! You have returned at last!" The words continued, but Elizabeth's attention did not, her gaze arrested by the dark gentleman standing beside the fair-haired Mr Bingley. Their positions were almost completely reversed from when they first met, she at the window, and he at the door.

He still resembled granite, just as she had originally decided, his attractive sharp chiselled looks, brow and cheekbones so distinctly defined, Elizabeth imagined tracing her fingers across those planes, feeling the stubble abrade her fingertips. How disturbing! Guiltily her eyes jumped to Mr Darcy's fearing he could detect her improper musings, as if she had spoken the idea aloud. His stone eyes captured hers, a look so intense, so *hard*, Elizabeth felt the chill of her location intensify. An eruption of gooseflesh had Elizabeth scrambling to wrap her shawl even tighter about her shoulders. He appeared angry, in her estimation, perhaps resentful to be in her company once more, and the suspicion that the gentleman regretted his offer made her back stiffen and a brow rose in mocking inquiry. Yet to this show of defiance, there was little reaction. Mr Darcy shifted, breaking into the speech Mrs Bennet was still conducting.

That slight movement acted as if a ripple in a pond, sending waves outward. Mr Bingley coughed, Jane blushed, and her mother ceased her words mid-way.

His husky baritone, somehow an admixture of decadence and gravel, followed, "Pardon the intrusion Mrs Bennet, but I was wondering if I could meet with Mr Bennet."

Rattled, Elizabeth, composure thin, a simple sheet behind which she hid, felt the gravity of the moment. Mrs Bennet nodded wordlessly, before turning to her daughter, "Lizzy, take Mr Darcy to your father's book-room, and see Hill, that she has prepared refreshments for our callers."

Elizabeth nodded in acquiescence, leaving

her safe haven, closer and closer still to the man who seemed as solid as the earth, and just as immense as mountains. His stone gaze tracked her path across the room, stalking her steps, until she reached his side, whereby Elizabeth gestured for the gentleman to follow, the silence between them a physical presence. His heat reached for her, the scent of him, sandalwood and something else, his own natural scent? Both twined about her, weaving them together, an unfinished tapestry. Elizabeth wove through Longbourne's hallways, until finally, her father's sanctuary was before them. A soft knock, and then Elizabeth heard her father's call to enter, the presence of Mr Darcy a looming shadow at her back. Elizabeth could not define the intensity between them, it was outside her world of experience. Gentlemen were entertained by Elizabeth's clever wit, but they fell in love with her sister's beauty. This, Elizabeth knew as fact. And yet, Mr Darcy's focus had never strayed to her sister. His attention, once turned upon her, had rarely shifted. The novel experience was unsettling, leaving Elizabeth feeling uneasy, robbing her of wit, until she felt as muffled as Mary often claimed she too suffered.

"Shall we not go in?" the deep timber vibrated through her, sending shivers tracing down her spine.

Confused, she stared blankly at the door, until an arm moved around her to grasp the handle and push the door open. Embarrassed, Elizabeth felt colour suffuse her cheeks, but she moved into her father's room with as much of her natural confidence as she could muster. Her father looked up, his book forgotten when he noted the dark presence at her back. He rose, closing the book, and setting it aside. The clap of the book was like the fall of a gavel. Judgement.

"Ah, Mr Darcy. Good afternoon." Her father gestured to the seat before his desk, and Elizabeth moved to the armchair, refusing to be dismissed from this meeting that would canvas *her* future. Seeing the signs of her obstinacy, her father chuckled but said not a word.

"Good afternoon Mr Bennet. I hope you and your family are well?" was the solemn reply to her father's greeting.

"Tolerable, Sir. For we are grieved to have lost the company of my cousin, who only departed yesterday." Elizabeth rolled her eyes without remorse at her father's quip. Mr Bennet had almost packed Mr Collins bags himself, he had been that eager to see the repellant rector depart!

"While I am sorry for your dismay, I must say the situation we are in will be all the more manageable to resolve without Mr Collins presence." Mr Darcy pulled a packet of paperwork from his coat, and Elizabeth watched them in fascination. That was a considerable set of documents. How had the man accomplished so much in such a short period of time?

"Ah, straight to the matter I see. Very well." Her father retook his seat, settling in to review the sheets he had been handed. Watching her father's brow rise and fall set Elizabeth's nerves on edge, and she felt horrified to feel sympathetic to her mother's complaints.

Unable to bear the silence further, Elizabeth interrupted, "I see that you have come prepared, Sir. But I must ask, are you certain it is necessary for us to wed? I have heard no word or rumour pass through Meryton, or from that of my neighbours either."

Mr Darcy turned, giving her his full attention. The sight of his handsome features studying her own modest appearance, her hair in an askew bun, her dress thrice mended, more comfortable than pretty, left Elizabeth feeling inferior. The thought made her itch to snap out a retort, but her wits had deserted her.

After another moment of extended study, Mr Darcy attended her question, "While little may have been said in *your* hearing, I am familiar with how gossip such as the ball and Bingley's absence will only grow, now that he has returned to the area." Mr Darcy paused, eyes of stone still pinning her in place. The fact that he had raised no complaint about her presence was a point in the gentleman's favour, but the truth was, he expended little energy in softening her resentment. "Yet, no matter what gossip does or does not arise, I know my friend. Bingley's honour would compel him to remedy the situation, and again, I state that this would only bring heartache."

"So, you are fixed on this course of action? You feel no qualms about marrying a woman so much lower than your own station?" Elizabeth heard the challenging tone, but was helpless to prevent it.

Smiling wryly for the first time, Elizabeth watched transfixed as the expression turned his hard features soft, warm, and welcoming. "I am bound by honour and inclination, Miss Elizabeth. And as to station, I am a gentleman, and you, a gentleman's daughter, in that we are equal."

"But what of my family, Sir? While you may *say* my situation warrants no issue, I will not give up my relations, married or not." Defiance dripped like venom, and Elizabeth watched in regret, as Mr Darcy's smile disappeared.

"I would not ask it of you, and little appreciate the implication. Marriage is a partnership between two people, and will require adjustments on both our parts."

Frustrated, Elizabeth tossed her head, eyes blazing in agitation, "Tis easy for you to make such remarks, when tis not *you* who must leave your home, your family, your friends."

Her father, not lifting his head from

his reading, silenced her, "Hush, Lizzy. That is enough of such missish behaviour. You are better than this, to attempt to tear down what has not yet been built." Looking up, Mr Bennet continued, "You are my clever little Lizzy. There is no challenge you cannot overcome when you set your mind to it, of this I am confident. And while you are correct, that the lion's portion of change falls upon a woman, this is not news to you. You have always known you are to wed and leave Longbourne behind. Do not begin, what I can see, has the potential to be a fulfilling marriage, in animosity and affront." Mr Bennet rubbed the bridge of his nose, dislodging his glasses higher, "I know, trust me, I know, from experience how little rewarding that is."

Elizabeth remained quiet thereafter, listening as her father questioned particulars within the settlement, but paying little attention to much more.

It was real, then.

She was to wed this tall, dark, mountain of a man, who incited such alarming reactions and responses, alteration Elizabeth welcomed not at all.

Words caught her attention, and Elizabeth asked in alarm, "Three days! I am to wed in three days time?! That is not possible!"

"It is, Lizzy, love."

"But Mamma cannot prepare anything in that amount of time! My dress! The wedding breakfast!"

"Hush, child," her father spoke, his words carrying a bite of irritation, "None of that will be half as important as saying the vows, Lizzy. And I am confident your mother will accomplish all that is necessary in the time given."

"As to your dress, your aunt has provided one she feels will fit the occasion, and has had it included in my own trunks." Mr Darcy's words had Elizabeth's eyes swinging to his, shock and surprise displayed without hesitation.

"My aunt?!"

The gentleman nodded, his eyes roaming her face, such that Elizabeth imagined she could *feel* a path blazing across her skin.

"Yes, Mrs Gardiner, your aunt provided a dress she considers sufficient."

Her shock apparent, Elizabeth whispered, "When did you meet my aunt?"

Mr Bennet answered, "I had Mr Darcy deliver a note of introduction and requested your aunt's assistance. Being best placed in providing the necessary accessories, it seemed expeditious to delegate the undertaking to one whom, I am assured, you would have no cause to censure, their style and taste much to your preference. And with the arrival of our Gardiner relatives, your aunt will ensure the event will proceed without issue, and thereby we all may be congratulated."

Mr Bennet nodded in conclusion, leaving

Elizabeth overwhelmed, and as a result, she excused herself from the room. Her need for peace, a moment to accept such sudden changes, had her donning her cloak and slipping into the denuded gardens. Her steps were much closer to a run, but Elizabeth felt too much to uphold any precept or ideal of feminine grace. Her hurried flight, she hoped would go unnoticed, yet with a barely audible growl, Elizabeth accepted it was not to be so, at the sight of Mr Darcy heading her way.

"I mean no disrespect, Sir, when I say, that I would dearly love to be left with my thoughts." Her need to be alone waged a war with the need to show this man that she was not so easily directed. To be added to his collection of *possessions*, set in her place, compliant in every way. Her quiet growl of moments before, repeated.

"I can appreciate," Mr Darcy said, face expressing a silent apology, "that you may wish to be left in solitude, but your father directed me to follow, therefore I am under obligation, your wishes not withstanding."

Outraged, Elizabeth fumed aloud, "How typical! Of my father. Of you. Men! To make these decisions that affect us women, those lesser in sphere! To command and instruct as you please, ignoring the truth that we, that *I* Am not lacking in intellect, and am more than capable to resolve my fate!" She stalked away, ignoring the hidden bench, beneath a barren arch.

She knew, knew, that her fate was bound to this man. But to be expected to be passed from father to husband, from pillar to post, to have no say! The *one* choice she had the *right* to decide, and it was stripped away! Logically, Elizabeth understood her anger was not directed upon Mr Darcy, but her circumstances. Yet reason and her own character demanded she expend some of this broiling resentment and frustration upon the gentleman, the only quarry available.

Her path took her back, whirling to face him, victim to her wrath, "I! I, am not property. And while your *experience of such matters* lends you the assurance that our course is set, I am not yet in your power!"

Mr Darcy's aspect stiffened the longer Elizabeth railed at him, and just as swiftly as her temper flared, so too did it dissipate, leaving only shame in its wake. The man was to be her husband and she would have them begin their union as confederates, not combatants. Contrition consumed Elizabeth as she bit her lip and moved towards the gentleman. A softer expression spread as she studied her companion. Her ire, flaring brightly often burned away after very little time, her temper suddenly cold ashes in the grate.

"Forgive me, Sir. I should not have spoken so precipitously." Elizabeth watched Mr Darcy's eyes as they pinned her to the spot, his refined and rugged face unchanged from its stiffness, "You are not to blame, and my impetuous and unladylike manners will surely have you think poorly of me."

In the next breath, Mr Darcy strode forward, his hand rising to cup the back of her neck, and then his lips covered her own. The kiss so wholly unexpected, so unfamiliar and foreign, she stood compliant in his arms, as his lips caressed her own, the soft, warm sensations giving her a liquid feeling all over, while her heart raced. What was this? She gasped, as the warm pressure at her neck was partnered with the strength of his arm banding about her waist, folding her closer into the gentleman's chest. His lips continued to move over her own, and without thought, Elizabeth leaned in to deepen the contact, her eyes having closed at the overwhelming sensations. Languid ease stole away every other thought. There was no pressure for further intimacy, no dreaded fear claiming her, warning Elizabeth to fight, to flee.

Eventually, Mr Darcy ended the kiss, but not his embrace, tucking her head close to his chest, his chin resting upon her hair, while the hand at her neck, stroked her skin softly, the one about her waist remaining still, fixed. Shaken to her core, breath sawing in and out, every long-held belief regarding passion, love, romance, had just been vanquished with one kiss. Her first. Limbs heavy and sluggish, Elizabeth had no experience with gentlemen, no little encounters that would explain why she felt so relaxed, so at ease and safe. Was it always this way? Is that why ladies were counselled to maintain proper conduct, else fall so easily under a man's power? Mr Darcy was still a relative stranger to her. She knew no more of him than she had moments before, yet the embrace, that kiss, felt filled with *something* undefinable, and the not knowing was frustrating.

Shrieks from the house broke the quiet moment, easing her away from her chaotic thoughts, and eyes closed in mortification, Elizabeth promised herself she would resume pondering this encounter much later. Presumably, from the sounds her mother was making, Mrs Bennet had just been informed of the engagement. This was confirmed with a sudden exclamation of, "Bless me! What pin-money!" and then, "Ten thousand pounds!" Burrowing further into Mr Darcy's chest, Elizabeth groaned, only to hear Mr Darcy chuckle dryly, "Tis somewhat more than that..."

Elizabeth decided she was staying right where she was, Mr Darcy's wishes and intentions, she would dismiss. There was no reasonable temptation that would lead her back into her home, to endure her mother's theatrics. Elizabeth refused. Perplexingly, Mr Darcy possessed an ability to comprehend the subject of her thoughts.

"We will have to return some time, for the weather is not conducive to be comfortable for any true respite."

Reluctantly, Elizabeth pulled away, missing the warmth and security, the comfort of his arms, sentiments which made her uncomfortable. Another loud shriek was heard, this time far less exuberant.

"I must assume your father has informed your mother, the date we are to wed." Mr Darcy matter-of-factly stated, tickling her ire back into existence.

Turning back to Mr Darcy, arms clutched tightly to her chest to maintain the borrowed warmth, she asked, "Explain why we must wed so soon?"

"Any delay permits Miss Bingley further opportunity for mischief, for she is bound and determined to keep her brother from tying his lot in with that of the Bennets, nor will she remain silent on *your* circumstances, feeding the gossip mill malicious tales, all in the hopes it will deter me from my course."

Accepting the truth and sense of Mr Darcy's words was like swallowing bitter medicine. Mind racing, Elizabeth returned to a safer topic, "And my aunt?"

"Yes? What of Mrs Gardiner?"

"I know my father provided you a letter of introduction, but I still cannot account for you acting as my aunt's agent in regards to my dress, rather than see to the matter herself." Her aunt Gardiner was more maternal and nurturing than her own mother; Mrs Bennet could not forget her own concerns long enough to attend to those of her daughter's.

Mr Darcy's smile caught her off-guard, his stone-granite features softening to such an extent, Elizabeth felt her already unsteady pulse skip a beat, her palms sweaty, she discreetly clutched her dress to mask their state. Her soon-to-be husband was breathtaking when he smiled. Thank heavens he seemed to possess a disposition that made this occurrence so infrequent, that witnessing the sight, was all the more a privilege.

"Your aunt is an excellent woman, Miss Elizabeth, and I was only too happy to make her acquaintance, and that of your respected uncle also." Mr Darcy took her arm in his, sheltering her from the cold winds with his own body. His steps guided their return back to the house, though they were unhurried and leisurely. "As to the matter of your dress, I believe your aunt thought only of you, that you may rest easy with it in your possession. Mrs Gardiner has additionally been instrumental in having your measurements sent round to my sister's modiste, who will hopefully have arranged for a selection of dresses based upon your own personal style and preference." They had just reached the portico of the house, when

Mr Darcy softly whispered, causing Elizabeth to blush, "The necessary undergarments and accoutrements have also been ordered, to be delivered to my home this coming week."

Her embarrassment was extreme, but the opportunity to express her gratitude to her aunt and uncle would be underscored by this private moment. She had railed at him, ranted, only to apologise, to then be gifted her first passionate embrace; it seemed her interactions with Mr Darcy were forever to bring with it some extreme emotion, for had she not undergone them all in the span of a half hour or less?

The next hours passed too quickly for Elizabeth to track, from the warm embrace of her mother's reception on their return to Longbourne, followed by the continual exclamations of all that Mrs Bennet claimed could not be done, while she simultaneously made lists and preparations with the steady support of their housekeeper. The gentlemen remained for dinner, yet Elizabeth knew her sister was uneasy in Mr Bingley's company, that selfsame gentleman fared little better. A chance for private speech came much later that night, when all had retired, their guests having long departed.

"Lizzy?" Mary called from her bedroom door, and Elizabeth turned from unpinning her hair, to note both Jane and Mary, sombre and serious.

Welcoming them in, a bright smile for them both, Mary and Jane were already attired for bed, their warm dressing gowns and slippers keeping the frigid chill at bay.

"I see tis to be a council of comfort then?" Elizabeth teased, but neither Mary nor Jane's smile were very convincing.

"Out with it then, for you are both sorely troubled." Elizabeth resumed plucking pins from her hair, only to have Jane step up behind her and assume the task. Elizabeth smiled in thanks from the mirror reflecting them both, catching Mary once again tidying away after Elizabeth, her preference for order ever present.

"Lizzy, I know not what to think of your engagement." Jane kept her gaze upon her task, "but Mr Bingley was very conscientious of the debt he owes to his friend. I fear I cannot know what to think of him, not now that I have had my eyes opened to his sister's character... and yet Mr Bingley desired to speak nothing of his sister's doing, of what occurred during the ball." Jane did not meet Elizabeth's eyes, her hands having completed the task of plucking up pins, turned to brushing and braiding Elizabeth's hair. "I know that from what both you and Mary have said, Miss Bingley acted unreasonably, especially when Mr Darcy provided Mr Bingley a way free, despite being ready to offer for you, in the name of friendship and the interest of preventing any broken hearts. But I feel aggrieved...it all feels so wrong."

Jane dropped the hairbrush, a sob escaping her, and Elizabeth turned, stood, and swept her sister up in an embrace. Poor Jane's heart was struggling, the knowledge of Miss Bingley's manipulations, or as the possibility she was responsible, sat ill. Mary stepped up and patted both hers and Jane's shoulders, and Elizabeth giggled at the sight of it. Mary had no misconceptions about people's motives, her ability to empathise however, was somewhat limited by her constrained straight thinking. Jane smiled softly at them both, before shooing Elizabeth off to change and don her robe.

Over the screen, Elizabeth answered Jane's unspoken plea, "Jane, you are free to behave however best suits your own conscience and heart. Permitting Miss Bingley to hinder or halt your own interests, gratifies the woman with success, and I would hate for that to be the case." Elizabeth returned to the bed, settling in at the headboard, while her sisters sat at the foot. "In relation to Mr Bingley, Mary has attested he would have done the honourable thing, but that he felt all the struggle of going against his own heart and interest. While I do not know the gentleman anywhere near as well as you both do, I believe Mr Darcy did more than save his friend from committing himself to the wrong sister, he prevented three hearts from being broken."

Mary looked back at her puzzled, "Three?"

Elizabeth explained, her smile loving, admiring the stark contrast of beauty that encompassed her sisters, one light and fair, kind and gentle, the other dark and subtle, her appeal elusive, while she hungered to learn, to discern all that she could.

"Yes, three, Mary. For Jane's heart would have suffered to see the man *she* feels an affection for, wed her own sister. Mr Bingley's heart would have ached, to wed the wrong sister. And mine would have broken, to be the cause of my dear sister's heartbreak. So, yes. Three."

Mary nodded, while Jane looked away, fighting to confine her tears.

"Dearest, why does my marriage to Mr Darcy pain you?" Elizabeth asked, her affection colouring her tone.

"Because it is all *my* fault!" Jane mournfully complained, surprising both sisters.

"How so?" Mary asked before Elizabeth could.

Slumping, Jane answered, "Because, the affection I feel towards Mr Bingley, my hopes of a union with him, must have been readily apparent. For Miss Bingley to be so desperate to seperate her brother and I, she would seek to entrap my sister in scandal! I know you Lizzy, you would have refused Mr Bingley! You would not have wed the man you know I possessed feelings for."

Stupefied, Elizabeth negated Jane's

illogical reasoning, "Jane, sister, let me assure you, that in no way, is this situation, a making of your own. That is entirely nonsensical, considering the point that your exemplary behaviour would not have you be so overt in signalling your affections!"

Mary agreed, "Assuredly so, Jane. Your conduct is unimpeachable."

"Then why else would Miss Bingley seek to cause harm to my sister?" Jane cried, and Elizabeth's simmering anger towards Miss Bingley grew.

"You give Miss Bingley far too much consideration, dear Jane. And that, I will not allow. Choose to remember this time, as if I am a gothic heroine," theatrically, she laid the back of her hand against her forehead with a dramatic flourish, "the young lady swept away from her beloved family, with a dark, brooding and handsome stranger." Elizabeth's coloured her voice with exaggerated feeling, an attempt to lift Jane's spirits.

Jane's smile fell flat, while Mary's gaze wandered off thoughtfully, "I would not want you to meet a grisly end." The only reply to her efforts, and Elizabeth sighed in defeat. She had not the strength to support her family with their acclimation to her upcoming marriage, for she was too consumed with coming to terms with it herself.

CHAPTER 7

Longbourne, December 3rd

T he next morning, Elizabeth woke bright and early, escaping outdoors for the shortest of walks, before rushing home to clean up in anticipation of abating her mother's haranguing. While the morning passed apace, the time for her family's arrival quickly approached, and before long, Lydia could be heard shouting of a carriage. Unfortunately, that was not the only arrival, for several officers followed behind.

Lydia's squeal of delight was not as attention drawing as it normally would have been, drowned out as it was by their four cousins descending from the carriage, succeeding her aunt and uncle. The general noise and hubbub was a soothing background, and Elizabeth greeted her aunt and uncle with all the warmth and affection that was reserved for them.

Her cousins good naturedly filed off to the nursery, looking forward to rambles through the fields later with their older cousins. For now, Elizabeth looped her aunt's arm through her own, and guided them indoors, leaving her to get refreshed before returning downstairs once more.

The parlour on her entrance was almost bursting with bodies, for not only were all her sisters present, but four officers too. Lydia had invited them in regardless of the fact they had visitors, and Elizabeth looked to their mother in the hopes she would quietly dispatch their company. Such was not to be the case, and so Elizabeth sat and waited, thankful only that Lydia had been warned to not discuss her pending marriage. The officers were too unknown to Elizabeth for her to wish them present, therefore, they were not to receive an invitation, much to Lydia's displeasure. Discussion of her upcoming nuptials was neglected as a result. Elizabeth could only hope her youngest sister would hold to her promise of discretion, rather than cause further embarrassment to the family.

"Lieutenant Denny, do you think Colonel Forster will really throw a ball? It would be just the thing to begin the Christmas season!" Lydia happily cried, to which Kitty gleefully concurred.

"Miss Lydia, if you could but convince him, I believe our commanding officer would be more than happy to arrange the occasion!" was the officer's glib answer.

Elizabeth rolled her eyes, but the action was swiftly noted by one she had rather avoid.

"Miss Elizabeth, I see that the thought of a Militia Christmas ball would bring you little pleasure." Lieutenant Wickham commented, his well-favoured features bearing a charming grin, sharp green eyes focused intently upon her. "I did hear mention of how sorely you were missed at the Netherfield ball. I, sadly, was not to attend as I had orders that took me to London that day. A convenient command, one could almost say." The implication was obvious.

Her sister sighed in sympathy, and Elizabeth speculated if her aunt's cousin had yet to agree to host Lydia, for only with some distance from their mother, would such coy displays be moderated. In essentials, her youngest sister straddled the youth and womanhood divide, her open disposition that of an innocent child, while her bold determination to think well of *all* officers spoke of more feminine curiosity. It would be a challenge to correct, else Lydia's open nature combined with the hunger for adventure made her ripe for those with less than honourable intentions.

"That is correct, Lieutenant Wickham, I *was* absent from the latter half of the ball, being struck with a frequent indisposition." Elizabeth emphasised.

"Then we are both to be pitied for missing the occasion, for we have that in common. I even heard tell of the *host's* absence! Is that not so Denny? His sister was determined to locate him for he had missed several dances!"

The officer agreed, and Elizabeth watched in dismay as Jane unhappily flushed red. Of course, the eagle-eyed Lieutenant caught the reaction and smirked. Lydia, bored with being ignored, redirected conversation more to her liking, and from there, Elizabeth ignored the company until her aunt could join them. Yet once more, Lieutenant Wickham was dissatisfied with being dismissed, and moved to sit closer to her. The attention disturbed Elizabeth, for no matter how little she engaged with the officer, he seemed to exercise great delight in seeking her out!

"It appears as if you are to have a full household, Miss Elizabeth. The Bennets are much in demand it seems, and I can only hope, that these relatives are an improvement upon your previous houseguest. Are we officers to be introduced, do you think?" The genial statement, made with casual eloquence, conveyed something of significance. However, in no mood to give consequence to attractive gentlemen who imagine themselves of more relevance to ladies, Elizabeth exercised her wit.

"Why, Sir, I did not think you had an interest in trade? If this is the case, I shall happily introduce you to my uncle!"

"I am not," Lieutenant Wickham amiably replied, "averse to those who earn their living honestly, and trade is just such an occupation. By all accounts, your uncle seems to be a successful businessman, and I would delight in knowing more of your family. Further intimacy with those who know you dearly, would only heighten my own delight."

Ignoring the glib inference, Elizabeth neutrally replied, "The distinction between those of gentle descent, versus less salubrious origins, is an antiquated condition, that I am sure cannot always hold firm with such changes that I have heard occurring." Her eyes watched the door, hoping to display by posture and demeanour, that no further discourse was desired, yet the Lieutenant was undeterred.

"While I may admire your uncle, it is not *him* I wish to know more of." was the seductive whisper her companion made.

A shudder ran down her back at his words, and Elizabeth almost leapt into her aunt's arms when that good lady entered moments later, having never been more delighted to see her relative than she was then.

"My dear aunt, I am sorely pleased you have arrived!" was her fervent greeting.

Mrs Gardiner smiled wisely, having witnessed the overly familiar behaviour of the officer. "Dear Lizzy, I shall be sure to visit if this is to be my welcome." Aunt Gardiner went about the room being introduced, her innate poise and grace a stark contrast to that of Mrs Bennet's effervescent, if ineffective manners. Eventually the officers departed, the Lieutenant lingering overlong at her side, making love with his eyes and charm. Only Lydia's naïveté prevented her from withstanding such regard.

When they left, it was with a heavy sigh of relief overshadowed by Lydia's complaint, "I cannot see why father says we are not to invite officers to Lizzy's wedding! It shall be such a dreadful bore without them to keep company!"

Kitty, having distanced herself to some degree from the overall obsession with redcoats, carefully replied, "Mama has not the time to arrange an extravagant affair, and adding further guests will only cause our mama more work."

Mrs Bennet seemed to feel all the compliment this consideration gave her, and openly expressed her pleasure, "Very true, my dear Kitty. Tis a shame, Lyddie dearest, but there is more than enough work as it is to have our close neighbours attend!"

Her aunt supporting Elizabeth's mother, while soothing Lydia's hair as the girl leaned against Mrs Gardiner, "Your mother has a considerable task ahead, and I am sure, if she could, she would delight all with a worthy celebration. However, we must focus our efforts on what *can* be accomplished and ensure we send off our Lizzy with the best possible preparations!"

From there, the conversation moved on to Elizabeth's trousseau, the dress Mrs Gardiner had sent with Mr Darcy, and all the little details that would provide a semblance of the ceremony she had little given consideration. Before long, Lydia's sulks were forgotten, and her sister threw herself into the preparations, working happily upon a veil, while Kitty and Mary settled to sewing some new chemises. Her heart warmed by her family's efforts, Elizabeth fought falling into maudlin introspection as she to her own tasks.

That day and the next passed far too swiftly for Elizabeth. The furious occupation of her and her sisters made her grateful, as there was hardly enough attention to spare for the myriad worries she had buried under her confident composure. Her neighbours wished her well at church, where they had excitedly discussed Elizabeth as if she were not present, and rather than exert herself to feel any offence, Elizabeth allowed her attention to wander. Charlotte, her dear friend, had been given little chance to have all explained, for Mr Darcy, stone persona firmly entrenched, all but conquered those who would use sly commentary to whisper of her swift union. The warmth he had displayed to her in the garden seemed a figment of her imagination, an ephemeral phantasm, but Elizabeth could not fault the gentleman, for he diligently stayed by her side, receiving congratulations with cool reserve. Mr Darcy remained as much a mystery now, as he did when his name was first mentioned, and the enigma frustrated Elizabeth, but there was little time to devote to deciphering the puzzle, her attention consumed with her family. Sitting with Mary at the pianoforte, listening to Kitty and Lydia share their excited hopes and dreams of what her *grand, rich life* would be. Admiring Jane's calm manners anew, delighting in her father's humour while silently wishing he would not torment his family so, and finally, listening to the ridiculous and wild excitement of her mother. They were all so dear to her, and expending introspection upon her future husband would be for some other time.

The night before her wedding fell heavily upon the Bennet household, everyone sharing eloquent looks and loving embraces, until all that was left once the chaos and unrestrained animation ceased, family settled in their rooms, was silence. Aunt Gardiner arrived, and Elizabeth felt cowardly fear choke her, as she watched her aunt shoo Jane and Mary back to their rooms. Grateful as she was to her aunt, holding her hands and sharing the much dreaded private conversation in place of her own mother, the topic was not one in which Elizabeth relished. The wedding night.

"You needn't look so afeared dear Lizzy, for I assure you, there is much to look forward to in the marriage bed." Her aunt's words failed to suppress the rising dread of every maiden's great unknown. She felt as if she stood upon an icy lake, hearing that first crack spelling danger, stalking your every step.

"Easy to say, when you are in love with your husband." Elizabeth retorted.

Her aunt ignored Elizabeth's curt response, "That may be so, but the fundamentals are all the same, and that we have already canvassed. My word of advice is to be as welcoming and warm as you are naturally. Be yourself, dearest, and you and your husband shall easily overcome this first challenging period. Do not dwell on the now, but think instead of what you hope your marriage to be; one of distance and cool civility, or two people who work together, live together, love together?"

"Thank you aunt," Elizabeth quietly replied, grateful anew for the words of wisdom, "I shall endeavour to keep your advice close and work to overcome my modesty, no matter how difficult it will be, vulnerable with a gentleman so wholly unknown to me."

Aunt Gardiner laughed delightedly, "Lizzy, dear, I understand this is not a circumstance any of us had envisioned for your future, but you are a bright and intelligent girl. I trust you to work to make your marriage a success, and assure you, intimacy between a husband and wife *can* be a solid foundation to build from. Before you argue that the marriage bed will only be difficult for you, bear in mind that *both* of you shall be vulnerable," Elizabeth snorted in disbelief, "Yes, you may well disbelieve that, but in this you must trust me. Unions such as yours will no doubt be fraught with difficulties, but *this* need not be one of them, therefore I encourage you to allow yourself to be open with your husband, not just physically, but emotionally as well." With a pointed look, her aunt grinned mischievously, "And to aid you in that regard, I have packed you a particular gift in your trunks that you are to wear tomorrow night. Do you understand?"

Aunt Gardiner's arm was wrapped about her, so Elizabeth just nodded her head, then rested it upon her shoulder.

"Do you really think Mr Darcy and I can have a happy union?" was her quiet and soft query.

To this, her aunt replied in kind, "I do. I really do."

CHAPTER 8

Longbourne Church, December 5th

D arcy paced the church ante-room, where he and Bingley awaited the Bride's arrival. The church had quietly filled, guests encouraged to sit as they desired, for there would be no kin-folk of his own to show their support in attendance. To distract himself from the ticking of his time-piece, Darcy had been quizzing Bingley as to how he got on with Miss Bennet.

"I have hope," was Bingley's serious answer, his gaze tracking the white and heavy clouds out the window, "but that is all I have. Miss Bennet has been as polite and kind as ever, yet I can see how distant she has become. For all you accused her of smiling too much, even you must admit how coolly I am received."

"I would encourage you to persist, but I admit I am not a natural lover, unlike you and my cousin." It was nearing time to take his place, but Sir William had yet to signal them, and so Darcy continued to pace. His anxious thoughts whirled about, in particular the wedding night, and whether it was kinder to give his new bride time to know him better. Yet, he would then place the burden upon *Elizabeth* to signal her willingness, and that seemed a heavy encumbrance to lay upon such small shoulders. Nay, Darcy counselled himself, he would *question* Elizabeth, and he would then know how to act, once they had spoken.

"-sister. Yet I cannot think that would help, but what else am I to do?" Bingley asked sourly, and Darcy flailed to form a reply, having completely neglected to heed his friend's words.

Before he could beg pardon, Sir William was coughing to catch his attention.

"The Bennets have arrived, Mr Darcy. If you would like to take your place?"

Nodding, he and Bingley moved to stand before the altar, acknowledging the guests with a tip of his head, but blind to aught else. Bingley's nervous shuffling was an irritant that did nothing to ease his mounting tension, yet Darcy held himself perfectly still. The organ music began, and Darcy turned, expression tightly controlled as he watched Miss Bennet gracefully walk up the aisle, taking her position, before turning to watch her sister and father step in.

Darcy could not have controlled his

expression then, as he sighted the woman who would soon be his wife, her soft pink dress bringing to mind cherry blossoms in spring. Her white veil kept him from seeing her face clearly, but he noted her confident steps, the strength in how she carried herself boldly towards him, and he sighed in blessed relief. Their time together before this hurried wedding had been intentionally limited, after their brief kiss, Darcy had not wished to test his resolve, knowing that to be in her company would compel him to seek such rewards repeatedly. Yet the relief in seeing how bravely Elizabeth took up her place beside him, filled his heart with elation. A grimly determined wife would not be an easy state of affairs to settle. That Elizabeth appeared amenable was a comfort.

Elizabeth let the words of the wedding ceremony pass her by, her attention fixed upon the gentleman at her side, the man who had just smiled so warmly at her, that her breath caught in her throat. If her father had not been guiding her steps, Elizabeth may have paused to admire her soon-to-be husband, but Mr Bennet had taken her forward, and to his side she had been conveyed. Into his keeping, her hand was placed, and when prompted, they had both spoken their vows without hesitation or dismay.

It was alarming how comfortable she felt at this man's side, her hand held securely in his own, uttering words of promise, receiving her ring in surprise that the token fit so perfectly upon her small hand. Then they were rising from their kneeled position, being united as husband and wife, the solemn look in her husband's eyes as he lifted her veil, his stone gaze so hard to read as he lowered his head to kiss her gently on the lips. There was the sound of applause and happy expressions, before both her and her *husband*, Jane and Mr Bingley moved to the antechamber and signed their names to the register, the last time she would ever sign as Elizabeth Bennet.

Her fingers placed the pen aside, as her eyes read her husband's name, *Fitzwilliam Anthony Darcy.* She was married. The thought had yet to penetrate, before her husband, *Fitzwilliam*, was taking her hand and tucking it in his arm, leading her out and back into the assembled guests, who had hurried to exit the church to bestow upon them the grains and what few petals could be found at this time of year.

"Well, Mrs Darcy, how does it feel to be wed?" were the first words her husband spoke after they had reached and entered his carriage, conveying them back to Longbourne for her wedding breakfast, after receiving the many well-wishes of their guests.

Assessing him, Elizabeth answered, "I have to say, *husband,* that at the moment, it feels no different, apart from the fact I am alone for the first time with an unrelated man in a carriage." Her tease was not up to her usual standard, but her circumstances had discomposed her more than she had anticipated.

"Forgive me, it cannot be easy to adjust to so much in such a short space of time." Her husband appeared genuinely contrite, and Elizabeth realised her tone may have been sharper than she intended.

"I shall not deny that, Sir, but I have faith in your character and will not assume you meant any ill." Her smile was genuine, expression open and relaxed as the rumble of the carriage made a cheerful background to the silence within.

Suddenly, Mr Darcy moved across the bench, to her forward facing one, capturing her hand in his, the one that now bore his ring. "You look exceptionally lovely, Elizabeth." He kissed her palm, the soft tickle of his lips, sending a flurry of butterflies in her belly. "Yet, perhaps, you may consider calling me by name?"

To this, Elizabeth's smile grew further, her spine relaxing from the tension of his sudden movements of moments before, "Of course Fitzwilliam." was her soft reply.

Her husband's own smile appeared, it's curved edges melting the severe granite expression, making him impossibly handsome. The rumble of the carriage wheels against the cobbled drive signalled they had reached their destination, and Elizabeth shuffled her dress to accommodate exiting the carriage. Her husband moved to help, whispering quietly in her ear, "This colour makes you look as if a spring blossom has fallen into my hands." and then he was stepping free of the carriage, turning back to aid her.

Unknowingly, Elizabeth's cheeks were rosy with a blush from his sweet comment, yet others made their own assumptions. Elizabeth was not ignorant of her neighbours gossip, it having filtered through her sisters to her own ears. They assumed some compromise or other, some scandal being averted by her rushed marriage, but their words did little to dispel her own innate assurity. This was her path, and Elizabeth would make the best of her condition.

Some hours later, having spent time with her friends and family, came the moment for her departure, Mr Darcy, Fitzwilliam having come to her side and spoke of the turning weather.

Teary-eyed, Elizabeth farewelled her family. Her mother's eyes were wet, her cheeks flushed from her mixture of elation and sadness.

"Oh! My dear Lizzy!" Her handkerchief fluttered, a sodden cloth, ineffectual to its purpose, "I know not when we shall meet again!"

"Dear mama, you have oft wished us all wed and out from underfoot, do not say that such is the case, you shall become despondant."

Her mother's state improved, yet before her ire could be roused by her daughter's tease, her husband shuffled his wife aside.

"Well, my little Lizzy. You are married now, and a grand lady you shall be, is that not a fine thing?" Elizabeth rolled her eyes at her father, kissing him on the cheek as his wiry arms embraced her, before he too trailed away, yet Elizabeth caught the evident emotion her father attempted to conceal.

Jane, Mary, Kitty and Lydia stood to one side, waiting their turns for their own farewells. Beginning with her youngest, Elizabeth entreated them all to write, reminding Kitty, that she would hope to see her in town in the new year, when her sister returned with their Gardiner relatives. To Mary, she promised quietly to have her join her as soon as could be, and then it was Jane.

"Write to me very often, my dear Jane." She pulled back, her gaze tracking Mr Bingley near her husband's side, his forlorn gaze following Jane. "He is a fine fellow, I like him immensely for you, but tis for your heart to decide and no other. I will wish to hear everything from you directly, sister dearest."

Jane avowed she would, her expression sad and despairing, for entirely different reasons to that of her admirer. And then she was being ushered into the Darcy carriage once more, waving woefully to her disappearing family, before turning back and facing her husband. How quickly her world had changed from the last time she had driven away from Longbourne, her time in Bath seemed so long ago. Then she had been excited to encounter new places and meet new people. Now she would be doing much the same, but under considerably more different circumstances.

Now, she was Mrs Darcy.

Darcy studied his new wife as she collected herself from farewelling her family. She did not appear unhappy, merely dismayed by the inevitable parting from her relations. He had yet to experience the same, his own family being so small, that separation of one kind or another was just another aspect of life.

"Are you well?" he asked, his heart stuttering in awe when her luminous eyes took possession of his. Darcy wanted to kiss her misery away, would wish to hold her comfortingly in his arms, ensure her every day was spent gifting him with her laughter and joy. But Darcy was familiar with his desires, and further intimacy between him and his wife would not be so foolishly rushed. Elizabeth deserved more from him than such behaviour.

"I am, Sir." Darcy winced when she failed

to utter his name, and Elizabeth caught it, a little sigh huffing from her lips, "Forgive me, I meant Fitzwilliam."

He waved her apology aside, "It is new for the both of us." Shifting, Darcy indicated the space at her side of the bench, "May I?" he enquired.

Her small nod was slightly hesitant, but Darcy accepted Elizabeth was adjusting to being alone with a man. How strange this all must be for brides, for one simple ceremony to rearrange all the rules by which a young lady is guided by!

With a quick movement and slight adjustment for his legs to become more comfortable, resting in the corner of the carriage, Darcy could more easily converse with his beautiful companion. Her veil from the ceremony had been removed, and in its place was a small bonnet, it's short peak and soft cap, covering the majority of her hair. Her dress remained unchanged and Darcy was thankful he would have the pleasure of seeing it on her for longer. The colour really did enhance her chocolate-coffee hair and delightfully sweet brown eyes.

"I imagine today was not quite the wedding you had envisioned." Internally, Darcy winced at his bluntness, but prevaricating would not answer. He was forthright by nature.

He watched as a thoughtful expression bloomed across Elizabeth's delicate features, her soft lips pursing in thought, distracting him from the question *he* had asked, until after a moment, she answered, "I cannot say I ever pictured myself marrying. My mother often complained my headstrong and obstinate nature would never win me a husband!" A self-deprecating chuckle, then his *wife* expounded, "I felt Jane would not complain if I were to remain in her household, following her own marriage." Again, Elizabeth chuckled, darkly this time, the sound difficult to abide when compared to her natural beautiful laughter, "I do not say this to beget compliments, but it is hard for gentlemen to see past my sister's beauty, so there has never been an occasion for me to picture how this day should be."

Darcy was moved to object, but his wife had not yet finished, "I am thankful my Gardiner relatives could be there, however. My aunt, you understand, has been a guiding influence, and is the best lady I know."

"Having spent some little time with your uncle and aunt, I hope we may invite them to dinner, perhaps have them take tea on occasion. Them residing in London will make it all the easier to be in company, when we are in town." His offhand suggestion was greeted warmly, a beautific smile broke across Elizabeth's face, and it suddenly became hard to calm his passionate musings.

"I had not dared to hope you would be

so welcoming, husband, but to hear you say so, makes me inordinately happy."

Unable to help himself, Darcy leant across and graced those smiling lips with a lingering kiss, nowhere near expressing his ardent admiration, but it was impossible to restrain the impulse now that there was no impediment to such activity. Drawing back, he pulled in a deep breath, kissed Elizabeth's brow, then began the topic of conversation he was of two minds broaching.

"I will not apologise for that, Elizabeth, but perhaps I should." His new wife shook her head, her smile gone, and in its place an unreadable tilt of her lips. "However, this does bring forward a topic I believe we should discuss." Darcy paused, his gaze fixed upon Elizabeth. "I would wish to have your thoughts on how we should proceed from this point forward. I would wish for us to be a true husband and wife, not only to beget an heir in truth, but I am willing to wait-"

"We should not wait." Elizabeth's words broke in, her cheeks flushing scarlet as she glanced away.

"Beg pardon, but you must clarify your intent further for me, I will be guided by your wishes in this, so I would not wish to have any misapprehension between us." Darcy felt a cad for pushing for clarity, but ultimately, what propelled him on, was the dread he would feel for starting their marriage on the wrong foot.

Elizabeth's bright eyes flittered about the carriage, struggling to fix upon one object, until eventually, "My aunt...that is...I was counselled to be open to my new situation, to begin as I mean to go on, and I believe...that is, I think... we should not-delay-the-wedding-night." the last breathless sentence rushed from her lips, and Darcy sat back against the plush squabs of his carriage, caught between bemused and jubilant, silently studying his bride.

◆ ◆ ◆

Elizabeth paced her new bedroom in nervous anticipation and dread. Perhaps dread was too harsh a term, yet the heavy feeling in her belly had yet to abate since her hurried remark in the carriage earlier that day. Her new husband had thankfully turned the subject upon other matters, allowing Elizabeth to regain her equanimity, yet the feeling remained. Her arrival into her new home had been all that she could expect, meeting the servants, beginning with the stately butler, Mr Nevins, followed by a slim and stern housekeeper, Mrs Carroll. Both had behaved as correct and proper town servants, stiffly introducing the lower ranked members of the household, such as the cook, her husband's valet, and her new-on trial lady's maid, a young girl slightly her junior, called Ivy Allen.

Her maid had been quiet and composed while assisting her change for the evening, her husband encouraging her to rest, and arranged for a light supper to be served in their quarters. Elizabeth's thoughts had been crowded and busy, and so she had spared little attention to the girl, other than to think it would be difficult to warm to the maid if she continued thus. Her own warmth and energy made her feel wild and untamed in comparison, and it was a struggle to adapt her view of herself as someone more refined and composed. Miss Allen left her feeling wanting, no doubt aided by her own fears.

Perhaps she was being unkind? Perhaps she was seeking some distraction as she awaited the knock to signal that supper was ready, for here she was, bedecked in her aunt's *gift*. Gift! Elizabeth snorted aloud, grateful to be alone. Her aunt Gardiner had provided her with a blush pink silk robe, with unconventional *pink* lace at the neckline, waist and bell-shaped cuffs. Beneath this, Elizabeth wore a silk gown, cut so cleverly that it flowed over her form, as if water itself. In the same shade of pink as the robe, a darker shade than that of her wedding gown, Elizabeth felt almost naked in the slippery sheath that reached the floor, two thin straps holding it up at her shoulders, it's cowl-like neckline the most modest thing about the whole ensemble, gathering just beneath her collarbone! To add to all of this, Elizabeth was *bare* of aught else, and this was how she was to greet her new husband. While they ate!

Her face flamed in mortification, but her faith in her aunt's wisdom would not be shaken, and therefore, Elizabeth held her head high as she heard the anticipated knock. The door led to a shared sitting room, between the master and mistress's chambers, and to that door, Elizabeth stepped lightly, entering the candlelit room with her courage rising to the occasion.

Her step faltered however when she was met with the sight of her husband, dressed casually in loose shirt and breeches, his banyan discarded upon the nearby settee. Of the room, Elizabeth took little note, her attention fixed upon the gentleman who stalked slowly towards her. Her throat dried, sighting his fierce expression, the fire in his eyes, and for a moment, Elizabeth feared she had displeased him in some way. However, that was put paid, when Fitzwilliam reached her, sweeping her up in an ardent embrace that stole her breath and had her heart pounding.

He pulled back, his eyes burning, her lips missing the feel of his, feeling pleasure rush through her core, she watched his mouth move as he spoke, "Tell me now, are you certain this is what you would wish?"

Her thoughts attempted to align, to discern what it was she was being asked. His strong arms were wrapped about her person, his embrace providing her with an upwelling of emotions and sensations, none she had ever experienced before. Her chest crushed against his, Elizabeth realised how much she *enjoyed* his embrace.

"Elizabeth?" Fitzwilliam asked again, before his head swooped down to hers, his lips melding with her own, and Elizabeth followed his lead in the kiss, responding felt as natural as breathing.

Once more, he pulled back, and a soft whine of complaint left her throat, causing him to chuckle.

"Well? I will not go further unless you reassure me you are certain this is what you wish to happen?"

Finally, Elizabeth's mind emerged long enough from the heated haze she had succumbed to, to accomplish connecting her thoughts together in order to answer him.

Wrapping her arms about his neck, reaching up on her toes, Elizabeth could not reach his lips unless he bent down, to which he granted her silent request. Against his lips, she replied, "I am certain, Fitzwilliam."

With a growl of satisfaction, no further words were spoken.

Elizabeth awoke the next morning, relieved to see her bed empty, grateful for the solitude to align her thoughts and come to terms with her new reality. She was now a *wife* in entirety, and Elizabeth would have to apologise to her aunt for any doubts she had held regarding the truth of Mrs Gardiner's assertions.

Her wedding night had not been something she had dreaded these past few days, not like she had feared yesterday evening. But she *had* held reservations on how well she and her husband would deal with each other. At least this was one concern she could lay to rest, safe in the knowledge her union could perhaps have a solid foundation of intimacy, upon which more could be built upon. Now as Elizabeth looked about her room, she pondered what the day would bring, and how she would accomplish settling into life as Mrs Darcy.

The room was filled with an abundance of yellow roses, from the papering, to the bed linens, through to the window dressings. Elizabeth, while fond of the flower and the colour itself, felt the room was little to her liking. She would have to discuss with her husband how free she was to redecorate, but for now, it could be tolerated. Thankfully the adjacent sitting room was more neutrally toned, blending warmer colours of browns with red and copper shades. That was enough rumination, Elizabeth decided, and summoned her maid, who arrived looking pin-sharp and just as quiet as she had been the day prior. Hoping to soften to her maid, and perhaps discover more about the young girl, Elizabeth attempted to discuss family, with little triumph. In resignation, she relinquished the task, exited her rooms and attempted to locate the breakfast room.

Masculine voices could be heard from further down the hall off the main foyer, and Elizabeth moved towards the noise, hoping to find aid, else guidance in which room to proceed to. Instead of the breakfast room, Elizabeth reached what looked to be a library, a large and imposing desk set facing a bank of windows, while a welcoming arrangement of seating was clustered about the roaring fire. Here, Elizabeth found her husband, seated opposite an unknown gentleman, his back to her, as she entered the room, catching the tail end of discussion.

"- nearest relation she has in the world, excepting you of course, and am entitled to know all her dearest concerns!" stated the gentleman officiously, to which Elizabeth could not help but raise a brow.

Her husband, his attention fixed upon his companion had not sighted her, and so, replied without hesitation, "Georgiana is *my* sister, Richard. And while I do not refute you are entitled to such concerns, you are not entitled to know mine; nor will such behaviour as this, induce me to speak as freely as I once did!"

From his tone, Elizabeth surmised her husband's displeasure, and felt it wisest to depart without drawing notice, yet just then Mr Nevins cleared his throat behind her, and Elizabeth was almost certain the sound implied heavy criticism aimed upon her back.

Both gentlemen startled at the sound, turning abruptly to face the doorway where she stood, the butler behind her. Fighting a rising blush, Elizabeth attempted to smile at her husband.

The butler, seeing he had gained his master's attention, spoke, "Pardon the intrusion Sir, but Cook was wishing to know if Mrs Darcy will be taking breakfast this morning, the footmen having not yet cleared the sideboard."

Internally, Elizabeth commended the butler's ability to condemn her for both her presence and its lack, and therefore sought to find amusement in her current position. No one had seen fit to direct her to the relevant room, nor had any footmen been present, and without a tour, there being little time to accomplish such the day prior, Elizabeth was intrigued to discover how she was to be present in the *right* place. Therefore, before her husband could reply, Elizabeth did so.

"Mr Nevins, organise a tray to be sent up to my private sitting room. I shall breakfast there this morning. Then instruct Mrs Carroll that I will wish to speak with her before lunch." Turning to leave the room, wrapping about her dignity like a fraying cape, she directed her next words upon her husband, "Excuse me, Mr Darcy, for the interruption with your guest. I hope I may rely on you joining me when opportunity permits."

With that, Elizabeth returned to her chambers, pacing about the sitting room like a caged animal. Her first day had spiralled swiftly, an aloof maid, servants set against her, their dislike painfully apparent, and to conclude, disharmony between her husband and his relations! Her dreams of contentment following her revelatory wedding night, her intentions to learn more of husband would have to be set aside in favour of fixing her current predicament. With that decided, Elizabeth admitted the maid bearing a breakfast tray, mulishly delivered. A sibilant voice in her head was quick to point out however, that her husband had failed to introduce her to his sister, and this, Elizabeth hoped, was only in respect of affording them some time alone.

She refused to believe it was any more than that.

Darcy clapped a hand against his brow, angered by both his cousin's bullheaded-ness and apparently his servant's antipathy. What Elizabeth could have done to have turned his loyal staff against him, Darcy could not fathom, but Nevins behaviour was severely out of character, but his treatment of Elizabeth was not to be tolerated.

He had meant to be present when Elizabeth had risen, hoping to provide a tour of her new home, enjoying a leisurely breakfast together, watching as soft blushes rose and dimmed as memories of their wedding night passed through both their minds. Yet, due to his cousin's intrusion, that had not come to pass. And his new wife had been left alone. What Elizabeth had overheard before Nevins rude interruption, he could not fathom, but all in all, his first day of married life had been completely turned on its head.

"Whew, looks as if your little wife has some spark to her. That" Richard cheerily noted, "and the servants dislike. I almost pity the poor thing." Richard's tone returned to his ire of before, "Yet I cannot take a concern for the new Mrs Darcy when tis *my* ward who has been shifted from her home."

Here, Darcy abruptly strode from his cousin, summoning his servant with a tug of the bell-cord.

"Oh, cease your ill-conceived complaints cousin. Georgiana was only too pleased to spend further time with her aunt, *your* mother! While, I and my wife begin our married life!" Darcy moved over to his desk, briefly scanning the paperwork he would conclude this week,

"Furthermore, if Georgiana has been filling your head with tales of woe, than I am only sorry you did not think to read your *own* correspondence that kept you abreast of all that occurred!"

Darcy ignored his cousin's guilty look, instead focusing his attention upon Nevins, who had just entered.

"Yes, Sir?" the man enquired, and Darcy's already chafing temper, unravelled further. How dare he stand before him, polite and cordial, after behaving so rudely to his new mistress?

Darcy failed to answer, signalling with a raised finger to wait, then moving to pull the bell-cord once more, his butler at last looking uneasy. Further minutes passed, before the housekeeper arrived, her uniform and hair as neat and tidy as ever, her expression set in her habitual attentive mien. Both upper servants had been with his household since before he became master, and he had never once had cause to speak poorly to either, yet now, when he had hoped to welcome his bride to her new home, he was sorely disappointed.

His cousin looked on expectantly, his posture upright and proud, yet Richard's eyes told the truth of his mood, watchful and observant. With his servants before him, Darcy quietly studied them both, allowing the silence to build uncomfortably.

At last, Nevins cleared his throat, "Ahem, Sir, how may we assist?"

Still, Darcy remained quiet, his expression hard. Indomitable. Both servants shuffled their feet, the glances they shared showing their growing consternation.

Finally, Darcy softly queried, "Tell me, Mrs Carroll, on whose authority, was Mrs Darcy *not* guided to the breakfast room?"

Mrs Carroll, startled, answered, "I cannot say, Sir. Surely Mrs Darcy could have requested her maid-"

He interrupted, "Nevins?"

"Yes, Sir?"

"Where were the footmen?"

"I cannot say, Sir. They are always present and attentive to their duties."

Silkily, Darcy spoke, "You both *'cannot say'*, how curious, that my two most senior members of my household, on the first day with their new mistress *fail* to be in a position to answer." Prowling round his desk, Darcy seethed, "I *cannot say* what this reflects, because I *refuse* to descend to such insipid and underhanded depths that both of you have sunk to!"

"Mr Darcy, Sir-" Mrs Carroll, her worried tone and expression failed to induce him to a softer frame of mind, attempted to disrupt.

"No! Mrs Carroll. You were both presented the opportunity to speak, and that time has now passed. There will be no further warning for you both, or any of the staff for that matter! Whatever discontent or schemes this household holds for the new Mrs Darcy will not be tolerated! Am I rightly understood?"

Both his housekeeper and butler assented, and he dismissed them, his mood black. With his servant's absence, he returned his attention to his cousin.

"Now. You!" Darcy pointed rudely at Richard, "You, are going to take yourself off, and out of my house, and you will not return until you are invited to do so."

Richard, palms up in an appeasing manner, "Darce, I can see you have matters to address, but you cannot deny me-"

"I can, and I will deny you Richard. If you had but taken a moment to read your correspondence before hastening over here, intruding where you were most unwelcome. Acting as if some white knight to your ward's rescue, you would have comprehended that I was to spend the week in my new wife's company, while my sister, *your ward*, was to be introduced, *after* you had called upon us!" Darcy's temper, severely tested this morning, had yet to run its course, and so he bore no patience for his cousin's apologies. "Now, you are to depart, and I will send a note round soon enough."

Obdurately, Richard left him in peace, to which, Darcy slumped against his desk. Why did so many issues seem to arise whenever Darcy had found a piece of happiness? Straightening, Darcy went in pursuit of his new wife, an almost desperate need to apologise for everything, and anything. His pace hurried, he obviously startled Elizabeth amidst setting her cup down, for the article rattled in its saucer.

"Forgive me, Elizabeth, for my arrival. I had not thought you to be still at breakfast."

A becoming blush stole across her cheeks, and Darcy's mind jumped to the night they had just shared. Clearing his throat, Darcy strode across the room, and leaned down bestowing a kiss upon her brow, before taking a seat across from her. The small table still had not been cleared, prompting him to ask, "Have you summoned a maid to clear away the breakfast things?"

Elizabeth looked down, her hands clutching a small volume of poetry.

Angered anew, Darcy rose and tugged the bell-cord, coming to the correct conclusion Elizabeth's first summons had been neglected. Retaking his seat, he waited quietly, the tension between him and his bride simmering. Almost a quarter of an hour passed before a maid knocked, entering when Elizabeth called for them to do so.

The maid, on sighting him, paled, and Darcy failed to soften his demeanour when he asked, "What can be the meaning of this?"

"Beg pardon, Sir?"

"I have never known my summons to be so poorly addressed before, so I must assume it to be deliberate now."

Darcy would have said more, but Elizabeth broke in, "Would you clear the table-" Elizabeth waved to indicate the table behind her, then continued, "and inform Mrs Carroll I will speak with her *following* lunch. That will be all. Thank you."

The maid bobbed a hurried curtsey, before scurrying to accomplish her task, exiting as swiftly as she could manage. Darcy was still scowling at the door the maid had left through, but his eyes jumped to Elizabeth's when she spoke.

"I must assume I have seriously displeased the household, Fitzwilliam, but rather than scowling so ferociously, perhaps you will allow me to manage the concern as I see fit?" Her brow rose delightfully, and Darcy squashed the temptation to drag her back to her bedroom. His bedroom. Here would work wonderfully too.

Nodding when it seemed clear she awaited some reply, Darcy listened as Elizabeth continued, "Now, I apologise for intruding upon your conversation in the library earlier, but perhaps you will provide me with a tour of the house, to ensure I do not become so turned about again?"

Her sweet, arch tone had him smiling in delight, but still, he could not completely put off his displeasure. Darcy House had never suffered such poor service before, and he would get to the root of this aberration, sooner, rather later.

CHAPTER 9

Darcy House, London December 8th

"**W**ould you be averse to my making some changes to the decor?" Elizabeth was grateful to be taking their meal once again in their private sitting room. Having toured the house, the current dining room was a vast space that would be ridiculous for just the two of them. The house was so much grander than she was accustomed to, that her contentment was most assured when she could gradually grow adjusted to her new station in life.

Her husband looked up from his plate, "Which rooms would you wish to redecorate?"

His tone implied neither hesitation nor concern, so Elizabeth continued, "I meant to begin with my own rooms? And then perhaps the dining room?"

"I can see you would wish to tailor the mistress's suite to your own tastes, but it might be easier to accomplish the changes when we travel to Pemberley." Fitzwilliam gently observed, causing Elizabeth to accept the wisdom, pleased he was making a relevant contribution, rather than dismissing the concern entirely, much as her own father was wont to do. "How would you wish to redecorate the dining room? For it might be easier to begin there, while you make plans for your rooms."

Nodding, Elizabeth detailed her ideas, "Tis not that the dining room is not to my taste, I merely thought some lighter colours would balance out the darker furnishings. And yes, I can see how being at Pemberley would make any works in my own rooms much easier to complete. Your home is on the whole so very grand, that were I not quite so resilient, I might have felt overall overwhelmed." It was decidedly difficult to sound complimentary without bordering on avaricious!

"You may make whatever changes you wish to *our* home, but I recommend you delay works until we depart. Tis difficult indeed to navigate our home with so much disruption."

Agreeing, Elizabeth listened to her husband issue further instructions upon which businesses they had accounts with, in addition to arranging to complete her wardrobe order that had been begun by her aunt, before she left for Longbourne. As she listened, Elizabeth pondered how to bring up the issue with the servants. Perhaps, being as forthright as her husband, she would just have to be blunt.

When Fitzwilliam resumed eating, she began, "Fitzwilliam?" When he returned his attention to her, "I know we casually addressed the issue, but I thought you would prefer my frankness?"

Fitzwilliam nodded, "I overheard my maid and the housekeeper talking in my dressing room." Her husband's brows rose in surprise, "Yes, I know, eavesdropping is poor manners, but neither woman was discreet in their defamation of my character." Her husband's scowl was a fierce sight, but as she was not the intended quarry, Elizabeth felt no alarm. "It has been spread about below stairs, that I entrapped you, and as such, the servants, in a show of loyalty to the Darcy name mean to punish me for the insolence."

Unable to conceal her amusement, the unladylike laugh was free and uninhibited, especially when she observed her husband's consternation, his bemusement tickling her puckish humour. The sound dispelled her husband's black mood, his eyes studying her with a familiar intensity, that she now grasped.

Her mirth wound down slowly, and breathless, Elizabeth heard her husband ask, "How can you find this all cause for amusement?"

"Because," Elizabeth had to bite her lip to stop another giggle, before she could explain, "the whole situation is beyond farcical!"

"You will excuse me if I fail to agree."

Elizabeth ignored the stiff reply, and resumed her point, "But it is! Can you not see how your servants-"

"Our servants." Fitzwilliam sternly pointed out, and Elizabeth smiled wider, refusing to be intimidated by him.

"*Our* servants, being so set against me, for 'compromising' their master, when instead, *you* saved me from being ruined by the machinations of the woman who would have happily done so!" Her giggles were quieter, but no less amused, her smile remained in place, eyes dancing with lively mischief.

"While I can agree, that, taken in that light, our current circumstances are somewhat reminiscent of a shakespearian play-"

"One of the comedies!" she exclaimed proudly, causing her husband to kick his lips up in a parody of a smile.

"As you say, one of the comedies. I still do not like how you have been treated thus far in your new home. Nor will I tolerate it to continue. The servants will not be given leeway to proceed as they have thus far."

Rising from her seat, her husband swiftly followed suit, trailing her to the generously padded and upholstered settee before the fire. Feeling the December chill stealing her warmth, Elizabeth scooped a shawl up to wrap about herself, yet before she could, her husband's arms came about her waist, pulling her back to his front.

"I am sorry, Elizabeth, more so than you can imagine, for you to have been treated so poorly."

At first having stiffened in his embrace, Elizabeth softened at his words, hearing his genuine pain and remorse made her heart ache in sympathy. Dropping her head back against his chest, Elizabeth laid her hands over his.

"Tis not for you to apologise. But I do wonder where they got the idea from. I know it would not have been you, yet *someone* has given them the rumour."

The quiet grew between them, until Elizabeth suddenly felt compelled to address something she was truly unhappy about.

"I would like to interview for a new lady's maid."

She felt her husband's arms tighten about her, before he dropped a kiss to her hair, "Of course, Elizabeth. I will see to arranging interviews for you tomorrow."

The next day, Elizabeth woke in her own bed, alone once more, yet from the warmth on the other side of her, she knew her husband had not been gone overlong. Hoping to prevent yesterday's drama, Elizabeth hurriedly dressed herself, neglecting to summon her maid, not wishing to contend with the girl's quiet petulance.

Her wardrobe had received an influx of dresses, her aunt having included the purchases in her trunks without her knowledge, and thankful as she was, the sight of the garments made her long for her aunt's sound sense and comfort. Sighing deeply, Elizabeth pulled a striped green and cream dress from the rail, thankful it was one she could dress in, unaided. Accustomed as she was seeing to her hair, Elizabeth was swiftly ready, hopefully in time to take breakfast with her husband. Her tour of the house had canvassed the complete ground floor, including the fact that the room she had mistakenly taken as the library, was in fact Fitzwilliam's study. The library was considerably larger, and its vast quantity of books would equate to her father's version of heaven. Elizabeth smiled as she passed the *actual* library, promising herself the opportunity to write a long letter to her family, having only enough time to write a swift note the day before.

She reached the breakfast room, just in time to see her husband rising from his seat to greet her. Without any hesitation, Elizabeth reached him, leaning up to deliver her first kiss, rather than receiving his. She had not planned to do so, but the action felt so natural, that Elizabeth did not think upon it overly long, instead moving to the sideboard to select her breakfast. Fitzwilliam waited until she had taken her place beside him, rather than sitting at the further end of the table. His smile was so handsome, Elizabeth felt herself fall under his spell, until a cough from the footman drew her attention away.

"Yes Stennings?" Fitzwilliam coolly asked the footman.

"Pardon the intrusion, Sir. Cook wished to know if the mistress was wishing to have breakfast in her rooms?"

"Stennings, do you see Mrs Darcy before you now?" Her husband's words were sharp and lethal, stone mask in place, no sign of the softness he reserved just for her. Elizabeth assumed the footman nodded, before Fitzwilliam continued, "If that is so, you had no need to enquire. You could have quite easily taken a response directly back to the cook." Elizabeth poured out her tea, topping up her husband's cup with the coffee pot before him. She finished fixing her drink, choosing to ignore the plight of the poor footman, the hapless messenger facing Fitzwilliam's fury.

Elizabeth heard a loud gulp, before the footman was heard to say, "The mistress had not called for her maid, so Mrs Car-"

"Enough!" Fitzwilliam's voice sliced

through the air like a foil, controlled and sharp. "Mrs Darcy may find you all amusing, but I most certainly do. Not." Her husband flicked a hand out, silently dismissing the servant, whose steps hurried away. Into the quiet, Elizabeth sipped her tea, not daring to look at her husband.

"I must apologise dearest. I had thought-"

Elizabeth could not contain her amusement any longer, and a bright peal broke into her husband's apology. Without restraint, Elizabeth threw her head back and let laughter banish the sting of disdain. It was not in her nature to pursue darker thoughts, yet it seemed her husband needed little provocation to become stern and dour. Eventually, Elizabeth ceased, her amusement vanishing when she caught sight of her husband contemplating her. His stone grey eyes were just as unyielding, but now Elizabeth knew the look for the passionate intensity she was delighted to be educated in. Fitzwilliam's stiff and cool reserve was a veneer concealing a devoted and sincere man beneath. Seeing his mask cracked allowed memories to rise, and Elizabeth could not help but to blush.

Her blush intensified when he quietly stated, "I love the sound of your laugh."

"Then you are fortunate to have married me, for I dearly love to laugh."

"I had already reached this conclusion, but you must know it is not in my nature to wave off such follies as the servants have provided.

My temper I dare not vouch for. It is, I believe, too little yielding — certainly too little for the convenience of the world. I cannot forget the follies and vices of others so soon as I ought, nor their offenses against myself. My feelings are not puffed about with every attempt to move them. My temper would perhaps be called resentful."Her husband spoke with conviction, accepting this flaw of his own temperament.

"That is a failing indeed!" teased Elizabeth. "Implacable resentment is a shade in a character. But you have chosen your fault well, yet I must add to your list of faults, a tendency to overlook life's little pleasures! I admit, I am only too quick to find amusement in any given circumstances, and ours, well for our mutual happiness and contentment, I would rather look for the best in every situation, than seek out the less pleasant aspects."

"Tis true, you have had to contend with a considerable number of changes in so short a period, that I cannot but admire your resilience, your kindness, your wit and intelligence. I am fortunate to have the honour of calling you my wife." Pleasurable contentment eased the injury the servants' behaviour created, yet Elizabeth was determined to improve her consideration the only way she knew how. Her father did not regard her his favourite due solely to their shared wit.

Elizabeth spent the rest of her day in the library, her husband occupied in the same room with his own work, remained in her company. With her letters written, lists made for alterations to her new home, Elizabeth was most grateful for her husband's presence some time later, when conducting the interviews with the candidates for her lady's maid position prior to taking lunch. From the six that attended, it was clear that there were three strong potential applicants. Miss Sarah Trent, however, was who Elizabeth instinctively warmed to, and therefore, when her husband could claim no defect of the girl, she was hired. Fitzwilliam summoned the housekeeper, after offering Miss Trent the position, confirming she was free to start immediately.

"Yes, Sir?" Mrs Carroll announced as she entered, once again completely ignoring Elizabeth's presence. It was becoming harder and harder to find the servants' objection to her amusing.

"Mrs Carroll, Mrs Darcy and I have hired Miss Trent here as my wife's lady's maid. Please see to her introduction to the household. Miss Trent, Mrs Darcy is to visit the modiste this Wednesday, and is to depart here at two in the afternoon, you will need to attend."

"Mr Darcy...Miss Allen is alre-" Mrs Carroll's words dried up once she sighted the cold look from Fitzwilliam.

Turning to her, "Mrs Darcy, shall we take our lunch in the dining room or our private quarters?"

Considering it a moment, Elizabeth replied, "Perhaps the dining room would suit, for it would allow us to discuss the necessary changes."

"Excellent idea." It was clear from his manner, that the housekeeper had been dismissed, yet Elizabeth worried her new maid would have a difficult welcome. Once both women had left, her husband let loose a deep sigh. Sitting beside him, Elizabeth attempted to relax into his side, uncomfortable still with the knowledge she was free to do such.

Dropping a kiss to her hair, her husband muttered, "One way or another, all will be well. I promise you dearest." Elizabeth could only hope her husband's words would prove true.

CHAPTER 10

Darcy House, London December 11th

Dearest Lizzy,

*Longbourne has been so remarkably different without you here. Your lively presence has left a void that not even the Gardiner's considerable happy characters can replace. I can only hope we will all soon be in company someday soon. As you know, our uncle needed to return to town for his business interests, yet we are all **incredible** fortunate to have been given this time to spend in company with our aunt, and our little cousins, who have relished the extended time in the country. Mary and Kitty have been so very good to seeing to their entertainment, encouraging their play or resolving the many childish complaints that have arisen. Our aunt has remarked that this change in Kitty is most welcome, for she is assured our sister's time in Bath will be the making of her. Aunt was so good to share with me your efforts in guiding and supporting our sister's education, and I must admit to feeling heartily ashamed I have never once troubled myself to similar efforts. That is the true difference between us, dear Lizzy. You are so warm and giving, so loving and generous, I am but a pale facsimile.*

*Regardless, as your letter so gently distinguished, tis not your absence that has been something of a trial, but the **attendance** of other company. Mr Bingley continues to call with near routine visits, fixing his attention upon us all, yet it has been made plain, not only by our sisters and aunt, our mother too, but by the very gentleman himself, that his* *intent is to call particularly upon myself. Before everything had occurred with you and your husband, news of this nature would have made me the happiest of souls alive. But nothing is quite the same, my feelings are but one aspect.*

Two days following your wedding, I was feeling very bereft, missing your company dreadfully, and hating how selfish my thoughts and opinions had been during a time when you had far more to contend with. During my solitary ramble through our bleak winter rose garden, Mr Bingley came across my path, begging leave to join me. This was granted, and we walked on without many words shared between us. Mr Bingley's manners had suffered some alteration, sharing a stronger resemblance with that of your new husband, for he was unusually quiet.

A moment more passed, and then I had cause to be astonished by Mr Bingley's abrupt speech. He begged leave to be spared the condemnation of his sister's actions, that while he had struggled with his partiality for my company, he was compelled to consider the ramifications of forming more serious designs. That it was this, the inferiority of our connections, that I possessed relations whose behaviour was less than desirable, and that, despite our standing in the community, our wider place in society was much lower than he, nor his sisters, had hoped to make an alliance.

*I cannot tell you of the pain his words gave me, how my very breath stole from my lungs, and how my mouth struggled to form words, my head pounding so fiercely. I had never felt more in harmony with our mother than I did at that very point. And yet, I was finally able to draw words forth, and I asked, to what these sentiments pertained, only for Mr Bingley to exclaim a fervent desire to **court me**! My astonishment was so great as to make me once again mute. Why would a man who wished to seek a courtship, set about it with a desire to offend and insult?*

When asked this, Mr Bingley felt it was necessary to

avoid disguise of any sort, for that is what had led to his friend's marriage to my sister. My astonishment quickly morphed to anger, a feeling that took me quite by surprise. I ventured to ask, in perhaps a less than ladylike manner, how Mr Bingley expected me to reply to such incivility, only for the gentleman to look at me speechless, before asking if that was all I had to say.

My natural temperament reasserted before I could say more, and I begged leave to return to the house. Mr Bingley was gentleman enough to return with me, but I fled his company as soon as could be. Aunt Gardiner, in place of our mother, sought an explanation for my disposition, and what I said I cannot rightly recall, so out of sorts was I. Needless to say, I think any and all future interactions with Mr Bingley will forever be somewhat strained.

I know dearest sister, you would counsel me to think on the matter in the best possible light, but I fear that it will not be as easily forgotten as when John Lucas tipped you in the mud when you called him as clever as a tree stump. I had not thought I would have more to say than this, but Mr Bingley has called again today, and this time we remained in company, where he could not importune me with offences, yet with little to no encouragement, my mother hurried near everyone from the room, only for our aunt to return and take up a seat at my side.

She quietly stated she was fully informed, and asked Mr Bingley why he thought it was appropriate to speak degradingly of a woman's family that he hoped to court. Mr Bingley flushed scarlet, while I paled at the reminder of the hurtful words. In reply, the gentleman stated he had wished to exemplify through his words, the depth of thought he had given a connection with myself, that in laying such honesty bare, that he would prove that his affection was not the making of a moment. That the matter with his sister, how she had worked unceasingly to lower the Bennets in his eyes, had come to nothing. With some time and distance, he could see how his words had been hurtful, and he assured our aunt, that he was not to be deterred by small grievances, and that he would continue to prove himself every day, from this point on. I said not a word, and our aunt thanked Mr Bingley and sent him on his way.

Dear Lizzy, you have been my most steadfast and earnest friend, I trust your guidance more than any other. Tell me what I should do, for in my heart, I must confess to still holding such ardent affection for a man who has gone about his courting in the clumsiest of manners.
Forever your sister,
Jane

Elizabeth dropped her hand from her mouth, her eyes staring out the window sightlessly. Poor Jane. And foolish Mr Bingley. Whatever would make a man normally so amiable and charming, alter into an almost unrecognisable creature, spouting such thoughtless words? A ridiculous thought intruded, and Elizabeth wondered if her own husband had some hand in guiding Mr Bingley, for she could very easily picture her stern husband making such facts as her family's condition in life pertinent to a proposal. Just then, the gentleman in question entered, his habitual mask in place. Following in behind, was a broad gentleman, of a similar build to Fitzwilliam, dressed in regimentals, yet Elizabeth knew little of the insignia to note of which battalion.

Folding her letter away, Elizabeth smiled in welcome, while raising a curious brow her husband's way. Her query was answered almost immediately following the gentleman's introduction, and Elizabeth recognised the man's voice from her first morning at Darcy House.

"Elizabeth, allow me to introduce to you, my cousin and close friend, Colonel Richard Fitzwilliam."

Another brow rose at the name, and this time her husband replied with a silent nod and tilt of his head.

"Pleasure to make your acquaintance, Mrs Darcy." Colonel Fitzwilliam bent courteously over her hand, but thankfully avoided anything so gauche as allowing a kiss, which was a relief.

"Good afternoon, Colonel. Tis a pleasure to meet the cousin who has featured in near enough all of my husband's childhood tales of mischief."

The Colonel chortled, while taking up the opposing stance at the fireplace, mirroring her husband's position unintentionally, for both men appeared very familiar as they stood in such a fashion. Perhaps it was a way for ladies to admire their form, for did not gentlemen appear to the greatest advantage in such attitudes?

"Oh, ho, been telling tales, heh Darce?" Then turning to face her more fully, posture bolstering his caricature of the jovial and friendly relative. Elizabeth would have believed it, if it had not been for that initial encounter, listening to his angry, terse words. For most assuredly, that had been in reference to her. "Well, Mrs Darcy, I would not believe everything my dear cousin relates, for half the scrapes were entirely not of my making."

Neutral smile fixed in place, Elizabeth affixed a benign mien, concealing any hint of her thoughts, offering to pour each gentleman some refreshment, she accepted their decline and searched for some safe topic to continue this interview.

"Naturally, childhood adventures are to be exaggerated, told with some missing element of magic, known only to us in our youth." There, that was sufficiently innocuous, she thought quietly, as Elizabeth sipped her cooling tea. The arrival of the Colonel, while expected, on the tail of reading Jane's missive, caused her some consternation.

"Admirably phrased, my dear Mrs Darcy."

'I am not your dear' Elizabeth thought darkly.

"It is very good of you to call on us, Colonel Fitzwilliam, albeit, I hear from my husband that you are a frequent resident of Darcy House, despite the Matlock's address being only two streets down?"

The Colonel's brow rose in some surprise, "My cousin speaks true. I am fortunate enough to be welcomed to Darcy House at all times of day. Yet I expect that must change with a new mistress in residence, and I would not wish to make myself disagreeable so soon into our acquaintance, that you have me barred from your doorway!"

Despite the evident charm and urbane delivery, Elizabeth felt the Colonel hardly held true to such convictions.

"I expect *much* change occurs when a new mistress takes the reins of a new household, but I hope I have no reason to deny my husband's family from our home!" Looking to Fitzwilliam, "Do you not agree, Mr Darcy?"

Fitzwilliam had remained impassive throughout, but at this, he stirred himself to answer, "Of course. My family will always be welcome in our homes, and I trust that they look forward to making themselves known to you. My sister, Georgiana, is one who has been awaiting the opportunity to do so, is that not so Richard?"

Hearing the hard tone, Elizabeth fought back a smile, waiting to see how the Colonel would respond to such a direct enquiry.

"That she is, Darce! I do believe my mother is keen to descend upon you both herself, as soon as your knocker goes up! Eager to meet your new bride."

Elizabeth couldn't help raising a brow at this, for why was the knocker applicable to a girl who resided in the same house, yet was dismissed to one who did not?

"I believe you share guardianship with your cousin, of Miss Darcy?"

Nodding, "That is so, and a sweeter girl, you will be hard-pressed to find. To be her guardian is a priviledge and a delight. My uncle, the previous Mr Darcy, paid particular attention to his daughter's education and as such, Georgiana possesses excellent manners, and is extremely accomplished for her age. Her performance on the pianoforte is exquisite."

It became difficult for Elizabeth not to provoke some comment upon the necessary *accomplishments* young girls are expected to possess, but with some restraint, she checked the impulse.

A shift in the Colonel's countenance had Elizabeth paying particular attention, "I hear from my cousin, that you are one of five daughters. I imagine that must have been an impressive feat for your governess, to manage you all at once?"

Elizabeth fought the snort, "We had no governess, Colonel."

The man looked appalled, "What? No governess? Your mother must have been a slave to your education!"

Elizabeth could hardly help to smile as she assured Colonel Fitzwilliam that had not been the case.

With a studied frown, "Then who took up the duty? You must have been sorely neglected elsewise!"

Feeling irritated on her family's behalf,

the interrogation had veered to the heart of the Colonel's concern and so Elizabeth attempted to dismiss any insult, "Perhaps, compared to other families, but we were never denied the means or the opportunity to learn. And, with my father's love of books, reading was a pastime that was actively encouraged. However, I will not deny, that those who wished to be idle, certainly might."

The Colonel flicked a glance towards Fitzwilliam, and Elizabeth fought not to follow his gaze. Her husband's opinions upon her family, Elizabeth little wished to know.

"Well as to that, I should think your mother was heartily relieved to see one of her daughters wed, and so well too! Does this mean your younger sister may now have her come out?"

She little liked the insinuation, but her course could only be truthful, "In relation to my sisters, they are all out, and as to my mother's contentment, I imagine all mothers would feel thus, regardless of if they have one daughter, or twenty!"

"All! What, all five out at once? Very odd! And you only the eldest? Your younger sisters must be very young?" Her husband's cousin seemed to shrug off the query, choosing instead to focus upon another point, disallowing Elizabeth from disabusing him of her placement in the Bennet daughters, "And while your comment as pertains to your mother is correct, I imagine not many can compare to Society matrons, hey Darce?" The Colonel resettled himself against the mantle, "There was one particular lady who seemed most intent upon her hunt of my cousin here, Mrs Darcy. She would be ever present in whatever event Darcy chose to attend, her milk-sop of a daughter, a step behind. Eventually, after over a month of hounding my cousin at every occasion, the lady decided enough was enough and set about to conspire an entrapment of my cousin! Thankfully, Darcy was quick to navigate himself out of such a briar patch. But not this time, it seems."

At last, Elizabeth felt relieved the Colonel had reached his design. Choosing not to rush a reply, Elizabeth chose instead to set her cup down neatly, aligning the handle and spoon with more attention than the activity warranted. Fitzwilliam opened his mouth to speak, but Elizabeth would not have him defend her innocence.

"Rich-"

"-I imagine, being so closely bound as the two of you so clearly are, that any injury to one, may feel like a wound to both. In considering how *I* would behave, if my circumstances had been the fate of one of my own sisters, I do imagine there would be a fierce anger seething in my breast. It would be difficult to set apart the guilty from the innocent, but I hope I have the integrity to not condemn without caution." Elizabeth raised her gaze from her cup, locking them with that of the indolent Colonel, "To be blinded by prejudice, is all-together far too easy, and therefore it is incumbent upon us all to be secure of judging properly."

"Ah, I see how it is," the Colonel ambled across the quiet room, and in reply, Fitzwilliam moved nearer to her own seat, "You are wise to my intent to be uncommonly clever in my decided dislike of you, Mrs Darcy, for snaring my cousin in whatever scheme that saw the two of you wed, and now you raise the flag of empathy. Of symmetry in our demeanour. How remarkably astute!"

In his words, Elizabeth could still hear that first trace of anger and wrath, and Elizabeth felt helpless to defuse the Colonel's dislike of her further. Rising from her seat, Elizabeth turned to her husband.

"I can see that I am to have no effect upon your cousin, and while I am aware you do not misconstrue the events that led us to this point, I feel it would not work to my favour, if it were me that explained, explicitly, the circumstances of that night. Therefore, I shall away to my sitting room, for I have correspondance that needs to be addressed." Turning to the Colonel, "Regardless of what you think of me, I would ask that you not speak so, to me again, for I would not like to have to make changes to your long-standing arrangements with Darcy House, and it's inherent welcome. Good day Colonel."

◆ ◆ ◆

Darcy watched as Elizabeth swept from the room, before wearily turning back to his cousin.

"Well, that was badly done, Richard." was all he could tiredly say.

"She is not what I had been expecting, Darce, I shall give her that. And she possesses a conceited independence, and is most certainly a headstrong and impertinent creature, to be sure!"

Angry now, Darcy bitterly replied, "How easy it is for you, to sit there and judge, when you are ignorant of the facts. That the woman who is under my care and protection, you feel free to disparage and castigate, for doing nothing more than having the misfortune to fall victim to Miss *Bingley's* intrigues!" His temper wished to leap about and flay open his cousin's insulting approach, yet it would achieve no satisfaction, would not soothe his wounded pride. "You may not think you owe my wife much, but she most certainly deserves more than you gave her Richard, and I have never been so heartily ashamed of you."

Angered himself, Richard gesticulated, "Oh ho, so easy for you to point your finger at me, yet if I was wrong to wish to know the particulars, then you, good man, are the greater fool, for neglecting to inform *your family* of the pertinent details!"

Unbidden, Darcy recalled his words to the Matlock's when he had arrived to inform them of his upcoming nuptials. The dismay and pleas to delay, to allow his family time and opportunity to look for some other course. Yet none had dared to *ask* him what his own wishes were.

His marriage to Elizabeth was *his choice*. Not his family's.

"What do you mean, Mrs Darcy was a victim to another's scheme? What does Miss Bingley have to do with it all?"

Richard had calmed enough to take the opposing seat from his own, and so, on a miserable December day, Darcy dredged up once again, the night of the Netherfield ball, and Miss Bingley's deceptions.

On occasion, Elizabeth accepted her wit could be as sharp as her father's, her intent to dismiss her mother's repeated complaints, to allow for amusement and not shame to stalk her steps when her sister's performed poorly, to be the first to find the folly, so that others could not hurt with their expected scorn and disapproval.

Time in Bath saved her from needing to use her wit as a ready defence, and therefore left its mark, such that her return to Longbourne was hard, despite the love she bore her family. An overbearing weariness weighed heavily upon her shoulders. Longbourne's missives were filled with sadness, guilt and a host of other less salubrious tidings, such that her latest missive from Rebecca and Evelyn, filled with expressions of warmth and compassion was a breath of fresh air. The girls spoke of new friends, promises to visit in the new year, when they came to collect Kitty, eager to see her content in her new situation, eager to be in company once more. The promise of reuniting with such sweet girls enervated Elizabeth, freeing her from dark concerns following the encounter with Colonel Fitzwilliam, the day prior.

Now, having dismissed the housekeeper, following their discussion of Elizabeth's planned renovations and improvements, the disgruntled woman's attitude had almost managed to sink her mood anew. Sitting quietly in her room, Elizabeth had a full day planned, so with her usual verve, set about her agendum. First, the modiste, and as much as the prospect lacked much anticipation, the appointment went much swifter and passed in a far more pleasant attitude now that she was not only Mrs Darcy, but that her sisters and mother could not fray her good nature.

"Madam Darcy, we shall have your commissions *toute suite!* One of my assistants shall bring the finished garments to you, and see to final alterations, *très bien*."

"Very good Madam Fouchere. I shall be needing the morning dresses as a matter of priority, but at least two of the evening gowns as soon as may be." Elizabeth turned back before she reached the door, only for Madam to be offering the very item she had almost forgotten, the collection of fabric samples, "My thanks Madam, this shall make my afternoon all the easier."

Elizabeth parted from the establishment, settling into the plush Darcy coach, "Well then Trent, where to next?"

And so, Elizabeth accomplished her slow transformation from Lizzy Bennet to that of Elizabeth Darcy, purchasing the undergarments, the necessary accessories, the bonnets, capes, and suitable winter wear for Derbyshire's cooler environs. Exhausted, she and her lady's maid reached Darcy House in time for tea, only to have her repose broken when Lady Matlock, accompanied by her son and daughter-in-law, decided to call. Of her husband's whereabouts, Elizabeth knew not, and therefore held her courage close for the trial to come.

"Good afternoon Lady Matlock, Lord Buxton, Lady Buxton." Graciously, Elizabeth bobbed a perfect curtsey, acknowledging the slight head dips of her husband's family. The butler swiftly escaped the tense parlour without waiting for instructions, and Elizabeth sighed internally. She was utterly alone.

"Good afternoon Mrs....Darcy. Apologies for calling without notice, but we happened to be passing when we saw you return home, and thought, why not take the opportunity to– welcome you to the family." Lady Matlock's expression was at odds with her demeanour, but Elizabeth accepted the paltry excuse for what it was, the hope to catch her unguarded, and thereby determine her true character.

"Ah, I have just returned from some much-needed shopping, for my wardrobe is not equipped for the much longer Derbyshire winters I have been advised of." Settling herself into her seat, Elizabeth watched in fascination as Lady Matlock studied the room with a critical eye; such judicial observation was perhaps necessary to see if she had brought her own poor taste to mar the elegance of Darcy House! Appearing satisfied, the Countess and her party settled into their chosen seats, Lady Matlock sharing a settee with the Viscountess, and her son electing to sit in a chair mirroring her own.

"If you need any advice in your purchases, please do feel free to seek my opinion. Having spent more than two decades in the county, I am confident I am best placed to be of aid." Nodding, Lady Matlock perched carefully, as if poised to take flight at a moments notice, much as a bird. An apt description for the delicately framed countess.

Elizabeth smiled slightly in acceptance, but how one was to go about requesting undesirable and unsolicited aid, she had no clue.

"We must apologise for not being in a position to attend your wedding." Lady Buxton tittered, "It was of such short notice that there was hardly opportunity!"

"Indeed! Poor Darcy having to rush his own nuptials!" Lord Buxton chortled, his lean frame at odds with that of his wife's soft appearance, and entirely opposite that of his brother's, Colonel Fitzwilliam.

"Your poor mother must have been wretchedly heartbroken to not have time to arrange for a much grander affair!" Lady Buxton's manners expressed the horror of such a prospect. "Why I recall my own nuptials was the product of over three months of vigorous planning! And so perfect was everything, I am sure there has yet to be an affair that could match the occasion!"

Elizabeth dismissed the concern with a delicate wave of her hand, "My mother was most aggrieved, that is so. Yet with four other daughters, I am sure she will have an opportunity to host a suitable wedding in the near future. And as for your own ceremony, you shall have to describe your dress some time soon. I am sure it was everything becoming and perfectly suited for the bride of a Viscount."

Thankfully, the housekeeper ushered in a maid carrying a tea tray just then, and the next few minutes were taken up with seeing to everyone's refreshments. The housekeeper and maid left just as swiftly as they arrived, the silent atmosphere stiffening Elizabeth's spine, waiting for the next approach.

Lady Matlock fired the first volley, "I heard from my nephew, that you are the second eldest. I hope your elder sister was not dismayed to be passed over?"

Thinking of Jane, Elizabeth could not help but smile in genuine delight, "Heavens no, Jane is the sweetest, kindest lady I have ever known. My sister would not wish to deny anyone their joy." Hoping to avert further inquiry, Elizabeth went on, "Truthfully, I had never thought I would wed, for I have often acted as my father's agent in matters of our estate."

"How...original." the noble gentleman sniffed.

"Exactly so, Lord Buxton. Hence, my diffidence in my potential to find a suitable mate!" The faux geniality, perhaps a touch over done, however fatigue weighed upon Elizabeth. Her marriage was still in its infancy, and already she felt as if she was running a gauntlet, and it galled her to think that *this* situation was preferable to that of being tied to Mr Bingley!

The conversation wended on from there, where Lady Matlock and her daughter-in-law spoke of all the shops they frequented, and of acquaintances Elizabeth was to avoid. Thankfully, neither disclosed any gossip nor rumours, but the shared speaking looks between her guests made Elizabeth long for this interminable interview to end, else desperate for her sisters to be seated beside her, to join in the silent volley of conversations occurring in her drawing room.

At last, her guests rose and offered their welcome to the family once more, and Elizabeth bore it all with her customary cheerful disposition, concealing her true sentiments. Once the door closed, Elizabeth's strength deserted her, and she sank down into her seat, and rested her head in her hands. Whatever scrutiny her husband's family subjected her to, she would do her level best to ensure she did not cause further dissension than she already had. Her guilt over Fitzwilliam's sister's absence already tore at her conscience.

Longbourne House

Dear Lizzy

I struggle to envision you in your new home, sitting some place far more elegant and refined than Longbourne ever is, and yet to picture you thus gives me such hope that we all may one day share in a similar fate. I will confess, your husband frightens me terribly, and so I am mightily pleased you are to have Mary accompany you on your journey to Pemberley, and more so that I am to journey to London in just three more weeks!

*Since knowing of my future trip, I have spent more than a little time with our aunt Gardiner, hoping to discover more of her nieces, and whether she believes we shall suit. From her own words, I take it that you wish I were to model my behaviour on Evelyn, for Rebecca is still full young! How strange it will be to be the **eldest**!*

Not much has occurred at home, other than Mr Bingley calls daily, and in observing his attempted courtship of our sister, I have begun to see the attention of the officers in an entirely different light! Mr Bingley's earnest regard for Jane displays to the fullest extent, how shallow, how insufficient the officers pretensions to please truly are.

Yet Lydia has told me quite plainly to not say such utterances, for she believes me to be jealous of their attentions, and that they prefer her over myself! While this would normally stir me to a righteous indignation, I felt comforted by the truth that I would be spending my time in much happier circumstances only too soon, and that the only jealousy, was that of Lydia Of Lieutenant Wickham, we have seen much, and he often asks if we have word from you. I believe the officer feels heartbreak that he had no opportunity to win your hand, but Lydia throws herself at him with little regard for how ridiculous this makes her appear. Her happy laughter seems to have disappeared under an earnest desperation to succeed in securing her own husband! It is most unlike the sister we all know and love–I cannot understand what has come over her!
Aunt Gardiner believes jealousy is the cause, for she sees everyone around her discovering their own path towards happiness, and seeks to ensure she is not left behind. How strange Lydia is, for if she would think but a moment, she will realise she will be the only daughter and therefore have our mother's company and support whenever she wishes!

Dear Lizzy, I am excessively excited to come to London and visit all the shops with our aunt! I feel that the day cannot come too soon, and now must only hope that the time passes without much difficulty.
I shall take great delight in calling on you, in your new home. How grand a lady you are now!
All my love and affection.
Your sister
Kitty

Elizabeth sniffed into her handkerchief, tucking the short missive away with the rest of her keepsakes. Receiving any letter of merit from her younger sisters had never been a cause for contentment, but here, sitting miserably in her room, Elizabeth allowed herself to mourn. To grieve over the loss of her familiar and ordinary life. To regret the steps that had led her here however, was not possible. For the alternative was intolerable. Worry over her family made her long for their chaotic home with a deep ache, that the silence of this grand home exacerbated.

Her husband had sent a note to say he was dining with his sister, and so her evening had been immeasurably dull, despite the hustle of her morning, followed by the difficult attendance of the point the Matlock party. Now, post retrieved, her letters reread, Elizabeth admitted how gloomy she truly was. While she could accept her husband's attentions, and while his manner and deportment was everything that could be hoped for in a relative stranger turned intimate partner, Elizabeth was adrift in a sea of another's world. Missing her family and friends, old and new alike, Elizabeth cursed Caroline Bingley with every known epithet she could think of.

Unfortunately, she had failed to do this solely in her head.

"Elizabeth?" Alarmed, her husband strode further into the room, "What on earth had occurred?"

Startled, Elizabeth gaped unbecomingly, "Forgive me, I did not know you had returned!"

"Who, precisely, is a 'lick-spittel strumpet'?" hummed Fitzwilliam, a dark frown marring his brow.

Shrugging in mortification, Elizabeth attempted to brazen it out, striding across to her bed, "I was merely practising a method of expulsion I have long held, a means of prevention in performing poorly while in company. It is never wise to restrict one's tongue forever, you know Fitzwilliam."

It was impossible to play coy with her husband, even though the intimacy they shared had become a fundament of their relationship. It felt anathema to be so unrestricted with a virtual stranger, yet their nights had carried the warmth of their liaisons over to the day, according Elizabeth a sense of belonging, regardless of aught else.

"Very well," her husband, wearing only his banyan, shucked free of his robe, his bare form highlighted by the soft golden glow of the candles all about the room, the roaring fire limning his broad muscled frame in shadows and light, "I will accept that explanation for now, but perhaps tomorrow you might feel more inclined to disclose what preys upon your mind."

Blushing from the masculine virility being so flagrantly displayed, Elizabeth gave herself permission to revel in her husband's embrace, to find a sense of peace and belonging that was present nowhere else. Afterwards, as they lay entwined, her head resting upon his chest, his hands softly stroking through her hair, Elizabeth accepted her earlier state of unhappiness would be temporary. She would, as the wife of Mr Darcy, find a way forward to happiness, and yet, even as she lay replete in her husband's arm, Elizabeth repined the loss of her previous life.

CHAPTER 11

Darcy House, London December 13th

Darcy watched his wife over breakfast, where he had lingered overlong in order to build up the courage to discuss Georgiana's return, now that his cousin had been properly introduced to Elizabeth. The thought of that interview still stirred his blood to boil, but Darcy had sworn not to interfere, else wise Richard would have refused his consent. As it was, his cousin was mightily impressed with Elizabeth, to such an extent he had been effusive in his praise of the new Mrs Darcy. It was just like his cousin to perform terribly, yet with his boisterous good charm, smooth over any lingering discontent.

"Elizabeth?"

Broken out of her internal reverie, his wife startled, "Yes?"

"I meant to disclose this yesterday eve-"

flicking a glance to ensure no nearby footmen could overhear, "ning, but my sister is set to return this afternoon. Do you have anything planned for the day?"

Quirking a humorous brow, "Pardon me, Fitzwilliam, but precisely what plans could I have other than to spend my pin money frivolously and await the return of my London relatives?"

Refraining from commenting, Darcy sipped his coffee.

"Yet I must be content, for it seems that I have gained the good Colonel's approval! And if I am very lucky, then mayhap your Aunt, the countess, will find me less objectionable, now that the family has discovered I am not without taste, refinement and sense!"

"I beg your pardon, but when did you meet my aunt Matlock?!" The sharp words did not trouble his wife, who bit her lip enticingly, effectively drawing his attention to her decadent lips.

"When I returned from my shopping, the countess *happened* to be passing, and decided to pay a call, to welcome me to the family, or so I was told." Elizabeth shrugged, but Darcy could see yesterday had been difficult, and his wife had endured it alone and without complaint.

Darcy could not help but scowl at the truth of Elizabeth's comment, unaccustomed to being dictated to in his home, let alone in regards to his own sister. Richard's obstinacy would be difficult to forget, but he had expected the rest of his family to behave poorly, yet could not help being disappointed that they continued to disappoint him.

"Do not scowl so" Elizabeth's light tone could not mask her own uneasiness, "I am more than gratified to finally meet your sister, yet I must ask, how did she seem last evening, during dinner?"

Darcy shared his quiet and companionable evening with Georgiana and his cousin, in their aunt Matlock's home, its occupants having other plans that evening. Elizabeth asked pertinent questions regarding his sister's character and disposition, to such detail that even his sister's favourite dishes were canvassed, and Darcy could not help hoping Elizabeth would be an excellent guide to his young, emotionally bruised and sensitive sister. Overall, his morning began far better than the day later developed.

"Georgiana! Welcome home!" Warmly embracing his little sister, he noted her careful study of their family parlour, comforted by noting very little changes, other than the display of some careful greenery in the form of some perennial branches. The sight had become a common feature in his home, for his wife often walked their gardens, coming in with bright cheeks and glowing eyes, making her the picture of youth and vitality. His desire to remain in her company had only grown since their first meeting, since before that truthfully. Now as he finally welcomed his sister home, he waited to see Georgiana comfortable before calling for refreshments, and a footman to locate his wife in the garden and inform her of his sister's arrival.

"Mrs Annesley, I hope you are well?" At that good lady's reply, Darcy turned his attention back upon his sister, "Elizabeth is currently walking the garden, hoping to give you a chance to settle in, before making her acquaintance to ensure you are comfortable."

"That was thoughtful." Mrs Annesley carefully signalled Georgiana, who agreed with little interest.

"Indeed, it is just the sort of thing Elizabeth does without hesitation. She is ever attentive to the smallest details, seeing to my preferences without prompting, as just the other day, she saw to the purchase of a book I had mentioned an interest in passing. Elizabeth has done everything in her power to ensure our home is happy and content as can be, and that is just in the first week of our marriage."

Sullenly, Georgina claimed, "Is that not what a good wife should do? Is that not how it should be naturally? I see nothing special in such small attentions."

"Georgiana, that is uncalled for. You have failed to even consider this situation from my wife's position!" Sternly, Darcy watched his sister attempt to conceal her contempt, her shock at being reprimanded by him compounding her ill mood. During their evening together, Darcy had deliberately avoided any and all mention of Elizabeth, not wanting his sister to feel supplanted in his affections.

"Your wife manipulated the circumstances to her benefit!" cried Georgiana.

Appalled, Darcy could do nought but stare at his sister in shock, "How do you come to such a conclusion? Who has told you thus?"

Quieter now, her natural timidity reasserting itself, Georgiana answered, "Was that not what you yourself told me occurred? That due to cruel machinations, your marriage was the result of the lady's reputation being ruined, and to save your friend, Mr Bingley, from an unsuitable alliance!"

Dropping his heads in his hands one moment, before shooting up to pace the floor, ignorant of the plush Persian rug, the sapphire settees, the damask pattern paper in cream.

"Do you mean to tell me, that you thought it was *Elizabeth* who was the author of such loathsome trickery?" Unknowingly, there was a terrible iciness in his voice, his mien fixed in a fierce frown, "I clearly stated, that I *willingly* offered to wed Elizabeth, how could the lady have contrived to entrap *me* when I did such?" His thoughts scrambled to align, and a troubling thought began to intrude upon his notice, "Good God, Georgiana, she and I had only met twice! Twice!"

Her own disquietude had grown when faced with an irate and troubled brother, his sister attempted to explain, "I thought you had been maneuvered into offering for the lady. I did not think much beyond you suffering a similar fate to the one I so closely escaped. Forgive me brother, I never meant to-"

The pause became protracted as his sister further paled, and Darcy genuinely feared she would be ill precipitantly.

"Oh no!" his sister wailed, and immediately he felt his dark thoughts coalesce.

His anger made his speech cutting, the gravel in his voice smoothing to a silky edge, "Do you mean to tell me, sister dearest, that *you* are the source of the servants gossip?" Seeing Georgiana begin to cry, he turned his attention to her companion, "Mrs Annesly?"

Looking worriedly between the siblings, the lady bravely faced her employer, "Miss Darcy may have been somewhat intemperate while her maid was present."

"Have you any idea the trouble your words have caused? How difficult it has been for Elizabeth with the servants seeking to punish her, no matter her innocence? My god, Georgiana...!" Darcy watched in agitation as Georgiana dissolved into a state of sobbing misery, and into this scene, walked his wife.

"Fitzwilliam?" The concern in her beautiful warm brown gaze had his temper deepen, "What has distressed your sister so?" Not waiting for his reply, Elizabeth knelt down in front of his sister, "There, there Miss Darcy, you need not fear I will be such a wretched sister, for I have four currently, and I believe that I am a tolerable sibling, happy to give consequence to a new little sister, who I hear plays so handsomely, I am tempted to never again tickle those ivory keys myself!"

Elizabeth's gentle tease startled Georgiana to such a degree that she gave his wife her full attention, until with a wretched wail, his sister fled the room.

"If you will excuse me Ma'am, Sir, I think I had best see to my charge." and with that, Mrs Annesley left him alone with his wife, who had risen from her position and now stared bemusedly at the door.

"Well, that is sure to sink my character further with the servants, not even home a full hour, and I have made the poor master's sister cry."

"She was in such a state before you had entered." Darcy grimly declared, jaw clenching in frustration, yet a voice could not help but point out his wife's kindness and warmth towards his sister, and for the first time he felt how little Georgiana deserved such consideration.

"Do you care to share what caused your sister such misery?" Head cocked to the side, Elizabeth peered up at him.

Shame filled his breast, for he had failed to protect his young, new wife, and as such her welcome and start to her life as Mrs Darcy had been marred by *his sister's* intemperance! Pinching the bridge of his nose, he admitted, "Georgiana is the source of the servants gossip."

"Well, yes, I had already surmised as such."

Stunned, Darcy took a moment to collect himself, "How? You knew? Wh-"

Waving her hand in a familiar fashion to that of Mrs Bennet, the comparison made Darcy slightly nervous, "It could hardly have been anyone else, for no one but yourself resides here. And from what I can gather, only your Matlock relations, the Bingleys and your sister knew of our situation."

"You have known all this time? Have suspected? Why did you make no attempt to share this with me?" The ice in his voice gripped his throat, as his mind vividly recalled each offensive and disrespectful treatment Elizabeth had endured. "Do you think me such an unfeeling brute that I would not acknowledge the possibility? Have I been so wretched a husband?"

Where these words and thoughts were escaping from, Darcy could not name, but a part of him was so unaccustomed to being powerless, that vexation whipped through his bloodstream, slashing Elizabeth with anger he rightly felt was aimed upon himself. HE had failed to explain himself towards his sister, *his* words had misled Georgiana in mistaken pride, not wishing to explain *why* he felt so compelled to prevent Elizabeth being bound forever-more to Bingley. There had been no way for him to explain the situation that did not expose his personal concerns for all to judge and question. It pleased him to indicate that his union was necessitated by honour, such expectations would therefore do away with the need to permit such folly as allow *his* family to drive Elizabeth away. He saw his behaviour so clearly in that moment, self-loathing and dismay fed his fury.

Elizabeth remained mute, but Darcy caught the flash of hurt in her toffee brown eyes, concealed a moment later by her sharp words and mocking expression.

"Forgive me for not wishing to cause you pain. I am afraid you have long been desiring my absence, nor do I see any need to remain, though I would wish you pass on my consolation to Miss Darcy in her state of distress. Good afternoon."

The stiff speech, delivered with cold indifference made Darcy feel an even bigger heel. He had selfishly verbally lashed his wife, with ridiculous accusations, when it was clear Elizabeth deserved no such treatment!

In defeat, Darcy slunk back to his study,

and attempted to pass off an attempt at seeing to his work. Yet his thoughts could not help returning again and again to what had happened in the parlour. He knew without a doubt, he was entirely at fault.

"Miss Darcy, Mrs Annesley, how lovely of you to join us this evening." Genuine pleasure suffused Elizabeth at the sight of additional company, hopeful it would provide distraction from the cold atmosphere that strained the air between her and her husband.

Their disagreement of yesterday had successfully driven the two of them apart, leaving Elizabeth terribly alone without his warm and reassuring presence, his amiable regard. For some inexplicable reason, Fitzwilliam had become essential to her well-being. Her feelings of neglect, compounded by her husband failing to join her last night, made the cross words they had shared all the more difficult to overlook. Compounded by Fitzwilliam spending most of the day '*out*', according to Nevins. Therefore, extra faces at the dinner table was welcome, and perhaps would engender a step towards healing the breach between the two of them.

"Mrs Darcy, thank you. I apologise for not

joining you for lunch this afternoon. Miss Darcy was still not well enough for company, yet thankfully, I am pleased to declare my charge has improved since."

Elizabeth admired the companion's capacity to deliver the truth with such gentle effect, relaying neither censure, disbelief nor encouragement. Elizabeth would have to question Mrs Annesley at some point to discover her secret. Before more could be said, the butler announced dinner was ready. Nevins was even more disapproving than usual, and Elizabeth rolled her eyes, before taking her husband's arm when offered. The strength of his forearm beneath her hand sent shivers through her, and Elizabeth fought not to blush as memories and sensations attempted to distract her absent thoughts. She was too susceptible to her husband's charms.

Dinner passed just as awkwardly as Elizabeth had imagined it would, the shy and quiet Miss Darcy barely spared her a glance, keeping her attention fixed upon her plate, leaving the bulk of conversation to pass between herself and Mrs Annesley, with the occasional input from Fitzwilliam. It was a startlingly different scene than nights previous. A tired sigh wished to escape, but Elizabeth continued to stay attentive and engaged, enjoying the intelligent conversation with the companion. Perhaps it would do well to encourage the lady to tutor *her*, for Elizabeth could not help but to continue to admire that good lady's intuition and sensitivity. When dinner concluded, it was almost a relief to escape to the drawing room, yet the tension remained, her husband and his sister barely sharing two words, each too upset to find a way forward.

With clear intent, Elizabeth kept up a steady stream of discourse with Mrs Annesley, hoping that the brother and sister would make some steps towards mending the damage caused by misunderstanding and wilful principles. Of her own heart, while she could forgive the foolishness that had led to her husband's harsh words, his withdrawal was what had injured her acutely.

"Mrs Annesley that is a very capable stitch, I wish you would show me how it is to be executed?"

Mrs Annesley agreed, and then the next few minutes were spent in careful attention to the process. Once Elizabeth felt confident she could replicate the design, Elizabeth practised upon her own sampler, and could not help a short small, unladylike whoop at her success. Embarrassed, Elizabeth apologised to the company, but was relieved to see her performance had caused not just a moment of surprise, but of breaking the tension between the siblings, both smiling in shared humour. Mayhap Elizabeth should behave make a cake of herself more often, she pondered, only to dismiss the possibility. Capering about would resolve nought but for her new family to judge her to be nothing but a determined fool! But at least she could attest her father's wisdom held true, laughter was a reliable remedy to many ills.

"Mrs Darcy you are a very quick study! It took me inordinately long to master the design!" Mrs Annesley's praise broke the silence, and then the two ladies continued to discuss their occupation. Embroidery was the one quiet and still pursuit, other than reading, that Elizabeth actually enjoyed. The mending of seams, tears, hems, and such, bored Elizabeth to sleep to such an extent that Jane would oversee the task, while Elizabeth would repay the favour in her fine work.

Fearing she could not neglect her new sister any more, Elizabeth attempted to strike up a conversation, "Miss Darcy, my sister Mary is the most proficient player of the pianoforte in our family, I believe she would enjoy discussing her love of music with you." Miss Darcy fairly jumped at the sound of her name, her cool blue eyes jumping from her face to the floor, and back again.

"I-I...yes, that is, I mean, I do enjoy music, and playing...the pianoforte, although...that is, I have been..."

Shyly Miss Darcy's words petered off, as if she had lost them all, and instead she stared helplessly upon her companion, rather than Elizabeth. The poor girl found no spark of strength, and instead jumped up from her seat.

"If you will excuse me, I think I shall retire. Forgive me. Good night." And in a rustle of skirts, the young lady departed the drawing room as if being pursued by a vicious pack of wolves.

"If you will permit," Mrs Annesley rose, genially nodding to both Elizabeth and her employer, "I shall ensure Miss Darcy is well, before I too will take myself off to bed. Good night."

Then it was just her and Fitzwilliam, the crackling fire the only sound.

"You must forgive my sister, she has struggled to adjust to this change. Even before our marriage, Georgiana's spirits were much affected by some unpleasant events this summer past." Fitzwilliam spoke gruffly, his gaze pinned to the fire.

"Of course, Sir, I suffer no offense from Miss Darcy. Yet I fear her continual swift departure from my presence will have rather far reaching consequences." Elizabeth's tease attempted to mask her unease. Her husband's mood was impossible to decipher.

"And what of myself?" Fitzwilliam turned to her then, his stone eyes reflecting the flickering of flames, "Am I to be forgiven so easily?"

Tidying her embroidery away, Elizabeth

gathered the threads of her heart and bound them safely away as well. Her husband had too easy a power over her, his moods ever affecting her own, until she felt almost a different person entirely from the Lizzy Bennet of before.

"Elizabeth?" Fitzwilliam stood before her, no sign of emotion evident, leaving her adrift all over again!

"What am I to say Fitzwilliam?" She clutched a skein of thread, trailing the silk through her fingers, "Would you have me assure you I understand your distress? That I can see how much our current circumstances dismays you. That to see how the servants have taken against me pains you. The tension between you and your Fitzwilliam relatives! I comprehend it all, and I continue to do my level best to meet the expectations of your family and conquer the disgust of your servants. I cannot do more than I have, but I refuse to quarrel with you..." Rising from her seat, stepping beyond her husband, she ignored him as he turned to follow, his statue mask affixed, "You saved me. Saved Mr Bingley. Saved Jane! Yet, we are still strangers to one another. Still unknown! All I know of you, I have our first week of marriage to thank. I am grateful, Sir, I am. But for there to be more between us, I cannot settle that I must forever be in your debt. We have begun this union with an unequal equation, and I am yet further in your obligation, for I must needs uphold the dignity of your station, your connections! I have never before felt as less as I do now, when I possess more than I ever dreamed possible!"

"Your gratitude you may do away with, I thought of myself only when I made my offer, and for that I have no cause to repine. You have been more than I had dared dream to possess, so Elizabeth do away with this belief I acted nobly." Fitzwilliam stepped closer, hands fervently clutching her arms, "Darling girl, there is *no* imbalance between us, for I acted selfishly that night, and I will not apologise. Not now, not ever!"

Surprised by her husband's emphatic rebuttal, Elizabeth relaxed subconsciously in Fitzwilliam's arms. Feeling it, he pulled her closer, head lowering, until their breath was shared, "I will not deny there is a reputation to uphold, not just for Georgiana, nor my family, but for our children's benefit besides. Yet anyone privileged to know you, will not think less of you. I do not. And before long, I have no doubt you will have worked sufficient magic to have charmed not just my sister, my cousins, the servants...anyone, and everyone. To know you is to admire you."

Elizabeth was stunned speechless, allowing Fitzwilliam to sweep away her thoughts with ardent kisses, his attentions so passionate as to strip them both of almost every inhibition. With the door safely shut, neither bore the patience to delay their expressions of connection until they had retired for the evening, and so, the crackling fire and the hearth rug kept them warmly cocooned, an intimate bubble.

Much later, as Fitzwilliam helped her back into her dress, his kisses lengthening the process significantly, they were in much better accord. Her husband guided her through the house as if they were two mischief-bent children scurrying about; however Elizabeth granted her husband peace, for his method had them back in his rooms without catching sight of any servants.

Elizabeth was about to shuffle across to her room to change for the night, when Fitzwilliam caught her up around the waist.

"Stay. Please?" the cautious tone, wary of pushing, soothed away the bruises her heart held.

Turning, Elizabeth burrowed closer to his warmth, the breadth of his chest so broad, his shoulders eclipsed her smaller frame. "I was only going to change for the night. I will return if you wish?"

They had kept to her rooms since their marriage, but Elizabeth felt a delicious thrill being in this masculine space, the chamber smelling just as her husband did.

"You don't need to change, for I assure you, I have little intention to allow much between us, not cross words, not surly servants, and certainly not cotton robes!" Kisses interspersed his words, and Elizabeth felt that magnetic pull her husband held, felt herself succumbing to his every desire and dream.

Much, much later, Elizabeth lay relaxed, blissfully replete in her husband's arms, when she finally recalled his words. Attempting to sit up, Elizabeth was thwarted in this, by the tight grip Fitzwilliam had about her.

"Where do you go wife?" the vibration of his words rumbled through her ear, causing a wave of delight to shiver through her.

"I wished to clarify something you stated earlier, so will you not let me up?" Elizabeth pouted, her lips brushing Fitzwilliam's skin.

"Then ask, but my arms will not permit you to move. I am too content, to have you stir me further."

Outraged, Elizabeth attempted to scowl, only for a giggle to escape, therefore she relented, "What did you mean when you said you had been selfish? I cannot see how you can make such a claim!" Her words, spoken into his chest, his arms wrapped securely around her, her hand carefully smoothing across his sculpted torso, Elizabeth spun thoughts about, attempting to discover their meaning.

A rough groan escaped Fitzwilliam, and she waited impatiently for an answer.

"I had hoped to have sufficiently distracted

you from such a confession, but I was cork-brained to suppose that to be the case. As disguise of every sort is abhorrent, suffice to say, it suited me not at all to have you bound to my friend, not when you had bewitched me from the very moment I discovered your character."

"My character?" This time, when Elizabeth tugged free, Fitzwilliam allowed it, his hand coming up to scrub his face as he groaned anew, "Do you mean to say that from our first meeting, where we shared but one sentence, you asked me for a dance, was when you fell victim to my charms?" Elizabeth fairly snorted in disbelief.

Her husband, still shielding his face from her, confessed, "No. Not then."

"Not then? Then when Fitzwilliam?" Elizabeth asked, bewildered.

The sight of a blush rising upon her husband's cheeks, what little she could see, had her honestly desperate to discover the cause of Fitzwilliam's fluster.

"When you met with Miss Lucas upon the bridge between Longbourne and Lucas Lodge. I was dismayed to discover I could not safely escape overhearing your conversation in such a way that would not cause embarrassment."

This time, Elizabeth was the one to blush, for she was certain she had been alarmingly candid in her discourse with her dear friend, had she not canvassed her own family's failings with critical clarity?

With perturbation, she enquired, "What could you have possibly heard that made a union between *us* more desirable, than allowing for an alternate resolution to Miss Bingley's machination?"

Fitzwilliam dropped his palm, his hands trailing across her skin, until each one cupped her cheeks, his palms so large, that his fingers stretched down her neck. With an intense look, so dark and compelling, "I heard this unknown Bennet daughter who had been spoken of in such glowing language, dismiss the wastrel who had blackened my name, a man who has caused a trail of deceit and despair in his wake. I listened as this lively, vibrant girl sought to help her sisters, seeking to make their situation significantly improved all on her own and without any parental support or guidance. I caught the most beautiful sound, as this creature laughed with her whole being, lighting up my world, unbeknownst to her, as she sought a union of equal fulfilment, rather than one of comfort and assurity. Who could be exposed to such, and not wish to know more of this divine being?"

Cheeks flaming, Elizabeth sat stunned in her husband's embrace. Her heart sang in her chest, as the first stirrings of hope bloomed. Mayhap her most cherished wish to have a marriage of love and fulfilment was not the impossibility she had feared it was to be.

CHAPTER 12

Darcy House, London December 30th

T he two weeks between her first marital argument, and its resolution, and the start of the new year passed in easy occupation, a far cry from the tensions that had existed in the prior two weeks. Elizabeth endured the servants gradually decreasing disgruntled behaviour, her new sister's ongoing depressed spirits, and her own longing for the comforts of her family, because throughout it all, her harmony with Fitzwilliam remained steadfast. The Christmas season passed quietly, with little of the high spirits and lively environs that no doubt had filled Longbourne. Instead, Fitzwilliam, Georgiana, her companion and herself had attended services, a lavish meal in company with the Matlock's followed, everything so refined and polished, Elizabeth imagined none in attendance would dare hum a Christmas carol, or squabble over the sweet treats laid out, else fall asleep in their chair, as her father was wont to do.

No, the festive season had left her feeling cold and bereft, and only the warmth of her husband in the evenings made it tolerable. Therefore, with the advent of her Gardiner relatives return that very day, Elizabeth was more than a little excited to finally share in some cheerful company. She had sent a note round to Gracechurch street, inviting her aunt and sister to call as soon as they so wished, and her intention to host a small dinner party before twelfth night. That evening was unfortunately set to be her own introduction into London's first circles, Lady Matlock *generously* assigning the evening to be in her honour. Elizabeth had fought not to roll her eyes as the implication she should be inordinately grateful for this distinction, but as she had already sworn to do, her compliance was all on behalf of her husband. Fitzwilliam had indicated how little he enjoyed such events, whether they be public, or private balls.

"You can imagine how frequently I have been pursued as an eligible single gentleman, in possession of a fortune, for certainly I was in want of a wife!" Fitzwilliam sneered the last, remembered agitation affecting him.

"While I can say I have spared little thought for how a gentleman must feel to such pursuit, it is not much different from how we ladies are perceived. Only our attributes and charms are more in the way of brood mare or else financially motivated. I know it is difficult in either case, hence my own displeasure with the *hunt* for husbands." Elizabeth paused to reflect, "Truthfully, with the example of discord before me in the form of my own parent's union, I found it very hard to feel any desire to bind my lot to that of anyone who would see me for such attributes." A chuckle escaped, and Elizabeth answered Fitzwilliam's silent query, "I am just thinking that I should offer my thanks to Miss Bingley for removing the difficulty. And I cannot help but to think of her reaction to such expressions of gratitude!" The laughter bubbled over, and it was some moments before Elizabeth was in command of herself, for every time she felt she was, the distressed vision of Miss Bingley set her hilarity off once again.

Now, sat in her dressing room as Trent and she discussed the new gowns that had just arrived, Elizabeth was happily surprised by the arrival of Fitzwilliam.

"Forgive the intrusion, but I thought you might like to join my sister and I for tea, she has something in particular she wishes to discuss."

Concerned, Elizabeth hurriedly complied, taking her husband's arm as he escorted her to Miss Darcy's private sitting room.

"Georgiana, Mrs Annesley." Fitzwilliam greeted, and so too did Elizabeth, as she took the seat indicated on the divan by her husband.

"Brother, Mrs Darcy." the sheepish expression was the most feeling Elizabeth had witnessed, and it was a vast improvement to the morose version they had weathered since Miss Darcy's return to Darcy House.

"Mrs Annesley, I hear you wished to discuss your employment?"

Alarmed, Elizabeth switched her study to the genteel lady.

"Heavens, Mrs Annesley, do not say you wish to leave us already?"

A wary look descended the lady, leaving Elizabeth further concerned.

"Tis not so much that I wish to move on, so much that I wondered if my services were still required, now that Mr Darcy has wed. Therefore, I felt it merited discussion."

Before anyone else could answer, Elizabeth hurried to refute Mrs Annesley's words, "Why, Mrs Annesley, I fear you are needed now more than ever! I have much to accomplish in assuming the roles of mistress of Mr Darcy's homes, and the very knowledge of your presence has given me immeasurable relief!" Turning to Fitzwilliam, sighting his displeasure gave her momentary pause, but Elizabeth was unwilling to silence her opinions, "I cannot speak for Mr Darcy, Mrs Annesley, nor that of Miss Darcy, but in my view, you are as much, if not more, indispensable than before."

The lull that settled was uncomfortable, but Elizabeth failed to feel any regret, nor would she apologise for her hasty assertion. Mrs Annesley gratefully thanked her for her opinions, allowing nothing else to be said.

Attention shifted to Fitzwilliam, who had donned his inscrutable mask, until at last he spoke, "Mrs Darcy, while brusque, is correct. I have no doubt my wife will oversee the management of our homes with very little guidance, yet the fact remains my sister still requires the same consideration as before. Furthermore, Mrs Darcy will have a sister join us at Pemberley when we travel north, and so, I believe you would have two charges in your care."

Relieved, Elizabeth emphatically agreed, "Yes, just so Fitzwilliam! Mary, while accomplished, would do well with the structure and guidance Mrs Annesley so capably provides."

Nothing more was said on that score, and when tea arrived, the lady took herself off to see to some correspondence, leaving Miss Darcy to address whatever she wished in private.

"Well Georgiana?" Fitzwilliam prompted once he set down his cup.

Elizabeth had been studying the abundance of pink in the room, surprised to see how attractive the apartments were despite such a potentially overwhelming palette. The rooms appeared everything comfortable and delicate, perfect for Miss Darcy, Elizabeth thought. Her perusal continued, for Elizabeth had not missed the stern note in Fitzwilliam's prompt, nor did she wish for Miss Darcy to feel further pressure with her own gaze.

A timorous cough, and Georgiana carefully apologised, "I cannot......that is, I must beg your pardon for causing you such difficulty at the s-start of your marriage. If-if not f-for me, the servants would have been vastly more...more welcoming. I.. I spoke in intemperately, and for that, you-you must see..."

Desperate to ease the young girl's suffering, "Dear Miss Darcy, I cannot fault you for such sisterly affection and concern for your brother, for I would have been just as distressed if such had befallen a sister of mine."

Sternly, Fitzwilliam intervened, "Elizabeth, Georgiana has not finished."

With a snap, Elizabeth sent her husband a look of reproach.

Ignoring the byplay between her brother and Elizabeth, Miss Darcy studied her cup intently, "While I w-was aggrieved, I did not care to take the time to comprehend matters clearly, and I humbly b-beg your pardon, Mrs Darcy, for the injury to y-your character and t-the harm I h-have caused your reputation with the servants."

Elizabeth glanced between the siblings,

waiting to see if more was to come, and perceiving Miss Darcy had concluded, declared the matter resolved.

"Apology accepted, and forgiveness granted. I see no benefit in beginning our relationship with recriminations, and as I said before, I cannot fault you for feeling as you did. You are a most devoted sister."

Still smarting from her husband's scold, Elizabeth refused to afford him any attention, and soon after, Fitzwilliam excused himself from their presence, presumably hoping the two would grow closer.

With persistence and the correct topic of discussion, Elizabeth grew to learn more of her sister, listening as Miss Darcy, Georgiana, described her delight in music, her burgeoning talent in watercolours. The afternoon passed, and before long, it was time to dress for dinner. Returning to her rooms, Elizabeth was delighted to see a note from her aunt, assuring her of their safe arrival and the promise to call the very next day. This happy state continued, and dinner was far more animated now that everyone felt more approbation in their shared company.

It was not until Elizabeth was preparing for bed that she recalled Fitzwilliam's sharp tone and grim manner from earlier that day. Settled into bed as she was, Elizabeth resolved to discover the cause, but it was not long before sleep overtook her.

"Why Lizzy, it is wonderful to see you looking so well!" Aunt Gardiner's greeting was everything Elizabeth had longed for, and the embrace they shared lasted twice as long as was customary. A little gasp behind her aunt, had her witnessing the awe in which Kitty assessed the morning room upon which she welcomed her family into.

"Oh Lizzy! Everything is so...*fine*! I had no idea you were living in such luxury!"

Mentally wincing at Kitty's voluble observations, Elizabeth squeezed her sister in a tight hold, unequivocally happy to see her family after such a strained month.

"Come, both of you and take your seats. I have already called for refreshments which will be here shortly."

Elizabeth's firm handling of the housekeeper, Mrs Carroll, and the stiff Mr Nevins had set the tone for all future interactions, and while Elizabeth was no doubt abused mercilessly below-stairs, the behaviour of the servants had improved. Trent, her lady's maid, noted that her reception amongst the servants was still cool, but there was a marked lack of derision and disdain. It was progress, and Elizabeth was keen to celebrate each small success.

"I will not deny that Darcy House is elegantly appointed, I must say I have thankfully not been so ill-at-ease that I felt unequal to make a home here. There are already plans in place for my own apartments to be re-done, and some restoration to some of the principle rooms, such as the dining room, will be accomplished before spring."

A maid arrived just then, and aided by a footman, disbursed the tray, and removed from the room without any words spoken. A pointed look from her aunt meant that Mrs Gardiner had noted the lack of servility from the servants, and Elizabeth would canvas such a topic another time, for she was eager to discuss Longbourne and how everyone had got on in her absence.

"Truly Lizzy, you look very fine. I believe married life suits you admirably." Aunt Gardiner's tease made her laugh at the thought, especially considering her current pique with her husband.

"Thank you aunt, I think?" Elizabeth smirked, "I would hope I can adjust to most circumstances, and I have found having a husband no great encumbrance, for gentlemen are easily diverted by their clubs, their pressing business concerns and so on." Loftily, Elizabeth winked at Kitty, "I highly recommend the state!"

Kitty's giggles joined those of her aunt's and Elizabeth revelled in the light-hearted banter that continued throughout tea.

"Now Kitty, I believe our aunt has some entertainment planned?" At her family's nods, Elizabeth went on, "Well, to that we must add a dinner party held here, while I hope to escort you to the theatre one evening?"

With a wrinkled brow, Kitty queried, "Not something terribly confusing, like you and papa enjoy? For I doubt I would like that very much."

Composure lost, Elizabeth laughed unreservedly, not noticing the arrival of her husband and his sister, "Heavens no, Kitty! I am sure to discover one that I feel you would delight in, so worry not on that score."

A cleared throat, and Elizabeth finally marked the presence of Fitzwilliam and Georgiana, who appeared shyly daunted by her aunt and sister's lively spirits.

"Pleasure to see you again Mrs Gardiner, Miss Kitty. Allow me to introduce my sister, Georgiana, this is Mrs Gardiner, my wife's aunt, and this is Miss Catherine, Elizabeth's younger sister, often referred to as Miss Kitty. Ladies, this is my sister Miss Georgiana Darcy."

The solemn introduction did nothing to ease Georgiana's discomfort, and therefore Elizabeth, in concert with her aunt, set about alleviating the young girl's anxiety.

"Kitty, I believe you will much admire Georgiana's skill with watercolours. She is just taking up the skill, and already it is evident, she possesses a natural talent. I believe you would enjoy seeing some of her pieces."

Fitzwilliam, noting his sister's hesitance, sought to aid her, "Do you have any of your earlier drawings?"

"There are s-some in the music room." Flicking a glance up and aimed at Kitty, "I w-would be happy to convey you there, for your perusal?"

The eagerness Kitty displayed did much to dispel any lingering shyness, and the two girls departed moments later, a rapport growing between them.

"Mrs Gardiner, I hope your family is well? I believe you remained at Longbourne for the last month, did you enjoy the Christmas season at Longbourne?"

Elizabeth rolled her eyes at Fitzwilliam's scant small talk, however listened quietly as her aunt related her share of the past month. "The children were not especially keen to return home, where they are frequently confined to the house, unless their nurse is willing to afford them time in the nearby park. As such, I am inordinately grateful to my nieces who have spent the past month with the children, expending their energies in numerous outdoor pursuits. Kitty and Lydia, while both near in age, encourage the children to play in very different ways."

The conversation continued, until eventually Fitzwilliam excused himself to return to his work. Finally alone, her aunt gave her a searching look.

"Now, tell me truthfully, how have you got on?"

With a sigh, Elizabeth expounded upon the difficulties, the servants, the rumour accidentally begun by Georgiana, her husband's relatives and the chilly accord between the two houses.

"If I am honest, I had little expectations where his family were concerned, for I am hardly ignorant of the inherent evils of the alliance Fitzwilliam has made. Without dowry, connections and as a result of averting scandal, you cannot fault the Matlock's for feeling so little inclined to accept my husband's marriage. No, that will take time, and I am committed to ensuring there is little cause for acrimony from this point on. To that end, we are to attend the Twelfth Night ball held by Lady Matlock, whereby I will be formally introduced as Mrs Darcy to society."

Aunt Gardiner laughed, "You sound little enthused for the occasion, despite your sociable nature and love of dancing! Not that I can blame you, for little pleasure is sure to be had that night. However, I exhort you to be yourself regardless of the conceit you may face."

Nodding, Elizabeth vowed she would, then blushed crimson at hearing her aunt's next query.

"I have spent little time in company with both you and your husband, so have only a small margin to discern the matter, and not knowing how long until Kitty's return, I ask if you have taken the final step of intimacy with your husband?"

Nervous, Elizabeth asserted that, yes, there were no barriers between her husband and herself, but of more emotional matters, the situation was not as clear.

"While I laud your advice to take such a step, for I dare not think how alone I would feel, I do question how I can be so comfortable with a man I cannot vow my feelings for?"

Taking her hand in her own, Elizabeth listened to her aunt while refusing to look away from where they were joined, "Lizzy, it sounds as if you are placing upon yourself heavy expectations, rather than permitting your feelings to grow at a more natural pace. You must not push, dear girl. There is time."

Thankfully, by the time her sister and Georgiana returned, Elizabeth's blush had been quelled and the topic of conversation had moved on to the less contentious matter of the servant's disposition.

"I am grieved your marriage has suffered such challenges so early on, and yet I am confident you are well-equipped Lizzy to overcome such trials. I cannot think this difficulty could have befallen a more capable woman! However, now Kitty and I must return home to the children, but I look forward to your visit, and so too will your cousins. They missed you terribly while at Longbourne, Peter especially felt very down-hearted."

Peter was four, his elder sister, Felicity, six, while the oldest, Melody, was eight. The baby of the family was Henry, at just two years old, however this was no age for his older brother to feel anything but outnumbered by his elder sisters, and therefore Peter enjoyed Elizabeth's more energetic manners which closely matched his own. Elizabeth promised to visit two days hence, and from there they would discuss in more detail any planned excursions.

CHAPTER 13

Gracechurch Street, London January 2nd

"Evelyn! Rebecca! I did not know you were to travel to town so soon!" Elizabeth cried, overcome with delight.

"Lizzy!" Both girls cried on sighting her.

The crowded embrace was full of giggles and happy tears, Elizabeth taken back to months before as she bid these delightful girls farewell, unsure of when next they would meet. Pulling back, an arm upon each girl, Evelyn closer in height than Rebecca's much shorter stature, "You sly things, for there was no mention in your last letter of you coming!"

Rebecca's giggle underscored Evelyn's reply, "You can hardly fault us for wishing to be in company all the sooner! So when papa finally agreed we could travel, our trunks were packed within the hour!"

"Girls, while I adore seeing you all so excited to be in one another's company, perhaps we may all take our seats?"

Flushing guiltily, Elizabeth extended her apologies to her aunt and sister who she had quite forgotten to greet. Kitty's hesitance, so unlike her, also was cause to feel some guilt.

"Dear me, I quite forgot myself." Elizabeth took her seat, the girls seated either side of her, "You must excuse me aunt, Kitty-"

The arrival of Mrs Ashley, the girl's governess, along with the tea tray prevented further speech until everyone was settled.

"Mrs Ashley, it is wonderful to see you again."

The governess was a trim woman, her deep blue dress adding to her stately manner, yet Mrs Ashley was hardly stern and unyielding. Her kindness was evident in the small ways she extended correction and guidance to the young and impressionable girls who adored her unconditionally. Her charcoal hair was always perfectly coiffed, highlighted the defined bone structure of her classic features; Elizabeth had been in awe of the woman from their first meeting, impressed time and again by her grace and poise. Mrs Ashley was a refined and cultured lady of sense, and Elizabeth felt the time spent in her company had made a lasting impression.

"Tis a pleasure, Mrs Darcy. I am pleased to see you well and in good cheer." and with that careful declaration, Mrs Ashley addressed the circumstances of her marriage. And *that* was why Elizabeth admired the governess.

"Thank you, Mrs Ashley. I am much as I ever was." The speaking looks shared between the two ladies conveyed appreciation and sympathy in equal measure.

"Now. I insist you join my aunt and sister when they come to dinner. Mrs Ashley, that includes yourself, for I believe you would delight in meeting Miss Darcy and her companion, Mrs Annesley."

Discussion flowed then amidst them all, Elizabeth keen to encourage kinship between her sister and their 'cousins'. Kitty gradually relaxed the longer the girls continued to talk, clear there would be no rivalry or jealousy, that existed with Lydia.

"Kitty has begun a sketch of Longbourne, that I hope she has finished?" Elizabeth asked her sister, to which Kitty swiftly affirmed, "It is a gift from me to you, or perhaps it is better to say, from Kitty to you!" Elizabeth laughingly decided.

"Are you very good with charcoal? Or do you prefer to use watercolours? Pastels?" Rebecca's eager questions tripped forth, and Kitty was delighted to be engaged in a discussion she felt qualified to address at length.

Leaving the two be, Elizabeth focused upon Evelyn who, having turned seventeen the month prior, appeared so much more mature, and therefore could not help remarking upon the alteration.

"Any improvement you see, I must attribute to you, dear Lizzy!"

"Surely not," Waving to indicate Mrs Ashley, who only looked on in pleasure, "Your governess can attest to how hard you have worked to be ready for your come out."

Mrs Ashley softly agreed, "Mrs Darcy is correct Evelyn, your maturity has been a pleasure to witness." The governess turned to Elizabeth, "Evelyn is however, correct to point out that you, Mrs Darcy, played a significant role in my charge's improvement. Witnessing how you engaged with those in company regardless of their station and rank, your kindness tempered every interaction. You provided the best example upon whom the girls could model themselves."

"Then I must attempt to gracefully accept such accolades!" Embarrassed to be so lauded, Elizabeth fought not to blush and failed, "However, much of my own guidance came from my dear aunt, who truly is the best lady I know."

Mrs Gardiner grinned broadly, "I have no objections to bearing responsibility in seeing my nieces become such exceptional ladies. I shall happily accept the credit!"

Laughter was heard throughout the room, and in general, it was the most at ease Elizabeth had been since the Netherfield ball. The truth she would have to return to such stiff environs was something Elizabeth deliberately shunted from her mind.

The week was filled with outings, shopping trips and one quiet trip to the theatre, for a production that was out of favour within the first circles, and therefore Elizabeth and her party enjoyed the performance, without *being* the entertainment! It was indelibly rewarding watching Kitty flourish in the care of Mrs Ashley, relishing the attention of their cousins, Elizabeth could agree to feeling satisfaction with her achievement, to which her aunt was quick to agree.

"Dear Lizzy, what you have done for your sister is to be commended, not *because* she has improved, but because it was not *your* obligation! Kitty, for all her faults, is just as you said, a girl without attention and guidance, and if your mother or father had expended a modicum of effort, this entire enterprise of yours would not have been necessary."

"Thank you, dear aunt. This I accept in relation to my parents, but I cannot help feeling guilty for my own behaviour towards my younger sisters. They deserved my compassion, and instead I ridiculed them just as my father does." Ashamed, Elizabeth twisted her handkerchief, until touch from her aunt had her smoothing the square of cotton.

"Let me tell you, that while it is right

you review your own conduct, it does not mean you must castigate yourself for the faults of understanding of your youth. You have more than made up for any defect of thinking and have made every effort to engage *all* of your sisters with gentle encouragement and nothing of scorn or derision!"

Sighing, Elizabeth accepted her aunt's counsel, and instead turned the conversation, "What of plans for Lydia? Has your cousin replied to your letter of query?"

Aunt Gardiner sat back and sighed softly, "Unfortunately, my cousin is in the midst of an unexpected courtship, and having been married once only to be widowed not long after, her comfortable situation has freed her from *having* to remarry. This development has my cousin struggling to decide how to proceed and therefore we must consider another avenue."

Fitzwilliam was happy to listen to Elizabeth discuss her hopes to help her sisters, especially now that she was better placed to make a significant difference. "Last time I discussed my family, Fitzwilliam thought a seminary might be a suitable solution for Lydia?" She watched her aunt's brows rise, and hurried on, "I have been brutally honest with him, regarding the root of the problem and he has suggested he would cover any and all fees."

"You mean, you told Mr Darcy that your mother was the reason Lydia straddled the line between childhood and womanhood, and fluctuated so wildly between the two?"

Nodding in agreement with the summation, "Exactly, and with Fitzwilliam's connections, he believes we should be able to locate a school that will excite Lydia's interests enough to override my mother's rejection of her youngest leaving her care."

Her aunt agreed, "Then I shall leave such a task in your hands, while I tackle your mother, who will, I am sure, be difficult at the thought of such a seperation."

Elizabeth rolled her eyes at the truth of such a statement, and from there, conversation moved on to her own excitement of seeing Pemberley, and her aunt's reminisces of her childhood spent in the nearby village of Lambton.

The night of her first dinner, Elizabeth was a combination of excitement and nervous tension. The desperate wish for the evening to be well-received, not only by her relatives, but those within Darcy House, evidence of her ability to uphold the credit of her husband's name. The servants had unbent their stiff disapproval, some even smiled when she crossed their paths! And Georgiana appeared much more comfortable, which ultimately affected Fitzwilliam, who relaxed, relinquishing his granite mask. With her husband more at ease, Elizabeth had felt comfortable in sowing seeds of curiosity within Georgiana, enough for her to enquire of the events that led to her brother's marriage. The dear girl had risen early one morning, attending breakfast promptly, whereby she set about satisfying her suspense about the changes made in recent weeks.

"Lizzy?" Still quiet, Georgiana kept to her purpose, "Why has brother barred Miss Bingley from our homes now, and made it so clear to aunt Matlock that there is to be no connection between her and our name? He never troubled himself to check her before."

Ignoring the perked ears of the footman stationed by the sideboard, Elizabeth carefully enquired, "Has he not informed you? Hmm, well, I see no reason why you should not know!" And therefore, Elizabeth related the details of Miss Bingley's scheming.

"Why in heavens would Miss Bingley manoeuvre her brother to compromise you? It makes little sense!" Georgiana was genuinely upset.

"Forgive me, I had not thought you so attached to her friendship." Elizabeth bit her lip in worry, perhaps her design would work against her.

Puckered brow, Georgiana looked away, "Miss Bingley did not *really* like me, I knew that. I was just part of the strategy Miss Bingley employed to become closer to my brother.

Everyone knew, even my brother, but for the sake of his friendship with Mr Bingley, the lady's actions were ignored." Turning back to Elizabeth with a strangely pointed look, "Perhaps, the fault lies just as much with us, as it does with Miss Bingley!"

"Whyever would you believe that? No, I shall tell you what I believe governed the lady's actions. Spite. Miss Bingley took a decided dislike of me from the moment we met. I had the audacity to arrange for a rather unpleasant dancing partner for the night of her ball, add to this, her own brother's partiality for my elder sister? Miss Bingley was keen to avoid any alliance between our families."

Confused, Georgiana hesitantly questioned, "But would not causing her brother to compromise *you*, ensure there *would* be a union? For if my brother had not stepped in and offered for you in Mr Bingley's place, I am certain the gentleman would have paid his addresses to you!"

Grimacing, the thought entirely unpleasant, Elizabeth explained why that was not as comforting as Georgiana might imagine, "As much as Mr Bingley is an amiable and estimable gentleman, the thought of being tied to him in marriage is disagreeable. For you see, my sister felt very deeply for the gentleman, and it would have broken her heart. I would have been miserable, to be the cause of such heartache to a most beloved sister. No, your brother was the only one who prevented Miss Bingley's machinations causing much grief, but I am near certain the lady felt safe to assume neither her brother nor Mr Darcy would preserve my reputation at the cost of their own wishes."

Scowling, Georgiana said nothing, and therefore Elizabeth sipped her tea and finished her meal in peace, hopeful that the truth would affect a positive alteration.

They had gathered in the salon, tastefully ornamented with gilt frames and finishings, while burnished settees and armchairs were carefully grouped together. It was balanced with emerald toned drapes and papering, the rich colour the perfect backdrop to the ladies. Elizabeth was attired in a vivid bronze silk that made her peach toned skin glow, the fabric hugging her figure with a sensuous hint. Mrs Annesley was draped in green silk, fine work embroidery at her neckline showing the lady's skill with a needle. Georgiana glowed in the candlelight, her cream silk dress with a yellow lace overlay gave her the appearance of a spring daisy in the midst of a meadow.

"Do you think I have time to change? For I cannot like how I look? Mayhap I should withdraw for this evening? I am not feeling entirely up to company." Georgiana's ramblings distressed Darcy, but Elizabeth was quick to soothe his sister's fears, leaving him to his own thoughts once more. A careful study of his wife, showed her own anxiety about how tonight would progress, but having met the Gardiner's, Darcy felt confident all would be well. The addition of Mrs Gardiner's brother and nieces troubled him not at all. Time with Elizabeth had given him an acute understanding of her family, and to Mrs Gardiner, Fitzwilliam could accredit his current felicity in marriage.

Nevins entered then, admitting the guests in clear, deep tones, "Mr Gardiner, Mrs Gardiner, Miss Bennet, Mr Thompson, Miss Thompson and Miss Rebecca Thompson."

Darcy stepped forward to greet and welcome his guests, catching a frown on his wife's face, before she smoothed it away, stepping forward to make the introductions.

"Uncle, Aunt. Kitty. Uncle Thompson, Evelyn, Rebecca... *Mrs Ashley*," Ah, Nevins' dismissal of the governess had upset his wife, "allow me to introduce my husband, Mr Darcy, his sister, Miss Georgiana Darcy and her companion, Mrs Annesley."

"Welcome to our home, and thank you for joining us. I know how eager my wife has been for this evening to arrive, and to be in company with you all again."

Elizabeth nodded, "I have indeed, longed

for us all to be gathered once more, but I have looked forward to introducing you to my new family. And despite being vastly different from the liveliness of my childhood home, Darcy House is a lovely residence anyone would be proud to be mistress of! So now you must all take a seat, while my husband shall see to your drinks."

"Oh, Lizzy, I am just surprised you have not walked half of London already, for I am certain we did the whole of Bath while you resided with us." Miss Thompson looked on Elizabeth with a look of adoration, a sentiment unsurprising to Darcy.

"Lizzy walks the garden most m-mornings, before b-breakfast." His sister's addition had Darcy's brows winging upwards, delighted by Georgiana's engagement with their company.

As was to be expected, the room divided up, with the younger girls sitting close together, while Mrs Annesley and the governess kept company with Elizabeth and Mrs Gardiner.

"Darcy, how did your first Christmas as a married man pass?" Gardiner jovially enquired.

"We spent the day with my Matlock relatives who remained in town this year. My uncle does not find winter travel to be at all desirable."

Mr Thompson, his sandy brown hair swept neatly from his brow, a match to his sister's, tugged at his waistcoat, before saying, "If it were not for Lizzy, that is Mrs Darcy, I would have delayed my own arrival to London. But my girls were bound and determined to see my niece, and so I am only grateful the weather was not at all treacherous."

"Indeed, returning from Longbourne, can sometimes be cause for much concern, and I am only thankful the distance is not greater. Spending time with family over the festive season is one of the highlights of my year, watching the children enjoying themselves, surrounded by loved ones. I am pleased, Darcy, you and your family could be together for the occasion."

With ease, Darcy withheld the grimace these words inspired. His Matlock relatives had been offensively polite and proper, treating Elizabeth as an unwanted guest in almost every instance. To them, she was an interloper in their world, and while his aunt had promised to launch Elizabeth into society with the coming Twelfth Night ball, Darcy was little inclined to remain for further mistreatment of his wife.

"As much as my Matlock relatives are excellent people, I believe next year will be vastly different, for I would dearly like to spend the season at my home estate, in Derbyshire."

Gardiner chuckled, "You sound much as my wife and brother-by-law," here Gardiner clapped Mr Thompson on the shoulder, "for the two of them were born and raised in the county!"

"Lambton, Gardiner. Tis but five miles from Mr Darcy's principle estate, and a very fine village it is!" Mr Thompson affably stated, no undercurrent of flattery present in his tone.

"I know Lambton well, Mr Thompson. I have the gift of the living for Lambton and two others, and with its closeness, it is the main source of supplies to my home." Deep in thought, Darcy almost missed Nevins enter.

"Dinner is ready, Mr Darcy."

Nodding in distraction, Darcy collected his wife and sister and led the way to the dining room, absently agreeing with Elizabeth about how dark the room appeared.

Taking his seat, Darcy noted Mrs Gardiner at his side, Mr Thompson next, with his daughters either side of the table, next to the companion and governess. Miss Bennet was seated to his left, while Mr Gardiner and Georgiana were with Elizabeth. Overall, Darcy found himself in agreeable company, pleased to learn Mrs Gardiner and Mr Thompson's father had been the rector in the Lambton parish until his health failed, and had to remove to the family estate in Nottingham, residing with his brother and relations.

When studying Miss Kitty Bennet, Darcy was impressed by the improvement of manners and comportment, testament to his wife's wish to help her family better themselves. Miss

Kitty had obviously taken on board her sister's guidance, and was embracing the lessons, while not erasing her own character. In just one evening, Darcy witnessed his sister engage more in company, than she had ever done, before Ramsgate and since. His wife's magic touch fell upon everyone in her circle.

The pleasurable period was rudely intruded upon, by the alarming report one of the footmen brought to him, causing him to rise and excuse himself from his guests, ignoring Elizabeth's questioning glance. Unfortunately, Lady Catherine was determined to embarrass the family and herself, as she rudely marched into the dining room before he had left, ignoring the butler's direction to wait in Darcy's study.

"What is the meaning of this aunt Catherine?" Darcy forced himself to be calm, desperate to prevent a scene from occurring, embarrassment surging beneath his skin.

"You can be at no loss, Darcy, to understand the reason for my presence! A report of a most alarming nature reached me two days ago, by means of Mr Collins! He arrived in Meryton, to attend his own nuptials, only to be informed of this...this...mésalliance!!"

"Lady Catherine! I have guests, therefore do me the honour of allowing my butler to conduct you to my study whereby we may discuss-"

"Guests!!! Who are these people?

Georgiana! Come away at once! You are not to sit at table with a harlot such as she!" His aunt's finger pointed aggressively towards Elizabeth and Darcy's vision turned red.

Striding over to the lady, he took her forcefully by the arm and removed her from the dining room without delay. His butler strode alongside him, opening the study door with alacrity and snapping it shut smartly once they had entered.

"Darcy! How dare you! You ought to know I am not to be trifled with! I shall not allow this travesty of a union to stand! You are bound for *my* daughter, Anne! Not to that- that-"

Savage fury flooded his blood, and Darcy paced away carefully, afraid he would dismiss the principles that had guided him for so long and strike his aunt, so angry was he. "Lady Catherine, before you express yourself with your vaunted *sincerity and frankness*, I advise you to think carefully of all that is between us. One more word against my *wife* and I will permanently sever all ties."

Snorting, his aunt struck her cane against the carpet, the lack of noise frustrating the great lady, her lips twisted in a sour sneer, "Your *wife*! That title belongs to *my* daughter! That creature out there has stolen what was rightfully Anne's!"

Astonished, Darcy stiffly declaimed, "Indeed, you are mistaken!"

Her ladyship scowled, "I thought better of

you Darcy! To be drawn in by torrid arts and allurements of a strumpet! Of course, you will choose to neglect the principles of propriety, the wishes of your own mother, to satisfy those *base urges,* to disregard honour, decorum, prudence! How do you expect your *wife* to be noticed? Do you welcome the censure and slights that will fall upon the Darcy name?!"

With every word his aunt uttered, Darcy's boiling temper hardened into iron, disgusted with the cunning and manipulation that dripped like venom, with every word from Lady Catherine's lips. The violent rage waned, and in its place, was revulsion, "If you believe the truth of your sentiments, I wonder you took the trouble of coming. What could your ladyship propose by it? For does not your very presence lend a lie to your postulations?" Slicing a hand through the air, halting further words from his aunt, Darcy continued, grit in every word, "I do not pretend to your ladyship's equal frankness, nor do I feel compelled to gift you any words of consolation for your imagined loss, or slighted hopes. You are not entitled to know more of my concerns, than you ever had before, nor will such behaviour as this, ever induce me to be ever so open and considerate with a woman of your character!"

Lady Catherine hissed, "Obstinate! Headstrong! Callous boy! I am ashamed of you! Is this your gratitude for all that I have done in service to you? On your behalf! Heaven and Earth, for the shades of Pemberley to be thus polluted!"

"That is enough madam!" Darcy bit out, striding over to the door, dismissal clear, "You have vented your spleen, have disclosed your scorn, and I must be content that all ties between us are to be severed, for I never suffer a repeat of such an abhorrent display as you have importuned me with this night."

The snap and clack of his aunt's cane against the parquet flooring, was a thudding metronome, keeping time with her ladyship's continued insults as she exited his home, but to satisfy his relation with more of his time, he would not grant. She had wounded his pride and dignity enough. Now he must make his way to the drawing room, and beg pardon of his guests for such a scene as that played out. Pinching the bridge of his nose, Darcy gave himself one moment of silence in his study, before turning his steps to his wife and their guests.

CHAPTER 14

Pemberley, Derbyshire March 28th

Pemberley in early spring was a delight to witness, from the earliest of blooms appearing upon the magnificent magnolia tree in the structured gardens, to the delightful daffodils cropping up along near every path. The last of the purple crocuses with their bursts of colour, to the craggy peaks in the distance, stole her breath at their raw beauty. Into this wild landscape she had travelled, only a week following the dinner Lady Catherine had burst in upon, days after her introduction to society as Mrs Darcy. Her husband's family had been warmly cordial, an attempt to ameliorate the offence their relative had given, but while the Twelfth Night ball had been a memorable evening, the most significant of which was dancing with Fitzwilliam, while he seductively teased her with his solemn complimentary whispers; the many new people introduced, some kind and others less so, her pleasure in the evening had only come when she lay in her husband's arms. The passion that had arisen between the two of them had continued to build, to grow, flourish, such that no longer did Elizabeth see a reserved and dour gentleman when she gazed upon her husband, but a man she was beginning to unravel and decipher, like the greatest puzzle set before her, she delighted in the challenge.

This morning, she sat curled up in their private sitting room, the window seat the perfect spot upon which to revel in the sights of the unfolding season, while herself feeling somewhat unwell. Her correspondence had been delivered with her tray, and feeling all the more slothful for neglecting such tasks as her letters, Elizabeth turned her attention to them. Her sister Kitty wrote of her growing friendship with their 'cousins' and her developing artistic skills were clearly displayed in the small sketch of the three girls, posed carefully in the gardens of their uncle's home. Next came a messy scrawl from Lydia, sharing her pleasure unabated in the company of the militia, of which Lieutenant Wickham was just as prominently mentioned as the Colonel's young wife, Mrs Forster. Little progress had been made in sourcing an establishment that would interest her youngest sister, but Fitzwilliam continued to explore possibilities. It had been too easy for Elizabeth to forget, and the evidence of her laxity lay before her! Elizabeth promised herself she would speak with Mrs Annesley that very day. The lady may have some direction in which to point them! The next letter she read, was Jane's, and Elizabeth prayed matters were more comfortable for her sweetest sister.

Dearest Lizzy

I cherish each letter I receive relating how well you have settled into your new home, and must admit it all sounds much more than I had ever imagined, if I were to base anything upon Miss Bingley's reports. As such, it appears, Caroline provided an accurate assessment, and therefore, I must delight in your fortune in being mistress of such a grand home. However, I cannot deny much of your pleasure in your new home stems from your repeated mention of your husband's presence, his diligent attention and his care and support as you take up the mantle of Mrs Darcy. Furthermore, I gather from how frequently you praise the servants, you have faced none of the censure that so marred your time in London. This can only be a relief!

For myself, now with the absence of both Mary and Kitty, Longbourne is all the quieter, providing a sharp distinction against our youngest sister's high spirits that seem entirely ungoverned. The house is fractured by the repeated calls of our mother as she bemoans my incivility in inducing Mr Bingley to propose, and the inevitable furore Lydia's liveliness brings. Else wise, not even this evidence has bestirred our father to check her behaviour. I can hear you marvel at such an ungenerous report, and to that I must confess that I have never been blind to our sister's faults, yet to my shame must admit that I felt turning a blind eye would keep the peace, and prevent further discord and disharmony.

Elizabeth re-read the passage once more, before biting her lip in mortification and sadness, for how else could she view her father's indifferent parenting. Even with just *one* silly daughter at home, Mr Bennet still would not trouble himself! Lydia was indeed culpable for her zealous flirtations, but with no guidance, no repercussion, the dear child would sink further and further, aided by their mother who saw no wrong in her favoured child. Poor Jane, to be faced with such discomposing displays. Turning back to the missive, Elizabeth continued to read.

I see now, that it is this behaviour that I dislike above all in Mr Bingley, for did he not behave in the very fashion of our own father, with his own sister? I wish I could beg pardon for continuing to expound on such subjects, but as my dearest confidant, I am assured you will not judge me harshly for my ungenerosity. Yet, to this I must add some abhorrence for my conduct, for in many ways, I am just as guilty as our father and Mr Bingley! Having assigned blame to all quarters, I had steadfastly ignored a truth that disturbed my own sense of self; I have known all along that your acceptance of Mr Darcy was solely on my behalf. For no other reason did you accept a veritable stranger, if not to avert my own heartbreak. My gratitude, dear sister, can never be expressed, for your selflessness, your forgiving heart, I fear I may never be in a position to repay you.

With that in mind, I am decided to make your sacrifice worthwhile, and have accepted Mr Bingley's request for a courtship, to the raptures of our mother and the gentleman himself. He has shown he is constant in his affections, and therefore I must now decide if what I have learned of the gentleman and how he conducts his courtship are alike. There was one point upon which I felt you would take further delight in, however, I am of two minds myself. Taking a page from your own book. I endeavoured to discover what was to be done with Miss Bingley, for I could not countenance residing under the same roof as that woman. I was astonished to hear that Miss Bingley was most recently wed! I wish this knowledge gave me comfort, but it did little to soothe my concerns regarding Mr Bingley's discipline, for the union was the working of the gentleman's brother by marriage, Mr Hurst! I know few particulars, save to say the former Miss Bingley, now Mrs Bailey, was hard-pressed to accept and was given little recourse. It does give me some satisfaction, to discover that Mrs Bailey had her own wishes dismissed, much as your own were.

The tone was so unlike Jane, and yet, Elizabeth found little strength to argue with any of the salient points her sister made. There *was* a worrying symmetry of indifferent behaviour expressed by numerous parties, and yes, Elizabeth was churlish enough to feel some delight in Miss- nay Mrs Bailey's situation. The letter continued in more comfortable tones, relating news of the neighbourhood, and the progression of her courtship. Overall, Elizabeth felt it was a marked improvement on other more bitter missives she had received from her sister, and at last, it appeared as if her beloved Jane was emerging, just as the spring, with new life and fresh hopes. In her conversations with Mary where she had canvassed the cynical shade in Jane's correspondence, her younger sister had shown a degree of wisdom hidden to most.

"She cannot accept your marriage, Lizzy,

for if she were to do so, it would reveal to her, her own selfish desires." Mary clearly pointed out.

Elizabeth felt unequal to disagreeing, and the sentiment sat ill with her, leaving Mary to continue.

"A part of all of us will wish to seek our own happiness, without consideration to others, and we are taught to model propriety, decorum and character upon the foundation of Christian charity, in order to vanquish that selfish voice. For most, we are able to balance our own wishes with the teachings of the church, yet for some, such as our mother, anything that smacks of disagreeable, she wilfully disregards in order to sustain her own accord. Now, in the instance of our gentle sister, Jane must come to terms with her own selfish heart being at war with charity, for while you sacrificed-"

"Twas no such thing!" Elizabeth refuted, disliking the thought of her content marriage to be seen in such a mean light.

"I meant no offence sister, merely, what I perceive *Jane* judges the situation to be. For while you *sacrificed* your own wishes for love of her, she cannot help but to be *grateful* you did so! Therefore, until Jane can accept your marriage, I imagine the bitterness of spirit Jane experiences will persist."

Now, here at last was the proof of Mary's assessment, for it seemed with her own light-hearted letters, Jane could finally come to terms with her union with Fitzwilliam. The sudden admittance of the very individual strode into the room hurriedly, still attired in his riding apparel, bringing with him the smell of horse, man and the outdoors. A roiling in her innards, had her holding her breath until the nausea had settled.

"Are you well?" Fitzwilliam dropped to his knees before her, his gloves stripped off, left his warm palms bare as they gripped her own, an expression of severe agitation affixed upon his countenance.

"Of course, Fitzwilliam." Elizabeth assured, and yet the worry did not abate from his cool grey eyes. Clarity struck, and Elizabeth sighed, "Heavens, do not tell me you rushed up in all this agitation for news of my having yet to descend for breakfast?"

"Mrs Reynolds related you requested a tray, then Georgie and Mary said they had yet to see you, despite it being near ten. What am I to think, when I enter and see you tucked away as you are?" Her husband's words were stiff and quick, almost expressing his censure, yet Elizabeth knew Fitzwilliam retreated behind his reserve whenever he felt *too much*, his dignity protected him from the pain and fear that seemed to stalk him. Fitzwilliam would not soften until she teased him into relaxing his control. Sighting her correspondence, "Have you had news of Longbourne?"

Unable to contain her laughter, Elizabeth giggled, "Why, you are in a state!" Then leaning forward, brushing her lips against his brow, "You need not fear, there is naught in my letters to be cause for concern, no more than is typical, that is. Now, up," Ineffectually, she tugged her husband from his kneeling position, yet the gentleman stubbornly refused to be moved, "Honestly, husband, why all the concern?"

"You have not been yourself this past month! I fear I-...that is, you-"

The blossoming secret that beat in her chest thrummed anew, always cherishing each of these small moments between them, free of restraint, when Fitzwilliam exposed the diamond hidden amidst the granite.

Relinquishing her hold in pulling Fitzwilliam to his feet, Elizabeth decided to reveal something of what she had come to realise these last few treasured months in the north, in her new home.

"Whatever it is you fear," brushing a lock of his inky hair away from his brow, she leant forward and gifted him with another kiss, "you need not. I had never envisioned such a home as this, and each day, each week, each month that has passed since we wed, since our arrival here, I have grown so radiantly happy, I cannot account for how I have been so blessed with it all."

A frown marred his forehead, and loath to see him unhappy, not now that she knew the truth that beat in her heart, a drumbeat that whispered his name, the glow he sparked to life, the feeling so immense, so all encompassing, the truth still stole her breath.

"While I am beyond relieved you are comfortable-"

Elizabeth tutted, tapping Fitzwilliam on the nose like a naughty pup, "I made no mention of such bland flattery, husband. That is too small a word, too shallow, too confined to express the truth."

At this, her husband allowed a small smile to tilt his lips, and while his eyes heated, his words were at variance with his intense look, "Forgive me, I shall endeavour to find the words to express your joy, yet I cannot help to question if you would be just as happy were you to find yourself in much differing circumstances. You possess the nature to make you at ease, no matter the company you keep."

Sensing her husband's unspoken query, Elizabeth could not help arching a brow at the probing questions she saw hidden in his eyes, that iron grey gaze boring into her, making her heart flutter in anxious anticipation of revealing the secret feelings she had been nurturing for so long. A knock intruded, and with a muffled oath, Fitzwilliam rose abruptly and paced away, before barking a sharp 'Enter' into the coiling tension building between the two of them, snapping the skeins until the threads fell about her feet.

Kirk, her husband's valet opened the door to the sitting room, "Your bathwater is ready, Sir."

Nodding, her husband thanked his valet, before excusing himself, leaving Elizabeth to wonder how one was to go about informing their husband that they loved them.

Fitzwilliam had never envisioned what married life would look like, too caught up in managing the estates, ensuring his sister's welfare and avoiding the society matrons so intent upon their pursuit, to ever contemplate the matter.

"Brother?" Georgiana's query broke into his musings, her soft expression full of concern, and with a gruff pardon, the conversation resumed.

"I cannot say how I feel Georgiana, regarding Miss Bingley, forgive me, Mrs Bailey's marriage, I have little troubled myself with thoughts of the scheming shrew."

His sister's gasp, while Mary's chuckle could not deafen him to the soft scold in his wife's words.

"Fitzwilliam, for shame. You shall have your sister and Mrs Annesley assigning your intemperate words to my influence." Studying her, Darcy watched the candlelight glow in her eyes, making them shimmering brown pools that far too easily brought improper thoughts to the fore. Her burgundy ensemble bared enough décolletage as to make sitting opposite her the entire evening nigh on torture, yet with their sisters present, it was a heavy burden indeed that he could not hurry them both back to their rooms, where he could lose himself in her like he had near every night since their wedding. Yet not even his physical craving for Elizabeth could allay the quiet voice that begged to be desired for himself and not what he could bring to the marriage. To be admired for himself and nothing more, nothing less. This morning's conversations immediately came to mind. Elizabeth had looked so affectionate, so *loving*, that her words seemed strangely-.

"Nonsense, Lizzy. Brother is justifiably ill inclined to Mrs Bailey, and I can only hope with her marriage, we are little to cross paths with the- that...woman."

Elizabeth's laugh shivered across his skin.

"Why, Georgie, I am impressed! I was given to think you were such a gentle creature!" The tease had his sister shifting from her disgruntled mood, and conversation progressed, until the meal was concluded, and they made their way to the music room, where both Georgiana and Mary entertained themselves with playing, leaving Mrs Annesley close at hand providing a cheerful audience for the girls.

"Fitzwilliam?" a soft hand discreetly

stroked a hair behind his ear, and the chills of earlier returned ever stronger.

"Yes dearest?" and she was his *dearest*, his heart could no longer deny how deeply this woman had burrowed into his soul. The last thought on his mind before he fell asleep, and the first when he awoke, his arms seeking her presence before his eyes even opened.

"You have been very quiet this evening. Is everything well? Did your meeting with Wilson raise concerns?" The brush of her hand against his, had him gripping hers, unwilling to part from her touch.

Shifting in his seat, knees brushing, the subtle touches, a paltry way to soothe the hunger for her, his wife, his Elizabeth.

"No. There were no issues regarding the spring planting strategy, nor the provisions for the wool yields, however, it does look as if the ongoing difficulty with the Luddites will continue to affect the mills production. Yet I cannot see what can be done, as such there is a need to travel up to meet with the mill owners and managers."

He watched as Elizabeth considered his words, how her teeth sunk into her lip, how her glowing eyes sparkled with intelligence. His distraction almost caused him to miss her comments.

"I am concerned about such violence being the only means for these unhappy workers to voice their thoughts. Yet I would not wish for them to be unduly pardoned when they have hurt innocents. I am also loath to see you venture into the area where you may face such dangers, but, I agree it would perhaps best serve to have a direct involvement in such a situation. Have you made any plans to depart?"

They discussed his arrangements for the remainder of the evening, until, at last, their sisters retired, leaving him blessedly alone with his wife. They made their way up to their rooms, and before long, he was in her arms, the connection between them thrumming like a harpsichord, its tones a symphony, blending their bodies, desires together. Afterwards, as Elizabeth lay in his arms, her breathing slow and deep, Darcy felt a tickle of fear that he was the only one to feel as deeply as he did, the only one so lost in love, he had no wish to ever find his way without Elizabeth.

CHAPTER 15

Pemberley, Derbyshire April

"Mary, Georgie, have you heard?" Elizabeth rushed into the music room, keen to inform her sisters of her happy tidings. As both girls looked up, Elizabeth related, "Jane is engaged!"

"Finally!" Mary stated, while a small happy smile lifted her lips.

"Oh, I am so pleased! I cannot imagine how hard it has been for Mr Bingley and your sister after such a difficult..." Georgiana trailed off, unequal to finishing her sentence, while a soft blush bloomed upon her cheeks.

Laughing in delight, Elizabeth exclaimed, "Exactly! My sentiments are matched in you both!"

"Does Jane say when they are to wed? Are we to attend?"

Mary's questions were duly answered, "Jane states that her and Mr Bingley wish to wed the second week of June, in the hopes we are to travel to Netherfield and attend the wedding, and I believe Jane wishes to ask you, Mary to stand up with her." Elizabeth took a seat, a quiver of concern hidden behind her cheerful mien. "I cannot say how long Fitzwilliam will remain in York, but I intend to write to him to enquire, for I am unwilling to travel without him."

Both girls agreed, and Elizabeth happily discussed Jane's letter further, sharing how Mr Bingley had eventually proposed.

"Here, I shall read it for you;

There have been many rides the two of us have shared, but on this day, Mr Bingley arrived at Longbourne driving a curricle, the soft blue vehicle a delight for the eye! And when Mr Bingley was admitted, he requested my company, to which my mother was only too happy to comply. I am unsure if the gentleman had intended for it to be so, but his jacket perfectly matched that of his vehicle, and the sight was enough to have stolen my breath, his handsomeness, the elegant curricle and the fine spring day the backdrop to both. I was ably handed up, and then Mr Bingley took up his seat, and I cannot deny, the strange tension seemed to emanate from him, quite exciting my nerves. Truly, Lizzy, I fear our mother has made me utterly terrified of referring to my nerves! Regardless, we soon were off, and the curricle moved delightfully along the lane, the drive taking us much further than I had thought was perhaps appropriate, that was until we reached a stunning field filled with wildflowers.

Oh Lizzy, it was ever so romantic, Mr Bingley stopped the curricle, jumped down, and asked for a moment if I would grant him my company on a short walk. There amidst the flowers, Mr Bingley dropped to his knee and begged me to

*make him the happiest of men and consent to be his wife!
Oh, words failed me entirely, and so panicked was I that he
would mistake my silence for rejection, I could only nod so
emphatically as to almost dislodge my hair pins.*

There, is that not a most romantic proposal? I must say, I am inclined to think well of Mr Bingley with the pains he took to make Jane's proposal everything it ought to be."

Elizabeth watched her sisters reactions, so opposite to one another as to make the sight amusing, for Georgiana had allowed her eyes to unfocus as she smiled serenely with her internal happy daydreaming, while Mary frowned with a quizzical bent.

"I agree, it was a most romantic proposal." Mary allowed, "But I would like to know if Mrs Bailey is to attend her brother's wedding." Looking up then, fixing Elizabeth with a stern look, "I shall not wish for you to be in her company Lizzy."

Georgiana's daydream burst with that, and once more, both girls were in alliance, "Oh yes, I had not thought of that! I cannot think how I should act were I to be in company with that- that...woman again."

Elizabeth could only agree, while enjoying the care of her sisters. Mrs Bailey and she would never be in company, and one could only hope Mr Bingley would be sensible of that fact. Regardless of the circles they mixed in, any encounter with 'that woman' as Georgie phrased it, would be intolerable. Regardless, the day passed quietly, each in their separate amusements, the ladies coming together again for dinner, where the conversation once more revolved around Jane's engagement.

"In society, you will often face ladies who you cannot like, or do not share similar interests." Mrs Annesley commented, taking a sip of her wine, she resumed, "However, it will not be possible to cut the acquaintance merely because you do not like such people. Part of controlling your composure is to ably navigate such occasions with ladylike grace and discernment, Miss Darcy. I am confident, that however much you fear crossing paths with Mrs Bailey again, you have the necessary skills to behave just as you ought."

"Why, I thoroughly agree with Mrs Annesley," Elizabeth grinned broadly at the genteel lady, "however, I would not wish the evening to orbit one so wholly immaterial to our own contentment! Now, I do believe I ought to comment that I have noted a significant growth in your aptitude with your music, Mary, and for that I believe we have to thank both our sister *and* Mrs Annesley!"

The evening concluded early for Elizabeth, her fatigue having grown significantly these past few weeks, despite her walks being restricted with the variable April weather, the rain and wind making it feel still unwise to venture too far afield. Furthermore, Elizabeth knew her nights were spent unsettled, so accustomed to sleeping with her husband at her side, his absence made the empty space unbearable. Fitzwilliam had been gone a sennight, and according to his latest letter, was still to be absent another fortnight.

Lying in bed, Elizabeth studied the canopy above her, the curtains pulled partway to keep the heat enclosed in her small space. Tossing onto her side, Elizabeth tried to ignore the heavy secret she was keeping, yet her hand slipped beneath the sheets, caressing her belly where only the slightest bump existed. All this time and Elizabeth had completely forgotten about the details her aunt had imparted, the lack of her courses, the nausea arising from certain smells and especially on waking; Elizabeth had been little troubled by this particular trait, however the heavy fatigue and tenderness in her breasts had been a nuisance she had failed to connect to one another. All occurred so sparingly as to make it near impossible for Elizabeth to have equated it to her current condition. And now, with Fitzwilliam away, Elizabeth could not relate her news to anyone, without first informing her husband, but she had little desire to do so in writing. She wished to witness his expression, to watch as emotion overcame him, to guess his thoughts while his stone gaze absorbed her every change, cataloguing the little signs. *That* was what she wished for, yet how could she continue to keep this secret, all the while wondering if she should travel for Jane's wedding. At the same time, how could she miss her beloved sister's special day?

Thumping her pillow, Elizabeth shuffled around until she was hugging the soft cushion, a hopeless attempt to feel as if she was not alone in her bed, as questions and doubts swirled apace.

◆ ◆ ◆

Darcy read his wife's letter, a smile of heartfelt affection, gracing his hard features, unknowingly affecting the two ladies absorbed in watching his every movement. Elizabeth's words related Bingley's successful courtship and plans to wed this coming June, and yet his joy stemmed more from the phrasing his wife used, her radiant happiness flowing from the page as if she was before him that very moment. Instead, he sat with his host at the breakfast table, while his wife and daughter joined them. His work in the textile mills, those he not only had large shares in, but who were supplied by the wool from his estate, had kept him busily engaged during the better part of the day, but there was still little progress made in settling the disgruntlement arising from the smallholders whose livelihood were impacted by the production from the mills.

Folding his letter away, Darcy looked to his host's wife as she queried, "You seem well pleased with your news, is it impertinent of me to enquire?"

Hiding his frown, Darcy politely replied, "Of course, tis merely pleasant tidings from home, and a happy conclusion to a friend's hopes. I must thank you for permitting me no delay in discovering such news."

Marianne Harding, the daughter of Marcus Harding, his host, coyly answered in place of her mother, "Why Mr Darcy, you tease us with such modest responses! You must share what brought such felicity!"

Mr Harding's daughter had been a pervasive nuisance during near enough every breakfast and dinner he shared with the family, thankful for the occupation that kept him from the house throughout the day. He could not see the purpose of such flirtations when his host was entirely aware he was wed, yet no matter how forward the girl was, Mr Harding raised no objection to his daughter's behaviour.

Ignoring the flutter of the blond girl's lashes, Darcy replied, "Forgive me, I meant no such thing, yet I fear there would be little interest in discussion of those unknown to my present company." Turning to Mr Harding, Darcy stated, "If you will pardon me but a half hour, I will be free to join you."

And with that, Darcy excused himself

from the table and retreated to his quarters. Immediately he made his way to his lap-desk and settled in to reply to Elizabeth to share in her pleasure about his friend and her sister. The emptiness could not be assuaged by such paltry communication, not when he longed to have been present as she read of her sister's joy. However, there was still issues to be resolved, and so it was necessary he stay, regardless of his own heart's desire.

Two weeks later, and Darcy breathed a sigh of relief as his carriage wheels rumbled over the road home. He could finally turn his back on the Hardings, the mother-daughter duo had been especially irritating with their determined efforts to ingratiate themselves, a scarcity of encouragement had affected the ladies' enthusiasm not at all. His rigid control relaxed with his escape from his hosts, and Darcy slumped heavily into the squabs of his travel coach. His valet, Kirk seated opposite, said nothing, simply keeping his eyes fixed on the passing city streets.

York was a beautiful place, full of history and industry in equal measure. In other times, Darcy would have relished exploring the streets, Elizabeth at his side, but for now, he must content himself with his return, for in two days time, he would do away with letters, and have her in his embrace as soon as may be. His ache to be in her company had grown from an ever-present itch to a desperation that bordered on obsession.

"It has been a long three weeks, Kirk." Darcy sighed, as he too, kept his gaze upon the city streets.

"Indeed, Sir. I believe we will all breathe a sigh of relief once Pemberley is in our sights." Kirk concurred, a lengthy pause, then hesitantly continued, "If you'll pardon my saying, Sir, but I would advise not residing in the Harding household without Mrs Darcy in the future."

Sitting up, Darcy studied his valet, noting the small signs of tension Kirk struggled to conceal.

His careful "Oh?" was enough for Kirk to continue, mindful of the iron hidden in his master's careful prompt.

"I mean no insult to Mr Harding, but I doubt very much he would have any compunction with his daughter causing a 'difficult situation', in the hopes of some pecuniary compensation."

Kirk kept his hands locked together on his lap, unable to look his master in the face, but duty, obligation and loyalty compelled him to speak.

Quietly, Darcy acknowledged his valet's intelligence, "Very good, Kirk. I shall ensure no such occurence has opportunity to come about." The intelligence cast a light upon the ladies

Harding, and Darcy grimly considered breaking all business ties with Marcus Harding and his loathsome character. The matter would require introspection before he decided upon a course of action.

The carriage returned to quiet, the only sound the horses as they pounded the earth with their iron hooves, and the rumble of the wheels as each revolution brought him ever closer to his purpose. With almost a guilty start, Darcy realised he had spared very little thought for his sister in some time, yet the very next moment he assured himself that was only natural, now that Georgiana possessed a loving pair of sisters to oversee her welfare in his absence.

Nearing midday two days later, Pemberley rolled into view, and before he knew it, he was exiting his coach, tired of the sight of its confined walls and striding impatiently up the steps of his beloved home. Surprised to see no greeting from his loved ones, Darcy felt the first stirrings of concern, as not even his butler, Croft, was in attendance. Pacing across the foyer, Darcy listened for voices, unnerved by the waves of tension he felt without knowing its cause. Heading directly to his wife's favoured room in the house, Darcy reached the library without meeting any footmen, maids or even Mrs Reynolds.

Instead, he entered the room, to witness

a scene straight from a nightmare. Elizabeth slumped upon the floor, his servants attending to her, while Georgiana sat sobbing, Mrs Annesley standing at her side, her worry evident in her bearing. Mary kneeled at her sister's head, talking quietly to Mrs Reynolds. Croft was moving to the door, and so it was he, who announced Darcy's presence. At the sound of his name, the room erupted in noise, none of which Darcy paid the least of attention, ignoring his servants, his sister, striding immediately to Elizabeth's side, kneeling by her, while he barked his questions.

"What has happened here Mrs Reynolds?" When that good lady could not find the words to reply, he sent his gaze about the room, leaving Mary until last, when sense reasoned, she would know more.

"Forgive me, Sir, for not greeting you, but Lizzy has fainted on receiving ill news from Longbourne." Here Mary said no more, returning her attention to her sister, who was just slowly coming awake, "Lizzy!"

At this sight, Darcy surged forward, his heart soaring to see her eyes open, searching the room until they fell upon him.

"Fitzwilliam! You're home!" His heart could not help but beat violently in his chest, her pleasure in sighting him unfeigned, the greatest gift she had given him to date. Dropping forward, Darcy bestowed a kiss upon her, heedless of the company surrounding them. He felt her arms come around him and hold him close, and pulling back, he rested his head upon hers, as gradually his heart and breathing slowed from its terrible panic. A moment later, Darcy rose, scooping Elizabeth's small frame up confidently in his arms.

"Mrs Reynolds, summon Mrs Darcy's maid to attend her in her chambers, Croft, call for the physician. Mary, please follow and explain what has occurred that overset my wife." Without waiting for anyone else to interrupt, Darcy strode from the room and made his way up the steps to the first floor. The comforting feel of Elizabeth in his arms had not entirely dismissed his own horror in witnessing his wife near lifeless on the floor of the library. Squeezing her closer, Elizabeth murmured a protest, to which he eased his grip only slightly.

So quietly, he almost did not hear, Elizabeth whispered, "Oh Fitzwilliam, I am so glad you are home."

"I thank you. I am immensely grateful to have arrived in time to be of service to you!" He fervently whispered back, kissing her brow in desperate thanks to have her in his arms, but the uneasiness did not dissipate, not knowing what had caused such distress in his wife. Reaching their apartments, Darcy strode into the mistresses room, gently depositing Elizabeth upon her bed, to which she quickly refuted his retreat.

Thankfully, Mary entered just behind him and silenced her sister, "Hush Lizzy. Allow your maid to see to your comfort, and I shall relate all to your husband." In Mary's hand was a sheet, folded, which she waved at Elizabeth. The sight of the page had his wife paling, raising a hand to her mouth in distress, before she was quickly bolting across to the chamber pot, casting up her accounts in wretched affliction. Moving to her side, Darcy held her by her shoulders, murmuring soothing nonsense, thanking her sister as she offered a damp cloth upon which to aid Elizabeth cool her cheeks and head. As Elizabeth moved to walk to her bed, Darcy once more scooped her into his arms and laid her carefully upon the sheets.

"Mary, I fear to discover what has caused such misery in Elizabeth, and my mind has leapt to various conclusions. Please-," Darcy did not turn away from his wife, stroking the cloth over her pale skin, as her dark eyelashes kissed her cheeks like bruises, silent tears slipping from her eyes, "please, what has occurred?"

He could not hear the worry and strain in his voice, but his wife and sister did, both affected by his obvious agitation.

"I cannot think of how...of what you will think...yet, I fear, I am not... Forgive me Sir, but to put it plainly, our youngest sister has eloped with an officer in the militia, a man by the name of Wickham. Yet the truth is, that while our sister believes herself to have eloped, all signs suggest that this is not the case, and that instead the pair have hidden themselves in London."

His wife, his dearest, cherished Elizabeth crumpled, "I cannot believe I left my sister so unprotected! I, that knew him to be untrustworthy! How can I have been so selfish as to neglect my impressionable sister in favour of my own comfort?"

"Elizabeth, shush, say nothing of the sort. These many months you have made every effort to find a way to help your sister! You could not know, could not have foreseen this. Tis not in your nature to be suspicious." Soothingly, Darcy wiped away her tears, while inside his heart felt pierced with shame and contempt. Turning to Mary, he asked, "What has been done to retrieve Miss Lydia?"

Ice chilled his blood as he listened to Mary read aloud the letter, and determination arose, his intentions bluntly shunting other matters aside. Bestowing one final kiss upon Elizabeth, he whispered, "All will be well, my love. I will ensure it is so."

And then he left his wife's rooms, calling for Croft, Kirk and Wilson to meet him in his study. An hour later, several expresses dispatched, instructions left for both his wife and housekeeper, fresh horses hitched, Darcy made his way south, accompanied by Kirk, determined to prevent Wickham from obliging himself upon his family anew.

CHAPTER 16

Darcy House, London May 7th

A nxiety pulsed deep in his chest, self recriminations running rampant, shame twisted up with fury, stealing the joy that had been at his very fingertips. Now, he was left with ashes, raining down upon him in a mockery of petals blessing a new union, only this time, he was sure it was the ruination of his own.

"Darcy! Whyever are you holed up in here on your own? Where is that delightful wife of yours and Georgiana? I must say, I've certainly seen a change in the dear girl's spirits since she has returned to Pemberley your wife and sister as steady company! Darce? Good god, man, you look ill! Whatever is the matter?!"

"Tis all in ruins Richard. Wickham has finally succeeding in stealing it all." The apathetic reply was given from his slouched position, staring into the weak fire, glass half-full of brandy set beside him.

"Wickham!" Spat his cousin, taking the seat paired with his own, "What has that low-life cretin done now? I know it cannot be Georgiana, I had a letter but the other week from her, and all was well then!"

Darcy could not find the attention or energy to spare in reassuring his cousin, too lost to his own reflections of the past wretched week that had sunk him to such a state.

His arrival to town had been accomplished in near two and a half days, and the period spent travelling south had provided opportunity aplenty to plan and fret in equal measure. The letters he had sent, one to his London housekeeper, one to Mr Gardiner, the last to the investigator used on previous occasions. Having done as much as could be accomplished from a distance, all that was left was to count the hours until actions could follow the plans made. He would do anything to ease his Elizabeth's pain.

*How the dear girl could imagine she was at fault was nonsensical, for assuredly, **he** held more responsibility for allowing the scoundrel free to ruin other poor creatures, so easily preyed upon by the excessive use of his charm! Yet his fear for Georgiana had made him blind to ought else, when it should have sharpened it, should have put that fear to more use than senselessly fretting over the potential future damage! Damn it! Why had Darcy allowed fear to override his sense?*

Darcy worked in his study, as he sent notes relaying his arrival, and his intention to call upon the Gardiner's and replying an acceptance to the note from the investigator, Simpson, who would call first thing tomorrow. Time had crawled, conversations had seemed tedious and pedantic, but Darcy maintained his composure, even if inside, a seething hatred burned, an intense loathing for the waste of a human that was Wickham. And himself. His silence.

Mrs Gardiner graciously received him when he called, despite the trials having wore upon her equanimity, the elegant lady was everything mannerly. "There has been little to no success, no word of them, no hints as to their location has reached my husband or my brother, Bennet. The gentleman retired to his estate when his health suffered from the stress of fruitless searches, and so the bulk of the task has fallen to my husband, using whatever means at his disposal. Yet, I must confess, I worry. Too much time has passed."

Mrs Gardiner wiped away the small tear that escaped, and Darcy gave her a moment to compose herself. Shame swamped him, and he struggled not to hang his head, to confess and unburden himself from the ever present guilt!

"If you will permit, I have some avenues I would wish to explore, in the hopes I can discover the pair's whereabouts." Mrs Gardiner's look of hope was as a blade to him, "I make no assurances of my success, but having a history with that faithless

jade- my apologies, I hope to make headway."

Darcy cannot recollect how long he remained, a few minutes at best, and then he was back in his blasted carriage, the rumble of wheels against cobblestone, a clatter of noise pounding against his head.

Then came his morning meeting with Simpson, who having been informed of the subject upon whom the search related, had already made preliminary progress.

"It appears, Mr Darcy, as if Mr Wickham was noted arriving at his former compatriot's residence, a Mrs Young?" At his nod, Simpson continued, "The pair, a young lady, and this individual were seen arriving, unfortunately there has been no signs since. Neither leaving, nor returning. One must presume that this Mr Wickham had gained some intelligence that encouraged him to depart from Mrs Young's property with the utmost discretion."

"Have you called upon Mrs Young? Spoken to the woman directly?" Darcy queried, cool voice, masking the roiling thoughts burning in him.

"I have not, Sir. I felt, it would have been precipitous to do so, without prior agreement."

Nodding, Darcy stared at his clear desk a moment, thinking carefully of his next steps. "Very well, I shall make my way to the address, and speak with Mrs Young myself. She may well yield more information were it to come from me directly. However, continue the searches in those gaming hells Wickham has haunted in the past."

Simpson agreed, and left, while Darcy summoned Nevins to order a hack, not wishing his personal equipage to be recognised in so conspicuous an area. Wickham already wanted his attention, else he would not have conducted this scheme to harm his wife's family. Tension thrummed beneath his skin, doubts surfaced and were dismissed, a furious storm of plans and contingency plans revolved endlessly. For he was determined to find Wickham, but what would happen after would all depend upon what Lydia Bennet wished. And for that to happen, he needed to find her!

The questioning of Mrs Young was done with anger tempering every word, laced in his every expression, such that the woman could not help but to be afeared. She related that, yes, Wickham and a young spirited girl had visited, but that they did not remain above a day, before their room was empty, and had departed without paying for their room and board. Frustrated with another dead end, Darcy returned home, a mass of emotions with no safe outlet, dangerous and short-tempered. It took little persuasion from Kirk to see the wisdom in expunging some of the violent energy within the confines of Gentleman Jackson's club.

Hours later, spent and exhausted, his demons quiet for the moment, Darcy returned home, only to discover a note waiting for him. Recognising it immediately, he read the words taunting him to a meeting that evening, and with a hurried wash and change, Darcy departed, not even pausing to partake of a quick meal.

The location was dreadful. A hole in the wall public house catering to those seamen on shore-leave. Sighting his quarry, Darcy ignored the looks, the threat of danger, for in his present state of mind, Darcy exuded his own menacing aura. Sighting Wickham brought to mind Elizabeth's tears, Elizabeth collapsed, her grieving sickness. Teeth gritted, he took a seat, confident the footman stood at his back, attired discreetly, would alert him of any trouble. Dressed in his own workwear, there was nothing to indicate his wealth or status, other than the polished manners and his immaculate diction. Ignoring Wickham's sneer, he growled his own greeting, "Wickham! So kind of you to extend an invitation!"

The murmurs of conversations filled the smoky room, providing them an illusion of privacy. "How good of you to grace us with your presence, Darcy!" Wickham contemptuously spat.

Unwilling to waste further time, Darcy demanded, "Where is Lydia Bennet?"

The dark bark of laughter Wickham gave disturbed Darcy immensely, "Yes, that was a little bit of unfortunate impetuousity. But, come, come, Darcy, share a drink with me, before we ruin the night with such unpleasant business."

"No!" growled Darcy, "I want nothing but the whereabouts of the girl. Save your lies and your scheming! Where. Is. She?"

For the first time that evening, Darcy noted

Wickham's pallor. His unsteady hands that thunked his tankard down heavily. A tendril of dread began to twine itself about his chest.

"I shall happily disclose the chit's bearing, all I ask for is some little compensation...some small payment in lieu of you playing the hero...that's not much to ask, is it? You would not want your little wife to suffer the shame of a ruined sister, what will Mrs Darcy say when your stiff pride got in the way of rescuing her beloved Lydia? Hmm?" The scorn and jealousy Wickham usually spewed was suspiciously absent, but the nasty taunts were unchanged.

"You shall not receive one red shilling, you cur. A wastrel like you would only see it as incentive to keep coming back for more, like the mangy dog that you are! Now, I shall not ask again." His fists clenched in fury, sore from their earlier abuse, yet blood roared in his ears, screaming for vengeance.

Like the uncouth lout that he was, Wickham wiped his mouth against his sleeve after draining his tankard dry. His eyes shifted about the room, never settling on one person for too long, but doing everything possible to not catch Darcy's. Stronger, and stronger, the impulse, the dread, thickened, he could almost taste it.

"I doubt your father would take kindly to such treatment, Darcy. You should be ashamed for treating your father's godson so poorly!"

Ignoring the oft-repeated babble, Darcy stood, disinclined to waste further time in the mongrel's company. Throwing a coin on the table,

Darcy had one last parting shot, assured Wickham's location could be easily tracked now that Simpson had him in his sights, the investigator having arrived while the man bargained for coin.

"You have until midday tomorrow to present Lydia Bennet, else you will find yourself in much darker straits than you are currently."

His footman at his back, Darcy negotiated his way clear of the hovel, for once eager to reach the confines of his coach. With a clack of the reins, the carriage moved off, but Darcy could not escape the fear something was terribly wrong.

"Darce?" His cousin booted his foot, nudging him free of the revulsion the memory of his dealings with Wickham gave him. "Tell me what ails you! I have had enough of staring at your face willing you to empty your budget!"

Grimacing, Darcy explained what Wickham had accomplished while in the militia in Meryton.

"So? If you have found the devil, are having him followed, what prevents you from forcing him to marry the girl?" Richard asked, his confusion an irritant to his boiling self-loathing.

"Because," Darcy uttered through gritted teeth, "Lydia Bennet is dead."

He watched the colour drain from his cousin, who then took a hurried gulp of the brandy he had helped himself to.

"Bloody hell!" Richard's glass hit the table

at his side with a heavy thunk, empty of its contents, "What...? How...?"

The self-loathing was not going to diminish, and so knowing this would not be the first, nor the last time he would relate events, Darcy scrubbed his face. "I have nothing but a scribbled note, not even her body to take home, just that worthless bastard's words!"

He dug the note from his jacket pocket, its crumpled state attesting to how poorly Darcy had received the news.

Darcy

You would not indulge me when you deigned to meet me at my request, so I shall not scruple to inform you of the demise of Miss Lydia Bennet.

There was nothing havey cavey about what happened, merely a case of over-indulgence leading to even higher spirits than the normally boisterous girl possessed. As such, when the stupid chit decided to dance a jig, she was not sensible to her precarious state. Her bouncing and jumping around came to an inglorious end when Lydia slipped and fell.

I must admit I still cannot drown out the sound of that awful crack her head made when it impacted the corner of the fireplace. There was no time to call for a doctor, the girl was dead almost instantly.

Mrs Young helped settle the matter of burying the girl, so I cannot even help you in this, for I do not know where Lydia Bennet rests.

I leave it to you to inform the family, and I feel somewhat revenged upon you, for knowing that you will be the one to carry such tidings to your wife's family.

For how could they not hate you, for failing to warn them.

Curse you, Darcy.

W

"The putrid stain upon man-kind! How I dearly wish I could lay my hands upon him! You cannot let him escape his dues any longer, Darce! For I sw-"

Darcy raised his hand to silence his cousin, "Wickham currently resides within Marshalsea, where he shall remain, for you are aright, and so too was he, he has finally revenged himself upon me."

The next two days were dark with his overwhelming guilt and grief. Mrs Young had been dragged from her home by Simpson, the lies she had uttered forcing Darcy to act upon the quiet threat he had left her with. The theft of some of Georgiana's jewellery had been his ace up his sleeve; once Mrs Young could see her old employer was in deadly earnest, the lying creature revealed where Lydia Bennet had been interred. He had thought himself angry before, but the sight of the pauper's grave his wife's sister rested in had made him ill. As ill as Elizabeth had been.

Yet Darcy would not rest until everything had been set to rights, and so here he sat, travelling once again, but this time to Longbourne, his carriage leading the grim journey home for Lydia Bennet. Of course his passage through Meryton drew far too much attention, but with the curtains drawn, none knew just who escorted the casket onward. Thankfully, his coachman signalled for the wagon to be directed directly to Longbourne church. But now came the rehearsal of how he would inform his wife, with the upcoming morbid conversation with Mr Bennet.

"Mr Darcy, is Elizabeth not with you?" Mr Bennet looked a decade older than he had when they first met. The stress and strain leaving a physical mark upon the elder's features and posture.

"No, Sir. My wife remains at Pemberley." How was he to broach the topic?

"I am saddened she would not come to support her sister and mother during our time of need. Tis most unlike her." Darcy could not say he was not relieved Elizabeth was safely tucked away at their estate. It delayed the inevitable moment that would break the cornerstone they had begun to build together.

"Elizabeth allowed me to act on her behalf, and so quite rightly, has not descended upon Longbourne in anticipation of a quick resolution." His lips felt stubborn and unyielding, unwilling to open the painful topic.

Mr Bennet's humph was the precursor to silence that lasted as both men struggled with their own thoughts. Eventually, Darcy's conscience shouted loud enough to push him into speaking.

"Forgive me, Mr Bennet for being the one to relate everything to you, but I could not stand back and do nothing when I felt the burden of guilt command I work to recover your lost daughter. Unfortunately, while I was in London, I was swiftly able to locate the reprobate... I am grieved to tell you... Sir... Mr Bennet, I am grieved to inform you of Lydia's passing while she was in the company, of Mr Wickham."

CHAPTER 17

Pemberley, Derbyshire May 20th

Her husband had been away for near three weeks in London, six, if she were to account for his time in York, leaving Elizabeth torn between elation at his expected return tomorrow, indignation at his lack of correspondence, worry over the fate of her sister, and most pressing of all, the desire to share her growing secret. Her body had hardly shifted, despite being somewhat into her fifth month, and only her maid was aware of her expectations, for unclothed her condition was apparent. Trent had solemnly sworn to share nothing until Fitzwilliam was home, and he would be the first to hear, but the burden of her secret was heavy. Compounded by the stress and fear for Lydia, Elizabeth had barely managed to rest, only succumbing once Trent roundly scolded her for putting her baby's welfare in jeopardy.

"Mary, how do you get on with that latest piece you are practicing?"

Life had continued on as usual once the furore of her fainting had settled. While Elizabeth was sure some speculation had arisen as to the cause, the physician was a gentleman who prescribed to the nonsense of bleeding and purging. Once he realised Elizabeth would tolerate nothing of the sort, Dr Blake had left citing his assurity he would take no responsibility for the lady of the house's continuing failing health. Hah. Elizabeth had recovered apace, her disposition such that melancholy would not be permitted to overshadow everything.

"I find the piece particularly troubling, Lizzy. Georgie often tells me to connect with the music, to find my own rhythm, and yet, no matter how hard I try, I cannot accomplish more than pressing the keys in the right order, with a dearth of *feeling*."

Elizabeth, curled up in the library, her book open in her lap as her feet were tucked beneath her, thought on her sister's problem. "I fear, sister, you are complicating the matter," She ignored Mary's dark glower, "If you feel confused, then you are *feeling* something. Have you considered pausing between notes, to show your own struggle, the hesitation and doubt. Mayhap press harder upon the pedal when you feel frustrated, speed up and slow down to express your difficulty. I believe you have come to know the piece in that you recall the order of the notes, but now it is time to look inside as you play, and express all the struggles you are experiencing."

Mary's glower disappeared as Elizabeth spoke, her gaze losing focus as she turned inward with her thoughts. "Very well, if you shall excuse me, I shall attempt to put your suggestion into practice while the advice is fresh in my mind."

Once Mary departed, Elizabeth could not lose herself to her own dark musings, for Georgiana's expression had caught her attention. Mrs Annesley sat beside the dear girl, guiding some of her stitches, but her charge had completely ceased paying attention.

"Georgie?"

"Hmm?" Her sister, whose quiet, shy demeanour had seen a significant change, her confidence having grown considerably, seemed much as Elizabeth first recalled, "You must forgive me, but I have just realised something rather difficult to resolve... For you see, I cannot help but think I have been terribly naïve about what having sisters really means."

Listening, Elizabeth's confusion grew, "Whatever can you mean?"

Restlessly, Georgiana set aside her sewing, "I have shared how much I have longed for a sister, and despite my foolishness causing you such difficulties, you have been everything and more that I would wish for. Yet it is in seeing you with Mary, that I realise how selfish my desires were. I longed for someone to keep *me* company, to be *my* confidant, *my* likes and *my* interests! But you! You do not think of Mary as *your* entertainment, someone to share all the things you do. Lizzy, it is blindingly obvious that I have been a selfish and prideful creature, little thinking of others and their concerns outside my own circle! Especially now!"

Georgiana dissolved into tears, and Elizabeth looked helplessly between the miserable girl and Mrs Annesley. Whatever had brought this on? How could one small exchange between Mary and herself, much like many others, cause such heartache? Elizabeth would have moved to sit beside her sister, but the girl leapt from her seat, pacing in agitation before the fireplace.

"The arrogance! The conceit! To see you struggle and take your approbation, knowing full well that *I* am at fault for allowing that...that...miscreant! To impose himself upon me, but to beg my brother for leniency! How can you bare to suffer my presence when your youngest sister has suffered!"

Rising from her seat, having pieced together enough to understand Georgiana's disturbance, Elizabeth took the girl by the arm and led her to the settee, seating herself beside her. "Georgie, do you mean to tell me, that Lieutenant Wickham attempted an intrigue with you?" Georgiana's words were swallowed by the sobs that escaped, and Elizabeth soothed her as best as she could, wrapping her arms around her shoulders, offering her a handkerchief, stroking her back in slow circles. When she felt the girl nod, Elizabeth continued, "Then, may I presume he was unsuccessful, or was there an intervention of one sort or another?"

Mrs Annesley moved to explain, knowing enough to relate the facts as she knew them, "I believe there was some conspiracy with Miss Darcy's former companion and the...ahem, gentleman, in question, to encourage an elopement that would allow those...*people* access to Miss Darcy's dowry. I believe Mr Darcy was able to prevent any mischief by his abrupt arrival, and as such, sent the two away. However, Miss Darcy's spirits were not so easily restored."

While understanding came easily, compassion readily given, it felt tarnished with bitterness. Both her husband and Miss Darcy had known what kind of man Wickham was, and to this, they felt no compunction against remaining silent.

"So his character has ever been thus?" Elizabeth dully enquired.

Georgiana pulled herself together, "No, the boy I knew, the George I remember, was ever kind to me. That is what made it all seem so innocent, for George was so warm and generous in his speech and demeanour. He is terribly charming!"

Elizabeth could not agree, "When I met the man, I felt he sounded rather petulant, complaining about a living he was owed, despite having never taken orders. Yet I must grant you the greater knowledge for your long-standing history." Elizabeth felt a flutter in her belly, and it took effort to not gasp and clutch her bump in wonder. The movement reminded her of what truly mattered, "While I can understand your hesitance in disclosing what occurred, I cannot help but to think *some* good could have come from warning the neighbourhood to be on their guard. But, Georgie, this is no need to castigate yourself so severely for protecting your reputation. I can well comprehend your reasoning." Taking the young girl by the chin, Elizabeth used the cloth to wipe the girl's tear-stained cheeks, "Now, I fear you would like some time to yourself, so I shall venture out for a walk around the hedge garden." Elizabeth dropped a kiss on Georgiana's brow, and took herself off.

Garbed in a light shawl, and her half boots, Elizabeth considered everything she knew and feared, relating to Mr Wickham. His upbringing provided him with all the advantages of a gentleman, and yet rather than profit from such an education, the villain appeared to scorn not being bestowed with more upon his godfather's death. Retaliation, both for preventing Wickham gaining possession of Georgiana's dowry, and the loss of the living; the motivation behind his elopement with Lydia, a tool in his plans to hurt her husband. Her poor, bright and impressionable little sister! The reasoning, the comprehension behind the man's schemes only served to heighten her anger towards Wickham, yet there was a sliver of fury pointed upon the Darcy's. However, no good would come of casting blame, for the past was done, and the future was not yet written. Fitzwilliam had been working without cease to find her sister, to restore Lydia to her family. Yes she had been left here to worry, knowing nothing, hearing only second hand reports from her aunt and Jane. Nothing. No trace. And every day Elizabeth continued on, Lydia's fate unknown, her sister in the hands of a manipulative, deceitful, worthless man.

Mary joined her restless pacing, her expression blank, while her deep blue gaze conveyed her own sorrow.

"Back to feeling guilty, again?" she asked.

With a snort, Elizabeth shook her head, "Of course. It seems I can only go so long until the pitiable thoughts renew their efforts in making me miserable."

Mary said nothing, merely keeping Elizabeth company, for this agitated state had oft repeated since the day Fitzwilliam left for London.

"Georgie seemed overset when I went to

check on her."

Elizabeth answered the question Mary did not ask, "She is merely accustoming herself to discovering her own flaws. I am sure it shall pass soon enough, and Georgie will be much as she ever is."

"I gather then, that you are disinclined to aid Georgie in her adjustment?"

With a deep sigh, she explained something of what had been shared in the library.

"So, now, not only do you attempt to overcome your own guilt, but must apportion some responsibility to two whom you have come to care for."

"Yes, just so."

The sisters said no more, merely sharing a quiet bond that was more than eloquent in the silence. A heartache that had only grown as each day passed.

"What did Kitty say in her latest letter?" Elizabeth finally asked, their steps turning them back to the side door.

"She is relieved to not be called home and spoke earnestly of her appreciation for the Thompson's, and their unstinting kindness to her. Mr Thompson has even gone so far to as to state unequivocally that Kitty is welcome to remain for as long as she so chooses, to protect her from any spite and gossip arising in Meryton."

Nodding, "Uncle Thompson is just such a

gentleman, I am assured of Kitty's welfare under his guardianship."

"What of Jane?" Mary asked pointedly.

Elizabeth smiled distractedly at Croft as they passed in the foyer, making their way upstairs to freshen up for dinner. Elizabeth had requested the family refrain from changing into evening wear, until everything involving Lydia was resolved, therefore the sisters retired to her sitting room.

"Jane? There has been little change excepting Mr Bingley's assurances that he will not renege on their engagement. Otherwise, mother is as she ever was, overly dramatic, requiring every bit of Jane's goodness and fortitude in settling her. There was some request for us to travel and help support our family, in this most trying time, but I confess, I fear I am unequal to the undertaking."

"Yet another thing you place guilt upon your shoulders for. Neither you nor I would serve to calm our mother. Mrs Bennet ever declaimed my use, and she would merely abuse you, were you to be in company. No, as much as I dislike laying such burdens upon our gentle sister, Jane, next to Lydia, is the only daughter who would please Mrs Bennet."

Both sisters settled quietly to their sewing, Elizabeth to her embroidery, and Mary to her mending. The silence hung comfortably between the ladies, a restorative of familiar comfort.

Elizabeth tugged her shawl tighter about her, feeling the brisk May winds tugging at her clothes and hair. The carriage had been sighted, and Elizabeth watched as the horses clambered down the drive, until at last, the wheels were halted before the portico, footmen rushing to unload the carriage, while grooms steadied the horses. A footman moved forth to lower the step and open the door, all the while tension strummed, like a piano key held too long.

Then he was there, standing before her, and Elizabeth balanced between relief and anger, love and resentment. His cool grey eyes captured hers, and Elizabeth felt a coil of tension wind around her, the sentiment there gave her pause.

Softly she welcomed him home, her gaze tracking the marks of his fatigue and strain, all on behalf of her family, yet its cause was a creature of *his* family's making. The tug and pull continued to beat against her chest. Unwilling to be churlish, to mistake the signs of weariness, Elizabeth permitted Georgiana to welcome her brother home, her mood still subdued from yesterday's disclosures, and then she was sending Fitzwilliam to refresh himself, promising to have tea waiting in their sitting room when he was ready.

It was only as he thanked her with a kiss to her brow and walked past her to take the stairs, that Elizabeth stared at his sleeve in horror.

The sight of the black armband almost had her chasing after him, but their sisters needed to be advised of allowing her husband to take his leisure, now that he was finally home.

◆ ◆ ◆

How long could he hide in his rooms? Bile coated the back of his throat, and nausea bubbled in his gut. Was it even honourable to delay, when he had patently failed to uphold his promises? His fear of rejection was no pardon to his cowardice! Darcy had never felt himself to be such until now, confidence in his own conduct, his pride well-regulated and the dignity he upheld with the family name. No, Darcy had never realised how devastating it was to be the one to deliver terrible news. To be the one to witness their shock, crumpling in on themselves as they valiantly fought to keep their composure, watching as silent tears tracked across cheeks, as grief consumed the eyes. It had hurt to deliver the news to his father by marriage, to then stand by and watch as the man moved bravely forward, speaking to his wife and daughter. Silent and forbidding, he had watched grief overwrite their every belief, and all the while he stood vigil. He had made the gentleman no promises, but he still felt all the wretched guilt of an oath-breaker.

Unwilling to delay further, Darcy entered the sitting room he shared with Elizabeth, sighting her gazing out the window, tucked up in the seat, haloed by the clear sunshine streaming in. She stole his breath. Her beauty, her pleasing figure and the light and graceful way she moved. A hypnotic dance regardless of what occupied her. He swallowed thickly, desire and guilt a terrible admixture. He must have made some noise, for she turned to face him, gifting him with a careful look, before she strode across to the bell-pull. Then she faced him, silence so sharp it cut deep.

"I have missed you, so very much Elizabeth." Darcy had not meant to begin in such a way, but he was glad for it when he saw the marginal softening in his wife.

Tea arrived promptly, in addition to a cold collation to satiate his appetite, for he had not felt equal to partaking of the fare provided by the inn this morning. Elizabeth remained silent throughout serving tea, fixing him a plate, setting it all before him, only to sit back and pick up her sewing, allowing him grace to eat without interruption. When he finally pushed his plate away, having forced himself to eat, Darcy almost regretted doing so when he saw Elizabeth's gaze fixed upon the black band about his arm. He fought the rising gorge, and began his horrific news, for the third, and perhaps most significant time.

"I cannot apologise enough for failing to write, my only excuse, that of wishing to be in a position to relate *something*, and yet I imagine that is hollow comfort." Darcy shifted to sit beside his wife, taking up her hand in his own, desperate to rebuild the tenuous bond he feared would be torn asunder at the next words he had to impart, "There is no easy way to inform you, I assure you, for having done so twice before, it is just as difficult as the first-"

"Who?" Elizabeth whispered, her hand chilled in his own.

Closing his eyes, he breathed, "Lydia-"

Ripping her hand free of his, Elizabeth stormed away from him, "No!" Her hand slashed through the air, but he saw in her eyes, those golden toffee coloured eyes, that the truth had burned itself through her denial, "No!" The sobs came next. Silent, wrenching, breath stealing tears, as she crumpled to the floor, defeated. "No!" Elizabeth continued to cry, as her hands covered her mouth, and Darcy could remain away from her no longer. With one stride, he bent and scooped her into his arms, holding her close and her weeping became muffled by his cravat, her face buried against his neck. Body wracking grief consumed his wife, and Darcy was helpless, to do ought but offer such weak comfort as his embrace. He wasted no words on encouraging her to cease, knowing all too well the need to purge the agony of unexpected heartbreak and pain. The lament in loss, an age-old symphony, and one he was too closely familiar with.

Her sobs quieted, her body lax in his arms, her spirit screaming despair. He pulled a handkerchief from his pocket with a little shuffle, cursing himself for failing to offer it sooner. Elizabeth took the white cotton, wiping her eyes that looked dull, absent its familiar glow.

"How? W-Why?" Then with a small fist, Elizabeth beat against his chest, "You never wrote! How could you leave me in suspense? Desperate for news, even if just to know you were well!"

"I have no excuse other than not wishing to deliver such tidings indirectly, to not be here for you would have been cowardly of me. I could not leave you to suffer, without wishing to provide comfort whenever you had need of me." Thumping his head back, Darcy pulled in a breath, before letting it gust out, then tipping forwards once more, he explained the circumstances of Lydia's demise. Her tears began anew, quieter than before, but no less grievous.

"I cannot beg your forgiveness enough, Elizabeth, for I am the reason for Wickham's perfidy. If not for his hatred of me, your sister would still be with us."

Elizabeth's hand came up to stem the flow of words, her plea for peace easily granted. The quiet grew teeth, biting into Darcy for his paltry appeal for absolution a selfish desire. His love for Elizabeth cried a demand to be shared, to lay his heart before her, to feel the soothing elixir of her forgiveness that would banish the wretched guilt that stalked him every day, every night.

With a start, Elizabeth tried to pull herself from his arms, and he was reluctant to comply until she cried, "Mary! My sister should hear this from me!" Having stood, once free of his arms, Elizabeth hurried away to the door, before turning back and saying, "Please, I doubt we will be down for dinner tonight, may I ask that you inform your sister? Mrs Annesley and Mrs Reynolds also. If you excuse me, I will go to my sister."

An instant later, his wife was gone, leaving his arms empty and his heart aching in abject misery. Damn Wickham to hell. He had successfully revenged himself upon Darcy at long last.

CHAPTER 18

Pemberley, Derbyshire May 24th

Elizabeth remembered little of the past two days, insensible to everything as she moved from place to place, the motions of routine unable to break through that invisible wall of grief. However, that morning, the rolls, fluttering and most likely wriggles of her baby had Elizabeth snapping up in bed, banishing the depressed fog hovering over her. She could not afford to be so selfish as to forget the life she was growing! Soothing the small bump beneath her nightdress, a glorious smile broke over her as the sun breaks through the clouds, a small trill of laughter escaping at the burst of joy she experienced. When Trent answered her summons, the relief her maid felt was evident when she witnessed Elizabeth's clear gaze and concise instructions. The first of her black-dyed gowns were laid out, and Elizabeth readied for the day with grim focus.

Mary had taken the news of their sister's passing quietly, her sorrow solemn. Both ladies had spent that first day together, but following, Elizabeth cannot recollect how Mary spent her time.

"Mrs Darcy?"

"Yes Trent?" Elizabeth collected her shawl, somewhat distracted.

"Shall you be wishing to make an appointment with the modiste in Lambton?"

Elizabeth turned to face her, detecting something in Trent's tone. Her lips turned up in a half-smile at the sight of her maid's huffy expression.

"If you'll pardon my saying, Mrs Darcy, but considering your current wardrobe will soon be...insufficient, I thought you may wish to consider having some more accommodating dresses made up."

The light of comprehension struck, "Of course, Trent. That makes perfect sense. I shall see about sending a note, for I believe my sister and I could both do with the relevant mourning wear."

"Will you be seeing Mr Darcy ma'am?" Again, the heavy suggestion had Elizabeth's lips smiling more fully.

"I will indeed, Trent. Thank you, not just for this..." here Elizabeth rested a palm against her modest bump, "but for everything. You have been an invaluable support, I would not have managed near half so well without you."

Trent blushed, only to bustle about the room, tidying the almost pristine space further, "Nonsense, Mrs Darcy. I am certain that is not the case, but I thank you. Tis an honour to be your lady's maid."

The two women smiled, in perfect harmony, before Elizabeth slipped away.

Having missed her husband at breakfast, Elizabeth went in search of him, attempting to ignore the little looks of relief the servants gave her, most assuredly a welcome alteration from her previous state.   Mrs Reynolds crossed her path before Elizabeth located her husband, wondering if he had departed to manage estate matters.

"No, Mrs Darcy. The master is in his study, ma'am." The sturdy woman clasped her hands together, her white cap perfectly affixed to her slightly greying charcoal hair, lending her a more distinguished air, "Shall I have tea delivered in a half hour?"

Elizabeth agreed, "Yes, that will suffice. Have it served in Mr Darcy's study, and ask my sister, Mary, to join me at that time?"

Mrs Reynolds continued on with her work, but Elizabeth also noted the good woman's easiness, her demeanour much softened now that not only was Fitzwilliam home, but that Elizabeth's own humour was much improved.

Hesitation had her palms clammy as she knocked on her husband's door, hearing him call to enter, she moved the handle and admitted herself. The light streaming in from the enormous windows, framed by silver damask drapes, fell upon her husband who had yet to register her quiet presence. She watched as a curl of hair fell across his brow which he flicked impatiently away as he continued to draw his pen across his page. When the silence lingered, Fitzwilliam looked up in irritation, only for the expression to morph into wary appreciation.

"Elizabeth! Forgive me, I did not mean to keep you waiting." Fitzwilliam rose with fractious jumpy movements. That was new. Her husband possessed a liquid grace, movements assured and confident, her eyes were compelled to follow and admire.

"Good morning, Fitzwilliam." Moving forward, Elizabeth crossed the room, meeting him halfway, leaning up to grace a kiss to his cheek. Her emotions where her husband were concerned were complicated, but there was no rush to resolve them all today, instead, what she *did* have to tell him would be enough.

Fitzwilliam halted his steps at her side, seeming frozen in place, her kiss having affected him more than she realised, no doubt he too was just as surprised by her elevated spirits as the servants, but her grief had to be set aside for the moment; it had no part in this. Guiding him by the arm, Elizabeth settled them both in armchairs before the fire, noting for the first time, the absence of a settee upon which they could share.

"Tea will be along shortly, so I hope you will forgive the intrusion." Nervously, Elizabeth straightened her gown, surreptitiously drying her palms on the black fabric.

"You are welcome to intrude. I do have some meetings scheduled for later however, matters I have delayed requiring attention."

What was this stiff formality between them? Not even when they were first wed, did they struggle to converse thus.

Awkwardly, Elizabeth rehearsed her words, her attention fixed upon her hands as they repeatedly stroked the skirt of her dress.

"Are you well?" Fitzwilliam quietly enquired, causing her head to flick up.

"I am. I must apologise for-"

"You owe me no apology dear girl. No one could judge you severely for suffering such acute grief." Her husband swallowed thickly, "You seem much improved, which is good to see!"

Unable to sit still, and struggling to put anything into words, Elizabeth bounced up from her seat, pushing Fitzwilliam back into his when he moved to rise. Instead, she took his hand, which he granted with a look of bewilderment. Stepping into the lee of his legs, his knees bracketing hers, Elizabeth moved his hand to rest against her belly, where he could feel the bump, and then she watched his face like a hawk. At first Fitzwilliam appeared puzzled, but then realisation dawned and delight blossomed for a minute, until it was wiped away by a blank mien.

Mystified, Elizabeth spoke at last, "I could not write to tell you my news while you were away in York. I longed to share this moment with you. I hope you can you forgive me for delaying so long?" The relief and joy she expected to feel when she related her news never came, instead the fear of losing Fitzwilliam's approbation overshadowed all. Fitzwilliam's warm palm carefully smoothed over her bump, the touch reverent. A glow of contentment sprouted, a tiny seedling, and she dared hope all would be well.

"When?" so softly uttered, Elizabeth almost failed to hear.

"From what I can gather, I expect to be delivered sometime in September else October." Biting her lip, Elizabeth felt it necessary to disclose, "I have yet to see a midwife for fear of word spreading. I could not risk the gossip, not when y-"

"So who *is* aware?" Fitzwilliam asked pointedly.

Elizabeth retreated to take her own seat, not wishing to face that stone mask.

"Only my maid."

Her husband stood then, pacing to the fireplace, leaving Elizabeth to feel like a disobedient child awaiting a scold. Leaning against the mantle, Fitzwilliam did not turn, "You could not have foretold all that has occurred, yet I feel you have taken an unnecessary risk with your health and that of our child. It cannot have been good for the babe, all the stresses of this past month. Nor yourself for that matter."

The misery and sorrow she had so successfully put in abeyance wished to return. His lack of joy, the cool reception...it hurt. And that pain only compounded her silenced grievances. How she longed to present a passionate rebuttal, but Elizabeth refused to serve incivility with it's like.

"I have suffered no ill affects, and have been conscious of my condition. However, my health has ever been lauded as robust, my regular exercise laying the foundations of my strong disposition. Yet, despite my ignorance of all that my state entails, I have made concessions. I no longer indulge in lengthy walks, confining them to easy rambles through the formal gardens. Neither did I agree to travel to Longbourne at my sister's behest, fearful of how well I would tolerate the journey, or how my mother's agitated spirits may lay further stress and discord upon my shoulders. For all this, you must allow me to have taken prodigious care of my health and my babe." Tugging a handkerchief free of her pocket, Elizabeth wiped away the angry tears silently.

"This does present an explanation of your absence from Longbourne." muttered Fitzwilliam.

How could he scorn her for her decisions? Having put everything aside in order to inform Fitzwilliam, the familiar press of grief wished to swell, but Elizabeth refused. When she looked back upon this moment, she would not allow sorrow to steal her modest joy. Silence grew, its black void filled with sharp edges, ready to slice the unwary. There was no ticking of a clock, no soft notes of music filtering in. Elizabeth remained still. Fixed in her seat, hands clasped tight. The sound of a knock shattered her composure, as she jumped as a startled doe.

"Come!" barked Fitzwilliam, his posture straightening from his leaning.

Mrs Reynolds herself bore a tray, Mary following quietly in her wake.

Depositing her burden on a table set before Elizabeth, Mrs Reynolds tucked her clasped hands close to her middle, "I should like to take this opportunity to convey the household's condolences on the loss of your young sister."

Throat tight, Elizabeth nodded, "Thank you, Mrs Reynolds. If you will agree, I would like to meet following the midday meal? We can discuss the household and the necessary alterations I feel would be suitable in light of our current circumstance."

Mrs Reynolds agreed, then departed. Mary having seated herself to Elizabeth's right, unruffled by the tension, waited calmly for whatever purpose she had been summoned. Stealing herself, Elizabeth saw to the tea, fixing her husband and sister a cup each. "Mary, Trent suggested we attend the modiste in Lambton for some appropriate mourning gowns-"

"I need no new clothes Lizzy. My maid has dyed enough of my current wardrobe to suffice."

Giving her sister a stern look, "Mary. Do not think that will serve. We will not entertain, but already word has spread that Fitzwilliam is home, and I am sure we will receive several callers, hoping to be introduced to the new Mrs Darcy."

If there was a hint of asperity in her tone, she could be forgiven for such.

Seeing her expression, Mary acquiesced, "Very well. Are we to attend our parents?" At Elizabeth's bemused look, Mary continued, "I presumed that was the reason for my attendance? To discuss such arrangements."

Looking away, feelings of guilt assailing her, "For myself, I will not be travelling south." Turning back, "However, that does not mean you must not." Taking Mary's hand, "You are free to return to Longbourne, if that is your wish."

Mary shook her head, "Nay, I would sooner not, for I doubt my presence is much missed, and I cannot see Mama finding much comfort by my attendance."

"There is much truth in that, and while I am sure our mother would take comfort in seeing Mrs Darcy, Fitzwilliam has already done more than enough on our family's behalf." Seeing Fitzwilliam's back stiffen at her words, Elizabeth set her empty cup and saucer back on the tray, "If you will both excuse me, I shall make the necessary arrangements and send a letter to our parents, Mary. So fear not on that score. I shall explain and bear responsibility for our absence."

Elizabeth hastened her steps, leaving an ache in her breast, racing away from the resurgence of pain and loss, only this time it was not on Lydia's behalf.

Several days later, Elizabeth thanked the midwife for her call.

"You should have summoned me sooner, Mrs Darcy, but I ken why you delayed." Mrs Dixon remarked.

"Thank you. I can assure you, I have been blessed with an easy time of it, such that I was almost upon the quickening before I had become aware of my condition."

"Hmm," scowled the midwife, "Can happen, that some are more fortunate than others. If you can get those who are sorely afflicted, then makes sense for others to pass their time with fair to no trouble."

Elizabeth desperately wanted to giggle at the woman's displeasure, her offence seemed disproportionate to the situation.

Mrs Dixon accepted the purse Trent passed across, "Well then, I shall make no assurances that all shall be well. Only a fool would make such a pledge, and I am no fool. If you wish for my presence for your lying in, then I would be happy to attend." And with that, Mrs Dixon departed, no doubt leaving a wake of hopeful expectation in every servant who heard tell of her presence.

"Trent?"

"Yes, Mrs Darcy?" Her maid stood expectantly by the dressing room door.

"I shall not adjure you to gossip, but I would be grateful if the date of my happy expectation is relayed?" Elizabeth felt it best to prevent any speculation, especially in light of her husband's lengthy absence.

Trent, cognisant of her mistress's meaning, nodded, dipped a curtsey, then left Elizabeth in her chambers.

While the midwife's words had supported Elizabeth's own thoughts, it was somewhat of a relief to finally be able to openly acknowledge her condition. Her words to Mary before they attended the modiste the other day had been greeted with a firm nod and a keen embrace from her most placid sister. Mary's pleasure in Elizabeth's news was displayed in her quiet attention, the shared tranquil company and her sister practising charming lullabies in anticipation. Each instance was a balm to the ache Fitzwilliam's coolness had caused, his distant treatment wounding her deeper each day. Twas cold comfort to note Fitzwilliam was the same with everyone.

Georgiana suffered keenly from her brothers dismissive behaviour, fearing his disappointment. No matter how Elizabeth attempted to reassure the girl, her words fell flat and upon deaf ears. Eventually, there was nothing to do but endure a household much subdued, a river of sorrow and grief an undercurrent, the cracks in her heart and soul widening every day.

A knock at the door and Mary, followed by Georgiana entered.

"Lizzy? Is all well?" Mary enquired.

Both girls stood hesitantly by the door, so Elizabeth assured them while ushering them from the room and into Georgiana's own sitting room further along the hall.

"I am perfectly well, as Mrs Dixon was so good to assure. In fact I would say she seemed most discontent I had not suffered much at all." Elizabeth could not keep a tinge of amusement from her words.

Comfortably arranged, the girls appeared relieved to hear such tidings.

"And?" Mary pointedly asked.

Huffing a short laugh, Elizabeth allowed, "And according to the midwife, I am not far wrong in my happy expectation for the autumn. Yet Mrs Dixon did think I was a little small." she sniffed at the thought, for she was hardly a large framed lady., and yet worry niggled, for Mrs Dixon had planted a concern she could not silence.

"Well, our endeavours must necessarily turn to seeing to the nursery and all the associated accoutrements. Furthermore, tis good we shall be in half mourning by that time. Shall you have our aunt Gardiner attend you?"

Looking away, Elizabeth considered the letters she had sent informing her family of her news, while condoling with them over their shared loss. Would it be fair to ask her family, her aunt, to travel, merely as comfort during her time of need? Did not many women labour without such support near daily? Would not her mother claim ill-use if our aunt attended, when she did not?

"I am undecided Mary. I had hoped to have our Gardiner relatives visit over the summer, but considering our circumstances, perhaps next year would serve. Perhaps tis best to see how my news is received?"

Georgiana, having only gained the briefest of familiarity with the Gardiners, looked moderately uncomfortable at the idea of her home hosting Elizabeth's family, therefore,

Elizabeth teased her younger sister.

"Poor Georgiana should fear an invasion of our relatives, should she not Mary? For certain our mother will make herself heard despite the numerous rooms Pemberley boasts of if she were to make the journey."

Abashed, Georgiana denied, "Oh, of course your family should visit! You need not deny yourself their comfort on my account!"

Laughing unreservedly, Elizabeth soothed the shy girl, "I do nothing of the sort, Georgie. I am merely inclined to suit my own needs, while hopefully avoiding riling the feelings of others who are dear to me. For now, I am content as I am, with both yours and Mary's company, and that of Mrs Annesley."

"What of my brother?" timidly, Georgiana worried her hands together.

Mary and Elizabeth shared a look. Despite Mary's own unruffled temperament, the discord between Elizabeth and her husband was appallingly evident.

"Fitzwilliam will presumably be barred from admittance during my delivery, however I hope your brother is tolerably content with his impending fatherhood. But I shall not hesitate in observing my husband is uneasy at present, the cause of such remains a mystery to me.

"My brother, despite your assurances, has avoided my company Lizzy. I cannot help but feel he holds my failings against me. But no. I will not mar this time with such thoughts, instead, Mary, will you allow me to look over the music you recently purchased? The one of lullabies?" Georgiana's mood ebbed and flowed as the tides of the sea, however both Elizabeth and Mary were accustomed to such shifts.

With a genial expression, Mary agreed, "Once you have completed today's lessons with Mrs Annesley, we shall both look over the sheets." The girls continued to discuss plans, before Georgiana excused herself to return to her lessons, while Elizabeth turned discussion upon estate concerns. Mary had accompanied her already on many of the tenant visits, but now they put their attention upon the harvest fête Pemberley was to host.

"Do you think, considering your time, you still wish to manage the arrangements?" Mary asked, having moved to the blue salon, her sister sat at the desk making notes for the event.

Unpicking her faulty stitch, Elizabeth shook her head, "While I shall not get about as much as is my usual wont, if we do not have some occupation for the next few months, I am certain the two of us shall find ourselves fit for bedlam. You, Mary, most of all, cannot stand to be idle!" Rethreading her needle, now that her work was set, Elizabeth continued, "As for myself, I am bound and determined to uphold the expectations placed upon Mrs Darcy. To do aught else would be most ungrateful for my fortunate circumstances." Grief attempted to steal her words, but Elizabeth fought the hold, while a surfeit of tears escaped, "If I am to overcome what happened with Ly-Lydia, I cannot, I must not, hide away, to wallow in our loss, to rail against the fates that saw our sister..." Arms embraced her, and Elizabeth sobbed into Mary's shoulder, her grief once more encompassing.

"Hush, now, Lizzy. None of that. You will do all that and more, for you have already impressed the servants, the tenants, and even won over some of the local gentry! No one can have anything to repine in the new Mrs Darcy, Lizzy." Mary continued to utter soothing words, until at last her tears abated, and Elizabeth was once more composed, though her head ached fiercely.

"I fear I had best rest now, I can feel one of my megrims coming on."

Mary tutted, but agreed nonetheless. Elizabeth kissed her sister's brow, before returning to her rooms, hopeful the darkness that could be achieved from her closed bed-curtains would offer some respite. Unfortunately, her escape was hindered as she crossed paths with her husband. There were strain lines about his eyes, and he looked as if sleep had eluded him on more than one occasion. Yet his appearance was as impeccable as ever, his grey eyes piercing her, pinning Elizabeth to her spot in the centre of the hallway, his handsome visage smoothed to a neutral mien.

"Elizabeth."

Feeling the pounding in her temples, Elizabeth distractedly acknowledged him, "Mr Darcy." Then stepping around him, "If you will permit, I must find my room."

A harsh bark of concern had her tucking her chin and forging forward. "Elizabeth! Are you well?"

With a dismissive wave over her shoulder, her attempt to assure him never slowed her steps, "Just a megrim, Sir. Nothing to be concerned over. I hope to be well enough to join you all for dinner." If Fitzwilliam was reassured, she could not tell, but retreat was paramount if she was to avoid the full escalation of her head paining her more.

CHAPTER 19

Days passed, and life continued on in this stiff and awkward quality cloaking Pemberley. The servants witnessed the strain their master's aloofness placed upon their mistress, but none were brave enough, or indeed held the necessary intimacy to find a method of healing the breach. The interminable days of Mrs Darcy and Miss Bennet garbed in black, a sombre sight, would have cast a greater pall upon the great house if not for both estimable ladies striving to conduct themselves peacefully.

Georgiana, opting for neutral shades to dress, soft greys and lavenders out of respect for her new sisters, having never been introduced to Elizabeth's family, found it much harder to mourn Lydia Bennet's senseless death. Georgiana's shy and quiet demeanour remained, but the experience matured the young girl into a thoughtful and considerate lady, emulating both Mary and Elizabeth's character in numerous ways.

With the quieter and more withdrawn period of mourning draped over Pemberley, the ladies carried out tenant visits, received calls from neighbourhood gentry, and saw to their own interests without ceremony. Visits from both parish rectors of Kympton and Lambton were conducted with regularity, both eager to make headway in improving the lot of those less fortunate. The Lambton rector, Mr Farnsworth, a gentleman of years similar to that of Mr Darcy, and though not in possession of quite so fine an appearance, was well favoured by all the young and hopeful local ladies. However, it was to Mary, that Mr Farnsworth paid particular attention. Mary's connections being what they were, was also pretty, sensible and a practical lady worthy of consideration, and as a result came a hint of blossoming interest, despite the state of mourning.

Elizabeth refrained from the intense desire to tease and torment her young sister. Knowing full well Mary would ill receive such well-meaning remarks, she permitted her sister to enjoy the subtle attentions the rector bestowed every other Sunday at church, and every other week in their twice monthly charitable meetings. Without having ever asked, Elizabeth was delighted at the prospect her sister might remain nearby, if Mary was to accept Mr Farnsworth's address, and while she still missed

Jane terribly, their mother would not hear of her daughter leaving Longbourne, not until she wed Bingley that is.

Sighing deeply, Elizabeth accepted her husband's arm as he stood to lead them out of church, their sisters and Mrs Annesley falling in behind them.

"You seem tired Elizabeth. Shall you rest on our return home?" Fitzwilliam's soft rumble carried down to her.

"Mary and I are in the midst of a book we are reading to one another, so I shall spend my time thusly. Yourself?"

Elizabeth nodded and smiled to those who attempted to catch her attention, while the forward motion of her husband guided them to the exit, his confident steps slowing not at all. Fitzwilliam's poor performance in social settings had been notoriously difficult to assuage recently. Thankfully his character was well known in the area, and none took offence at his swift removal from company.

"Mr Darcy, Mrs Darcy–I hope you enjoyed today's sermon?" Mr Prentiss, Kympton's parish rector enquired, his greying blond hair at odds with his strong voice. While not handsome, the rector was of modest looks and a placid temperament, his confirmed state of bachelorhood a well-known and much discussed theme amongst the local matrons.

"We did," Fitzwilliam answered, and

Elizabeth had to bite back the retort of 'did we?' considering she had given no indication of her thoughts.

"Excellent. Excellent. I must say, Mr Darcy, it has been a welcome pleasure to work with your esteemed wife and sisters these past few months! I have never felt such satisfaction in being so excellently placed to improve the situation of those less fortunate! How propitious for us all, that you have selected for your life partner, a lady so generous and kind!"

Her husband agreed, perhaps wishing to forestall further words of praise, the tension in the arm Elizabeth's hand rested upon, mounting. "I cannot but agree Mr Prentiss. If you will excuse me, we would not wish to preclude you speaking to our neighbours."

Fitzwilliam dipped his head, and Elizabeth tipped a shallow curtsey, before allowing herself to be steered to the awaiting carriage. She was handed in, took her seat and remained silent throughout the short journey back to Pemberley. Every day, the grief of her sister's passing was buried under the grief of losing her husband's good opinion, for how else could she perceive matters between them? Her husband no longer spent his nights in her company, abandoning the blossoming intimacy between them, kept himself apart from her daily, and while she could allow he attended dinner each night, Fitzwilliam had made it abundantly apparent he wished to be anywhere else but where she was.

Oh, Lydia, you poor foolish child! Why could you not wait and allow yourself to be courted, rather than scramble away like a thief in the night? To be so wild and lost to any common feelings of decency, to throw yourself upon the less than tender mercies of a man so immoral!

Such thoughts continued to assail her. Grief blending with anger. Sorrow mixed with resentment. Almost listlessly, Elizabeth descended from the carriage, completely unaware of the worried looks sent her way. Too wrapped up in her own concerns, Elizabeth found solace only whilst thoughts of her unborn child consumed her attention.

"Lizzy?" Mary loosely held her by the elbow, "Shall we sit out in the courtyard? We can have Mrs Reynolds bring us out some cool lemonade?"

Agreeable to the idea, Elizabeth assented, handing over her pelisse and bonnet to the maid waiting.

"I shall fetch the book and my sewing basket, for I am confident it is to be your turn to read."

"May I join you?" Georgiana stood slightly apart, her dove grey gown a compliment to her fair hair and soft grey eyes. Mrs Annesley slightly behind her, and Elizabeth felt a gradual awareness of how carefully she was observed.

"Of course! And Mrs Annesley, you must

join us, for it is a fine summer's day." Her words pushed through her pensive mood, reassuring her company with a false gaiety all knew she did not feel. The ladies agreed, and Elizabeth meandered her way to the chosen destination. She paid no heed to Fitzwilliam, not until he called her name a moment after she had settled upon her seat.

"Elizabeth." Flicking her head in his direction, she waited for him to relate his purpose. Her husband had abandoned keeping her company, and she had come to expect his swift removal. "I have a letter here for you in amongst my own correspondence."

Accepting the missive, Elizabeth instantly noted the author, but could not help exclaiming, "Tis from Jane! She wrote the direction very ill, which is most unlike her. Thank you, Fitzwilliam. I had begun to wonder at the delay."

Unwittingly Elizabeth dismissed Fitzwilliam from her company, resigned to his aloof manners.

"Elizabeth?"

Surprised, her gaze returned to Fitzwilliam, where he stood just by the door leading back inside, "Yes?" Her husband hesitated, but no words escaped. Instead the soft voices of their sisters and Mrs Annesley caught their notice, and her husband quit her company with a stiff nod. Sighing in defeat, Elizabeth greeted her sisters, and settled herself in pursuit of a gentle and restful Sunday in good company.

That evening, Elizabeth recollected the letter from Jane once she had readied for bed, and settled in to hear of her sister's news. Happy tears rolled down her eyes moments later as she read of Jane's quiet wedding, and her much happier situation within Netherfield. Jane's next words cheered her immensely.

Oh, Lizzy, I cannot tell you how good it has been in my marriage to Charles. This past year has been perhaps the worst of our lives, but we have both come out of it wiser, warier and with wonderful husbands. My grief over the loss of our sister goes unabated, much as it does for you, but Charles has been the perfect husband in his support of me. Despite our much lauded kindness however, it has become increasingly difficult for our mother to be without any of her daughters. With Kitty being encouraged to remain in Bath, both you and Mary comfortably settled at Pemberley and now my own removal, Mama chooses to alleviate her sorrow by continuing to remain at Netherfield long after a visit should cease. I believe, as does Charles, that in order to be free of such imposition, we should look to the north for a property my husband can purchase. If your husband could aid in the search, both Charles and I would be most grateful.

In that light, would it be very terrible if you could extend an invitation for us to visit with you? I have missed you terribly dear Lizzy!

The next morning, Elizabeth could not help but invade her husband's study to canvas the subject of her sister and Mr Bingley. "Fitzwilliam! Jane and Mr Bingley are married!" For a moment Elizabeth caught the flash of pleasure in those cool grey eyes, then her husband turned away and hid his expression from her.

"I am pleased for him. I had hoped Bingley and your sister would finally unite and make Miss Bingley, pardon, Mrs Bailey's machinations for naught."

Glancing about the room, Elizabeth made a note to shift some of the furniture to make it more suitable for their needs. Deciding not to take a seat, either before her husband's desk, or over by the silent fireplace, she chose to saunter to the edge of the heavy piece of furniture and rest a hip against it.

"Poor Jane, to be forever tied to Mr Bingley's sister, yet I must admit I was pleasantly surprised by Mr Hurst's scheming to declaw the menace."

"It was indeed most unlike the man, but I imagine there is some degree of pleasure Hurst took in arranging matters to everyone's satisfaction."

Elizabeth fought not to roll her eyes at the bland remark, "Admittedly I held some reservations, but Jane seems much improved since enduring the loss of our sister, having born the brunt of our parent's grief, now that she has wed. However, my sister has expressly stated their intentions to relocate and are in want of a property further north; do you think you may know of anything that would suit?"

An almost churlish grunt and considering expression would commonly be deemed ungentlemanly, but Elizabeth was simply grateful her husband had yet to politely dismiss her.

"Excellent, I shall inform Jane of such when I send my invitation to join us here!" Elizabeth popped from her restful pose and had almost made her escape when Fitzwilliam called out a halt.

"When were you going to enquire of my desire to host guests?" The churlishness of moments before had turned surly.

Turning, Elizabeth politely refuted, "The mistress of Pemberley does not *need* permission, or am I no longer Mrs Darcy, mistress of this estate?" Before Fitzwilliam could argue further, her words became a rant, "I cannot fathom what mischief I have done, what error I have made, but this senseless and callous behaviour has continued long enough! If you can object to my invitation of a beloved sister wed to one of your dearest friends, then you must accept my own resentment, such that I have refrained to display until now!"

Fearing the tears she was holding at bay with the flimsiest of strength, Elizabeth departed before further words could be exchanged, only allowing her misery to escape once she had reached the sanctuary of her chambers.

Darcy stared hard at the door, such that if he were so endowed, the wood would turn to ash from the admixture of censure and desire surging through him. How could he suffer his wife's passionate embrace, when *he* was the cause of her grief? She was radiant, magnificent in her fury as she boldly called him to task; what else was a man to do when bound to such a glorious creature! Desire, his carnal hunger for Elizabeth had not waned as her shape altered with the burden of bearing his child. No, she became more desirable, more tempting at every alluring shift of her feminine form!

And yet, guilt ate at him. The conviction *he* was ultimately responsible for the death of Lydia meant he could not look at the glory that was his wife without feeling that awful weight crushing him. Six weeks had passed since his return and every day he felt himself unable to bridge the gap that grew between them. His throat constricted, choking the words before they could be spoken. He would beg for Elizabeth's forgiveness, but how selfish would that make him!

Already bearing his child, Elizabeth need not be burdened with *his* failings. His mistakes! The small consolation of seeing Wickham incarcerated in debtor's prison was but a paltry result, considering the libertine's ultimate responsibility, and did little to ease his conscience. Scrubbing his hand over his face, his hands dragged through his hair in agitation. A knock disturbed him, but before he could call to enter, Georgiana approached on eager slippered feet.

"Oh, brother, you must come! Mary and I have almost perfected our lullaby concert! Shall you not come and hear us play?" Bright and cheerful, here was another example of how unworthy he was to possess Elizabeth as his wife. Georgiana, delighted with her new 'sisters' had transformed from a shy and withdrawn girl, into this delightful lady. And what had he done for her sisters? Allowed Wickham to prey upon them! If only he had taken a moment to think of what designs the dastard would concoct!

The sharp thought had him curtly reply, "Not now Georgiana! I have no time for such frivolous pursuits!"

The light drained from his sister, but where his wife would deliver a witty and pert set down, Georgiana was made differently. Felt things differently.

Face downtrodden, his sister apologised before escaping. Dropping his head in his hands, Darcy groaned. At this rate, he would set his whole household against him.

"Lizzy! You must speak with him!" Georgiana

cried, her entrance dramatic and entirely unexpected of the normally reticent creature. The sight made her recollect the many times Lydia had rushed into a room in some form of pique or another.

Without needing to clarify, Elizabeth resumed her attention to her even stitches, "I have attempted to do so, sweeting. He spares my words the barest attention." Elizabeth pulled back, studying her embroidery on the small baby frock Mary had already sewn up.

Huffily, Georgiana accepted her words, but it was not a moment later that her complaints renewed. "He looks so unlike himself. So unwell. I cannot help but worry." Georgiana's soft words only echoed Elizabeth's own disquiet.

Fitzwilliam remained distant and aloof, his stone mask firmly affixed in any social setting. His ability to make even his own sister worried spoke of the tension that prevailed around the beautiful rooms of Pemberley. A painful discordant note.

Sighing, Elizabeth folded away her work. She had to admit Georgiana made a fair point, and so, Elizabeth could postpone the coming confrontation no longer, this merely provided the impetus to act.

"Very well. I make no promises, and ask that you go and find Mrs Annesley to keep you and Mary company. I doubt we will receive callers, but I shall inform Mrs Reynolds we are not at home to anyone."

Sitting up, Georgiana gave her a worried look, "You begin to alarm me Lizzy. There seems to be something more to your intentions that I cannot determine." Elizabeth did nothing more than to give her sister a blank expression, "As you mean to deprive me an explanation, I shall make myself absent, however, allow me to speak with Mrs Reynolds?"

Agreeing, Elizabeth made her way through the bright morning room, her steps slow and steady despite the heavy burden that prevented the sight of her feet. She was now near seven months along and the August heat was gradually dropping away, leaving the first blush and hints of autumn. The last two months had been difficult, the distance from her dearest Jane, who had been put off from visiting in order to spend some time in London. Now that their half mourning was fast approaching, the need for a new wardrobe allowed her eldest sister some escape from their mother's frequent visits.

Entering her husband's study without invitation, closing the door firmly at her back, Elizabeth was pleased to note the settee placed just where she had wished, the memory of her husband's frowning countenance as he mentioned the addition jumped to the front of her thoughts. Taking a seat there, Elizabeth patted the space beside her, noting how her husband acknowledged her presence without ever looking up from his work, suffering anew the sting of his disapprobation.

"Fitzwilliam. Please, join me for a moment." Taking care to sound warm and inviting, Elizabeth kept the truth of her feelings buried beneath her fragile composure. A wriggle in her belly helped to firm her resolution.

"I am set to meet with one of the tenants shortly, Lloyds has an issue he wishes to discuss." Looking up from his desk, Fitzwilliam gave her his attention, his grey orbs distant and cool, "Can this not wait until this evening?"

Feeling more heartbreak than such a dismissal warranted, Elizabeth felt her love of him, for him, crack. Standing, she gripped the reins of her control, and held tightly to them. "As you will. I shall not trouble you further, than to state my purpose, for I little like this propensity of yours to dismiss me out of hand."

Pinching the bridge of his nose, Elizabeth witnessed her husband take a deep breath before his powerful gaze caught her up in his grasp. If it was possible to crumble, she felt it then. Felt her resolve to hold everything together, to be *fine*, to be *well*, when she was anything but, disintegrate like the cracking of a frozen lake, the chill depths blooming up to take her under.

In an aggrieved tone, Fitzwilliam denied, "I am not dismissing you Elizabeth." Pushing back from his seat, he went on, "But as you wish, my time and attention is yours. How may I help you my dear?"

The time had come for her to accept that to go on as she was, to accept the crumbs of his attention was a pittance, an offence to the babe she carried, one she had been sure was conceived in love and not duty.

"I feel it is time that you establish a home for myself and my family to reside."

She watched alarm spread across his handsome features, followed by the paleness of confusion. "I can comprehend your wishes to have a home for your family, should anything happen to your father–have you had news from Longbourne to warrant such concern?" There was nothing in his tone that betrayed his worry, but Elizabeth could see the signs in his wary eyes.

"You misapprehend me, husband. I desire a separate establishment for *myself* and any of my sisters who so choose to reside with me." She kept a pleasant mask on, denying Fitzwilliam the sight of her pain, her sorrow and heartache.

Standing up in anger, Fitzwilliam slammed his palms down upon his desk, "You cannot be serious!"

Before further words fell, Elizabeth calmly argued, "I am perfectly serious husband. I feel it is near enough necessary to reside elsewhere. Where my presence will not offend my husband into further ill-health!"

"How can you say such?" Fitzwilliam stalked around the desk, steps powerful and commanding, "You carry my child!" He growled darkly.

Unruffled by such a display, Elizabeth answered, "You have not troubled yourself to be in company with me. Can not bear to remain wheresoever I am. You spare the barest of civilities, such that your disdain is all but evident. It, therefore behoves me to affect you no further." Hands clutched tightly together, Elizabeth kept her gaze fixed upon a point above Fitzwilliam's shoulder, her courage failing to keep her gaze locked with that of his.

"That is unduly harsh madam! I will not dignify such a request with a response." Fitzwilliam stood with hands braced, his dark scowl setting her heart pounding, but still she would not look directly upon him. "And while I cannot deny my conduct of late has been wanting, I have never failed to place your needs above those of any other! To suggest otherwise is a gross misconduct."

Throat clogging with misery, yet denying the luxury of tears, Elizabeth pushed, "You mean to tell me, you see no cause for concern in your behaviour? Your almost abject loathing of my person? You tolerate me, Sir, and that under duress! The servants tiptoe through their work, for fear of your dark countenance! Your own sister begged me to do whatever necessary to see you return to health. This cannot continue!"

"You convict me unfairly madam. I have

been all that is considerate throughout your recent travails. Would you have wished to have me burden you unnecessarily when you were so clearly grieving? And that even more so is compounded when one takes into account your expectant state!" Fitzwilliam paced away from the chair he had sought shelter behind. "As to the rest, I was not aware I had so offended my household to have you all whispering behind my back. I thought better of you madam."

Rising with some difficulty, Elizabeth addressed her husband's back, "You may comfort yourself with such sentiments, but for myself, I have found little solace in the treatment I have suffered at your hands. And no one is whispering anything. I am your wife, your wellbeing is my primary concern, or am I to have that denied too? But no matter, I shall absent myself from your company, and will send word with news of the birth of your child. Until that time, I see no reason to remain."

Before she had taken one step, Fitzwilliam whirled to face her, his steps taking himself into her path, as if a wall had spawned from the earth, "You cannot mean to leave!" His hands grasped her shoulders, and Elizabeth feared his touch would be harsh, only to feel an upwell of affection at the near reverent hold he had upon her. Almost brokenly, Fitzwilliam spoke her name, "Elizabeth?"

Her resolve began to tremble, "I can

and will, for you said yourself, prolonged strain and stress are harmful to a woman in my condition." Shrugging her shoulders, she affected a nonchalance she did not feel, "I merely abide by *your* edicts in removing myself from such provocation!"

An intense look of pain bloomed in those stone grey eyes, "I?" Words broken, Fitzwilliam asked, "I am that source?"

Her own anger escaped, the closeness between them breaching her defences, "Yes! *Your* silence! *Your* unfeeling neglect, impressing me with the fullest belief of your regret in our marriage and disdain for the shame such a connection has wrought upon the Darcy name! With such disapprobation before me, what else am I to assume! Faced with your darkly forbidding countenance, a departure seems the most sensible course of action; I cannot remain where I am not wanted, cannot continue to face such immovable disfavour, nor watch as you become this grim facsimile of the man I-." A few traitorous tears escaped, and Elizabeth let them fall unheeded, unable to let the words stuck in her throat, free.

Her husband's eyes tracked them, misery etched upon his granite hard features.

"You would truly depart?   Leave? Me?" Her heart clenched to hear his pain, to feel its twin in her breast, yet some part of felt reassured to note it. He could not be so unfeeling if the mere thought of her leaving wrought such an affect.

Her love for him softened her words, twined through each syllable, "If I were to be given a preference — I would not. But nor can I continue thus." Her palm beat heavily upon his chest, the firm and unyielding strength beneath lending itself to her, "Can you truly not forgive me for concealing the truth of my expectancy? Or have I committed some other sin that has you regretting our union?"

A huff of air escaped, and Fitzwilliam's brow dropped forward to rest upon her own, "You think that- Why would I hold such against you?" She felt him shift, pulling away minutely to drop a kiss upon her brow before returning to his restful pose in their constrained embrace. His hands no longer gripped her arms tenderly, but wrapped about her, her heart delighting in the pleasure of his embrace, soothing the ragged crags and peaks that had formed in her heart. Enveloped in his hold, every beat of his heart thudded against her palm, it's ragged beat a melody she had missed every night. "No, never mind. If you must know... I feel ashamed." Fitzwilliam drew in a deep breath, then pulled back, looking down upon her with an ardent expression tinged with misery, "The guilt of my inaction, my own foolish pride has wreaked irrecoverable harm upon you and your loved ones... How can I suffer your smiles when I am burdened with such guilt? You should loath the very sight of me!"

Tears fell in abundance and Elizabeth wiped them away impatiently, not wishing to lose sight of her beloved husband. "Oh, Fitzwilliam, you foolish man! Why in heaven's name would I feel such towards one who worked tirelessly to resolve my family crisis?" Her hands crept further up his chest, until they rested around his neck, "Yes, I cannot deny some asperity for your previous indifference, however I am not ignorant for the reasons for your silence; you were in an untenable situation."

Gruffly, Fitzwilliam denied, "I could have found some means by which to expose his perfidy to the neighbourhood. Yet I was too intent upon our own unexpected union and the difficulties you were to face when thrust into a situation so suddenly."

"Precisely!" Elizabeth reached up on her toes and bestowed a kiss to Fitzwilliam's chin, adoring the look of delight and pleasure he displayed, "The fault lies with Mr Wickham, who had he behaved differently, could have been in possession of so much more had he merely desired to apply as much effort to such endeavours. He instead chose to use his time less wisely, applying his skill upon his scheming and ploys. His bitter end to rot in debtor's prison is a waste of your father's patronage."

Wrapping her arms tighter around him,

Elizabeth rested her chin upon Fitzwilliam's chest, "Dearest, I must tell you how ardently I have come to love you," she watched the glow of elation spark in those stone grey orbs, "where it began, the genesis of my affection, I cannot name." Elizabeth paused to collect her thoughts, "Our union began so abruptly, and yet you never appeared ill-content. You provided me with your patient understanding and careful consideration, remained in such good humour, how could I do anything *but* fall headlong in love with you! You asked me what *I* desired, and I would choose never to be separated from you again; but if you cannot overlook, overcome this feeling...there can be no future for us." Once more, Elizabeth stretched up to bestow a kiss, ecstatic when he met her half way. Their lips brushed softly, before pressing more firmly against one another.

The pleasure consumed her, until with a ragged breath she pulled back, "Think on it Fitzwilliam, for our future depends upon it."

CHAPTER 20

Darcy bent low over his mount's back, feeling the brisk late summer breeze kiss his cheeks with stinging intensity. Elizabeth's words reverberated around his head for the past two days, his mood shifting between desperate hope and wretched guilt. The hoofbeats against the earth thudded in time with his near hopeless need to break the monotonous cycle of his thoughts. She was right. They could not continue on as they were, and nor would he accept a separation; already the absence of Elizabeth gnawed at him night and day, an ache never soothed unless he could caress her with his gaze, fulfil the promise in his eyes when alone — for there to be even greater distance between them...no, that path was not one he was willing to assent to, at any cost.

Therefore, he must overcome this wretched guilt, the history of Wickham's dissolute and wastrel exploits, tied up together with his happier memories of his boyhood playmate. What future was before him, could no longer be tainted by the past, not if he wished to keep Elizabeth. And his child.

Watching Elizabeth's slight frame shift with her burden had been a mixed blessing, as he longed to trace and map out her softness, learn her new curves, feel the shift of his unborn babe. His restrained joy sat like hot coals in his chest, warming and burning in equal measure. The snort of his horse's heavy breathing forced Darcy to ease up on the reins, turning them back home, to the stables, and once more, the place he had hidden these past two months, his study. Having failed to wash off the stink of horse and sweat, Darcy paced, a prowling and agitated creature. Dragging his hands through his hair one final time, Darcy accepted there was only one way forward. One path to take. With that, he pulled the bell to summon a servant to have water prepared for him, then moved to his desk to address an important missive he would have dispatched express.

Several hours later, he finally managed to track down his sister, hoping to offer her a much-needed apology, Elizabeth's would be given later, once their privacy was assured. For once, Georgiana was not to be found in the confines of the music room, and instead kept her occupation restricted to her sitting room.

With a light tap to her door, he was

admitted and could only wonder at the smile of welcome he received from his little sister. Her generous spirit, obvious in the hopeful expectation upon her features, made him feel all the more wretched for his callous treatment of late.

"Brother! Is aught amiss?" was to be his welcome, whereby his sister thought he only sought her out when something was awry.

"I hope I am not disturbing you?" he asked, seeing an array of sketches laid out, obviously interrupting his sister in her occupation. At her negation, Darcy stepped further into the room and indicated a seat, lowering himself to the divan once given approval. "There is...that is, forgive me, what I mean to say, is that I bring no ill-tidings. Instead I wished to offer you my abject and heartfelt apologies for my behaviour of late. There has been a total want of cordial and considerate behaviour that I have displayed and I can offer no justice, except to say that I have struggled mightily with the burden of guilt-"

"Nay brother! You have no cause to feel such! Not when I! I am the cause for such misery–had I but considered the consequences of my actions, had I not been swept up in the folly of my romantic and senseless wishes, *you* would have been better placed to hobble the libertine!" Georgiana wiped a tear away, and Darcy struggled to swallow the lump in his own throat, realising how blind he had been to his sister's misery. "All this time, I have fought not to trouble Lizzy and Mary with my self-recriminations, for what good would it serve to lay all before them; more than I have already exposed."

Startled, Darcy sat forward, "Elizabeth is aware of what occurred at Ramsgate?" Georgiana nodded, and Darcy dropped his face into his palm, comprehending how truly ignorant he had been of the words Elizabeth had spoken two days hence. His wife had absolved him of guilt, aware of all he had believed her to be ignorant of. Shaking his head abruptly, Darcy put such thoughts aside for the moment, "Georgie, please, I beg of you, do not allow that man to mar the truth of your own character. I wish I could say your words were without merit, but I cannot. Yes, naivete and folly guided your steps with one you had once been close with, aided by another who bore the charge of your care. Yet, as I am sure Elizabeth has told you, what girl of fifteen is without mistakes? Please dearest, do not allow Wickham to win."

Offering Georgiana his handkerchief, his sister wiped her eyes before looking at him with sisterly affection.

"Georgie, can you offer me your own forgiveness for my past behaviour? I promise to do better, yet I am sure I will err and will rely on you and my loved ones to correct me when needed."

"Heavens, brother!" Georgiana smiled wide, "You need not fear any sort of recriminations from myself! Truly, my only concern has been for you and your health and happiness. Seeing you much restored has me feeling all the gratitude of one redeemed! All I would wish for, is to see you and Lizzy reconciled once more."

"Thank you dearest," Darcy dropped forward to his knees before his sister to envelop her in his embrace. After a moment, he pulled back and took up a seat beside his sister, "In that, you and I are in accord. I have struggled these many weeks since returning to Pemberley, to come to terms with my own guilt, the part of my silence according the Bennets the acutest of suffering; ultimately, it has been difficult to reconcile that Elizabeth's sister bore the price. I curse the day I first chose to act thus, for it had oft become the pattern that led me to where I am now."

Darcy felt his sister's head drop upon his shoulder, and his arm clasped her closer to him, the very near miss of his sister's folly, brought forcefully to the fore once more. With a deep sigh, Darcy laid bare before his sister, his scheme for the rest of the day, pleased to have a confederate who wholly supported him, whether he deserved such was not to be addressed.

"Georgie?" Elizabeth studied her sister, her appearance brighter than it had been in days.

"Oh. Forgive me, I quite forgot what it was I was going to say!" Georgiana blushed becomingly, and Elizabeth wondered what had so offset the dear girl. Then with a sudden sound which quite startled Elizabeth, Georgiana jumped up from her seat.

"I remembered!" With an abashed expression, "I do beg your pardon, that was quite loud."

Chuckling, Elizabeth prompted, "And?"

"Yes? Oh, you meant for me to continue!" With a sheepish expression, Georgiana explained, "I had hoped you would select a new book for us to read!"

"I had not thought we had concluded our current selection?"

With a stuttering and halting explanation, Elizabeth came to understand that Georgiana was desperate for a new book to be chosen, as their current choice had the unfortunate affect of causing Georgiana to somnolence. With laughing compassion, Elizabeth agreed to discover a new title that might be of more interest, and therefore made her way to the vast library, quite possibly one of her three favourite rooms in the house.

The air was muggy and heavy with a brewing storm, the sultry August temperatures speaking of stultifying days craving a cool breeze to clear the air. Elizabeth felt much in harmony with the weather, or mayhap was simply keen for a break from the hold she and Fitzwilliam found themselves in. The library was much cooler than the rest of the house, being so much darker than the bright and airy rooms found elsewhere, and so Elizabeth was content to browse the immense selection in a leisurely fashion. A soft snick of sound reached her, and Elizabeth turned about to study the now closed doors. Raising a brow in curiosity, she was about to test the handle when a murmur of sound from before the fireplace caught her attention. Her movements near silent, Elizabeth reached the settee and could not help a sharp inhale at the sight.

Masculine glory stretched out before her, Elizabeth's gaze travelled the length and breadth of her husband and allowed her admiration for his physical perfection. Another grumble of sound escaped and Elizabeth checked his face for signs of him waking. When he stirred no further, Elizabeth gently lowered herself to the floor beside him and simply admired the hard planes, the shadows and textures that made up Fitzwilliam Darcy. His breathing was slow and deep, but she watched him begin to shift and stir. For such a private gentleman, he had such powerful strength running through him, such capability paired with gentle care and compassion. Soft words of love whispered through her mind, and suddenly a glaring memory jumped to the fore. He had called her *my love* once before, when he departed to search for Lydia. It was the last words he had spoken and how she could have forgotten that until now was stupendous!

Resting her arms upon the edge of the seat, Elizabeth dropped her head to rest on them, "Dearest Fitzwilliam," her words were the faintest sound, a whisper of breath, "you foolish beast, when will you allow yourself to be free of this heavy burden of yours? Do not mistake me, my love-"

"Am I?" the grave tone of her husband had Elizabeth jumping and her eyes searched his face; he had awoken then. Eyes open, the silver depths pinning her still, Fitzwilliam's vibrating tone travelled across her skin, an ardent touch to a woman who was starved for that connection. "Elizabeth?"

"Are you?" she hesitantly broached, relaxing her head back upon her arms, relishing the closeness, the anticipation of sensation tingling through her. Her head level with his, their breath mingled, the closest she had been with him for so long.

"Your love. Am I your love?" unmoving, his iron gaze never left her, his rumble affecting her attention.

"Without question, Fitzwilliam. You are. But as I was in the midst of saying, do no mistake me, *my love*, I am by no means equal to forgiving you for your behaviour. You have caused me grief in a way entirely unrelated to that of the loss of my sister. Her death was as senseless as you have been." Rising with difficulty, Elizabeth brushed aside the aid he presented, and found her feet, her steps slowly taking her across to the fireplace, its immense construct affording her the span to relay her thoughts as coherently as she could. "I absolve you of your guilt in bearing any burden of Lydia's folly, her loss, or even Mr Wickham's involvement. However, you left me without word, without thought!"

Fitzwilliam had risen when she did, and now he took two strides until he frustratingly growled, "My every thought was of you! Seeing you brought so low! The image haunts me still! I should have written, and I can only apologise that I was so compelled, so focused upon recovering your sister, that I allowed myself to set you aside and deny you the comfort of my assurances. I will plead for your forgiveness without cease. As to my own conflict, I have strived to move beyond my own feelings of complicity in this terrible debacle, but I will continue to always put *you* first. To think of your needs, and those of our children, and to never permit myself to be used for such ill purpose ever again."

Desperate love glowed in those stone grey eyes, heating them, and his gaze once more had Elizabeth transfixed. Her movements had ceased the moment he spoke, her attention solely for him. Her heart pounded in her chest, her fingertips itching to ease away the lines of stress and sorrow marring his beloved face. Yet no matter how her arms ached to hold, her skin yearning for his touch, she could not let Fitzwilliam sink into the dour and dark mood without comprehending how much it *hurt*, to be shut out, to be isolated and without the comfort of his solid strength.

"You *have* put me first, but you also put yourself first too! As much as you need *my* softness, my warmth, my *love*, I *need you*! Your strength, your comfort, your protection....your love! And you do not express such sentiments, walling yourself away. Shielding your feelings, leaving me alone. Tis unfair, cruel and...and.." Tears overwhelmed her, and Elizabeth searched fruitlessly for her handkerchief, only to have Fitzwilliam proffer his, his hands sliding about her waist, pulling her in close, shielding her from the pain, sheltering her from the loneliness and grief.

The storm of her emotions swept away her reason, and Elizabeth finally succumbed to the torment of all she had undergone these past few terrible months. Fitzwilliam whispered soft words of comfort against her hair, his strength banding about her, pulling her so tight, so wonderfully close, they were almost one. A roll of her belly had her hiccuping a giggle, especially when she witnessed the unfettered delight and awe in her husband's eyes. He dropped to his knees, his hands delicately spanning the small bump, his lips pressed against her belly.

The misery of before was banished. Instead, Elizabeth watched as Fitzwilliam communed with their unborn babe, absorbing the way his expression shifted from one emotion to another, a magic lantern of feelings displayed for her to witness. Brushing her hands through his inky hair, letting the soft curls slide through her fingertips, enjoying the pleasure in this precious moment, shared just between the two of them, the gift that came from such a whirlwind of experiences, struggles.

"Oh Elizabeth, I am so miserably sorry to have hurt you in any way. Twas my endless pride to believe I could resolve everything, to be your knight. I will spend the rest of my days ensuring no walls ever come between us. Please, dearest. Tell me what I may do to return us to how we were before?"

Enveloping him in her arms, his cheek tucked against her growing belly, slight though it was, "We cannot go back, love, we can only go forward. Build stronger foundations than before. Remind one another that what we have is a union of equal parts, give and take. You are my strength, and I am your comfort. And yet, that is not all we are to one another. I made the vow to be yours, to trust you with all that I am, so in turn did you. Therefore, if one of us pulls away, we must work together to bring us back to our foundation. Of Love. Trust. Faith in one another."

"My darling girl, I will spend my every breath being worthy of your love and forgiveness." With a final kiss to her belly, Fitzwilliam rose to his feet, towering before her, a column of virile strength. Heart racing for another reason entirely, Elizabeth felt the yearning to be with him, to seal their bond, their promise, their vow to one another, all over again.

Much later, Elizabeth lay in her husband's arms, content, replete and utterly ravished. Fitzwilliam had been a man possessed with an intensity yet to be experienced. The powerful ache he had inspired had been so intense, so consuming, Elizabeth was still settling back into her own skin.

"Am I to surmise, I have finally seduced you senseless?" The dark murmur was accompanied by firm nibbles, nips and kisses along her neck and throat, her husband having yet to let a moment pass where they were not touching, caressing, exploring. Her new shape fascinated Fitzwilliam, and despite being somewhat concerned about causing any harm, Elizabeth felt her husband knew her body better than she did.

Arching her neck further to allow for greater access, Elizabeth replied, "Senseless? No. Never. I am merely captivated by your careful and dedicated attentions." She smiled wide when she felt his low chuckle, his hands gently exploring her once more, roaming every hill and valley, without resting in one place.

"I will allow that to be so, yet I cannot promise you will be quite so content to remain in my arms when this babe demands to be fed."

Sighing deeply, she agreed. "True, yet I am sure, that as the architect of this little seduction, you have some measures in place that will address those additional needs?"

Sitting up, and looking down at her with a mischievous grin, one Elizabeth delighted in witnessing, "As the architect? Whatever can you mean?"

Rolling to her back, Elizabeth looked up at her husband, his skin gleaming in the soft light of the afternoon pouring in through the large bank of windows on the furthest side of the room. "You have not fooled me for one moment Sir. You successfully roped Georgie into assuring my presence in this room," Elizabeth raised a brow, "Perhaps in the hopes to recreate a certain important moment of our brief history?"

Saying nothing, Elizabeth closed her eyes as Fitzwilliam continued to study her features, before he resumed his soft nibbling, over her collarbone, following the valley between her breasts, each carefully tended, before his hands and lips worked together to map out her rounded shape.

"My clever little wife. I should have known you would discover my design. I could not help wishing to recreate our beginning, for I have developed an almost desperate fantasy to seduce you in a library, that it is our library makes it all the more satisfying. Well, as you seem quite content in your current condition, I shall worry not. Instead, dear" his lips peppered her with kisses between words, "darling" the rasp of his stubble grazed her skin, "girl" his hands caressed her curves, "you will tell me why your skin is so sensually soft, that I cannot tear myself away from you? Tis witchcraft, I assume?"

Ignoring the man's silly nonsense, Elizabeth allowed her own hands to map and explore his hair, neck, scalp, shoulders, ears–whatever she could reach, enjoying the moment. Relishing the hard-won peace. She more than deserved such.

The next moment, Fitzwilliam had her caged in, his arms bracketed by her head, as he looked down at her with such a burning look of love, Elizabeth found her heart racing, feeling the building tension, the power radiating from his frame.

"Elizabeth, am I forgiven?"

Unable to break from his gaze, Elizabeth realised her gentle husband needed more from her than love and comfort, he needed absolution.

"Yes, my love. I exonerate you of any ill-intentions. The mistakes made were done with the best of intentions and you are not to punish yourself further. Tis done. Let us think of the good, learn from the bad and work towards a brighter future."

Lowering himself, Fitzwilliam growled with the glorious sensations of skin against skin, the soothing bond, the healing connection and power of touch.

"Thank you, my sweet wife." Resting his forehead against hers, they shared a reverent moment of accord, before finally Fitzwilliam pulled away.

Rising, her husband sought his breeches, before pulling them on, only to disappear behind one of the bookcases. He returned moments later, wheeling a laden cart causing Elizabeth to giggle with his boyish delight in being so correctly sketched. After serving a cold collation, Fitzwilliam settled back down upon the rug, the scene an intimate indoor picnic. Few words were spoken, until both of their appetites were sated. Once the plates were cleared away, Fitzwilliam pulled Elizabeth back into his arms, whereby he pleaded to hear of all the childhood tales and memories involving Lydia.

"I wish to see her as you do. To know your sister through your eyes."

With a catch in her throat at her sweet and

kind husband, Elizabeth talked, and eventually, through the tears and frequent laughter, her grief was soothed, the jagged cracks, the yawning maw of pain, began to grow ever smaller.

CHAPTER 21

"**F**itzwilliam, what is this I hear of having visitors? Mrs Reynolds just confirmed that all is in readiness for our guests?"

Darcy looked up from the book he was reading, having found the need to remind himself the words to a particular poem he wished to whisper to Elizabeth that evening, and so only half paid attention. "Guests?" Then with a jolt, he was reminded that in all their time spent together reconciling, Darcy had failed to mention his invitation. With a guilty start, Darcy attempted to appear innocent, "Did I not mention anything? Well, too late now, they are to arrive shortly."

To his amusement, his darling wife, dressed in a stunning mauve morning gown, a blessed relief from the sombre black, her petite frame bearing his child, stalked menacingly towards him, until she could poke him sternly in the ribs, a particularly sensitive spot that made him jump more than it ought to.

"Fitzwilliam, so help me, if any of your relatives have decided to impose themselves upon us, and you have neglected to inform me, you will be back to sleeping alone for the foreseeable future!" This was emphasised by a further jab, and Darcy quickly caught the offending digit, bringing it up to his lips to kiss.

Before he could soothe his wife's agitation, Croft entered, "A carriage approaches, Mr Darcy."

Thanking him, Darcy steered Elizabeth out of the room and across the foyer, until they reached the portico, whereby he valiantly fought the twitch of lips at the sight of Elizabeth's displeasure.

"Do not think for one minute I have not noticed that smirk Mr Darcy."

He had to disguise his bark of laughter as a cough, but neither Croft nor his wife were fooled. Finally the carriage came to a halt directly before the steps, and before further words could be spared, Elizabeth's shout had everyone smiling.

"Jane!" Darcy caught Elizabeth before she rushed down the steps, her walk unsteady with her condition being some eight months along. With a frustrated huff, Elizabeth allowed Darcy to guide her down the steps with care, only for her to fling herself into her sister's embrace once Bingley had handed his wife down.

Both gentlemen stepped back, content to

watch their loved ones share a special moment of reunion. The tears were brushed aside, and laughter followed the happy greetings. Eventually both ladies pulled back enough for them to hook their arms together and be guided forward into the house.

Darcy quietly chuckled as he heard Mrs Bingley say, "Dear Lizzy, of all this you are mistress! Oh my."

Elizabeth effervescently denied any self aggrandisement, "Nonsense Jane, tis just a very lovely home that I am inordinately pleased to welcome you to at long last! I have sorely missed your company these past few months!"

Mrs Bingley looked steadily upon her sister, "And I you, Lizzy. Yet I can clearly see it could not have been any other way. Look at you, so lovely and radiant! I can finally be content to see you so well settled, happily so."

Darcy watched as Elizabeth felt keenly her sister's words, before she set the sentiments aside in order of seeing to her guests, "Thank you, Jane. Now, I am sure you are keen to refresh yourselves after your journey, so let us find Mrs Reynolds and see you to your chambers."

Realising he had been very much forgotten, Darcy turned to Bingley to offer his own welcome, "Welcome Bingley, you are looking well. Married life suits you indeed."

His friend followed, and Darcy took them to his study to offer Bingley a drink before he removed himself to his rooms. There was a hesitance in his friend's demeanour that indicated that not all was as it should be.

"Thank you, Darcy, I am delighted to have overcome Jane's concerns, and despite the somewhat sombre ceremony, in light of ...well...everything, I cannot but think matters have resolved themselves exactly as they ought."

Taking a seat in the armchair before the fireplace, he watched as Bingley paced about the room, drink in hand, yet forgotten, held almost absently.

"Elizabeth and I have been ardent supporters of your suit, yet we knew Mrs Bingley would have to approach the situation as best suited her own wishes." Waiting patiently was not his strong suit, yet Darcy could see something troubled his friend.

At last, Bingley burst out with, "I am unsurprised it has been some time that we were in company together, I am obliged you would house my wife and I in order for Jane and Mrs Darcy to be united once more." To say that Darcy was immediately alarmed by such a statement, that there was some truth in the words, was uncomfortable, and yet he could not comprehend his friend's distress. "Do not mistake me, I dare not presume that all is forgiven," Bingley thunked his glass down heavily, having drained the contents without pausing to savour the rich, full-bodied brandy, "nor forgotten, as I am very much aware that a longer road lays before me, before I can restore what once was so valuable to us both. I have made mistakes, have taken for granted what ought not to be and from here on out, I am committed to being a better man, a better friend,, a better husband." Bingley had paced to the fireplace, his bearing that of a man ladened with guilt.

Having only just restored his own sensibilities, Darcy was in every way sympathetic to his friend's condition, "You shall have to excuse my ignorance, and perhaps my neglect, for I have not the slightest notion to what has brought you to this state."

Bingley spluttered for a moment, before sitting heavily in the matching seat to his own, "Come now, Darcy, tis abundantly clear to all that I am long overdue such remonstrations as you ought to levy upon me. My obdurate and intemperate sister, her single-minded dedication to seeing herself as the mistress of Pemberley, was no secret that these were her intentions. And yet I did nothing to constrain her, allowing her the delusion for the peace and avoidance of bringing my will to bear weight. I ought to have done more, to have stood firm, to heed your own counsel that Caroline's behaviour would bring ruin to the family name and honour. Instead, my negligence, my disregard permitted my sister to arrange the very circumstances that led to your marriage!"

Darcy was speechless. Never before had he thought his friend would have troubled himself to consider his own behaviour under such a critical light. Yes, Bingley was the picture of modest humility, but this was not the same. This was such deep self-reflection of the nature of his own musings. Witnessing his friend's character grow and develop gave Darcy hope that he too could endeavour to become a better man, a lighter one, closer to Bingley's own carefree nature.

However, he could no longer permit his friend to continue to castigate himself, "Enough my friend, I bear no grudge for the circumstances I find myself in, I am far too content, too blessed, to worry over just how I have reached this point." Rising from his seat to set his glass back upon the tray, Darcy walked back to clap his friend on the back, "I am keen for you to witness the changes my own marriage has wrought in me, but I am impressed by such reflections. It shows maturity of character I have heretofore, not known you to possess."

Rising himself, Bingley attempted a rough smile, "My wife has much to be credited with, for it was her own harsh assessment that made me see how my behaviour led us to the point we were in. Jane could see shades of her father's character in me, in the poor governance of my sister, so much the same as Mr Bennet's...and look where that led." Darcy looked away, unable to fully concede nor refute Mr Bennet's culpability.

Turning back, "Then Mrs Bingley is to be commended. I am sure that was not an easy conversation to be a party to, but I believe you both shall be the better off for it."

And with that, Darcy guided his friend to the stairs, allowing him to seek his respite, while Darcy put away his work, for he would allow nothing to intrude upon his wife's felicity in having her loved ones united once more.

The drawing room was filled with the soft hubbub of content conversation amidst happy company, delighting Elizabeth and shaking her from the sticky strands of grief. She quietly sat back, allowing her family to converse, from Mary and Georgiana speaking of musical interests, to Jane and Mrs Annesley discussing with Mr Bingley and her husband the trials of establishing a household from nothing. While usually an equal participant in any conversation, her delight robbed her of words, forcing Elizabeth to cherish this moment, allowing it to lay a balm over the past few difficult weeks, months, mayhap the year in full.

Nay, Elizabeth could not discount her marriage so easily. There had been blessedly lighter moments, interspersed with the challenges of growing together in partnership. What little a woman learns before she is wed, her perception is bound to undergo a complete transformation; to no longer think of herself as 'I', and instead as 'we'. And Fitzwilliam had worked just as furiously to make their union one of joy and fulfilment.

"Lizzy?" Jane interrupted her ponderance, and Elizabeth marked the changes the time apart had wrought on her most beautiful sister. Shadows were just starting to fade beneath her eyes. Tiny lines traced a story around her mouth, and the soft serenity that forever characterised Jane was replaced with a quiet strength, the tilt of her head and the jut of her shoulders, no longer demure, but rather fixed in place with a feminine strength. This was who Jane was always meant to be, unconquerable, forcing those in her circle to 'be better', to work harder, else suffer her disappointment, far more terrible than disapprobation.

"I can see in you such strength, Lizzy. I had believed you to be indomitable before, but you are so much more now. Seeing you like this gives me hope that I can be just as capable in my home."

Elizabeth could not help but laugh aloud at the symmetry of their thoughts, and happily said so. To this Jane looked everything surprised, "I? How can you think I have changed when

I have spent the past few months doing much as I ever would, caring for our mother, while enduring all the gossip and tittle-tattle!" She could see Fitzwilliam watching her with his iron-eyes, could feel them caress her as if it was a tangible force. "Jane, in every instance, in every moment since I moved away, you have endured trial after trial. You are altered, and it feels as if you have grown into the woman you were always meant to be." Sending a stern look towards her husband, to which he did nothing but tilt his head in that adorably affected way, Elizabeth returned her focus to her sister, "Yet I can see you will not heed my view, so instead I shall ask you what you think of our Mary? Is she much as she ever was?"

Jane gazed thoughtfully towards where their sister had engaged Mrs Annesley, while Georgiana and Mr Bingley discussed entertainments. Fitzwilliam remained somewhat apart, much as she herself had been.

"Mary is in very good looks. I have ever seen her as content to observe rather than engage in conversation, yet I doubt she has done so once since our arrival." was Jane's candid opinion.

Nodding, Elizabeth agreed, "Indeed, Mary has suffered in the past from near constant comparison with her livelier and prettier sisters, yet at long last our sister has found her place here. I can empathise with the disparaging scrutiny she faced, for I have long been in the shadow of our mother's displeasure, suffering her words of complaint with jokes and impertinence was how I chose to escape. For Mary, she retreated entirely. Now, well, I shall allow her to share her news, and shall not ruin the surprise!"

"I am sorry Lizzy." Jane reached out to clasp hands, sorrow etched once more into the familiar lines of her dear face, "We all struggled under the burden of our parent's *care*." Elizabeth struggled to suppress the snort these words inspired, "From my serenity, to your wit, Mary's withdrawal, Kitty's imitation and...and Lydia's-"

"Liveliness." Elizabeth supplied, unable to amend her sister's obvious distress.

"Yes, just so. We *all* became distinct in one way or another, and truthfully, none of us are at fault for how we chose to address the instability of our home. No, father cannot be excused, and I beg your pardon Lizzy, for I know how close you are with him-"

"Jane, I cannot argue the truth with you. In every aspect, you are correct, and father does indeed carry the blame for the faults of understanding in our younger sisters." Sighing deeply, Elizabeth looked back upon Fitzwilliam, watching as he paced across the room, struggling not to interfere in the clearly difficult discourse Jane and she were engaged in. "Guilt has been born in partnership with grief in our home, both here and clearly within the walls of Longbourne. Why else would mamma continue to desire an escape by intruding upon you when at Netherfield?"

Jane, hand still tightly clasped in her own, looked intently upon her husband, Mr Bingley, having retreated to observe just as Fitzwilliam was apt to. "Mama and father are much altered, especially now that Kitty is fixed in Bath with the Thompson's. With no daughters running about, no boisterous arguments, the silence seems to have physical presence. Longbourne is nothing like it was."

"I am glad." Jane seemed shocked, so Elizabeth continued, "Seriously Jane, I am. I could not be happier that Kitty is free of mama's complaints, that she is best placed to allow her to grow and mature is everything I could wish for. And while I love our parents, they ought to feel the consequences of their behaviour." Another sigh escaped, and Elizabeth instead attempted to divert the talk to pleasanter topics. "Enough depressing talk, I insist we talk of something far more pertinent! I do believe, sister dear, that my husband has located two properties, of which could be considered appropriate for your needs!"

Elizabeth happily divulged the scant details her husband had shared, and listened as Jane enthusiastically shared her hopes for her new home.

◆ ◆ ◆

Darcy was just readying himself before joining Elizabeth in her room, his valet collecting the usual paraphernalia he carried about on his person, when Elizabeth stormed into his bedchamber. With a pointed finger, Elizabeth climbed upon the bed, until she was on her knees and of a height with him, "You wretch!" He had met her in front of the bed, stabilising her uneven weight, throwing off her balance, "How could you go behind my back and orchestrate such a scheme?!"

Kirk had discreetly escaped, leaving Fitzwilliam to enjoy his wife's fury alone. Fighting a delighted grin, Darcy addressed his little irate temptress, her hair wild and curly about her head, cheeks beautifully flushed and eyes flashing in the candlelight.

"You are not really angry dear girl. No matter how hard you try to appear so, you will not succeed in convincing me thus." Drawing closer, belly to belly, chest to chest, Darcy relished feeling the roll and fidgets of his unborn babe, and yet he could not imagine the furious movements were always so delightful when it was your own insides being pushed against. The glorious sound of Elizabeth's laughter chimed and Darcy grinned in response. Her own arms came about to wrap about his neck, where she proceeded to drop kisses along his chin and jawline.

Interspersed between kisses, Elizabeth allowed, "Very well, you dear man, I am so profoundly grateful for you arranging for my sister to be here. Seeing her so happily united with her Mr Bingley has given me such delight to witness! And I have you to thank!"

Pulling away just slightly, he ignored the seductive pout of her lips that begged for his kisses, "Tis but a small consolation, love. I should have, would have, had them here sooner, if I had but paused to think of the pleasure it would give you." Unable to resist further, he thoroughly kissed his wife, until they were twined together and he had tumbled her to the sheets, where he could tend to his Elizabeth in every way, "I would do so much more, anything, everything, for you love. If you but wish it."

While his arms wrapped about her, holding as close as could be, he heard Elizabeth whisper, "That is a terrible power you lay upon me, dear man. You rely on me to behave wisely and not have you flitting about fulfilling my every whim and fancy!"

Decided there had been enough talk, Darcy rebutted, while his hands were pleasurably engaged, "I know you, Elizabeth. Your heart is too good to ever use such power wilfully. I have every faith in you my darling."

CHAPTER 22

"Now Georgie, you have everything in hand for the games?" Elizabeth had lists before her, notes on sheets beside them, and numerous pencil markings with additions and changes. Overall, it looked to be complete chaos, but this gathering of women were sure to put everything to rights.

Mary was making the final draft of arrangements, her penmanship the neatest of them all, and so Elizabeth listened as Georgiana explained, "Well, having spoken to Croft, he tells me he was not yet in his post the last time a fête was held. However, the stable master, Gordon? He was, and knew just where to find everything! The quoits, bowls, croquet and such have been collated, and Gordon and I have gone over everything. There has been much cleaning, repairing, repainting, until we were both satisfied with the results. Therefore, everything for the games is set!"

Biting her lip, Elizabeth looked back to her notes to prevent her giggles from escaping over Georgiana's excitement. The dear girl was clearly and deservedly so, very proud of her accomplishment. The responsibility had at first daunted her sister, but once she had begun, Georgiana had delighted in discussing every last detail. It had been at times tediously painful.

A pang across her belly gave her momentary pause, but when nothing else occurred, Elizabeth resumed her work, "Mary? Music?"

"I have met with the fiddlers, the pipers, and happily we have a cellist player also. We have agreed the formation for the day and evening, divided up between them to ensure everyone has a chance to enjoy themselves and perform evenly."

The succinct summation was no surprise, "Oh, Mary what an excellent plan. I had not even contemplated the matter in such a light."

Jane's reasonable reply should have made Elizabeth feel at ease, but instead provided only mild irritation, "Well that is surely due to you having despatched the task to Mary, who you trust to arrange everything. If you had undertaken the matter yourself, I am certain you would have canvassed the same points. Your faith in our sister ensured you could direct your attention elsewhere."

With a forced nod of thanks, Elizabeth

could not help a slight tease, "I shall allow you to portray me in the best possible light, dearest Jane."

Ignoring the questioning looks from all the ladies, Elizabeth moved on down her list, only for Mrs Annesley to ask, "Mrs Darcy, how are we to arrange the judging of the contests?"

Fighting her frown, Elizabeth again attempted to answer politely, despite everyone muddling matters. There was a clear list for them to run through! "For the baking and embroidery, I had thought, yourself, Mrs Reynolds and myself could adjudicate, while Jane, Mary and Georgie could attend the singing competition? That allows for them to be arranged simultaneously, and I shall not be running hither and yon."

When everyone concurred, Elizabeth worked slowly down her list, grateful that near everything had been settled, and there were no further interruptions. Yet the irritation did not abate.

Over dinner, Elizabeth watched Georgiana enthuse once more about all that had been discussed that morning, and Elizabeth could attest to being somewhat wearied of talk related to the harvest fête.

"Oh brother, everything is going to be perfect! Lizzy has everything in hand, it is hard to fathom this is the first occasion she has organised an event such as this!"

Fitzwilliam seemed just as entertained by Georgiana's lively spirits, but his heated gaze appraised her as he said, "I have every confidence in the excellence of Elizabeth."

Blushing slightly, Elizabeth felt her irritation wash away, only for a swathe of pain to take its place. Conversation continued all around her while Elizabeth breathed slowly until the pain ebbed, and she could compose herself once more. Shifting in her seat as discreetly as was possible, Elizabeth ignored Fitzwilliam's concentrated gaze boring into her, neglecting to answer the question in those silver grey eyes, Elizabeth directed her husband's attention elsewhere.

"That reminds me Fitzwilliam, you, Mr Bingley and Mr Wilson are to judge the carving and herding contests, while Croft will replace Mr Bingley in the cider tasting. Please tell me you are prepared to decide a prize for the winners?"

Mr Bingley appeared flummoxed and turned to his friend, "Herding? What do I know of that, Darcy?"

Her husband jokingly replied it was much like matchmaking mamas in pursuit of eligible gentlemen in a ballroom, but Elizabeth could continue to conceal her pains no longer and begged to be excused.

Elizabeth noted the wary question in Jane's querulous, "Lizzy?"

Seeing the concern mirrored in Fitzwilliam's eyes, she attempted to allay everyone's fears and suspicions, "No, please do not disrupt your dining on my behalf, I am merely a trifle indisposed and would prefer to retire to my rooms."

Escaping, Elizabeth carefully made her way to her own apartments, summoning her maid on reaching its security, she paused as another pain flowed through her belly, but while the strength and frequency of them had gradually increased, they were yet of the strength and duration the midwife had warned her of.

A sound behind her had Elizabeth witnessing her husband's worried entrance, stepping through the door and carefully clicking it closed.

"Fitzwilliam, you should not abandon our guests without a host...and you need not attend me either." While knowing her time had come, and admittedly feeling some level of apprehension of the unknown, love for her unborn babe, love for her husband had her eyes glowing with warmth, pleased to have a quiet moment just between themselves.

He came towards her then, arms wrapping about her, enveloping her in his love, "Foolish girl, why would I be anywhere else? And our guests as you put it, are more than capable of entertaining themselves, so have no fear on that score." Dropping a kiss upon her hair, his hands wandered soothingly down her back, "Tis begun then?" Elizabeth nodded while remaining tucked within his embrace, "Allow me to remain for as long as I may? Please, dearest, loveliest Elizabeth? From my own misguided expectations, I have already missed so much, and I would wish to be near, to support you however I may."

Another pain seized her, stealing the words of assurance she would have offered, and then her maid Trent entered, and with one look immediately understood the state of affairs. Fitzwilliam murmured soft encouraging words while his hands continued to travel her back. Afterward, Elizabeth slumped heavily into her husband's strong arms. Without lifting her head, Elizabeth muttered, "You may stay for now, but I would not wish for you to be discomfited when proceedings develop accordingly."

Another kiss was to be her gift, her reward, "Thank you, my love. Until then, I am yours to command. What would you have of me?"

With her husband's help, Elizabeth was assisted into an old nightgown, and the pins gently removed from her hair. Three more pains delayed the proceedings, and further interruption came on the heels of Mrs Reynolds strong aversion of the master's presence.

"Now Master Darcy, you should know this is women's work we do here. Your presence is not needed, and I beg of you to take yourself off, until you are fetched."

Elizabeth could not help but laugh at her husband's mulish expression, "Mrs Reynolds, my wife has granted her leave to remain, and I shall do so until my presence is no longer desired. No words to the contrary shall I pay any heed."

The sight of the housekeeper's less than impressed aspect was further cause for amusement, and Elizabeth wondered if the woman's glowing opinion of '*Master Darcy*' was to be forever marred.

There was much shuffling and mutterings proceeding within the confines of her chambers, and Elizabeth was content to remove to her sitting room, Trent in her wake.

"Fitzwilliam, go take yourself to your rooms and allow Kirk to attire you more comfortably. If you could also ensure our sisters are assured of my well-being, and I shall remain thus until you return. I would have Trent attend to my hair, for it cannot remain thus."

A grunt was her sole reply, but her words were heeded, and moments later, another pain struck, this one by far more intense than the previous. What felt like minutes later, but was much less, Elizabeth breathed deep and relaxed, finally taking in her maid's concern.

"I am well, Trent, tis much as Mrs Dixon proclaimed." Turning, Elizabeth settled in place for Trent to braid her hair, only for Mrs Reynolds to enter, pleased to see no sign of her husband.

"He will return Mrs Reynolds, he is seeing to his attire and the comfort of our guests, though I am sure Miss Darcy will be ably assisted by Mrs Annesley."

Frowning slightly, "Very well Mrs Darcy. I have sent for Mrs Dixon and will direct her to your rooms anon. The maids have finished in your chambers, so you may return whenever you so wish." The housekeeper paused, excitement and anticipation quivering in every line of her strong figure, "Mrs Bingley has requested she be present when the time comes, but I am hesitant to encourage her presence..."

Elizabeth considered the affair, wondering at Mrs Reynolds caution, so with a breath, her housekeeper explained, "Mrs Bingley is only newly-wed, and having no immediate experience in a birthing... I would not wish to give a fear of what transpires from the proceedings."

With comprehension, she questioned whether Jane would be dismayed and truthfully could not answer. Her sister was a gentle creature, and would suffer to see Elizabeth labour to deliver her babe. Perhaps, despite the comfort her presence would provide, it might be prudent to rely predominantly on Fitzwilliam and her servants.

Nodding, yet feeling another pain intrude, Elizabeth paused to concentrate on breathing through the ordeal, "Forgive me, while I cannot say one way or another, I would rather err on the side of caution and delay any tribulations to Mrs Bingley. Would you assure my sister that I am well tended, and that I look forward to introducing her first niece else nephew?"

Fitzwilliam had entered part way through her reply, nodding stiffly to the women present, before making his way to her side. Seating himself behind her, he proceeded to massage her back with gentle pressure, alleviating the tension she held unwittingly. Once it was apparent that the master was not to be shifted, the other women in the room moved off, arranging items to some undefined design that eluded Elizabeth.

The crackling fire was the only sound for a while, that and Elizabeth's varied breaths, while occasionally pained moans escaped. Eventually, she accepted her husband could not be convinced to discuss idle topics in an endeavour to distract, but was fixed upon bearing her company in silence, a witness to her increasing pain as if it were penance for him to suffer. A light whisper had Trent scurrying away, only to return, hands tightly clasped and lips caught between her teeth.

Sensing her maid's anxiety, Elizabeth waited.

"Mrs Darcy, Mrs Dixon is currently assisting another birth, and is not at liberty to attend you. Her words were, to keep attentive to the timings between pains, to walk as much as you are able, and that as this is your first babe, not to be concerned if it takes much time. She is assured you will be well, so well tended as you are, and is near certain she will arrive in time to assist in your delivery."

The tension strumming in her husband's frame at her back was apparent, despite him being out of sight. His hands had stilled their soothing ministrations. Shooing her maid back to her chambers, Elizabeth leant heavily against Fitzwilliam, his arms quickly adjusting to take her weight against his chest.

"I can hear your thoughts, and your fears, and you are to banish them both. The birth of our first child will not be marked by ill temper or cross words." Her hands soothed down her belly and Elizabeth constantly shifted her weight, feeling more than ungainly, discomfort making her uneasy. "Truly my love, I am confident all will be well."

Another pain struck, intense enough to have her curling forward, and once it passed, Fitzwilliam tugged her up, cradling her in his arms, while his hands resumed their tender care. "I would wish for you to not suffer thus, but as I am helpless to do more than this, I shall be your strength, when you need it most. Lean on me, love. I promise we will both endure together."

Looking up, Elizabeth twisted and

wrapped her arms around Fitzwilliam's waist, the love and comfort in his embrace, a soothing remedy, "Then I am sure to succeed, for you are the strongest man I know."

Several hours later and Darcy stood enraptured as he cradled his newly arrived daughter, the quiet solitude of his shared sitting room his retreat while Elizabeth was settled more comfortably. The hours had passed at what felt like a crawl, his agony at witnessing his beloved suffer to labour, to bring this precious bundle into the world. Now, he could only stare in wonder, not only at the sight of his sweet daughter, the soft chocolate coloured down of her hair, a match to her mother's, but Darcy marvelled at Elizabeth's strength.

She forbore to scream and shout when her pains grew so intense speech was impossible, but bore them all with a fierce determination that undermined the female as the weaker sex. No man who had witnessed the miracle of a woman labouring to bring a child into the world could ever dare to presume such boorish nonsense. The midwife, much to his own dismay, never managed to arrive in time to see to Elizabeth, and instead his wife had been waited upon by Mrs Reynolds and her lady's maid. Darcy himself should have departed, but with no sight of Mrs Dixon, had stubbornly rejected every expectation of his removal.

A soft knock interrupted his reflection, and Darcy looked up to see his housekeeper at the entrance of his wife's rooms. "Mrs Darcy is comfortably arranged, Mr Darcy. Shall I take the little one to the nursery?"

The thought of handing the care of his precious daughter over to another was abhorrent, and Darcy rejected the notion immediately, "No, Mrs Reynolds. My daughter is perfectly content where she is."

With a huff, his housekeeper moved on, "I shall look for a wet nurse, but for the interim, Mrs Darcy will need to see to feedings until then. I have settled upon two maids to handle the babe's care, and they will be along shortly. Would you like me to make the announcement to the household? Your guests?"

Helpless to keep his gaze away from his daughter, Darcy bestowed a soft kiss to her brow, delighting in the heavenly softness of her skin. Still looking down as his daughter slept, Darcy addressed the woman waiting patiently, "If you and Croft would deliver the knowledge to the servants, I would be most grateful. As for my family and house guests, if you would direct them to my sister's sitting room, those that are still awake that is, I shall speak with them as one."

When Mrs Reynolds left, Darcy slowly walked to Elizabeth's room, pleased to see her sitting up in a freshly made bed, enjoying her tea, looking far more at ease than he had anticipated. When his wife noted his presence, her eyes lit up with pleasure, love and joy shining in her eyes. Drawn to her as a moth to a flame, he was at her side and lowering his precious charge into eagerly waiting arms the very next breath.

Kissing those tempting lips, Darcy could not help but offer his unconditional devotion once again, "I love you, Mrs Darcy."

A wide smile was his reward, followed by a lengthier kiss, "And I love you, Mr Darcy. Are you disappointed to not have a son?" He could hear the concern in Elizabeth's words, could taste them in the air between them.

"I will *never* be disappointed in the children we are blessed with. Our daughter is everything I could dare to dream of. Thank you, loveliest of all Elizabeth's, for our daughter." Her laughter rewarded him once more, "I am in awe of you, my love. I cannot see how you are not laid flat out exhausted after the ordeal you have undergone!"

Settling back, Darcy watched Elizabeth marvel just as he had done, her fingertips gliding over skin, fingers, cheeks, brow, kisses interspersed. "While I am not eager to experience it all again, holding her in my arms is thanks enough." Elizabeth only spared him a lightning quick look, her attention fixed upon their child.

"She is as beautiful as her mother, and I am privileged to call myself her father. But that brings me to ask, what are we to name her?"

So softly Darcy had to strain to hear, Elizabeth spoke, her words falling like a benediction upon their daughter, "I am not one to hold with using names of our nearest and dearest, for I would wish each child to forge their own path, their individual blessings to be as varied and diverse, to follow no mould, no pattern card. With that in mind, I do desire to honour the woman who helped form me into the woman I am today. Without her care and guidance, I am certain you would not have spared me a thought." Looking up, Elizabeth solemnly stated, "Would you be averse to naming her Madeleine, after my aunt?"

Darcy took a moment to consider her words, feeling the veracity hit home. No he would not wish his daughters to grow up into ladies who would one day pursue a gentleman just for rank and fortune, and despite having never considered it at all before now, Darcy was determined to be the type of father that would educate his children equally regardless of their sex.

With a dimple wide smile, after all, his wife had at long last admitted how devastating she found them to her composure, Darcy agreed,

"Madeleine Anna Darcy it is. Anna for my sister."

At long last Elizabeth looked to have wearied, and so with genial words, Darcy collected his daughter and urged his wife to sleep, promising to return once their family had been informed. The perfect feeling of *rightness* followed his steps as he paced to his sister's sitting room, excited to begin this new stage in his life.

EPILOGUE

Dear Kitty

While I cannot claim to have shared a close bond with our youngest sister, nor yourself for that matter, I believe I would like to correct this breach in sisterly affection. Please do not fear I will importune you with boring, staid platitudes, for I can clearly see that such behaviour is unlikely to endear myself to you. Nor would I wish for you to inundate me with the latest styles in fashion that are au courant.

Instead, allow me this opportunity to relate all that has occurred since the birth of our niece. Lizzy had everyone alarmed when she would not remain abed, following her lying in, stating unequivocally that remaining such would only prolong her recovery. In truth, our brother is hard-pressed to deny her anything, and instead trails her about the place, seeing to Lizzy's every comfort and requirement. Lizzy has further tormented the staff by refusing to engage a wet-nurse, and instead keeps Madeleine Anna with her throughout the day. The poor maids, turned Nurse, have very light duties, but they remain devoted to their charge's care.

Our niece is a beautiful baby, and I consider myself typically void of any such sentiments about babies in general. However, there is something delightful about watching our tiny niece toted about by her besotted father, while he carries on running a vast estate and his many interests. Mr Darcy can still be the 'stone-masked' menace, as Lizzy calls him, infant baby in arms or no.

Well I shall spare no further commentary on our niece, ever hopeful you will agree to visit in the very near future so that you may greet her in person.

Instead I shall turn my attention to the harvest fête, of which you had shown so much interest. As you know the music fell under my purview, and I flatter myself that I did a commendable job, and hope to repeat the endeavour in years to come. From the music to the games, from the dancing to the contests, the day could not have passed better. The weather was everything fair, and the grounds of Pemberley were the perfect setting for such a cheerful event. While the day was mostly on behalf of the tenants and local towns and villages, there were other prominent figures who hoped to find something to critique or disparage, and you will celebrate with me when I say they went away with disappointed hopes, but I shall think of this no more. There is far more pleasurable news to relate that the day bore witness to, that of Mr Farnsworth proposing. While I am not of a romantic nature, I do believe the rector ably achieved a memorable address, one I will be proud to relate to our children, if god-willing, we are so blessed. Therefore, you have further incentive to visit, that of attending my nuptials.

Our father has given his blessing, but has opted to remain at home, granting his blessing for us to be wed from the parish Mr Farnsworth presides over. Mrs Bennet sent her own agreeable wishes, but feels she is not equal to attend a celebratory event just yet. The loss of Lydia has wrought a formidable change in the Bennet matron.

I shall close with an added message from Lizzy, that of further desiring you and the Thompson's as a family make the journey to visit, if not now, then for the festive period. I urge you to make the trip, in the hopes the Bennet sisters may pour into each other, the solace of sisterly affection. You are not under any obligation to remain, nor to return to Longbourne. We all would simply wish to assure you of our love and affection.
God bless you and keep you well.
Your sister

Mary

Dear Aunt

Thank you for all of your well-wishes and words of love and support. I am blessed to have such a loving and wise aunt to offer counsel whenever the occasion demands. In light of this, I am delighted you have accepted my husband's invitation to join us, have agreed to journey to Pemberley, for Christmas, but am grieved my parents declined to join you. As much as Mrs Bennet is a woman who expresses herself with energy and volume, the desire to see my parents well goes unabated. I have nothing from my father since Lydia's situation, and must assume his shame makes it impossible to accept my current felicity.

Please do not feel you were not wished for when I entered my confinement, for that is hardly the case. I simply felt it would raise in my mother's breast a slight to her own presence being undesired. I doubt I could have tolerated my Mrs Bennet's theatrics on such an occasion, and perhaps more concerning, nor could my husband! And yes, I shall admit, Mr Darcy was present during the birth, though he remained firmly by my side, lending me his strength. I cannot deny, his presence was of great comfort for me, but whether Fitzwilliam would wish for a repeat, I cannot answer.

Now that my confinement is concluded, I am willing to wax poetic about my little girl and the many delights' parenthood, motherhood has brought about. My daughter was named in your honour, for how else would I have come to accept my marriage, without you and all you have done for me? Just like her namesake, Madeleine has won the hearts of near all the servants within Pemberley, especially because I keep her with me for most of the day rather than the nursery. The footmen and maids seek any means to catch a glance, hoping to be assigned a 'little miss' related task. It is delightfully funny to witness, but even more so when another attempts to poach my daughter from her father's arms!

*Will you think me odd for confessing, that often, when I sit with her in my arms, I consider her future? The choices she will face, the paths that will be open to her, and I make a promise. I promise to permit my daughter to be who **she** is meant to be; I vow to not demean, play favourites, or push my children where **I** wish them to go. I swear to not make the choices **my** parents made. I sound bitter, when in truth I am not. No matter how it came to be, I love and cherish each and every one of my sisters. I love their characters, their spirit, their flaws. Oh dear, aunt, I appear to have become some emotional creature with the advent of becoming a mother! How lowering.*

Heaven forfend!

On to other matters, the search for a property continues for Jane and Mr Bingley, although I expect Jane simply is content to remain in company with us all Pemberley. She has lost much of the strained look about her, and her glow has gradually returned. Has Kitty written? If not, I ask you prompt my little sister in making arrangements to travel up with you. How long she remains, we shall canvas during her stay.

And finally, Mary has given me leave to relate that she and Mr Farnsworth have set a date to wed three days after Christmas. She wishes for a small private ceremony, but asks that Mr Gardiner give her away, in the absence of our father. She plans to ask Kitty to stand up with her, so perhaps a new dress could be acquired for the occasion for your niece? And no, this must be placed on my account, for it is part of my wedding gift to Mary, to see to that of the outfitting my sisters.

I must leave off here, for Fitzwilliam has been walking Madeleine for some time while I wrote, but the 'little miss' has become most insistent for my attention.

All my love to you, my uncle and my cousins.

Your 'ever-grateful' niece
Lizzy Darcy

AFTERWORD

Thank you for taking the time to read my own twist on the much loved P&P. I try to consider, from all the stories I've read, what I have yet to see, or what I would most delight in. I have to thank the entire length and breadth of similar authors to myself, who continue to inspire and fulfill my own burning need for 'more' Darcy&Elizabeth.

As ever, it would mean a lot to me as baby author, if you could leave a review...or just some stars...yes we are that needy! :)

ACKNOWLEDGEM ENT

I have to thank my Beta Readers, Eliza Jones, Nikita Sridar, Sara S. & Michelle David who took the time to read and feedback to me in one weekend! Legends!

I'm very grateful to the team of Beta readers, who not only keep me motivated to conclude, but also, to add just that little bit more...for them.

BOOKS BY THIS AUTHOR

Indifference & Indecision

What if the Netherfield party are not the only eagerly anticipated guests for the Meryton Assembly?
What if Elizabeth and Jane are no longer bound by the bonds of sisterly affection?
And what if Mr Darcy is the one to be snubbed?

Welcome to a beloved story retold, introducing characters old and new, where the true challenge is not so easy as saving a foolish younger sister.
When Darcy encounters Elizabeth at the Meryton assembly, he's unfortunate enough to not even warrant a smile from the lady who fascinates him. For Elizabeth, paying any heed to the dour and dark gentleman is the last thing on her mind. She has much bigger matters to tackle - that of seeing to her sister's welfare.

This is a story that takes Darcy and Elizabeth on

a journey of self discovery and healing.

Not So Easily Persuaded

What if Anne was not so easily persuaded?
Who wants our sweet Anne to get her happily ever after without the years of heartbreak?
What about Frederick?
Who wants to hear him rumble his affections persuasively?

Let's remake a story and experience the right way for Anne to find her happily ever after.

ABOUT THE AUTHOR

A.s. Bishop

Married, mum of three with a full household that spans three generations, writing has been there in the background for me and finally, I returned to my pleasure of the written word, but this time with the commitment to see it all the way through to publishing. I've been a small business since before the pandemic, so  apart from the books I love to read, the books I write, I'm a dedicated sewist of things small and large, to bake and craft.

Currently I have several books in the works, the next one due beginning of 2024, but am also writing my first original romance story, to be released around the same time.

Made in the USA
Las Vegas, NV
03 March 2024

86642703R00249